Green Wellies and Wax Jackets

Morag Clarke

Kindle Create

To our much loved family horse, Fliss.
Without her equine antics, this book would never have been written.

Contents

Chapter One

It should have been a day for remembrance, a day for quiet reflection and contemplation.

Ella smoothed the yellowing newspaper cutting between her fingers, and stared wistfully at the grainy black and white picture of her father.

'Tragic death of talented sportsman', proclaimed the headline. 'The sporting world is in mourning for the loss of one of its finest show jumpers, Robert Johnson, who was killed in a car accident late last night.
The BMW he was driving was in collision with an articulated lorry five miles north of the Dartford Tunnel...'

'Ella! Ella!'

The hall door slammed back on its hinges. Ella had seconds to snatch up the paper and stuff it into the nearest chest of drawers. She could hear the thud, thud of footsteps coming up the stairs.

Her stepmother, a stout, grumpy looking woman with bleached blonde hair wound tightly into a bun at the nape of her neck, and eyes as sharp and narrow as a hawk, glared at her from the doorway. 'What are you doing? I thought I told you to start cleaning the tack.'

'I know.'

'Well, get a move on,' she said. Her chubby hands were planted firmly on each side of her generous hips. 'You do know what day it is, don't you?'

'Yes.' Ella paused in the door and glanced tearfully back at her. It had been five years since the accident. She was surprised her stepmother had remembered it.

She hadn't.

'The film company are coming at nine thirty, and if that saddle isn't up to scratch, there's going to be trouble, my girl. Big trouble. Now then...' She thought for a moment. 'Saddle, bridle, oh, and make sure Jasper is groomed and ready. And you'd better get Nero tacked up as well.'

'Nero?'

Ella pulled a face. The black gelding was hard to handle, and bad tempered at the best of times. The only thing in his favour was the fact that he was a magnificent looking animal, with his dark glossy coat and long, silky mane and tail.

'Just do it!' she said. She glanced at her watch. 'Vanessa? Caroline?' She breezed past Ella to the other side of the landing, and rapped lightly on one of the bedroom doors. 'It's time to get up, darlings. We want you to look your best for our visitors, don't we dears?'

Ella made her way outside and across the dimly lit stable yard to the tack room. A 'please' or a 'thank you' wouldn't have gone amiss, she thought, grumpily. Ursula seemed to take it for granted that she would willingly do anything for the horses, and normally, she would. But, unlike some, she had other things on her mind today.

It was a little after seven o clock, and the sun was starting to edge its way over the distant rooftops. The horses whinnied a greeting, their heads bobbing up and down over the stable doors. They had been fed and watered, and now they were looking forward to being let out for a few hours.

Hollyfield stables and stud boasted thirty-two horses, mainly used for riding lessons, show jumping and hacking, and another twenty-four on private livery. Ursula Johnson, as Ella's legal guardian, had inherited the pride of Robert Johnson's life when he died. Technically (and according to the terms of Robert's will) she should have handed over control of the estate to Ella on her eighteenth birthday, but Ursula was never one to let the finer points of such matters concern her. In her eyes, Ella was nothing more than a child, and totally incapable of handling the business side of things. No, it was far better for her to remain in charge, a point she made quite clear when one of the trustees had questioned her continuing control of the stables.

'I'm doing it to protect the child. You must see that it makes sense. I'm quite sure that when Robert wrote his will he had no idea he was going to die whilst Ella was still a teenager. It's far better for all concerned if I keep on running the business until she's older and more mature. And Ella agrees with me, don't you Ella?'

At eighteen, Ella would have agreed to anything as long as she got to spend as much time as possible with her beloved horses. And Ursula had been right in one respect; she didn't have a clue about running a thriving livery yard and stables.

So, Ursula continued to keep control of the business side of things, and Ella managed the welfare of the horses. It was a seemingly satisfactory arrangement for all concerned.

Except on mornings like this, Ella thought, when she was quite tempted to tell her stepmother to go take a running jump.

'Now then, Miss Ella, up with the larks again, I see.' Thomas Button tipped his laden wheelbarrow onto the muckheap, before hobbling back across the yard towards her. He was a small, wiry man, who'd been a former jockey in his youth. A severe fall had left him with a pronounced limp and one leg shorter than the other. It had not, however, put him off his great love of horses. ''Tis the Irish blood in me, you see, Miss Ella,' he had once told her. 'The Irish blood.'

Her father had employed him as a groom. Ursula Johnson had downgraded him to a stable hand, (although even she admitted, begrudgingly, and not to his face, that he did have a way with animals).

'I've got to get Jasper and Nero ready for some film company,' she said.

'For those two great lumps of daughters to ride, I'll be bound,' Thomas muttered. His eyes narrowed slightly. 'You've been crying, Miss Ella.'

'It's nothing, Thomas.' She wiped the back of her hand

across her eyes.

He looked at her thoughtfully, and frowned. It was the anniversary of that awful day, so it was. A day he would never forget. 'He was a good man, Ella. A much-loved man. Aye, and well-remembered in these parts.' He jerked his head back at the house. 'By most folks, anyways,' he sneered. 'Here now, you come into the tack room, and I'll make you up a warm brew.'

'Thanks, Thomas,' she sniffed. 'I mean it. Thank-you. But there's no time for tea. I've got work to do.'

'Sure, you have. Sure, and we all have.' He grinned, and his blue eyes flashed with a hint of mischief. 'And I'm thinking a nice round thistle under a saddle might be a good idea.'

Ella laughed. 'Don't even think of it, Thomas.'

'Oh, I can think of it,' he chuckled. 'Sure, and I can think it.'

So too, could Ella. Vanessa and Caroline were not built for the show-ring. Oh yes, they could ride, but not with the grace and finesse demanded by the sport. They could kick and whip and beat a horse into clearing the jumps, but neither had the art of making a partnership with their mount. But their mother – their oh so determined mother - had sights on her daughters being the next big thing in the show jumping world. Even hinted that they might stand a chance in the Olympic team.

Some chance, Ella thought.

'So, what's it all about, this film thing?' Thomas said, as he filled the kettle from the tap above the white enamel sink, and plugged it in to boil.

'I don't know for sure,' Ella said, as she lifted Jasper's saddle down from the rack, and started to rub it over with leather soap and a sponge. 'Ursula muttered something about it a couple of weeks ago, but I wasn't really listening. All I know is that they're filming in this area and they apparently need a couple of show-jumpers for one of the shots.'

'Anybody famous in it?'

She shrugged. 'I haven't a clue. I didn't ask.'

'More's the pity,' Thomas said. 'See, I can see you on a show horse, Miss Ella. Sure, with your style and grace. You've got your father's skill, and that's saying something. But those two puddings?' He shook his head. 'Ever seen a sack of potatoes on a trampoline?'

'Thomas!' she groaned, but she was smiling all the same as she buffed the dark brown leather of the saddle.

'Did your mother ever ride?'

'Yes, I think she did. Not professionally, of course. Not like Dad. But she used to enjoy hacking out over the moors. That's how they first met,' she added.

'What, your ma and pa?'

Ella nodded as she unfastened the stirrup leathers and stretched them out to clean them with the soapy sponge. 'She fell off. She was out riding with an old school friend, and Dad was the first on the scene, and picked her up out of the mud. It was love at first sight, so I was told.'

'I don't suppose you remember her that much. Weren't you just a nipper when she died?'

Ella felt the wetness of a tear start to form in the corner of her eye. 'I was nearly five,' she said. 'Old enough to know what I'd lost, Thomas.'

'Aye, you're right there.'

Her mother had died of a particularly virulent form of cancer. Ella's memories of her were hazy with the passing of time. But she knew she had been loved, and cared for and that, as an only child, she had been the pride of her mother and father's life.

What she remembered more than the loss of her mother, however, was the immense sadness and weariness that had affected her father in the years following his wife's death. The laughter and happiness had gone out of him. His only joy seemed to come from being with horses, and being with her.

She could remember, even as a tiny child, being swung up on the saddle in front of him, his strong arms around her, holding her secure. The gentle swaying motion of a slowly plodding horse beneath her, and his hands over hers, helping her to hold the reins. 'Like this, Ella, darling. You hold them like this.'

She could ride on her own at the age of five, courtesy of her first little pony, Darkie – a stubborn Shetland, with a penchant for parsnips - who had been nicknamed, 'The Thief' by the gardener, who was forever having to extricate him from the vegetable patch. Her father would take her out on a lead rein, riding his own gentle schoolmaster alongside her. They must have looked an odd pair, him on his huge, bay hunter, and she on a squat little shaggy coated pony.

Later, she owned Bayleaf, a pretty New Forest pony, who excelled at gymkhana games. His stable was bedecked with coloured rosettes and ribbons. Long gone now, Ella kept a boxful of photographs and mementoes of him, including a brass plated horseshoe, engraved with his name, under her bed.

As the years passed, so too did the overwhelming air of sadness that hung over the stables. Gradually her father, her much loved and cherished father, began to enjoy life once more. His natural ability, coupled with a finely tuned competitive streak led to him becoming a British champion show-jumper, who won more awards and trophies than any other rider of his ilk.

Ella smiled proudly, remembering.

Thomas handed her a steaming mug of thick brown tea. 'Here you are, lass, and I've put two sugars in it.'

'But I don't take...'

'Drink it,' he said kindly. 'And pass me over that bridle. I'll give you a hand here before I put the mares out to grass.'

Ella buffed the leather saddle until it shone. The job kept her occupied, but it didn't stop her thinking about how things had changed over the years.

Hollyfield Stables had been a happier and more prosperous place when her father had been alive. In those days they had bred horses, as well as competed with them. Her father had brought a stallion over from Ireland – Devil's Eye, he was called – a magnificent animal, coal black, like the horse in her favourite storybook. He had sired a string of top-class foals. She had been forbidden to ride him but one day, at the tender age of thirteen, she had sneaked onto his back, and ridden him bareback across the fields. No bridle, no saddle, just her and the horse, as free as the wind.

Her father had been secretly impressed.

The housekeeper, Mrs Wallace, had gone berserk. 'That child's running wild,' she told him. 'She needs a mother and brothers and sisters. I'm getting too old to be a nanny to her.'

It was soon after the 'wild riding incident', as it became known, that Ursula Pendlebury appeared on the scene. She had been pleasant enough to her then, Ella recalled, always buying her presents and making a fuss over her. Acting like the mother she had never really known. But it had all been a charade, a ploy on Ursula's part to secure herself another wealthy husband.

No sooner had Ursula flounced down the aisle in a cloud of ivory taffeta and lace, than her true colours had started to show through.

Little things had niggled at first. The way she took over the running of the riding school, and the manner in which she dispensed with the services of the ever loyal and elderly Mrs Wallace.

'We don't need a live-in nanny now, darling,' she told her husband. 'Ella's got me to look after her.'

What she failed to mention was the fact that her own two spoilt daughters, Vanessa and Caroline, would be given preference over Ella in everything, be it for shopping, toys, clothes, holidays or outings.

'Well, they have lost their *real* father,' Ursula would say, as if that would explain her biased behaviour.

What it meant was that Robert, always eager to please, indulged them as best he could, and Ella – agreeable, easygoing Ella – didn't complain.

Instead, she devoted all her time and effort to the horses. She had her father's competitive streak when it came to competitions. She was regularly the Ponies UK junior champion, and she competed in several major National events. Her bedroom was full of cups and trophies. Awards that Ursula felt sure would have been given to *her* daughters, if only they had been given the right horse or pony to ride.

It was Ella's great love of horses that kept her going after her father died. She threw herself into her work, and began to train through the British Horse Society to become an instructor, so that she could pass on some of her knowledge to other riders.

She had really wanted to go away to college, but Ursula soon put paid to any of those (as she put it) fanciful ideas.

'We need you here, Ella,' she said, appealing to her better nature. 'There's no point in wasting good money when you can learn all you need to know at the stables. And if that's not enough for you, then get some books from the library. You can't abandon the horses for three years just to do a degree. It's madness. And if you won't do it for us,' she added, 'then do it for them. They need you here.'

That much was true, Ella recalled, judging by the way Vanessa and Caroline behaved around the yard.

'Like two pompous ladies,' Thomas observed dryly. 'You won't see them getting their hands dirty.'

And he was absolutely right. Her stepsisters had no intention of exerting themselves over the mundane tasks of mucking out and grooming. Oh no, they were perfectly happy to ride and to compete, but they made sure the necessary jobs were left to somebody else, that person usually being Ella.

She didn't mind, not really, she thought, as she polished the bridle and stirrup leathers until they were gleaming like new. At least she was doing a job that she loved and was working with the animals she adored. It could have been worse. A lot worse.

'How are you doing?' Thomas asked. He had soaped up the bit and cheek pieces, and polished the metal stirrup irons until they glittered like silver.

'Nearly done,' she said, giving the leather a final rub.

'When did you say these people were coming?' He fastened the last bits of tack together, and hung them over a hook on the stable wall as he spoke.

'Nine thirty,' Ella said, glancing at her watch. 'Blimey,

Thomas, it's after nine now. I'll have to get Jasper and Nero saddled up.'

She jumped down from the bale she was sitting on, and brushed the strands of straw from her fleece jacket and jeans. Her blonde hair had fallen loose from its ponytail, and swung forward over her eyes. She ran her fingers through it and expertly coiled it into a loose knot at the nape of her neck. It wouldn't hold, but it was better than nothing.

'Ella!'

'Oh God, that's Vanessa,' she said. 'Can you give me a hand, Thomas?'

'Sure, I can. Do you want me to fetch in Nero?'

'Please,' she said, nodding. 'He's always a bit of a handful. I'll get Jasper.'

'There you are!' Vanessa pushed open the tack room door and glared pointedly at the pair of them, her pale blue eyes flicking over the empty mugs and the pile of cleaning cloths and soap. She was wearing a pair of skin tight, cream jodhpurs that looked as if they had been sprayed on, and a checked hacking jacket. Her mousy brown hair was stuffed into a hair net, which made her look twenty years older than she really was, and her plump, pink cheeks shone where she had pulled the strap of her riding hat far too tight under her chin. 'Why isn't Jasper ready?'

'He is ready,' Ella said. 'He's been groomed and all he needs is his tack put on.'

'I see.' She wrinkled her nose. 'Well, I'm waiting.'

She thwacked her whip against her leg as she spoke.

Thomas muttered something unintelligible under his breath, as he snatched down Nero's head collar, and strode out across the yard.

The way they treated Ella made his blood boil, acting as if she was some sort of skivvy. It was her father who had started up the stables, and given the place such an enviable reputation. It had nothing to do with Ursula Johnson, and her two spoilt offspring. Yet they lorded over the place as if they owned it. Truth be told, they wouldn't know a nag from a stallion if they were stood side by side in front of them. It was the image of the landed gentry and the distinctly upper-crust class that they were interested in.

Ursula and her daughters liked mingling with the nobs.

Thomas spat forcefully on the ground, as he unlatched the gate into the black gelding's paddock. 'Come on, me darling,' he muttered, waving the head collar. 'Let's see you do your worst.'

Vanessa sat perched on a bale of hay, twirling her whip between her fingers as she watched Ella tighten the girth on Jasper. 'Don't you think it's exciting,' she said.

'What?'

'This film they're making.'

'I don't know much about it,' Ella said.

'Oh. I thought mother had told you.'

'No,' she said. Or at least, if she had, she obviously hadn't been paying her much attention. Ursula talked such a load of twaddle at times it was hardly surprising. Name dropping was one of her fortes. She was forever trying to outdo her neighbours by boasting of her various important acquaintances. Ella would find herself listening with half an ear, bored stiff, whilst Ursula launched herself into the latest topic of country gossip.

'Well, they're looking for experienced show-jumpers,' Vanessa explained. 'So naturally, someone told them about us.'

'Naturally,' Ella muttered, as she yanked Jasper's girth up another hole. The bay gelding snorted and tossed its head in protest. That "someone" was a person who obviously needed their head examined.

'Vanessa! Vanessa! Oh my God, I don't believe it, Vanessa!'

Caroline came hurtling into the stable yard, her face pink and flustered with excitement. Her large breasts bounced visibly under the tightness of her velvet show jacket, and her sturdy thighs were quivering as she ran.

'He's here!' she panted breathlessly.

'Who's here?'

'Lewis!' she screeched, waving her arms excitedly. 'Lewis Trevelyan.'

'No!' Vanessa jumped down from the bale, her cheeks rapidly flushing with colour. '*The* Lewis Trevelyan, from Blackwater Films? Oh my God! Where is he?'

Caroline smirked as she sucked in a breath of much needed air. 'He's talking to mother. Can you believe it? *He* is talking, to *our* mother.'

'No!' Vanessa gasped.

Ella stroked Jasper's nose, and patted him fondly on the neck. The shrieking from the two girls had unsettled him, and he seemed tense and nervous.

'Yes! And you'll never guess what.' Caroline paused a moment, for good effect. 'This film he's making, it's got Simon De Silva as the main star.'

'You're joking. Simon De Silva?' Vanessa clutched at her sleeve.

Caroline nodded, beaming.

'Oh my God!' She snatched Jasper's reins from Ella's hand. 'Well, what are we waiting for? Come on, Ella, move. Give me a leg up. Now!'

'But what about Nero?' Caroline protested. 'He's not ready, yet.'

'Sod Nero.' Vanessa thumped her backside down into the saddle, and jerked the nervous horse's head around.

'Wait for me, Vanessa.'

'Get stuffed.'

Caroline looked as if she was going to burst into tears.

'This is all your fault!' she snapped, glaring at Ella. 'Where's my horse?'

'Thomas is bringing him in.'

'Well, he should have been tacked up by now. It's not fair.'

Ella shrugged. Life was full of disappointments. That much she had learned in the past few years. You either got on with it, or you didn't. In her experience, complaining and moping around didn't do anyone any good.

She hurried to lift down Nero's saddle, as she heard hooves clattering over the cobbles in the yard.

'Where the hell have you been?' Caroline snorted crossly.

Thomas shrugged as he tethered the black gelding to a ring in the stable wall, and undid its rug.

'He's filthy! Well, you'll have to brush him. I can't ride him with all that mud on his legs.'

'Suit yourself,' Thomas muttered. 'I've got to set up some show jumps for your mother and that producer chap who's hanging round.'

'Lewis Trevelyan.' Caroline positively swooned. 'Ella, do hurry up.'

A quick flick over with a body brush, and Nero was ready to be saddled up, allegedly. He, however, was not in a good mood. He had been enjoying a lazy morning in the field with his stable mates, and he did not relish the idea of work. His black ears lay flat against his skull as Ella tried to soothe him. He snorted and tried to nip her when she tightened his girth.

'Oh, for goodness, sake, let me do it!' Caroline snapped. She whacked him on the side of his neck with the flat of her whip. 'He just needs to know who's boss. You're too soft with him.'

Ella winced, and stepped to one side. She could see the whites of Nero's eyes. It was patently obvious (to her, at least) that he wasn't in the right frame of mind for any of this.

'Stand still, you stupid horse!' Caroline said, as she thrust her polished boot into the stirrup. 'Give me a leg up, Ella.'

'Caroline, I don't think...'

'You're not here to think,' she snapped. 'You're here to help me, so hurry up. I'm fed up of Vanessa getting all the attention. I want Lewis Trevelyan to notice me, not her.'

With a sigh, Ella cupped her hands around Caroline's podgy knee, and thrust her upwards on the count of three. She thumped all of her weight (which, admittedly, was quite considerable) onto the horses back.

Nero's eyes rolled in their sockets, and he snorted angrily.

He could have done without the thrust of Caroline's spur capped boots, or the whack of her crop across his rump. In fact, he didn't need anything to make him move. What he did need, however, was something to make him stop.

A horse in full flight is a splendid sight to see. A horse in a panic stricken, headlong bolt is terrifying.

'Sweet bloody Jesus!' Thomas swore, as he scuttled to one side to avoid being trampled in the mayhem that ensued. 'What the devil does she think she's doing?'

'Riding to impress,' Ella said sweetly. 'What does it look like?'

Nero soared over the five-bar gate and took off like a black demon possessed, across the adjoining field, the hedge, and the field beyond, with Caroline clinging on for all she was worth.

In the sand ménage, Vanessa was busy jumping a round of coloured poles, and doing so quite successfully until Jasper, startled by Nero's headlong dash for freedom, swerved, spun around, and promptly deposited her in a rather undignified heap on the ground.

Ella didn't mean to laugh. In fact, she was quite mortified by what had happened. But there was something uniquely satisfying about seeing Vanessa sprawled on her backside in the sand school, and Caroline screeching hysterically around the neck of a maddened horse, which was rapidly disappearing into a cloud of dust on the horizon.

And the subdued giggle, which she had tried in vain to suppress, erupted into a loud and mischievous laugh.

Lewis Trevelyan was standing by the white post and rail fencing of the paddock, and trying desperately not to appear bored. (It wasn't good for PR reasons). But the inane chatter of this annoying Mrs Johnson woman was driving him nuts. As far as he could see, her daughters couldn't ride, weren't photogenic, and would look hideous in any kind of movie, bar a B group horror spoof.

He raised his eyes skywards, as he caught the amused, sideways glance from his personal assistant, Lucy. He would have words with her later. It was her suggestion that they come to these stables in the first place.

The thunder of galloping hooves distracted him

momentarily from his thoughts. The sound of mischievous laughter distracted them more.

And that was when he saw her.

It was only a fleeting glimpse, but it was enough for a snapshot impression to implant itself in his brain. The girl was stunning, but in a natural and unassuming way. She had long blonde hair, and she was wearing casual clothes, jeans and a sweatshirt, nothing fancy. But even from this distance, he could see she was something special.

My God, he realised, *she really was quite beautiful.*

Ella, oblivious to this sudden interest in her, clamped a hand over her mouth in dismay and ducked back into the stables. Goodness, she hoped no one had heard her. Ursula would go berserk if she thought she was laughing at her precious daughters.

'Didn't need no thistle, then,' Thomas observed dryly. His eyes sparkled merrily.

'Shush, Thomas,' she said. 'That's wicked. I suppose I'd better go and see if I can help catch those horses.'

'Don't you dare. You know you'll get the blame. If I was you, I'd sneak back to the house, and pretend you saw none of it.'

'I can't do that.'

'Now how did I know that's what you were going to say,' he sighed, picking up Nero's head collar, and tossing it over to her. 'Come on, let's go.'

Vanessa dusted herself down and remounted Jasper. She was sure she had Lewis Trevelyan's attention now, and she wasn't going to let an opportunity like this one go to waste. Especially as Caroline was out of the picture. (And for good, if she had her way.)

But sadly, she was mistaken in her beliefs. For the man who could make her dreams of fame and fortune come true, was no longer watching her.

Lewis Trevelyan's gaze was fixed on the distant horizon, where he had spotted a far more interesting proposition.

The girl he had seen earlier was walking back across the

fields leading the black horse. It was following her quietly, as docile as a lamb. A short way behind her came a small limping man, supporting a red faced and hobbling young woman.

'So, Mr Trevelyan, what do you think? Has Hollyfield stables got what your company is looking for?'

Lewis Trevelyan glanced with a certain degree of distaste at the simpering smirk Ursula Johnson was giving him, and then looked again at the trio on the far horizon. A slow and steady smile began to spread across his face.

'Actually,' he said, stroking his designer bristled chin thoughtfully, 'Yes, I rather think it has.'

Chapter Two

'I think I've broken something,' Caroline moaned, as she draped herself over Thomas' shoulder.

'Nay, lass. You'll be a bit bruised, that's all.'

'And winded,' Ella said. 'That was quite some tumble you took.'

Caroline had managed to pull Nero up before he jumped the boundary hedge, which was fortunate for her, because it was all that came between them and the main road.

What wasn't so fortunate, however, was the way she had been tossed over his head like a champagne cork going off, when he jerked to an abrupt standstill.

By the time Thomas and Ella caught up with her she was sprawled flat on her back, groaning (having made quite sure they were coming after her first), and Nero was munching contentedly on a clump of meadow grass a short distance away.

Ella caught hold of the horse's reins, as Thomas administered his own version of first aid to the prostrate Caroline.

A poke here, and a prod there, and a muttered 'You'll live,' seemed to be enough to galvanise her into action. (After all, there was still the matter of the Blackwater Film Company to contend with).

Ella crouched down and ran her hands over the black gelding's legs. The front nearside was warm to the touch.

'It's a bit hot,' she said, glancing over at Thomas.

The small Irishman frowned, more from the weight of Caroline leaning on him than anything else. 'I'll cold hose him when we get him back to the yard,' he said. 'He'll be fine and dandy in no time.'

'Unlike me,' Caroline sniffed, smearing a patch of mud across her flushed cheeks with the back of her gloved hand. 'I ache everywhere. Stupid horse.' She glared at the offending beast.

'Still, he looked a picture sailing over that gate, so he did,' Thomas said. He winked at Ella.

'Did he really?' Caroline's voice sounded hopeful. 'Do you think Mr Trevelyan saw me?'

He could hardly have failed to miss her, the noise she was making.

'Possibly,' Ella said. 'Although I think his attention may have been diverted slightly when Vanessa fell off.'

'No!' Caroline gasped. This was news to her. 'She fell off Jasper?'

'Quite spectacularly,' Thomas assured her.

Caroline beamed. 'I hope she wasn't hurt.'

'No more than you, by the looks of things.' He pointed a finger in the direction of the sand school. The people from the film company were standing around watching the proceedings. Vanessa had managed to get back on her horse, and was in the process of completing the course of jumps. She looked as if she was doing rather well at it, too.

'Right!' Caroline announced, straightening her shoulders, and deciding she no longer hurt as much as she had first thought. 'Give me a leg up.'

'No,' Ella said. She laid a warning hand on her stepsister's arm. 'You can't ride him. I don't want him going lame.'

'He won't go lame if I just sit on him,' she said. 'Please, Ella. I want Mr Trevelyan to see me.'

'I think he's seen you already,' Thomas said. 'Leastways, he keeps staring over here.'

'Does he? Does he really?' Caroline peered around the horse's neck. Why yes, the young man in question *was* looking across the fields at her. In fact, he had one hand raised to shield his eyes from the sun as he did so.

Caroline thrust her bosoms out and held in her stomach. She risked a tentative wave back at him.

'I can't believe he's actually here,' she said excitedly. 'He works with all the top stars, you know. It was his PA who phoned mother to ask if she could suggest some suitable riders.'

'And your ma thought of you,' Thomas said, trying hard to keep a straight face. 'Well, I'll be.'

Ella smiled as she walked on ahead with Nero. The gelding had stopped snorting, and was plodding calmly, his long black tail swishing behind him at the ever-present cloud of flies.

Her stepsisters never ceased to amaze her. Both were under the illusion that they were talented riders just waiting to be discovered. The fact that they never won anything, and were frequently disqualified from jumping competitions for riding the wrong course, didn't seem to dissuade them.

Ursula couldn't be swayed in her beliefs either. She was the one who bolstered their confidence, blaming the horse, the ground, or even the judges when things went wrong. Anything, it seemed, other than to accept the plain truth that her daughters were not top-class riders, and never would be.

Back in the arena, she was acting true to form by trying her best to convince the Blackwater Film Company that Hollyfield stables could and would produce talented show jumpers for them.

There were four people in the visiting party - the producer, Lewis Trevelyan, (A very nice young man. Quite charming, actually, Ursula thought) - and his personal assistant, Lucy. (A thirty-something beanpole with flame red hair and an appalling taste in clothes.) The two other young men were introduced as Matthew, the assistant locations manager, and James, the technical adviser. Since neither of them looked old enough to have left school, Ursula paid them very little attention. Instead, she concentrated her efforts on the rather distinguished looking producer.

'Take Jasper over the poles again, Vanessa,' she instructed. 'Now watch this, Mr Trevelyan. I'm sure you'll be impressed. My daughter's been riding since she was four years old.'

'Has she really,' Lewis said politely. He presumed that included rocking horses, by the way the woman was rolling round in the saddle.

He was beginning to think that Lucy's idea of using real show jumpers in the film instead of stunt riders was not one of her better suggestions. Not with this rider, anyway. The girl was capable enough (once she'd stopped falling off, that is) but she wasn't what he had in mind.

But the blonde-haired girl – his gaze drifted over to the distant field, where he could just see the hapless trio disappearing from view – now she was something else entirely.

'Who is that girl?' he said.

Ursula followed his gaze with an irritated look on her face. He had missed Vanessa doing a perfect double spread. And Jasper was behaving impeccably now he wasn't being watched.

'Oh, that's Caroline,' she said. 'My youngest daughter.'

'Really?'

'Yes,' Ursula assured him.

(She was, in fact, speaking the truth, because when she glanced into the distance the only people she could actually see at that moment, was Caroline and Thomas. How was she to know (as she was quick to point out later) that a split second earlier, Ella had been in the picture?)

'I'd like to meet her,' he said.

Ursula beamed. Well, it was tough on Vanessa, but what the heck. At least he was showing an interest in one of her girls. 'I'm sure she'll be thrilled,' she said. 'Why don't you come up to the house with me and we'll wait for her to come back? I don't suppose she'll be very long.'

Vanessa felt a wave of despair surge over her, as she watched her mother and the group of people surrounding Mr Trevelyan turn and walk away from the arena. It wasn't fair. Jasper was jumping magnificently now. Why weren't they watching her?

'Mother!'

Ursula glanced back over her shoulder. 'Ah, Vanessa,' she said, as if suddenly remembering she was there. 'You might as well finish now. Oh, and can you tell Caroline to come up to the house when she's ready. Mr Trevelyan wants to speak to her.'

It was perhaps as well that the film company had moved out of earshot at that moment, because Vanessa uttered a particularly loud expletive as she dismounted and looped Jasper's reins over his head.

Her face was flushed with anger. What the hell did they want to speak to Caroline for? Hadn't they noticed the way she'd ridden like a lunatic, totally out of control, and with no regard for anyone else's safety?

She slid up the stirrups and loosened Jasper's girth. And if her mother thought she was going to tell Caroline that they wanted to talk to her, she was going to be disappointed. If they wanted her sister, they could find her themselves.

'Is he lame?' Ella asked, as she watched Thomas patiently hosing Nero's leg with cold water. The black gelding fidgeted as the icy spray ran down him and settled in a spreading lake around his hooves.

'No, no, he'll be fine,' he said. 'But this won't do him any harm, seeing as how he took off without being warmed up properly.' He gave Caroline an irritated scowl, but she was oblivious to it, seeing as how she was bent double at the time, and fiddling with one of her boots. 'Bloody woman,' he muttered, under his breath. 'You might be best to take him for a gentle hack,' he added, glancing back at Ella. 'It would stop him stiffening up.'

'Good idea,' she said. 'I'll walk him round the cross-country course. No one's riding it at the moment, and the track's pretty soft and sandy there.'

She tied her hair back, and retrieved a riding hat from the tack room. 'I won't be long,' she said, as she swung nimbly into the saddle and gathered up the reins.

Not a moment too soon, either, she realised. It looked

as if battle between the two warring stepsisters was about to commence.

Vanessa came stomping into the yard, hauling a sweaty looking Jasper behind her. 'So, there you are!' she said, glaring pointedly at Caroline, who was now sitting on the ground trying to untangle the piece of baling twine from the zip of her polished leather riding boot. 'What the hell did you think you were doing?'

'Me?' Caroline spluttered. 'Huh! You're a fine one to talk. You're the one who fell off in full view of everybody.'

'Only because Nero startled Jasper.'

'Yes, well, if you'd been paying attention to what you were doing...'

'I *was* paying attention. It was your fault...'

'Oh no it wasn't. You were the one...'

The voices faded into a distant muttering of accusation and counter accusation, as Ella rode Nero away from the yard, and headed out on to the track leading into the woods.

'All this fuss about a film, Nero,' she said, rubbing the black horse's withers. 'I don't know. Whatever next.'

Ella couldn't think what had possessed Ursula to recommend Vanessa and Caroline for the part, other than maternal pride in her offspring. Nature was very good at ensuring most parents saw their children as perfect, even if nobody else did. It was just as well, really. She dreaded to think what Mr Trevelyan had thought of the whole sorry spectacle.

She guided Nero down a grassy bank and paddled him through the shallow water jump. The horse seemed to be enjoying himself. His ears were pricked forwards, and his manner was calm and unruffled.

It was amazing what a bit of kindness and attention did. No one seeing him now, would believe he was the same maddened creature of a few short moments ago.

She loosened the reins and let him pick his own way through the stream.

The sun glinted off the water's surface, and warmed the

faint chill in the breeze. Above her, the sky was clear and blue, with only a few wispy white clouds drifting past. It was going to be a glorious day, she thought.

Unfortunately, it wasn't glorious for everyone.

'More tea, Mr Trevelyan?' Ursula said, holding up the pot and beaming at him. She had laid out the best tea service especially. It hadn't been used for years, but a quick wipe over with a damp cloth had rendered it serviceable. It wasn't often she had such genuinely important guests. 'Or a custard cream, perhaps, or another fig roll?'

'No, I'm fine thanks,' Lewis said, risking a surreptitious glance at his watch. 'Do you think she'll be much longer?'

'Caroline? No, I don't think so. In fact, I really don't know what's taking her so long. Do you want me to go and have a look?'

'If you wouldn't mind,' he said. 'I've got another engagement to go to, you see.'

'Oh.' Ursula tried to hide her disappointment.

'Actually, we are running a bit late,' Lucy said, declining Ursula's offer of a second cup of tea up with a quick shake of her head. She had managed only a few sips from her first cup. It was so strong and bitter that she marvelled at the way her boss had managed to drink any of it.

Matthew and James had been wise to decline the invitation all together. (When last spotted, they had been having an animated conversation with a couple of young stable girls they had bumped into in the paddocks, and had said - well, practically insisted really - that they would stay outside until Lewis had finished his business at the house).

'How late?' Lewis said.

'Well, you did say ten thirty, Mr Trevelyan, and it's after that now.'

'So it is,' he said.

Ursula looked almost panic stricken. 'I'm sure she won't be long.' She peered anxiously out of the front window as she spoke. They couldn't leave now, not now. Not when he had shown such an interest in Caroline. Oh, where was she, the stupid, senseless girl?

'Perhaps we could call back later?' Lucy suggested, looking at her phone. 'I don't expect this meeting with Mr Fitzgerald will take very long, and you've nothing else booked after that.' She glanced over at Lewis. 'What do you think?'

'Yes. I think we should,' he said. He was actually torn in two directions. He was desperate to get away from Mrs Johnson, who was trying his patience by the second. She had spent the best part of half an hour extolling the virtues of her daughter. He had yet to meet a more pushy mother, and he had met several in the course of his career. On the other hand, he really did want to see this girl. She had caught his attention and intrigued him, which was always a good sign.

'That's agreed, then,' he said, standing up. 'We'll call back later.'

'Oh yes, yes,' Ursula cooed. 'Come back anytime. I'll make sure Caroline is ready for you. I expect she's got involved in something down at the yard. She does love her horses, you know.'

Caroline was, indeed, involved in something down at the yard – a rather vicious battle of words with her older sister - which was starting to turn into a nasty case of push and shove.

Thomas despaired of the pair of them. There was Jasper standing, hot and sweating, and neither of them saw fit to fetch him a sweat rug, or a damp sponge to wipe him down.

He lifted the saddle off and thrust it at Vanessa. 'Hold this,' he muttered.

'Me?' she said.

'Well, excuse me if I'm mistaken, but it is your horse.'

'Yes, but...'

'And you,' he continued, his eyes narrowing on Caroline's sulky face. 'You can take this.' He handed her the bridle, which was flecked with foam and smears of grass coloured slime. 'And don't forget to give the bit a good rinse before you hang it up.'

Caroline was incensed. 'I don't see why I should clean her smelly tack,' she said. 'I don't suppose she'll clean Nero's.'

'No,' Thomas sighed resignedly. 'I expect Ella will do that.' He picked up Jasper's feet, and started to clean them with a hoof pick. 'I thought you wanted to create a good impression for this here film company.'

'We do,' Vanessa said, and Caroline quickly nodded her agreement.

'Well, then.' He straightened up and rubbed the small of his back. 'How do you know they haven't been watching you all this time?'

'Oh my God!' Vanessa looked aghast. 'You don't think...? No, they couldn't, could they?'

Thomas gave a nonchalant shrug. 'There were four of them in that car,' he said. 'I only saw two people go up to the house with your ma.'

'You idiot!' Caroline shrieked, pointing an accusing finger at her sister. 'If they've seen us, it's your fault. You started this.'

'Me?' Vanessa swung round and almost dropped the saddle as she did so.

'Yes.' Caroline shook the bridle at her. 'It was you who came storming into the yard shouting your mouth off.'

'With good reason.'

'God give me strength,' Thomas groaned.

Shaking his head, he turned and walked into the peaceful sanctuary of the tack room. Someone needed to find a sweat rug for Jasper. The way things were going it might just as well be him.

'Well?' Lucy said, glancing across at Lewis as he clipped on his seat belt, and turned on the ignition.

'Well, what?'

'You know what,' she said, grinning. 'You've got that dreamy look on your face again.'

'I don't know what you're on about,' he said gruffly.

'She means the look you get when you think you're on

to something,' Matthew said cheerfully, waving out of the rear window to the stable girl with whom he had been having a most interesting flirtation. He turned back to them. 'So,' he said. 'Are you on to something?'

'Possibly.' The car wheels scrunched over the gravel, as Lewis drove them down the impressive driveway. 'I'm interested in seeing that girl again, anyway.'

'What girl?' James's ears had pricked up.

'The one with blonde hair,' he said.

James looked quizzically at Matthew. He hadn't seen any blonde-haired rider. Matthew hadn't either, judging by the puzzled shrug of his shoulders.

'She wasn't actually riding,' Lucy explained, craning her neck round to talk to them. 'We saw her in the distance. Apparently, she's the youngest daughter. Caroline, I think her name is.'

'Right,' Matthew said. 'So, you don't know if she can ride.'

'I think it's fairly natural to assume that she can,' Lewis said. 'I mean, she's living at a pretty well-established riding school.'

He swung the wheel of the BMW round to the right. The road was narrow and full of sudden twists and turns. 'Map, Lucy,' he said, pointing a finger at the glove compartment.

'Please,' she said airily. 'Well, I thought it was ideal, for a location shoot, anyway.' She opened up the folded map and peered intently down at it for several moments. 'I think you want to take the next left.' She glanced up at the road. 'There should be a sign for Ecclestone.'

'How about a Ridgeway?' He indicated the sign at the side of the road.

'No.' She stared down at the map again.' At least, I can't see a Ridgeway.' She turned it upside down and squinted sideways at it.

Lewis gave a soft growl. 'Perhaps if you gave it to James...'

'No. No, I've found it. Yes, I was right.' She flapped a well-manicured hand to the side. Her gold and silver bracelets jangled. 'You need to turn left. Here.'

'To Ridgeway?' Lewis said.

'I guess so.' She smiled sweetly up at him.

Lewis shook his head despairingly, as he swung the wheel round.

And that's when he saw her for the third time.

The black horse was walking along a sand covered track on the other side of the hedgerow, its thick black mane and tail blowing and ruffling in the breeze. The girl was riding one handed, using the other to rub his gleaming withers. She looked happy and relaxed, without a care in the world.

Lewis slammed on the brakes, propelling the occupants of the car abruptly forwards. The rear wheels skidded on the gravely surface, and the front wheels bounced over the grass verge, bringing them to an emergency stop.

'Bloody hell!' James swore, rubbing his cheek, which had connected with the front passenger seat's headrest. (That would teach him to fasten his seat belt *before* they set off.) 'What was it? A pheasant?'

'No,' Lewis said, flinging open the car door and climbing out to get a better look. 'I think it's her.'

'Who?' Lucy mumbled, from her doubled over position in the front seat. The contents of her handbag had spilled out like a shower of confetti, and she was groping around trying to retrieve money, make-up, cigarettes and other assorted items from the foot well of the car.

'The elusive Caroline,' he said. He was peering over the hedge like an ardent bird watcher, who has just spotted a rare species of the feathered variety. 'Look. She's over there.'

When no one responded, he glanced back at the car. Matthew and James had seized the moment to climb out and have a quick drag on a vape. They were standing, puffing away quite merrily, without paying him, or the girl, for that matter, the slightest bit of attention.

'Oh, please,' he muttered, his voice heavy with sarcasm.

'Sorry boss.' Matthew grinned sheepishly. 'Where did you

say she was?'

'Jesus Christ, I've broken a nail!' Lucy's alarmed shriek drew another irritated glare from Lewis. 'My best one as well.'

'Is anyone remotely interested in making this film?' he said wearily.

James gave a low whistle, as he stepped onto the verge and peered over the hedge. The girl had ridden into the distance, and was heading through a small copse of trees. Her long blonde hair cascaded over her shoulders and gleamed in the sunlight as she moved from side to side in rhythm with the horse's movements.

'She looks the part,'

'Thank you,' Lewis said.

Lucy emerged from the car, clutching her tan leather handbag under one arm, and peering hopefully at the pair of them. 'Where is she? Have I missed her?'

'Over there.' James pointed.

They stood watching for a moment, until she rode out of sight.

'Interesting,' Matthew said, nodding his head. 'I certainly didn't see her at the stables.'

Which was probably just as well, Lewis thought. Matthew's reputation as a womaniser was not without strong foundation.

'Told you we'd find somebody suitable,' Lucy said, sucking her finger. 'You didn't believe me, did you?'

'Not when I saw those other girls,' Lewis said, grinning. 'Come on, we'd better get a move on. Mr Fitzgerald will be wondering where we are. Don't forget,' he added, as he climbed back into his seat and slammed the door. 'We need his approval if this venture is ever going to get off the ground.'

'And then we're going back to the stables, right?' James said, glancing back over his shoulder at the distant copse of trees.

'I am,' Lewis said. 'But you're not. I'm going to drop you off at the hotel. You've got work to do, remember?'

'Can't it wait,' Matthew protested. He was looking forward to going back and seeing if he could fix up a date with the young stable-girl he'd been chatting with earlier.

A withering glare from his boss persuaded him not to push the matter.

'This is a business trip,' Lewis informed him, as he bounced the car gingerly back onto the road. 'Try and remember that. Now then, Lucy. Do you think we could try the map again? The right way round, this time, otherwise I'll give it to James.'

'I can manage,' his assistant said huffily. 'You know we always get there in the end.'

'Yes, but we'd get there a lot quicker if you'd remembered the sat nav,' he said, grinning. Four hours from London, when it should have taken them two at the most, all because his delightful PA had missed the turning off the M25, (supposedly because a juggernaut had blocked her view of the slip road exit).

If Lucy noticed the irony in his tone, she ignored it. She felt she was quite capable of reading the map. And if he didn't agree with her judgement, then he was perfectly at liberty to read it for himself. Or look it up on his phone, she thought, although the likelihood of getting a decent signal seemed remote.

'Turn left at the end of this road,' she said.

'The Ridgeway road?'

'That's what I said.'

Lewis switched on his car indicator, and glanced across at her pert little face, with its stubborn, don't-mess-with-me expression.

'Right,' he said calmly.

'No!' She flapped her hand at him. 'Left.'

'Left it is,' he said, grinning. 'I was only agreeing with you, Lucy.'

'Oh,' she muttered, peering down at the creased map once more. A thoughtful frown wrinkled her brow. 'Actually, maybe we should go right.' She spun the map round.

'James,' Lewis pleaded, rolling his eyes in exasperation. 'Get us out of here.'

'Whatever you say, boss.' He plucked the map from Lucy's hand, and ignored her immediate yelp of protest. 'You want to turn left here, and then right at the next junction. Ecclestone is about two miles away, and the Fitzgerald place is the first house on the left. Got it?'

He folded the map up and handed it back to Lucy with a grin. 'Simple,' he said.

'Like your brain, Connors,' she snapped.

Lewis smiled. He hated them teasing Lucy, but he had his own reason for getting this visit over and done with quickly. The sooner he finished his appointment with Mr Fitzgerald, the sooner he could get back to Hollyfield Stables to meet the elusive Caroline in person.

Had he but known it, the encounter was going to be a disappointment for both of them.

Chapter Three

'I don't believe it,' Caroline said, her face beaming with obvious pleasure. They want to meet me?'

'Indeed, they do,' Ursula said, taking her daughter's muddy riding hat and gloves from her and placing them on the kitchen table. 'I don't know why you were so long at the yard, but it doesn't matter. They're coming back, so you've got time to smarten yourself up a bit.' She peered closer. 'What's that red mark on your cheek?'

Caroline reached up tentatively. 'I think it's where I fell off,' she said. Or where Vanessa had thumped her, but she didn't want to tell her mother that.

'Well see if you can cover it up with a bit of foundation or something. Oh, and Caroline,' she added, lowering her voice a fraction. 'I haven't told Vanessa they're coming back to see you. She was in rather a bad mood when she came in. I think she felt a bit embarrassed falling off in front of everyone.'

Caroline nodded. She wasn't surprised. It was fortunate for her that her own little tumble had taken place out of sight of the main arena and the watching spectators. 'Where is she now?' she asked.

'Gone for a long soak in a hot bath.'

'Right. Well, I won't say anything to her.'

Not yet, she thought gleefully. Oh my God, she couldn't believe it. Lewis Trevelyan wanted to see her. It was so exciting. He must have been really impressed by the way she had ridden Nero. She was impressed with it herself. At least she had managed to pull him up before he jumped the hedge, even if she had catapulted over his neck at the same time. It took skill and courage to halt a bolting horse; skill, and courage.

The fact that she had never been so terrified in her life before, had nothing to do with it. Appearances could be deceptive, and if Lewis Trevelyan had been deceived, it was all well and good. She wasn't going to tell him otherwise.

'Tea?' Ursula suggested. 'And there's some biscuits left on the plate.'

A brandy would be more welcome, Caroline thought, for medicinal purposes, naturally. She shook her head. 'No thanks. I think I'll get changed.'

'Wear those dark blue jodhpurs.'

'Mother,' she groaned. 'They're far too tight. I told you that last week.'

'Did you, dear? Oh well,' she shook her head. 'I must have forgotten. The tartan checked ones look nice, though.' At least, they did when she was about twelve, she reflected.

Caroline made her way upstairs, a thoughtful frown on her flushed cheeks. What did one put on, when one was destined to meet a film producer who could be her gateway to the stars? And how long was Vanessa planning to lock herself in the bathroom? She wanted to get in to wash her hair.

'Will you be long?' she said, knocking on the door.

'Ages,' came the grumpy reply.

Vanessa had no intention of letting anybody in. She lay back in a steaming mass of frothy bubbles, her eyes closed, inhaling the subtle perfume from several fragranced candles, which she had lit and placed strategically around the room.

The knowledge that the Blackwater Film Company was showing an apparent interest in Caroline was partly to blame for her foul mood. The ache in her left thigh and arm, where she had landed in her fall, was also contributing to it. What made things worse, however, was the fact that she felt as if she had been publicly humiliated, and her mother didn't seem to care. Jasper had been performing really well, and they had all walked off and left her. How did they expect her to feel?

She raised her leg and turned the hot tap on with her toe. A spout of gushing water rekindled the mass of bubbles, which were now threatening to spill over the sides of the bath.

'Hurry up!' Caroline said, banging on the door.

'Get lost!'

'I bet you're using all the hot water.'

'Quite possibly.'

'Cow!'

Ursula raised her eyes to the ceiling as she heard the violent slamming of a bedroom door.

'That sounds like fun,' Ella said.

Ursula dropped her gaze, to see her stepdaughter standing in the doorway, levering off her boots on the kitchen step.

'What's going on up there?'

'Oh, nothing,' Ursula said. 'You know what they're like. Well actually,' she paused, wondering if she should say something. Ella was bound to find out one way or the other. And she was too excited not to mention it. In fact, she was positively bursting with excitement. 'Actually, it's about this film company.'

'Oh, yes?' Ella draped her riding jacket over the back of a chair. 'Impressed, were they?'

'Yes, as it happens.'

'They were?' she said, in disbelief. She stopped washing her hands at the kitchen sink, and glanced back at her.

'Yes.' Ursula was beaming like the proverbial Cheshire cat. 'Isn't it marvellous? That young man, Mr Trevelyan – ever such a nice young man - he's the producer you know,' she added. 'Well, he wants to speak to Caroline.'

'He does?' Ella said. 'Why?'

'Because he saw her, and he wants to meet her.'

Ella was surprised at this, to say the least. She had seen Caroline's performance, and at close quarters too, and it had not been a pretty sight.

'The trouble is,' Ursula said, lowering her voice. 'I think Vanessa is a little bit jealous. In fact, I think she's sulking.'

That figured. Ella dried her hands on the kitchen towel. 'But they've gone, haven't they?' she said. 'I thought Thomas said he'd seen them drive off.'

'Yes, but they're coming back.'

'When?'

'I don't know. Later today, I expect.' Ursula opened the fridge and peered hopefully inside. 'I thought I'd do us a salad for lunch. I don't want to be fiddling about cooking when they return.'

'I won't be eating,' Ella said.

'You won't?'

'No, I'm meeting Kate. She's picking me up in her new car. We,' she added, smiling, 'are going to be "ladies who lunch".'

Ursula's face fell. 'But you've got a class at two.'

'I know. I'll be back by then,' she said. 'I've asked Kelly to tack up the horses for the lesson, so it won't be a problem.'

'You could have told me,' Ursula muttered.

'I just have.' Ella picked up a soggy custard cream from the plate and popped it into her mouth. 'Besides,' she added. 'I want to go down to the church, and Kate has offered to take me there.'

'The church?'

Ella's smile faded. 'I wanted to leave some flowers.'

'Ah, right.' Ursula had the decency to look guilty. 'I hadn't forgotten, you know,' she lied. Goodness, was it the anniversary of Robert's death again? The years seemed to be whizzing past. 'In fact, I had planned to go this afternoon.'

'It doesn't matter.'

'I could go tomorrow,' she said. 'Yes, that's what I'll do.' She fiddled with the pin in her hair as she spoke. 'I'll pop down tomorrow, and I'll get a nice bouquet from Madisons, that florist in the village.'

An over-the-top, once-a-year, token gesture, Ella thought, as she filled a glass of water from the tap, and drank it slowly.

'It doesn't do to brood over the past, Ella,' Ursula said. 'We've got the future to think about – the future of the stables - your future. You, me, and the girls,' she added hastily.

35

It still irked her that Robert had left the house and the stables to Ella in his will. As his loyal wife, she had expected to inherit the house at the very least. But no, she was only allowed to remain in residence there, although she could, of course, move to the groom's cottage if she so desired.

Ursula shuddered at the thought. A pokey little two bed-roomed house was not what she aspired to, and she couldn't understand why Robert had left it to her in the first place. Besides which, Ella needed her around to run the business properly. A young girl like her couldn't be expected to take on a managerial role. She was far too soft with people. The feed merchant would eat her alive, if she tried to haggle with him.

Of course, the girl excelled in her work with horses. Ursula couldn't deny it. She had a natural affinity with them, and it was only to be expected, given her parentage. But she couldn't delegate and a firm hand was needed when dealing with the motley assortment of staff, customers, and businesses that used the stables.

The bank manager, for one, was giving her a lot of grief at the moment. She could handle him. She was quite sure that Ella couldn't. (Although a fluttering of those long eyelashes and her sweet and beguiling smile might help.)

Ella leafed through the pile of letters on the kitchen table. 'Anything interesting in the post?' she asked.

Although the main bulk of the mail came addressed to her, Ursula, as manager in charge, tended to open anything that looked remotely businesslike or official.

'No. Only the usual junk,' she replied, quickly plonking a plate on the brown envelope marked "urgent", which had come from the bank that morning. 'There's a card from the vet about Wilson, though. He needs a booster.'

Wilson was the family dog, a huge Great Dane, with an appetite second to none, and manners that left a lot to be desired. He had never really grown out of the puppy stage, and was forever bounding about and upsetting the furniture. Now that he was fully grown, Ursula found it quite off-putting to have him leaping about and slobbering over her every five minutes. Yet whenever she shouted at him, he tended to give her a look of aloof disdain, and then ignored her completely.

Ella, however, could control him with a click of her fingers. The wretched dog appeared to adore her, and followed her everywhere, loyally obedient to her every command.

'I'll make an appointment for him next week,' Ella said.

'How about next month?' Ursula suggested. She had yet to pay the vet's bill, and didn't want to run up another one.

'Whatever.' Ella drained her glass of water. 'Right. Well, I don't suppose Vanessa will let me in the bathroom so I'll have a quick wash downstairs, and then I'll be off.'

'But you will be back at two?'

'Yes,' she said. 'I will be back at two.'

Half an hour later and Vanessa decided it was time she surfaced from the now tepid bathwater, with its sparse covering of bubbles. Caroline had given up banging on the door, and was no doubt fuming in her bedroom. Well good, she thought. Serves her right. She draped herself in her bathrobe, and blew out the spluttering candles. A waft of fragranced steam followed her as she opened the door and stepped out on to the landing.

'About bloody time,' Caroline snapped, rushing past her, and slamming the door. It was too late to wash her hair now. She would have to make do with tying it up instead. She wiped a circle of condensation away from the mirror, and peered at her reflection. Her skin looked blotchy, and she was sure she was starting a new spot. Well, she didn't have time to worry about that now. She brushed her teeth and then fastened her hair in a ponytail, before darting back into the bedroom to put on some make-up. She had already changed into a pair of black trousers, and a neat fitting blouse – rather too neat, if the truth were known - but at least it showed off a good portion of her cleavage. She squirted perfume on her neck and wrists, and applied some more lip-gloss, a free sample from a magazine but she rather liked the finished result (the wet look was so in these days), and then she hurried downstairs to wait for her expected visitors.

Vanessa was in no such hurry to get dressed. She lumbered round the house in her towelling dressing gown, feeling dejected and miserable.

Her mournful face was putting Ursula off her lunch. 'Do try and eat something, darling,' she said, offering her the bowl of prepared salad, and a crusty roll. 'I've said I'm sorry.'

'I'm not hungry,' she sniffed.

'It's not as if we meant to abandon you,' Ursula soothed. 'It's just that Mr Trevelyan and his colleagues had a more pressing engagement to attend.' She helped herself to a liberal portion of grated cheese as she spoke. 'They only travelled up from London last night, and they had a lot of people to see.'

Caroline sat smirking by the window seat as she munched on a stick of celery. (Anything more than that, and her trousers would probably burst at the seams.)

'It's just that Jasper was jumping so well,' Vanessa sniffed.

'I know, darling. I know.'

'He's here!' Caroline shrieked, almost dropping her stick of celery into the dog's drinking bowl, as she leapt to her feet. 'It's him, mother! He's here.'

'Oh my God!' Vanessa ducked behind the curtain and peered through the window. Her sister was right. It *was* Lewis Trevelyan of Blackwater Films. He had come back. In fact, he was at that very moment, striding purposefully up towards the house.

He was wearing dark jeans, which fitted him perfectly, and a pale blue shirt. A pair of sunglasses poked out of his top pocket. His sun-bleached hair was tousled and windswept, and a shadow of stubble covered his jaw. He looked every inch a movie producer; the sort of person splashed all over the celebrity magazines, shaking hands with all the major Hollywood stars.

'He can't see me like this,' she screeched, darting back from the window. Her cheeks were red and shiny, and wet rat's tails of hair dripped down the back of her lumpy towelling robe.

'It's probably not you he's come to see,' Caroline said airily. She examined her immaculate nails, and buffed them with an

38

emery board as she spoke.

Vanessa gave her a sudden hard look. She was suspicious of the fact that her sister was dressed to impress. Had she known about this surprise visit, and not had the decency to tell her?

'What do you mean?' she said. 'What do you know about this?'

'Shush!' Ursula said, rubbing her hands on a damp kitchen cloth. 'He's coming to the door.'

'Stall him, mother!' Vanessa pleaded, as she made a frantic dash for the stairs. 'I won't be long.'

'Take as long as you like,' Caroline said, smugly. 'I'm sure I can keep him entertained.'

Vanessa looked as if her cheeks would explode. They were scarlet with rage. How dare she! The Bitch! Well, she would get her for this. She would. She would!

She galloped up the stairs and burst into the bedroom, flinging the towelling dressing gown onto the bed as she ran. Naked and glorious, she yanked open the wardrobe door, and began snatching down jumpers, shirts, trousers...no, they wouldn't do. Where were her show breeches, the black ones? Oh damn! She thrust her foot into the narrow elasticated leg, and stumbled sideways, fighting to keep her balance. She could hear voices from the hallway, his voice. Oh, what a wonderful, deep voice with just a trace of an American accent. Must come from working with all those famous actors like Julia Roberts and Brad Pitt.

Oof! She staggered onto the bed, and sat down, panting. Shirt. Shirt, which shirt? Polo shirt. That would do, that would be quick. Bra? Where the hell was her...Oh, stuff the bra.

She snatched up the yellow polo shirt and dragged it down over her head. There! She was ready.

'Well, thanks again.'

'Yes, I'm sorry about the misunderstanding.'

Oh No! No...ooo!

Vanessa stumbled to the top of the stairs, but she was too late. The front door was closing, and Lewis Trevelyan, had gone.

'Mother!'

'He wouldn't wait, darling. I did try.' Ursula clicked the latch on the door.

Hot angry tears pricked at the back of her eyelids, as she thumped her way downstairs. She glared at her sister who was perched on the window seat, staring outside. 'Cow!'

'Oh, shut up,' Caroline snapped. 'It's not me you should be cross with.'
She looked almost as shattered as she felt. Defeated, humiliated, and bitter to boot. Her one chance, her one real chance to impress, and it had all been in vain.

'What do you mean?'

'It's bloody Miss Perfect again.'

'Who?' Vanessa's breasts bounced uncomfortably as she strode across the front room and peered miserably over her sister's shoulder at the rapidly departing and godlike, Lewis Trevelyan.

'It's got to be Ella, of course,' Ursula said, coming to stand behind them. 'It can't be anyone else.' She rested her hands on both girls' backs. 'He saw someone riding the cross-country course this morning, and he wants to know who she is and where he can find her.'

'Oh no! Oh Mother!' Vanessa looked quite distraught. 'He can't want her. It's not fair. She always wins at everything, every competition, every show, everything.' She sucked in a deep breath. 'It's our turn now. Oh, it's not fair.' She glanced sideways at her mother, her voice rising. 'You didn't tell him who she was?'

'No. Well, not exactly,' Ursula faltered. 'I said I didn't know who it was, but I'd make enquiries and let him know.'

'And he believed you?'

'Why shouldn't he,' she said.

'So, he'll be coming back?'

'I expect he will.' Ursula smiled a trifle sadly. 'He seemed keen enough.'

'And he's still planning to make this film?'

'I think so.'

'If he can find the right rider,' Caroline said, sniffing miserably.

She didn't know when she had ever felt so wretched. She could tell, the moment her mother had proudly introduced her to Mr Trevelyan, that she was not the girl he was looking for. Disappointment and disbelief had been etched all over his face. 'He wants someone with long blonde hair,' she added sulkily.

Blonde hair, hmm? Now there was a thought. Vanessa chewed on her top lip for a moment, and then turned and glanced at her reflection in the mirror on the wall. Her hair was long, as long as Ella's when she brushed it out loose. She curled a tendril of it around her finger, and tried to imagine the finished result. Already, her spirits were starting to rise. 'Mother,' she said. 'Can I borrow the Range Rover? I thought I might pop into town. There's something I want to buy at the chemists.'

Caroline jerked her head up. 'Like what?'

'It's none of your business,' she snapped.

'You're going to dye your hair, aren't you?'

'I might be.' She shrugged. 'Anyway, why shouldn't I?'

'Because...because...' Caroline was lost for words.

'Actually, that's rather a brilliant idea,' Ursula said.

'It is?'

'Yes, it is.' She glanced from one expectant face to the other. 'Don't you see, Lewis Trevelyan wants to see a blonde-haired rider. Who's to say that the girl riding the cross country-course, wasn't you?'

Caroline's voice dripped with sarcasm. 'Because he saw her riding Jasper?'

Ursula shook her head. 'No, I've been thinking about that.' She looked back at Vanessa. 'You were wearing a hair net under your hat, weren't you?'

Vanessa nodded.

'Excellent.' She beamed. 'I don't suppose he even noticed the colour of your hair. It's only because Ella was riding with hers hanging loose that he saw it was so long and blonde.'

'So technically, it could have been me?' A look of glee

41

settled itself on Vanessa's face.

Caroline's scowl deepened.

'Exactly.' Ursula dangled the set of car keys in front of her. 'Now off you go, and make sure you buy a good make. We don't want any more disasters, do we? I've always gone for ash blonde, myself.' She patted her tightly coiled bleached bun with the tips of her fingers as she spoke. 'And in the meantime,' Her eyes narrowed slightly. 'I'm going to have to think of some excuse to keep Ella out of the way. If you're serious about going through with this, we can't have her wandering about the place.'

Vanessa had never been more serious about anything in her life.

'You'll think of something, mother,' she said, clutching the keys to her ample and bra-less chest and heading for the door. 'I know you will.'

Ursula wished she had her confidence in the matter. She glanced at Caroline, who was weeping a tearful mixture of misery, anger and resentment, and then back to Vanessa, who was positively glowing with her new found energy and excitement.

'Yes, darling,' she sighed. 'Don't worry. I'm sure I will.'

Chapter Four

The Church of St Mary stood tucked away down a side street, appropriately named Church Lane, a few hundred yards away from the centre of the village. It was one of the oldest buildings in the area, with parts of it dating from the fourteenth century. The huge oak door was locked, with a notice pinned to the handle, stating the church would be open for private prayers from two o clock.

'Or when one of the church wardens or the flower arranger turns up,' Kate said.

A spate of local robberies had necessitated the locking of the doors. Ecclesiastical furniture such as solid wooden pews and kneeling stools, were forever turning up at car boot sales and auction rooms, supposedly salvaged from derelict churches. The local constabulary had other ideas.

'I think it's sad,' Ella said. 'You'd think people would have more respect.'

'Not these days,' Kate said scornfully. 'There are a lot of valuable things to be had in these old churches; brass candlesticks, gold plate, even the lead off the roof. Nothing's sacred these days.'

They strolled round the back of the church, and into the neatly tended graveyard. The smell of newly mown grass and the tidy flowerbeds showed that the groundsman, Arthur Billington had been hard at work. Clumps of fading daffodils had already been deadheaded and crimson tulips and creamy coloured primroses were blooming in their place.

Ella laid the bunch of fresh flowers and greenery, cut from the gardens of Hollyfield Stables, beside the engraved marble headstone of her father's grave.

She no longer felt sad about coming here. In a strange way it gave her comfort. She crouched there for a moment, tidying away a few stray bits of grass, and a handful of stones. It didn't seem possible that five years had passed, five long years since that awful day.

Kate stood a short distance away, reading the epitaphs on various weathered and lichen covered headstones. They never failed to intrigue her. Goodness, four children from the same family, "Gone to sleep with the angels". How tragic was that? Or the one with mother, father and son, all dead by drowning, in "the year of our Lord eighteen hundred and one".

'Ready?' Ella said, standing up, and brushing the soil from her trousers.

'Hmm,' Kate murmured. 'Look at this one, Ella. "Mary Martha, spinster of the parish, one hundred and three years old." And that was in the last century as well. I didn't think people lived that long in those days.'

'Well, she obviously did,' she said. 'Anyway, don't be so morbid. I can't see what you find so fascinating about other people's headstones.'

'I'm just interested, that's all.'

'Nosey, more like,' Ella said. 'So, tell me, where are we going for lunch?'

Kate linked her arm through hers. 'I thought we'd go to the Red Fox.'

'That's a bit pricey, isn't it?'

'Yes, but this is my treat.'

Ella raised an eyebrow at her. 'Got promotion, have we?'

'Not yet, but I'm working on it.'

Kate was one of Ella's closest friends from the village. They had known each other since primary school, but even she would be the first to admit that in lifestyle and circumstances, they were miles apart. Kate worked for one of the major insurance companies in town. She wore smart and fashionable clothes, and had a string of well-heeled boyfriends falling in her wake.

Ella spent her days in muddy green wellies and wax jackets. The only men she seemed to attract were those of the farming variety, or the occasional (elderly) vet, or the arthritic blacksmith. She shuddered at the thought. Tom Bluntesham, the lecherous farrier, had been making suggestive remarks to her for years. She would be glad when he retired, but Ursula insisted on using him, since he was the cheapest farrier she could find.

'Watch this,' Kate said, as she unlocked the doors of her sporty looking blue car. The roof collapsed back on itself with a gentle whirring sound.

'Wow,' Ella said. 'That's cool.'

'It is, isn't it?' Kate grinned. 'Come on, hop in.'

The lounge bar of the Red Fox Hotel was bustling with lunchtime customers. The food was reputed to be delicious and all home cooked and freshly made.

Ella had never eaten there before, but knew it received a favourable mention in a Good Food Guide, a recommendation that was truly justified. The avocado and pancetta salad, with honey and mustard dressing, was divine, and the vanilla cheesecake that followed it, utterly delectable.

'I'll never be able to work after this,' she groaned. 'I feel stuffed.'

'Don't go, then,' Kate said, reaching in to her handbag to find her lip gloss, which she carefully reapplied, pouting her lips as she did so.

Ella looked appalled. 'I've got a class to take.'

'So? Can't Ursula do it?'

'Not today, she can't,' she said, stirring a spoonful of sugar into her coffee. 'She's expecting a very important visitor. Did I tell you about this film company coming to the stables?'

'No.' Kate's eyes widened visibly.

'Oh, well they turned up this morning,' she said. 'They're looking for locations in this area, and they also want some show-jumpers, so Ursula recommended Vanessa and Caroline to them.'

'That ought to put them off for a start,' Kate said bluntly. 'I'm sorry, Ella, but it's the truth. I'm no rider, but I can tell a good one when I see one, and those two ain't it.'

'Yes, well that's what I thought.'

'But?'

She shrugged.' Oddly enough, they seem to be interested in Caroline.'

'You're joking?'

'No. In fact, they're coming back to see her this afternoon.' She took a mouthful of strong coffee. 'That's why I've got to get back.'

'I don't believe it,' Kate said. 'What's the film? A comedy or something?'

'I have no idea,' Ella smiled.' But it's got someone called Simon De Silva in it.'

'Simon De Silva?' Kate's jaw dropped.

'You've heard of him, then?'

'Heard of him,' Kate gasped. 'Ella, he's drop dead gorgeous. You must know who he is?'

'Nope,' she said. 'I haven't a clue. Mind you, that might explain why Vanessa and Caroline were in such a state this morning.'

'Too right,' Kate sighed. 'Ella, you need to get out more.' She popped her lip gloss back in her handbag and pulled out her purse. 'I'll just pay for this, and then I'll run you back. What time are they coming?'

'Not you as well,' Ella groaned.

She honestly couldn't see what all the fuss was about. It wasn't as if this Simon De Silva, whoever he was, was going to turn up. Only the producer and the locations manager were involved at this early stage, and the shoot may not even happen, if things weren't right for them. This, she suspected, would probably turn out to be the case.

She stood up and pulled on her suede jacket. Kate was standing at the bar talking to two well-dressed young men. Both wore suits and ties. The taller of the two, the one with short dark hair, was carrying a black leather briefcase. They were probably people she knew from work, she decided. The Red Fox was the kind of place that business people came to for working lunches.

She waved, and caught Kate's eye. 'I'm going to the loo,' she mouthed, pointing at the sign above the door.

Kate nodded, and turned back to her companions.

Ella felt distinctly under-dressed as she peered at her reflection in the floor to ceiling mirror of the Ladies powder room. Her jacket was faded in places, and her pale blue jumper had seen better days. Even her smart navy trousers looked a tad jaded under the harsh and unforgiving lights above the mirror.

Beside her, a woman with a mass of dark red hair, and a figure to die for, was leaning towards the mirror and applying a thick covering of scarlet lipstick to her lips. She was wearing a pale green jacket and a matching long skirt that screamed "designer label". A chunky gold chain hung around her neck, and her wrists jangled under the weight of matching bangles and bracelets.

Ella fluffed up her hair with her fingers. It was the best she could do. She didn't have a brush with her.

The woman beside her was spraying herself liberally with a flowery fragrance that reminded her of jasmine and roses.

Ella had to make do with a squirt from the complimentary bottle of perfume left in a straw basket on the Formica-topped dressing table, alongside the pot-pourri and tissues. It reminded her strongly of the lavender water old Mrs Wallace used to wear.

The woman gave her a polite smile, as she breezed past her on a pair of high-heeled shoes that Ella could never have managed to stand up in, let alone walk in.

How the other half live, she thought glumly, as she made her way back into the crowded bar.

Kate didn't look out of place at all, dressed as she was in a smart knee length skirt, with an off the shoulder blouse. Her dark curly hair had been pinned up in an artistic arrangement of tufts and tendrils, which looked as if it was going to cascade free at any moment.

Ella's spirits sank still further when she saw that the glamorous woman from the Ladies had joined the two men with whom Kate was having such an in-depth conversation.

She stood shyly behind her friend, clutching her shoulder bag under one arm, and trying to ignore the fact that she felt like a country bumpkin.

'Oh, hi,' Kate said, swinging round to face her. 'Are you ready to go?'

She nodded quickly.

'Okay, then. We'll make a move.' She turned back to the two men. 'We might see you there,' she said, fluttering her long dark eyelashes at them. 'If you're lucky.'

'See who, where?' Ella asked as she followed Kate across the crowded room.

'The Jazz Club on Sunday,' she said, fiddling in her handbag for her car keys.

'What?'

'I only said, maybe. Anyway, didn't you think they looked nice?'

Ella glanced over her shoulder. The two men had their backs to her, and were leaning over the bar, trying to attract the attention of the barmaid. 'I thought they were someone you knew from work,' she said.

'I wish.' Kate grinned at her. 'No, we got chatting while you were in the loo. They're up here on business, and they were asking what the local nightlife was like.' She pointed her key at the car, and the doors clicked open. 'So, what do you think?'

'I think they were with that woman.'

'What woman?'

'The glamorous looking one with the red hair and the armfuls of gold bangles,' she said. (The one who had made her feel decidedly dowdy and frumpy, and old before her time.)

'So?'

Ella pulled a face at her. 'Kate, you're such an impossible flirt.'

'Rubbish. I'm only trying to find a handsome young man

for you. You need a man, Ella. Someone strong, someone who'll look after you.'

'I don't need looking after,' she said crossly. Her encounter with Miss Glamour Puss in the Ladies had shaken her confidence somewhat. 'Anyway, I'm of the fervent opinion that horses are much less trouble than men. They're always pleased to see me, and they never answer back.'

'Yes, but you can't cuddle up on the sofa with a horse, darling. Believe me, I know about these things.' Kate switched on the ignition, and grinned wickedly across at her. 'Now then, two o'clock, you said?'

As her blue sports car negotiated the narrow exit from the car park, a silver-coloured BMW was manoeuvring itself into the newly vacated parking space.

Lewis Trevelyan was not in the best frame of minds. His return visit to the stables had been a complete waste of time. He still hadn't found out who the blonde girl was, and negotiations with the County Showground committee had yet to be finalised. To crown it all, the director was agitating for a progress report as filming was about to commence at the studios, and they still hadn't resolved where they were going to do the location shots.

He strode into the bar of the Hotel, and ordered himself a non- alcoholic beer, before glancing around for his colleagues. They were sitting at a corner table, tucking into some gastronomic delight, which would no doubt cost him a fortune in expenses.

He took a much-needed mouthful and wiped the frothy moustache away with the back of his hand, and then strolled over to join them.

'Aha! The main man!' James said, popping an olive into his mouth. 'How did it go?'

'Not too good,' he said, pulling up a padded stool, and sitting down beside them. 'Whoever that blonde girl was, she certainly wasn't Caroline. How about you?'

Lucy flipped open her phone. 'We've had confirmation

from Mr Fitzgerald that we can film at the show,' she said. 'And, barring any last-minute hitches, we're still on schedule for next month.'

'Excellent.' Lewis felt himself relax slightly. At least they were getting somewhere now. 'When can Phil and the crew get up here?'

'Two weeks,' she said, scrolling through the pages.

'And Simon?'

'Ah, we've got a slight problem with Simon,' Matthew said.

Lewis glanced over at him. 'What?'

'He's contracted to do a commercial in June. It's not too serious, because we can work round that, but he'll be out of the schedules for at least a fortnight.'

'That's okay,' Lewis said. 'As long as we're aware of it we can warn Miles in advance. Anything else I should know?'

Lucy shook her head. 'No, I think that's it.'

'Good,' he said, picking up the menu and studying it carefully. 'Because I'm starving. Anything here you can recommend?'

The goat's cheese tartlet with sun-dried tomatoes was as good as it looked, and the apple granny that followed was even better.

Lewis was beginning to find himself warming to this particular neck of the woods. It had been a while since he had been anywhere but London. The country air must be doing him some good.

'What's happening about the stables situation?' James asked. 'Are you planning to go back there?'

'Yes,' he said. 'But only to find that girl. Now we've got the permission of the County Show ground, we don't need to use it as a location anymore.'

'Well, I liked it,' Lucy said sulkily.

'Only because you suggested it,' Matthew reminded her. 'How did you hear about it, anyway?'

'I asked Lucinda,' she said. 'She still keeps in touch with

the horsy world, even though she hasn't competed for years. She used to know Robert Johnson.'

Lewis glanced up at her. 'I've heard of that name somewhere before.'

'That wouldn't surprise me. He was quite big in the show-jumping world. He won at Hickstead and Olympia, and all the major events.' She took a sip of her iced water, before adding, 'His stables and stud were renowned for churning out champion show jumpers, dressage and event horses. And then he was tragically killed, oh, about five or six years ago.'

'In a fall?'

She shook her head. 'No, it was a car accident. Sad, isn't it? All those years of jumping, and he never had so much as a scratch.' She drained her glass, and hooked out a cube of ice with a manicured finger. 'I don't suppose Lucinda knew what an oddball he'd married when he hitched up with that Ursula, though. She always spoke very highly of him.'

Odd being the operative word, Lewis thought.

'Coffee, anyone?'

'No thanks.' Lewis smiled at the young waitress, and glared at Matthew, who was eyeing her up quite blatantly. 'Do you have to?' he muttered.

'You'd think he'd had enough for one day,' Lucy sneered. 'What with those two girls at the stables and the one he chatted up in here.'

'Ah, but she had a friend,' he said, grinning. 'She wasn't bad looking either.'

'Who, the girl, or the friend?'

'Both,' he said, swallowing the last of his beer. 'If you're interested, we're meeting them at the Jazz Club on Sunday night.'

'No, I'm not bloody interested,' Lewis said. 'Some of us are here to work, not to chase the local talent.'

'Unless, of course, they're blonde and beautiful,' James observed, with a wry smile.

'That's different.'

'If you say so, boss. By the way, one of those girls had

blonde hair. Didn't she, Matt?'

'I'm not after *any* blonde,' Lewis said. 'It's this one particular girl I'm after, which you would appreciate, if you'd been doing what I pay you for, and spotted her at the stables. I'm telling you, guys, she's stunning, and I mean, stunning.'

If it hadn't been for the fact that they had seen her riding through the woods that morning, he would have thought he was imagining her. But no, she existed all right. The question was where was he going to find her?

Ella's friend, Kate was more than disappointed to discover that she had missed seeing the producer of Blackwater Films by a little less than half an hour.

'Oh blast,' she said. 'Was he on his own?'

'That he was,' Thomas informed her. 'And he didn't stay long. About five minutes, at the most, I reckon.'

'What, you mean he didn't have any actors or famous people with him?'

'Nope.' He glanced at Ella, who was reading the list of names on the class lesson schedules. 'He didn't stay to see Caroline ride, either.'

'Didn't he?' Ella looked up from her sheet of paper. 'That's a bit odd.'

'He wasn't looking best pleased when he left,' he added. 'Mind you, neither was Ursula. She's been in a right bad mood every since.'

'What's new?' Kate said. 'Right, well, I'd better be going, Ella.'

'Yes, okay.' She gave her friend a hug, and a kiss. 'Thanks for lunch, Kate. It was lovely. And I think your new car is brilliant.'

'It should be. It's costing me enough.' She popped a pair of sunglasses on as she climbed into the driver's seat.

'Poser!' Ella yelled.

'Yeah.' She grinned. 'Great, isn't it?'

Ella had barely enough time to get changed into her

riding clothes before the start of the two o'clock lesson. She rushed upstairs and pulled on her jodhpurs without stopping to check with her stepmother what had happened. It seemed clear enough, anyway, from what Thomas had said that the omens for Caroline were not good.

She grabbed a riding hat and a pair of gloves from the tack room, and hurried into the yard, where the first of her students were arriving.

'Thanks, Kelly,' she said. The teenage stable girl had been as good as her word, and ensured that all the horses were tacked up and waiting for her.

'Now then, Sarah, you're on Paddy, Beth, you've got Jonty, and Rebecca, you've got...' She scanned the list of horses. 'You're on Tuppence. Is Jennie here, yet? No? Well, we'll get started, and she can join us in a minute.'

The group lesson consisted of what Ella termed the intermediate riders. No longer novices, they could control and ride their horses with a fairly secure seat. She was planning to introduce some jumping poles into the class structure, as some of the more confident girls had expressed a desire to give it a go.

Ursula was mortified when she saw her setting up the jumps in the middle of the sand school. She couldn't have this. What if the film company came back, and decided to use the youngsters, instead of her daughters in the film. Worse still, what if they spotted Ella? No, no this wouldn't do at all.

'Ella!' she said. 'Ella!'

What now? Ella glanced up to see her stepmother standing at the gate to the arena, with her arms folded in front of her, looking anything but pleased.

'Keep on riding round, girls,' she said. 'I won't be a moment.' She ran over to the railings. 'What is it?'

'You can't do jumping with them?' Ursula hissed.

'Why ever not? They're perfectly capable of it.'

'Think of Caroline,' she said.

'Caroline?' Ella looked confused.

'It's a long story,' Ursula sighed. 'I won't bore you with the details. All I'm asking is that you postpone any jumping classes until next week.'

'But I promised the girls...'

'Please, Ella?'

'Oh, all right,' she sighed. 'If you insist. They won't be happy about it, though.'

That was the least of Ursula's worries. She was more concerned about keeping Ella out of the way. What could she ask her to do that would keep her out of sight without arousing her suspicions?

And then the thought came to her. It was perfect, like a bolt from the blue.

'You want me to do what?' Ella said later, as if she could hardly believe her own ears.

'An inventory of tack,' Ursula repeated firmly. 'I've detailed it all here. It's time we had a sort out of all the stuff we've got around the place. Every bridle, saddle, bit and stirrup iron needs to be accounted for. I mean, it's for your benefit as much as anyone else's,' she added slyly. 'You need to know how much tack you've got. What better way than to do it yourself.'

'But I've got lessons booked, and exercise sessions with the event horses.'

'Yes, yes, I appreciate that, but this is more important, Ella.'

'It is?'

'Of course,' she assured her. 'But don't worry. I've re-scheduled some of the other staff to take over your classes.'

'But what about Majesty?' she said. 'You know Heather doesn't like anyone else riding him but me.'

The horse in question was a stunning bay gelding who had been at the stables for less than three months. His owner, Heather Hutchins, had put him into livery when she started a full-time job in a solicitor's office, on the proviso that he was not to be used in class lessons, or ridden by anyone other than a very experienced rider.

'Heather Hutchins pays for us to keep her horse fit and exercised,' Ursula said bluntly. 'I don't suppose she gives two hoots who rides him as long as he's kept in top class condition. That's the trouble with these weekend horse people,' she added with an unpleasant sneer. 'They've no idea of the work involved. But don't worry. I'm sure Vanessa will do very well on him.'

'Vanessa?' Ella choked. Things were going from bad to worse. Ursula surely didn't think that Vanessa was the right rider for a horse of Majesty's calibre.

'If it doesn't work out, we can always have a rethink,' Ursula said firmly. 'Let's just give it a go, shall we?'

'Starting from when?' Ella said.

'I think now, is as good a time as any,' she said, handing her the list she had drawn up. 'And while you're at it, perhaps you could make sure everything has a proper clean as well. It would be nice if we could get everything into show condition before next week.'

'Next week?' Ella echoed. Was the woman going mad?

'It's for your benefit, dear,' she assured her. 'After all, no matter how much you try to ignore the fact, Hollyfield stables is your business, so really, these sort of tasks should be up to you.'

And with that parting comment, Ursula turned and marched gleefully back towards the house, her mission accomplished.

That had sorted out the little madam. There'd by no chance of her riding over hill and dale in full view of any lurking film crew. It would take her a week or more to sort through the jumble of mildewed leather harnesses and tarnished bits of tack. And if she finished that, there were dozens of other "essential" jobs she was sure she could think of to keep her safely out of sight.

All she had to do now was to convince Lewis Trevelyan that the girl he had seen riding the cross-country course really was her own fair daughter, fair being the operative word.

'No! No! Oh God! Mother! Mother!'

Vanessa's hysterical screeching roused Ursula from a rather pleasant dream she was having about attending the

Oscar's ceremony in Hollywood. Simon De Silva looked so nice in a dark dinner suit. And Vanessa was particularly fetching in the crushed purple velvet dress she was wearing...

She blinked, and peered, bleary-eyed at the bedside clock.

'Mother!'

The door crashed open, and Vanessa stood quivering, in her nightie, a large towel draped around her head. She was silhouetted in the doorway like an oversized lampshade.

'It's gone orange!'

'What has, darling?'

'My hair.'

'Orange?'

Vanessa hiccupped loudly as she ripped the towel from her head to reveal the fact that, yes indeed; her hair had turned a rather brassy shade of carrot.

Ursula tilted her head to one side, as she fumbled for the light switch. 'Oh my God,' she murmured, horror etched on her face.

Vanessa flumped onto the bed, and heart-rending sobs erupted from somewhere deep inside her chest. 'It's not fair. It's not fair. I followed the instructions on the packet.'

'Did you do a strand test?'

Ursula flicked on the light. My goodness, it looked worse, more marmalade, than carrot, she supposed.

'Strand test? What's that?'

'A sample of hair, before you apply the whole packet. Well, obviously not,' she observed.

Vanessa's cheeks looked podgy and tear stained in the artificial light. Her hair, released from the all-encompassing folds of the towel, hung in bright orange strands around her face.

It was a disaster.

'I wanted strawberry blonde,' she sobbed, plucking at a clump of hair and holding it out as if, by examining it, the colour would miraculously change its vibrant shade to a more satisfactory one.

'Did you leave it on for the correct length of time?'

'Longer,' Vanessa sniffed miserably.

'Longer?'

'Well, I wanted to be sure.'

Ursula groaned.

'Mother, what am I going to do?'

'God knows,' she muttered.

'Mother!'

'All right, all right, I'm thinking.'

Fat shiny tears trickled down Vanessa's cheeks. She had so wanted this to be right. She would do anything to meet Simon De Silva. He was the most vibrant, passionate, man she had ever seen. Her walls were plastered with pictures of him. Her notebooks were scribbled with the name Vanessa De Silva. (It had a nice ring to it.) And she was certain that if he got the chance to know her as a person, he would see that she could be the love of his life, just as he was in hers.

'We'll book you into Michael Robbins salon first thing. He'll do it as a favour to me, I'm sure,' Ursula said, taking charge once more. 'You should never have trusted these home colouring kits, not without a strand test. I always said you were too impulsive, darling. But don't worry. Mummy will sort things out for you.'

'Will it be all right?' Vanessa sniffed. The carrot-coloured mop on her head bobbed up and down like a Muppet. The sobs had subdued to a mere shuddering every now and then.

'Of course, it will, dear,' Ursula sighed, though she was beginning to have her doubts. She had never seen such an adverse reaction before. 'But we need to get you down to Michael's salon as soon as it opens, darling. You go and get dressed, and I,' she said, glancing at her watch, 'will put the kettle on. I'll phone him as soon as the doors open at nine.'

Chapter Five

'One hundred and forty pounds!' Ursula gawped at her daughter, who was doing a kind of pirouette in front of her, and tossing her newly coloured hair (a perfect blonde), over her shoulder in a veritable imitation of Miss Piggy. 'Is that what he charged you? One hundred and forty bloody pounds?'

'Yes, but it's worth it, isn't it?'

'Yes, yes, I suppose so,' she grumbled. Some favour that turned out to be. The next time Michael Robbins wanted riding lessons for his precocious six-year-old, she'd up the price and get her money back that way.

Vanessa stared gleefully at her reflection in the hall mirror, and pursed her lips expectantly. 'Has he been back to the yard?'

'Who?' Ursula said, looking distracted, which, indeed, she was. Blasted hairdressers. She hated being taken for a ride.

'Lewis Trevelyan.'

'No, of course he hasn't.'

Vanessa's face fell.

'But in case he does, you'd better get changed. I want you riding that course from dawn to dusk, if need be.'

'I'll get saddle sores.'

'No pain, no gain,' Ursula snapped, a trifle inconsiderately. 'You want a part in this film, don't you?'

'You know I do,' Vanessa sighed. To star in a movie with Simon De Silva would be like having all her dreams come true. He was so gorgeous, so handsome, so daringly devilish…

'Mother,' came Caroline's rather petulant whine. 'It's not fair. Why can't I ride the course?' She tossed her hair over one shoulder, and glared at her sister. 'I don't mind riding. In fact, I'll ride all day long if I have to.'

'I know, my sweet, but the sad fact is that Mr Trevelyan knows it wasn't you. He saw you in the house, remember?' Ursula tried to sound sympathetic. 'I'm sure if Vanessa gets the part, she'll persuade them to take you on as an extra.'

Not bloody likely, Vanessa thought. If she got the part, it would be her moment of glory and hers alone. No way was she going to share it with her sister. Caroline could go suck sour plums, for all she cared.

She stuck her tongue out at her, a gesture not spotted by the keen eyes of their mother, and then scuttled up the stairs to get changed into her riding clothes.

'Thomas, for goodness, sake. Make the bloody animal stand still!'

Vanessa scowled, as Majesty swung his quarters towards her every time she approached to put her foot in the stirrup.

'I'm trying, Miss, but he's being a bit temperamental today.'

He didn't like to add that perhaps it was the rather overpowering smell of hairdressing chemicals that was putting the horse off. Some beasts reacted quite strongly to off-putting smells, and this smell was more off-putting than most. The stench of hydrogen peroxide was making his eyes water. God only know knows what it was doing for the horse.

He groped in the pocket of his baggy cords, and found a half packet of mints. 'Shush now, my beauty,' he soothed, as he rustled the paper.

Majesty's ears pricked forwards.

'What have we here, now?'

Vanessa teetered precariously on the edge of the mounting block. 'Move him closer, you idiot,' she snapped.

Thomas gritted his teeth into the semblance of a smile, as he backed the horse towards the block.

'There now,' he murmured softly, as he slipped a mint onto the palm of his hand, and held it to the horse's muzzle. 'I think you're going to need this, my boy.'

Vanessa thumped her weight down into the saddle, and snatched up the reins. 'I hope you're not giving him titbits, Thomas?' she said.

'No, Miss,' he lied.

'Because it's a very bad habit, you know. He'll come to expect it, and that leads to nipping and biting.'

So speaketh the mother, Thomas reflected crossly. 'Right you are, Miss. Have a good ride.' He stood to one side as she yanked the horse's head around, and trotted him across the yard.

And don't fall off and break your bleeding neck, he thought, because I, for one, won't be coming to pick up the pieces.

Ten Snaffles, three Pelhams, four Kimblewicks – Ella counted out the number of bit pieces, and marked them off on a sheet of paper - as she went through the inventory Ursula had provided her with the previous day. There should be a rubber Mullen mouth snaffle somewhere, a vulcanite, and a happy mouth. Oh God, this was so boring!

She glanced out of the storeroom window in time to see Vanessa riding past on Majesty. The large bay was frothing at the mouth, and tossing its head up and down in an agitated gesture that didn't need interpreting.

Don't look, she thought miserably. It wasn't worth it. But even as she turned her head away, she found herself forced to do a quick double take.

What on earth had Vanessa done to her hair? A long blonde plait escaped from the back of her riding hat, and was hanging down over the padded folds of her jacket. Blonde hair? Had she dyed it, then?

As she was considering this point, she caught sight of Caroline, stomping across the courtyard, in what appeared to be a foul mood. (Nothing new there, then).

She rubbed at the dusty pane of glass, and peered closer. It was Vanessa who was catching her attention, though. Her stepsister was now blonde, unashamedly, brassily blonde. How odd. Perhaps her mother had leant her some of her bleach.

Maybe this was the new look for the season. Ella smiled. Well, she wouldn't call it an improvement. Vanessa, with her mousy brown eyebrows, and florid complexion, should really have plumped for a darker shade. Blonde really wasn't her colour. Deep rust might have gone better, especially with all those freckles. Still, there was no accounting for taste, good or bad.

She ducked back from the window as she spotted Ursula making a beeline across the yard, her mouth set in a tight-lipped scowl. She was gesticulating wildly at the departing horse and rider.

'Get him on the bit, Vanessa. You won't have any control if he tucks his head in like that. On the bit, I said,' she repeated, somewhat needlessly, because Vanessa was, by now, well out of earshot.

'You should have let me ride,' Caroline complained. 'You know I'm better than her when it comes to cross-country.'

'Yes, I know, my sweet, but your turn will come. You'll see. Why don't you go and help Stella with the dressage class.'

'Because I don't want to.'

Ella grinned. Dissent in the ranks. Oh dear. This wouldn't do at all. Ursula would go mad.

She didn't.

She placed a tender arm around Caroline's shoulders, and gave her a hug. A hug? Ella blinked in disbelief. Was her stepmother going soft in her old age?

Puzzled, she knelt back down on the floor. The heap of assorted tack lay spread out before her in a jumble waiting to be sorted. It would take her the best part of the day just to count everything, let alone put it in some kind of logical order. Then there was the task of cleaning and oiling all the bits of leather, and buffing them until they shone. "Show condition", was what Ursula wanted. "Show condition", was what she was going to get.

If that was what it took before she was allowed to ride Majesty again, then she had better get on with it. Otherwise, Vanessa was going to do irreparable damage to a beautiful and naturally talented horse.

'My, but you've been working like a little Trojan,' Thomas observed, as he came into the storeroom to collect some spare tack.

Ella had laid out everything in order; stirrup leathers in one pile, reins and bridle pieces in another. A plastic crate full of gleaming stirrup irons sat on the bench, and a box full of bits was at her feet.

'If she thinks I'm doing this for one more day, she's mistaken,' she said, as she finished polishing the last Pelham, and dropped it into the box. 'Honestly, Thomas, some of the junk that's in these boxes must be twenty years old or more. Half of it needs chucking out, let alone cleaned and polished. I don't know what she's thinking of.'

She stood up, and brushed the dust and dirt from the front of her trousers. 'Anyway, I've had enough for today. I'm going to have a long soak in a hot bath, and then I'm going out with some of the girls.'

'What girls?' Thomas asked.

'Oh, Laura, Kate, the usual crowd,' she said. 'Why don't you come along? We're only going to the Mariners, and we won't be back late.'

Thomas considered the matter for a moment. A good pint of Guinness sounded tempting enough. 'Sure, and why not,' he said. 'I'll meet you in there, once I'm done here. I'll pop in about eight?'

'Good man,' Ella said.

The bar of the Mariners was crowded by the time Ella had washed, and changed, and met up with her friends from the village.

'You're just the person to ask,' Laura said gleefully, as she motioned her to sit down in the chair, she had been saving for her. As always, she was impeccably dressed, in a pale lilac cashmere jumper, with a brightly coloured scarf draped flamboyantly around her neck. Her long brown hair had been wound into a knot and fastened at the back of her head with a deep purple ribbon.

'Ask me what?' Ella said, wishing she had worn something other than her usual jeans and the navy sweater she had put on.

'About this film crew at Hollyfield, of course. Kate tells me you've had the people from Blackwater Films wandering round the place and that they're planning to make a film with Simon De Silva in it. Simon De Silva,' she repeated dreamily.

Not another one, Ella thought wearily. Who was this Simon De Silva?

'Come on, Ella, we can keep a secret. It is a secret, isn't it?'

All of a sudden, she was surrounded by a group of eager faces, and everyone started talking excitedly at once.

'What film is it? Zac says he's heard they're making a rerun of the Dark Spy series.'

'I heard it was the Blaydon Files.'

'...And Tom says they've been in touch with the committee of the County Show...'

'I don't know,' she said loudly. 'I mean it.' The voices dropped off and faded, one by one. 'I really don't know. Honestly. You guys probably know more about it than I do. All I know is that yes, the producer, Lewis Trevelyan, and some of his colleagues came to the stables, and yes, they're making some sort of film, which allegedly, is going to star Simon De Silva, but that's all I've heard. They came to see Vanessa and Caroline ride.'

'Ella I'm very disappointed in you,' Laura said. 'I thought you were going to give us all the gossip.'

'Sorry,' she said.

'I heard they were looking for show-jumpers,' Becky said shyly. 'I overheard Vanessa going on about it. We thought you might be doing it, Ella.'

'Me?' She almost choked over her glass of chilled cider. 'Fat chance. I haven't even met these people. Honestly, I've been too busy. And I'm not likely to meet them either. Ursula has given me the crappiest job imaginable, doing an inventory of the tack, of all things. Look at my hands,' she added, holding them out to everyone. 'I've been cleaning stuff all day.'

Thomas stood by the bar, listening, as he supped a mouthful of rich, dark beer.

Everything was starting to fall into place now; the reason Vanessa was riding the bay horse over the cross-country arena, and the fact that Ella had been shut away in the store room for the best part of the day.

He picked up the pint glass, and carried it over to the table.

'Oh, Hi, Thomas,' Ella said. 'You can vouch for me, can't you? I haven't been hob knobbing with the people from the film company, have I?'

'No,' he said, frowning thoughtfully. 'Ursula's made quite sure of that.'

Ella's smile faded. She wasn't quite sure what to make of his troubled expression. 'What do you mean?' she asked

'Yes, Thomas,' Kate leaned forwards, and rested her chin on her hands, as she smiled sweetly up at him. 'What do you mean?'

The small Irishman glanced down at Ella, and then across at her friends.

'It's obvious, isn't it? I mean, if I was a film producer looking for a pretty young girl to take part in a show jumping scene, would I be picking those two great galoots, or would I be picking someone with real beauty and flair?'

'And blonde hair!' Becky announced loudly. 'That's it! That's why they didn't want Caroline. I heard Vanessa say they were looking for a girl with blonde hair.'

'Oh my God!' Ella groaned. 'So that's why she's dyed her hair.'

'And that's why,' Thomas said, 'you've been dissuaded from riding, and you're shut away in that pokey little stock room all day.'

'Wow,' she gasped, the fingers of one hand going to her mouth in surprise. She stared round at her friends, who were all

64

grinning and nodding at her. 'Do you think Ursula's worried that they might want me?'

'I'd say it's a dead cert,' Kate said. This was so typical of Ursula. She couldn't think why any of them were surprised. She'd do anything to make sure her daughters were in the limelight, even at the expense of others, Ella in particular. 'Aren't you going to say something?' she said. 'Or do something?'

'Like what?'

'Heck, I don't know, phone them up, and tell them you're blonde and beautiful, and you know how to ride.'

'Sounds a bit perverted to me,' Laura said.

'Trust you,' Kate snorted. 'Just because you've got a one-track mind. I'll phone them,' she added brightly. 'I could pretend to be your agent.'

'Steady on,' Ella said. 'I'm not sure I want to be in this film, anyway. Not if it means incurring the wrath of Ursula and her daughters. I mean, I do have to live with them, you know.'

'Why?'

'What?'

'Why do you have to live with them?' Kate said. 'The house is yours, the business is yours. Heck, if I were you, I'd have hoofed them out a long time ago.'

'Yes, but you're not me,' Ella said simply. 'And Ursula does a good job of managing the stables.'

'Does she?'

'Yes,' she sighed. 'Well, better than I could. I haven't the time or the inclination to do the accounts or the book-keeping. I hate paperwork. You know I do.'

'Which is why computers were invented,' Kate said, with more than a hint of sarcasm in her voice. 'I don't know why you let that woman run rings round you. She treats you like a servant, and you don't seem to care.'

'Life's too short.'

'It's also for living,' Kate said, as she raised her glass and took a mouthful of some brightly coloured cocktail.

'Tell that to your liver,' Laura said, laughing.

'You know what I mean,' Kate said.

'I do. And I know you're only looking out for me,' Ella said, 'but I'm okay. Really, I am. It's sweet of you to be concerned about me, but I'm happy as I am.'

Kate frowned at her, obviously not convinced.

'Besides which, I must be the only one of you who hasn't heard of Simon De Silva, so it's unlikely that I'd harbour any great ambitions to want to star in a film with him. But if that's what Vanessa wants to do, then fine, she can go for it. I won't stop her.'

'You're mad,' Kate snorted, fumbling in her bag for her purse. 'Thomas, be a love, and go to the bar for me. I think we all need another drink.'

'I'm being realistic,' Ella said. 'You know I am.'

'More's the pity,' Laura muttered.

'It's perfectly simple. If Vanessa gets the part, Ursula will be happy. If she's happy, then I'm happy. End of story.'

'And you might still get to meet Simon,' Becky said, with a hopeful look on her face. She'd never met anybody before who knew somebody famous.

'Exactly,' Ella said, with a smile. Though whether she would recognise him or not was another matter entirely.

Thomas handed over the money at the crowded bar, and carried a tray of drinks back to the table.

'Aren't you having one?' Ella said.

'No. I'm away off home now. One's my limit when there's work to be done in the morning.'

And by God, was there work to be done.

He hitched his jacket collar up against the driving drizzly rain that was sweeping down from the hills. The lights from the pub window spilled onto the pavement, as he walked outside, and glanced up the street. The phone box was outside the post office. If it was empty, it was more than likely to have been vandalised. There was only one way to find out. Thomas limped his way along the pavement, his fingers fumbling for loose change as he did so.

'Sweet Jesus,' he muttered, as he cranked open the door.

One of the last remaining red telephone boxes in the country, and it had been used as an opportune urinal. It smelled to high heaven. Condensation and numerous trickles of water ran down the glass panes; such a charming combination. He kicked a crumpled beer can and the remains of a chip supper to one side.

The number was written on a piece of paper stuffed down the inside zip of his wallet. He smoothed it out and stared at it thoughtfully. Then he picked up the receiver, jabbed out the numbers, and waited patiently, as somewhere on the end of the line, a telephone started to ring.

Chapter Six

The following morning saw the team from Blackwater Films gathering to discuss the day's agenda in the dining room of the Red Fox Hotel.

Breakfast had been laid out on an open styled buffet table at one end of the room, and James was heaping his plate up with bacon, sausages, scrambled egg, mushrooms, hash browns – in fact everything on offer - until he had a veritable mountain of heart-attack inducing food on his plate.

'Steady on, James,' Lewis muttered, selecting a more modest portion of toast and scrambled egg for himself. 'They'll think we don't feed you.'

'He's such a pig,' Lucy said, pouring herself a glass of fresh orange juice.

'Only getting my money's worth,' James said. 'Hey, Matthew.' He waved at one of the silver-covered serving platters. 'Over there, the bacon's really crispy.'

'Seen it,' Matthew said, waving a fork at him. 'Have you tried those sausages?'

'For God's sake,' Lewis groaned, carrying his plate over to a table in front of the window. 'Don't they ever think about anything else?'

Lucy smiled, as she sat down beside him. She was wearing a neat fitting sea blue trouser suit, with a cream blouse, and matching high-heeled shoes. 'Hmm, possibly sex,' she whispered, 'but not at meal times.'

Lewis spluttered helplessly into his cup of black coffee.

'So,' she said, seemingly oblivious to his amusement. 'What's the plans for today?'

'I want you to see Mr Fitzgerald again,' he said, trying hard to keep a straight face. 'See if you can pin him down to times and places at the Show. Matt and James are going to look over a couple more locations for me, and I,' he added, taking a mouthful of coffee, 'will be going back to the stables.'

'You're doing what?' James said, dumping his over-loaded plate onto the table and stabbing his fork into a succulent, plump sausage before it rolled onto the starched white tablecloth.

'Going back to the Johnson place,' he said.

'Again?' James sat down and pulled up his chair. 'But I thought you'd decided to use the Showground for the shoot.'

'He's after his mystery blonde,' Matthew chuckled. 'Any tea in that pot, Luce, or shall I order us a fresh one?'

Lucy lifted the lid and peered inside. 'Better get fresh,' she said. 'This one's a bit stewed.'

'I know what it is,' James said, grinning. 'I think you secretly enjoy seeing that Ursula woman. Mature, single lady, wealthy, loads of dosh....'

Lewis gave him an exasperated glare. 'For your information, I have no intention of seeing "that Ursula woman", as you so nicely put it. I'm going to go there unannounced, and have a look around on my own.'

'Good thinking, boss.' Matthew tapped the side of his nose. 'You go case out the joint.' His voice had developed a heavy, American twang.

'Please!' Lewis groaned.

'No, I think you're right,' Lucy said. 'You'll probably find out more by having a wander round by yourself, than having her influencing who and what you see.'

'My thoughts exactly.' Lewis waved the waitress over. 'Could we have another pot of tea, and another coffee, here, please?'

'So, what if you don't find her?' James asked, through a mouthful of fried bread. 'Got any other thoughts up your sleeve?'

'Not so far,' he said. 'But I'll think of something.' Of that much he was certain. Admitting defeat was not going to be an option. He would find that girl if it were the last thing he did. But finding her was only the start of the matter. Next, he would have to persuade her to take part in the film. For all he knew she might be painfully shy, or tongue-tied, or embarrassed. Fame wasn't necessarily everyone's cup of tea, but that was something he could work on. It was tracking her down that was his main problem.

With that aim in mind, he left the hotel soon after breakfast, in a car hired from a local company. James and Matthew had already arranged to take his car on another location search, dropping Lucy off at the Fitzgerald house on the way, so it made sense for him to hire a car for the day.

The small red hatchback was ideal for the narrow, tree-shaded lanes with all their twists and turns. The fact that he was beginning to feel like a rally driver, turning the wheel first one way, and then the other in rapid succession, (and enjoying the challenge immensely), made him wonder if he had missed his vocation in life.

If anyone had told him, ten years previously, that he would be an independent producer of a small, but successful film company, he would have thought they were raving mad. His introduction to drama had come from a stint with the University amateur theatrical society. A girlfriend of the time had persuaded him to join, and as it meant he got to see more of her by going than if he didn't, he willingly went along to rehearsals.

His fascination for the whole production business stemmed from those heady student days. A degree in accountancy and business management was followed by a year doing a Media Studies course at the same University. (Which didn't please his parents, who thought he should be getting a 'real' job, instead of messing about "making movies").

Their attitude changed somewhat when his first film, a half hour 35mm thriller, (made as part of his course) attracted the attention of a wealthy sponsor, who offered to fund his next film. This subsequently won rave reviews at the London International Film festival, and prompted a spate of calls offering him some lucrative commissions.

A spell in advertising further honed his skills for producing gritty and realistic drama, and his eye for talent, and knowledge of current market trends, meant that most of his projects were successful. In five years, he had gained a reputation some producers had strived most of their lives for, and still hadn't managed to achieve.

Luck didn't come into it. Lewis worked hard for his success. He had a shrewd business mind, combined with the ability to deal with people from all walks of life, be they temperamental actors, or hard- hitting executives.

He also had, as James was forever pointing out to people, the strength of character to act on his hunches, even if everyone else dismissed his ideas as unworkable.

This blonde girl, for instance. He knew, the moment he had heard her laughing, and seen her leading the horse across the field, that she was exactly what he was looking for. She had something about her, something he couldn't put into words, but something that was unique and special only to her. He had to find her. There were no two ways about it. He had to find her.

The car bounced over the grass verge as he hit the corner too soon, and he braked sharply to avoid hitting the trunk of a tree. So much for his rally driving skills. He eased his foot off the accelerator slightly, and coasted down the lane.

Hollyfield Stables appeared to the right of him, through a gap in the hedge. He slowed the car to a gentle crawl as he passed the large billboard and the sign pointing to the entrance. Several cars were parked at the end of the long gravel drive. A horsebox and a couple of four-wheel drive vehicles were on the drive itself.

Lewis drove past the entrance and found a place to stop in what was supposedly a passing bay. Since he presumed traffic along that particular stretch of road was few and far between, he didn't suppose anyone would mind if he left his car there for a few moments.

That was his first mistake.

Taking a pair of binoculars with him was his second one.

Bethany Boggis was not the most elegant of riders. Ursula had likened her to a beached whale, when she had tumbled off her pony, Munchkin, at the gymkhana the previous week, and lain on the ground bawling. The fact that she wasn't hurt was neither here nor there. She was far too heavy, she said, for the pony she was riding. It was no wonder that poor Munchkin had overbalanced.

Her mother insisted it was puppy fat that she would grow out of given time, but Ursula begged to differ.

'She's too big for her pony, Mrs Boggis. It's time you started thinking of a replacement.'

'But Bethany loves her little Munchkin.'

'Of course, she does,' Ursula soothed. 'And it's hard to let go, I know. But for the pony's sake, she needs to move on. We've got a lovely little Welsh Cob which might suit her,' she added. The horse was stubborn, but incredibly strong.

It needed to be, she thought, studying the rather obese child with a dispassionate stare. 'Why don't we forget about Munchkin for today,' she suggested, 'and I'll let you ride something else for a change?'

'Don't want to ride anyfink else,' Bethany sniffed.

'I know, darling,' Mrs Boggis sighed, raising her eyes in a helpless gesture at Ursula, as if expecting her to perform miracles or something.

Shrink the child or stretch the pony, perhaps? Ursula smiled. 'You could always keep Munchkin here *and* buy another horse to ride,' she suggested. 'That's what some of my other clients have done.'

It was a lie, but the thought of double livery charges made it a wonderful idea, even if she said so herself.

Mrs Boggis looked doubtful.

'It helps ease the pain of parting,' Ursula added knowledgeably. 'And it doesn't have to be for long.' She lowered her voice. 'Only until the child gets to bond with her new horse.'

'Does that mean I can have two ponies?' Bethany said, looking a lot more cheerful at this suggestion and a bit sneaky too.

'Possibly,' her mother said, frantically adding up the figures in her head, and wondering what her husband, Robert, would have to say on the matter.

'And in the meantime, you can try out Minnie,' Ursula said, 'who just happens to be for sale. Her owner is giving up on horses. Pregnant,' she added as an aside to Bethany's mother.

The stout woman's mouth opened into a silent 'oh' of understanding.

'Kelly. Can you tack up Minnie, please,' Ursula said. Strike while the iron was hot. That was her motto. Bethany was skipping across the yard, no doubt heartened by the thought of having two ponies. Her mother, however, was looking distinctly uncertain about the whole thing. Ursula planned to have the child up and riding before she got the chance to change her mind.

Minnie, the Welsh cob, was a sturdy looking horse with a thick black mane and tail, and a blaze of white down the centre of its dark face. She had a kind eye, and a tendency for laziness, or stubbornness, depending on how one viewed the matter. She was, however, the ideal horse for a child graduating from ponies.

Bethany seemed thrilled at the prospect of owning her as well as Munchkin.

'Oh Mummy, Mummy, she's so sweet,' she said, jumping up and down in excitement as Kelly saddled her up.

It wasn't quite how Mrs Boggis would have put it. She wasn't really a horsy person. Still, she seemed placid enough, and that was the main thing. She risked giving it a tentative pat on the neck.

'Where can I ride her?' Bethany said, as she scrambled up on to the mounting block, and waited for Kelly to lead the horse alongside her. 'Can I take her to the four-acre field?'

'If you like,' Ursula said. 'Kelly will go with you, won't you

Kelly?'

The young stable-girl nodded, as she clipped a lead rope on to the horse's bridle.

'I don't need that,' Bethany said, as she flopped into the saddle. 'I've been riding Munchkin for ages.'

'Better safe than sorry,' Ursula said shrewdly. The last thing she wanted was the horse bombing across the paddock before the girl had got used to her. 'Off you go, and don't worry, Bethany. Mummy and I will be watching you from here.'

They weren't the only ones watching her.

Lewis had found a suitable vantage point behind an overgrown hawthorn hedge at the side of the road. Through a gap in the thicket, he could see the vast expanse of paddocks and exercise areas, and a good proportion of the cross-country course, as it wound its way through the distant trees.

The ground was sodden with overnight rain, and he trod carefully, trying to avoid the worst of the mud. Expensive Italian leather loafers were not the things to be wearing at a time like this. Still, if he could track down the girl it would be worth the inconvenience of ruining a decent pair of shoes.

He raised the binoculars to his eyes. Excellent! He could see the sand school and the entrance to the yard as well. He scanned backwards and forwards, taking in all that was going on. A class lesson was in progress in the arena, and in one of the fields, he could make out some youngsters riding a course of coloured poles. His view zoomed in on the person riding the sturdy bay cob. Hmm, it looked like a child, but who was that leading the horse? He twiddled with the focus. Yep, it was a child riding, but there was definitely someone leading. A young girl; she could have blonde hair. It was difficult to see when she was wearing that hat...

'Oi! What do you think you're doing?'

Lewis jumped at the sound of the gruff and rather belligerent voice that came from just behind him. The binoculars bashed into his eye sockets, as he staggered forwards, his foot landing in a squishy lump of something soft and foul smelling.

'I know your type. Bloody pervert!'

He turned round to find that his accuser was an angry looking man with the ruddiest face he had ever seen. He was wearing a muddy green-waxed jacket and stout walking boots. In one hand he carried a shotgun, and in the other was a walking stick, which he thumped into the ground by his feet. A black and white collie was lying inches away from him, its black muzzle resting on a pair of outstretched paws.

'I'm sorry?' Lewis said, a trifle disconcerted. This had all the appearances of turning nasty if he wasn't careful.

'You will be,' the man growled.

'What? Now hang on a minute,' he said, letting the binoculars dangle from their leather cord around his neck. 'I think you've got the wrong idea here.'

'Have I, by God?' The man hoisted the gun down from his shoulder.

Lewis took a step backwards in alarm. 'Yes. Look, I'm not doing any harm.'

'No?' The man snapped the gun together as he spoke. 'That's what they all say.'

Good grief, he looked like one of the deranged mountain men in the old Burt Reynolds film, Deliverance. Lewis had to think of something – and think of it fast. 'Steady on…um…Sir,' he said. 'Before you do anything hasty, let me introduce myself. I'm Lewis Trevelyan, from the film company, Blackwater Films.' He held out his hand, and then withdrew it sheepishly, when it was pointedly ignored. 'You must have heard of us,' he said.

'Nope.' The man's eyes narrowed suspiciously.

'Oh. Oh, that's a pity. Well, you see, we're filming in the area,' he explained. 'And I'm looking for a girl.'

Lewis knew the moment he had said it that it was the wrong thing to say, the very wrong thing to say. What an idiot.

'Clear off!' the man bellowed, waving his gun at him. The dog was starting to growl and creep towards him on its belly, dark hackles raised.

'If you'll just let me explain…'

Okay, maybe not. Lewis decided to cut his losses. The ominous click of a shotgun cartridge being slid home was the deciding factor. That and the way the man was staring at him, with a slightly maddened look in his eye.

'We don't want your sort round here,' he growled.

That much was bleeding apparent, anyway.

Lewis backed away from him, one eye fixed on the dog that was looking almost as menacing as its owner. 'It's all been a misunderstanding, you know,' he said, as he fumbled in his pocket for his car keys.

'I said, clear off!'

One didn't argue with a loaded gun, he told himself firmly. A loaded gun, a vicious dog, and a deranged local, (who would have been perfect for a thriller he had just finished making). He clicked open the door of the red hatch back, and scrambled into the driving seat, locking the door firmly behind him.

The notice, plastered over the front of his windscreen, informing him of the proper use of passing bays on country lanes, partially obscured his vision, but Lewis didn't give a toss. The sooner he was out of here, the better. He slammed the car into gear, and lurched forwards, narrowly missing an oncoming vehicle.

In perpetual slow motion, he saw the blue car heading towards him, saw the dark-haired girl at the wheel, and then saw the girl with blonde hair sitting beside her. She was laughing, her head tilted to one side, and her thick, glossy mane of hair tumbling freely over her shoulders. In the split second that their cars passed, he realised it was her. The very person he was trying to find.

'Shit!' He banged his foot down hard on the brakes. It really *was* her. He glanced quickly over his shoulder. The car was disappearing round a bend in the road.

Not so, the madman with the hunting rifle and the dog. He was standing by the side of the verge, the shotgun held across his stomach, and his legs planted apart like a gunslinger in an old Western movie.

'Shit,' Lewis said again. He didn't have any other option but to drive on. A braver man might have turned the car round, and gone after her. Lewis might have been brave, but he wasn't stupid. Not when he was looking down the barrel of a loaded shotgun, that is.

The detour he was forced to take took him down endless country roads, with no obvious signposts, and no hope of doubling back on himself to follow the blue car. All he was doing was wasting precious time and petrol. He was also getting himself hopelessly lost.

Burningstone, where the heck was that? He drew up by the village sign, and got out to remove the annoying piece of paper jammed under his windscreen wiper, (the one informing him not to park in passing bays on country lanes.) Well, he wouldn't be doing that again. In fact, he had no intention of going anywhere near the place again. Next time he would send Matthew – or James – or even the two of them together. That's what he paid them for. Let them get blasted sky high by the local vigilante.

He jabbed out a number on his mobile, and glanced up and down the street as the phone started to ring. The village was decidedly rural, with only a handful of houses, and no sign of life. 'Hello? Lucy?'

'Speaking. Is that you, Lewis?'

A friendly voice. He breathed out slowly. 'Yes. Hi. Lucy, I'm a bit lost. Are you still with the Fitzgeralds?'

'Yes, but I'm almost finished. Where are you?'

'Burningstone,' he said. 'Wherever that is. I haven't got the map. It's with Matthew and James, and I can't get Google maps on my phone.'

'Burningstone. Hang on a minute.'

He could hear her talking in muffled tones.

'Lewis?'

'I'm still here,' he said. He had absolutely no intention of going anywhere,   not without explicit and cast-iron instructions. His petrol gauge was in the red, and he had no idea how much fuel he had left in the tank.

'Apparently you're not far from the main road,' she said, having obviously discussed the matter with her host. 'It's about a mile through the village, and you want the first turning to the right.'

'Can you ask if there's a petrol station nearby?'

'Hang on.'

He glanced down at his watch as he waited. It was almost eleven o'clock.

'Lewis?'

'Yep?'

'There's one on the main road, about half a mile further on.'

'Great. Thanks, Lucy.' He pocketed his mobile and climbed back into the car. Now what, he wondered? Fill up with petrol, and go looking for a blue sports car, or cut his losses, and head back to the hotel?

In the end, he did a bit of both. With a full tank of petrol, and a newly purchased map from the shop on the garage forecourt, he spent some time cruising the country lanes, on the off chance that he might see the two girls, and be able to flag them down. (Though whether they would stop for a lone male in a red hatchback was another matter entirely).

He couldn't help wondering what it was about this girl that so intrigued him. She was incredibly beautiful, of course, but then so were several other girls on every casting agent's list. He only had to pick up the phone, and he could have his choice of any one of them. Maybe it was because she seemed so unattainable, he thought. He was forever seeing her, but never quite getting to meet her.

'Give it up, Lewis,' Matthew told him, over a late business lunch – a very late business lunch - in the Red Fox. 'No woman's worth that much time and effort.'

He was inclined to agree with him. Two hours he had spent, driving up and down country roads, and through little villages and hamlets (and that was after the embarrassing episode of being accused as a stalker), and all to no avail.

'Matt's right,' James said. 'You can take your pick of riders at the County Show. There'll be dozens of worthy competitors there. Take a look at this programme.' He handed him the brochure, which gave details of all the events. 'See?' he said, 'there's loads of show-jumping going on.'

'Yeah, yeah,' Lewis sighed. The trouble was, he'd never been very good at accepting second best, and this girl, he was sure, would outclass them all.

Matthew stood behind him, peering at the pamphlet over his shoulder, as he supped from a pint of warm and robust beer. The landlord had recommended it to him. 'It's real ale, lad, and brewed in our local brewery. It's well worth the extra expense.' It was cheap, compared to London prices, and fairly palatable, too. Matthew took another mouthful just to make sure. 'Why don't we run our own event at the show,' he suggested. 'I can see it now - the Blackwater Films Show-jumping stakes.'

Lewis darted him a look. That sounded interesting. 'Go on,' he said.

'Okay, well, let me see.' Matthew thought for a moment. 'How about this; Competitors need to be under thirty, blonde-haired, slim and female.'

Lucy pulled a face. 'Bit sexist, isn't it?'

'Not at all,' he said. 'We're talent scouting for a film, remember.'

'Yeah,' James agreed. 'And there are plenty of other events for everyone else to enter. This could be an extra competition.'

'Brilliant,' Lewis said. 'No, I mean it, Matthew. It's a great idea.'

'Well, I think it's absurd,' sniffed Lucy.

'I don't,' Lewis said. 'I think it's a bit of inspired thinking. Well done, Matt.'

Luckily, the Chairman of the Showground committee thought so as well. ('Splendid idea. That ought to bring the punters in. Bit of showbiz razzmatazz and all that.') By early evening, and several phone calls later, the arrangements were all in hand. Not only did Lewis have a film to produce, with the entire organisation that that entailed (securing finances, hiring the crew, and finding locations for starters), but he was now responsible for running a show jumping competition; the appropriately re-named "Simon De Silva stakes".

'Sounds like something out of a burger bar,' Lucy muttered sulkily, as she finished mopping up the last few morsels of strawberry gateaux from her plate. She still hadn't come round to the idea of the competition, and a mouth-wateringly delicious dinner in the hotel restaurant had not improved her mood either. 'Who's financing it, anyway?' she asked.

'We are.' Lewis drained his glass of chilled wine, and motioned to the waitress to bring them another bottle.

'We are?'

'Hmm,' he nodded. 'Look on it as a pre-publicity exercise. We could even put details of it on a Web site. You know, like the Blair Witch project.'

Lucy frowned.

'That film made megabucks.'

'Yes, but,' she sniffed. 'Anyway, Simon De Silva doesn't need that much publicity. Anything he's in is bound to be a success.'

'Not necessarily,' Lewis said, leaning to one side to allow the waitress to place a fresh bottle of wine in an ice bucket on the table. 'Remember "Oxford Sunset"?'

'Didn't that go straight to video?' Matthew said, topping up their glasses.

Lewis nodded. 'The critics hated it.'

'So?' Lucy said.

Lewis grinned. 'I'm only reminding you why we need good publicity.'

'Any publicity,' James added.

Lucy pouted and began twirling a strand of curling red hair around her fingertips.

'I take it we're almost finished here,' Matthew said.

'I think so,' Lewis confirmed. 'Unless you've got

something else you want to do? Got any more locations for me? Any last-minute change of plans?'

He shook his head.

'Well, I guess that's it, then,' he said, glancing at his watch. 'We need to leave first thing in the morning. I've got a meeting with one of the sponsors next week, and I need to see Miles. There are a few things I need to clarify with him about the shooting schedule.' He drained his glass and set it back on the table. 'Coffee, anyone?'

'No thanks.'

'Lucy?'

'No, I'm fine.'

'Right.' He leaned back in his chair, feeling pleasantly satisfied. The dinner had been excellent, and the wine, a young Australian vintage, quite superb. With the arrangements for the show-jumping competition all in hand, he decided it was time he had some relaxation. 'I'm going for a walk,' he said. 'Anyone else fancy some fresh air?'

'You're kidding, aren't you?' Matthew groaned. 'We've been tramping round that bloody showground all day. It goes on for miles.'

'A slight exaggeration,' Lucy said. 'What he means is, they're going to the Jazz Club tonight. This pair,' she added, 'have a pre-arranged assignation.'

'You're only jealous,' James said.

'Do me a favour,' she muttered.

'I take it that's a "no", then?' Lewis sighed. 'I don't know. All this beautiful scenery, and it's wasted on you lot.' He picked up his jacket. 'Don't make a night of it guys. I'll be knocking for you at eight o'clock. I want to make an early start in the morning.'

'Especially if it's going to take us four hours to find the M25,' James sniggered.

Lucy aimed a kick at him under the table with the pointed toe of her high-heeled shoe. Judging by his muttered grunt, she knew it had connected with some sensitive part of his anatomy.

'Eight o'clock will be fine, Lewis,' she said, smiling sweetly. 'Because I won't be the one nursing a hangover.'

The air was crisp and refreshing after the stuffy atmosphere of the pub. Lewis draped his jacket over one shoulder as he strolled through the village. It was a pretty little place, with a tiny church tucked down a narrow lane, a duck pond, complete with assorted ducks, and a couple of shops, now closed.

He peered into the window of the post office. Several notices were taped to the glass with yellowing sticky tape, advertising everything from jumble sales to playgroup bazaars. The local Women's institute was holding a produce sale, on the Friday of each month, and a tabby cat had gone missing from Fuller's Close. (A faded photograph accompanied the latter, and the name "Whiskers" scrawled underneath it in childish handwriting.)

'Evening.'

Lewis glanced round, startled, but the speaker, an elderly man with a walking stick and a shaggy looking spaniel at his side, had already walked on.

'Evening,' he said.

He couldn't get used to the fact that most of the people he had come across in this area were prepared to exchange a few pleasantries with him, even complete strangers. It didn't happen in London, or at least, not in his neck of the woods. There was a lot to be said for country living.

He walked on past the village green, admiring the quaint and picturesque cottages that fronted it. Bet they cost a fortune. This place would be ideal for a period drama; something turn of the century, perhaps, with coaches and horses. Or maybe early Edwardian, with servants and gentry. He turned the corner and found himself heading towards the churchyard. "The Church of St Mary," proclaimed the board at the arched wooden entrance. "Rector Jeffrey Green, The Vicarage, Church Lane". Now this was something else entirely. The graveyard was beautiful. It was neat, tidy, and carefully tended. Fresh flowers lay on several of the graves. Not a weed or a faded, dying bloom was in evidence anywhere.

Lewis wandered up to the heavy oak door of the church. It was locked, of course. He didn't expect it to be anything else. Shame though. He would have liked to take a look inside.

'Now then, Sir? Can I be of any assistance?'

The man was clipping a privet hedge behind the church. His cloth cap was jammed well down on his head, and he wore a faded tweed jacket, and baggy brown cords. His teeth were remarkable for their absence, all bar one, which poked out like a tusk from beneath his bushy moustache.

'Thanks, but no,' Lewis said. 'I was just having a look around.'

It was almost nine o'clock at night, and this man was out trimming hedges. Unbelievable.

'You'll be a tourist, then?' he said, in an accent that was pure Suffolk.

'Hmm? Sort of,' Lewis said who couldn't be bothered to go into details.

'You'll be going to the Club, then?'

'Club?'

The man raised his cap from his forehead, and gave it a scratch. 'Jazz Club,' he said. 'Down the road and round the corner a bit. That's where all the young uns go.'

Lewis supposed he should feel flattered. In comparison to this old boy, he probably was young. Not young enough, though, to feel like frequenting a club. It wasn't his scene, either here, or in London.

'Not me, mate,' he said, shaking his head. 'I've got an early start tomorrow. Business to attend to,' he added.

'Pity,' the man said, resuming his hedge clipping. 'They say it's a good do.'

Lewis smiled. Whether it was or it wasn't, he was sure he'd hear all about it over breakfast the next day. 'Think I'll give it a miss,' he said. 'Goodnight, then.'

'Aye, well, goodnight.'

Strolling back towards the hotel, Lewis paused to glance in the window of an antique shop. Most of the objects looked like junk, the sort of thing that could be picked up in any cheap second-hand shop, such as odd bits of cutlery and decorative plates, silver serving platters and pieces of old lace. But there was a picture on the wall that caught his eye, a watercolour painting of the village green. Very nice. Lewis squinted closer to see if he could spot a price tag.

With his attention fixed on the painting, and his concentration diverted from the road, he failed to notice the blue sports car cruising up the street, or the two young women sitting inside it.

One of them, however, did notice him.

Chapter Seven

Ella didn't usually spend her time ogling at passers by, but even she had to admit that it felt good to be sitting in such an eye-catching car, relaxing and watching the world rush by.

Kate had put the roof down, and Ella sat with her arm dangling out of the window, enjoying the feel of the breeze as it rushed through her fingers. Her feet were tapping in time to the steady drumbeat thudding from Kate's CD player.

'Call me Thelma. You can be Louise,' she said grinning sideways at her friend. And that's when she saw him. She could hardly have missed him. The streets were empty, so the stranger peering into the window of Ludlow's Antique Emporium stood out like a sore thumb.

At first, she gave him nothing more than an interested glance as they approached. Then she sat up, and stared intently, because her heart had given a sudden and unexpected jolt. 'Wow,' was the first thought that sprang to mind. She hadn't seen him around town before. He was in his late twenties – maybe early thirties - and dressed in dark trousers and a smart shirt. A jacket dangled over one shoulder. His hair was ruffled and windswept, and streaked gold with the sun.

The car drew level with him, and she saw the curious and thoughtful expression on his face as he peered into the shop window, the face that was causing her to feel suddenly and inexplicably hot and flustered.

'He,' she said, giving Kate a nudge with her elbow, 'is gorgeous.'

'Who?'

'Him,' she said, glancing back over her shoulder as they

drove past.

Kate was trying to dodge pot-hoes in the road and had missed the encounter entirely. She peered hopefully into her rear-view mirror.

'Want me to drive round again, so you can get a better look?'

'Don't be daft,' Ella said, blushing profusely.

'It's no trouble. I can do a right hand turn into Capel Close.'

'No, don't,' Ella shrieked, mortified at the thought. What if he saw them? What if he had seen her looking at him? Oh God. She would die on the spot.

'Well, it's not often you fancy someone.'

'I didn't say I fancied him,' she groaned. 'I just said...'

'That he was bloody gorgeous,' Kate finished for her.

'Well, he was,' she said, glancing back over her shoulder. Her heart was still thumping rather alarmingly against her rib cage. They had rounded the next corner, and were heading down the road to the club. The man had disappeared out of sight.

'Sure you don't want me to turn round?'

'Sure,' Ella said.

Kate grinned as she swung the car into the club car park. 'You never know. He might be coming here.'

'Not with my luck, he won't be,' Ella sighed.

She was beginning to wonder how Kate had talked her into going to the Jazz Club at all. It was the last place she felt like going. After a hectic day at work, bath, bed and cocoa seemed distinctly more appealing.

The "Jazz Club" was a bit of a misleading name, since the club hardly ever played jazz, apart from the occasional Sunday lunchtime. "Jazz" referred to the name of the owner, Jason Hardwick, an ageing rock star, who now spent his retirement pulling pints, and reliving his youth by hiring bands who mainly played rock and blues, or, 'real music,' as he called it. The place was always crowded, charged exorbitant prices for drinks, and relied on the fact that it was the only decent entertainment venue for miles, thus ensuring that people would turn up and part with their hard-earned cash.

'I don't know how you persuaded me to come here,' Ella grumbled, as she swung one trouser clad leg out of the car and wondered if she could balance on the high-heeled shoes Kate had insisted she borrow for the night.

'Because it'll be fun.'

'Hmm,' she murmured, unconvinced.

'It will be,' Kate said, tugging her micro mini skirt down. (Even then, it barely covered her bottom.) 'Anyway, those blokes from London should be here.'

'Great,' Ella groaned. 'That's all I need.'

To say she was not looking forward to the evening was a bit of an understatement. But, several hours later, she had to concede that Kate had, once again, been right. The evening had turned out to be not just fun, but brilliant fun. The live band had been a local group with a crowd of their own supporters, who just happened to be from her old school. Ella found that she knew loads of people, people she hadn't seen in years. She didn't have the time or the inclination to meet Kate's newfound London friends.

Not that that was any great loss. Self-opinionated and boring, was Kate's frank opinion of them. Or so she said, later.

Ella thought they looked nice enough, but she hadn't had a moment to say hello. She was too busy catching up on old news and long-lost friends. Added to that, the band had been excellent, the company stimulating, and the white wine more so.

Suffice to say she had woken up rather later than planned on the Monday morning, and with something of a headache. But, all things considered, she reckoned it had been worthwhile. The gang had agreed to meet up on a weekly basis. For Ella, it was a promising start to a social life she had never really been a part of until then.

She yawned, as she filled some hay nets and then dragged them over to the tap to give them a final rinse. It was a time consuming but necessary chore, since it reduced the dust and spores that were often present in the bales, which some horses were allergic to.

'Looks like someone had a late night,' Thomas observed, as he limped across the yard with a plastic carrier bag full of shopping. 'We missed you at the morning feeds.'

'Sorry,' she said, stuffing her hair behind one ear, and glancing sideways at him. 'I meant to get up, but I overslept.'

'Not long enough, by the looks of you,' he said.

Ella groaned.

'Fancy a ham roll?' He held out the bag to her.

'No thanks.' If the truth were told, she was starting to feel rather nauseous.

She turned off the tap, and shook the hay nets up and down. A scattering of water droplets splashed everywhere.

'Let me do that,' Thomas said. 'You look dreadful.' He handed her the plastic carrier bag and took the dripping nets from her. 'You go and put the kettle on, and I'll sort these out. Go on.' He waved her away. 'Off with you.'

Ella didn't need much persuading. She had felt all right when she first got out of bed. Now she was beginning to feel rather hung-over. The dull headache had intensified to a throbbing pounding in her temples, and the queasy, unsettled sensation in her stomach had worsened considerably.

'Lots of water for you, my girl,' Thomas announced cheerfully a few moments later. 'Coffee will only make it worse.' He poured her a mugful from the tap. 'Drink that, and I'll get you a refill.'

Ella sipped it slowly. Her stomach was heaving.

'Must have been a good night,' he said.

'It was.' She sat down on an unopened hay bale. She sincerely hoped that Ursula did not want her to do any intensive schooling on any of the young horses. She was not in the right frame of mind for a battle of wills with an uneducated beast.

'Never again,' she groaned.

'That's what they all say.' Thomas munched happily on his ham and cheese roll, the sight of which was making her feel worse by the second. 'Where did you go?'

'The Jazz Club.'

'The one on Fellows Road?'

She nodded.

'Ah well, it's good to see you getting out and enjoying yourself. You need to have a bit of fun when you're young.' He glanced at the door, and then back to her. 'I tell you this much, Ella,' he said, lowering his voice. 'There's not much that passes for fun going on around here.'

'Tell me about it,' she groaned. She took another sip of cold water, and could feel it going all the way down to her empty and rather sensitive stomach.

Thomas took her words at face value, and began to do precisely that.

'There's that Vanessa, parading about on Majesty like she knows how to handle him,' he grumbled. 'Sure, and doesn't she think she looks grand with her corn-coloured hair.' He shook his head despairingly. 'And there's six horses needing shoes, and no farrier worth his salt willing to come until Ursula pays what she owes them.'

'She owes them money?' Ella tilted her head to one side. This was news to her.

'Aye.' Thomas nodded. 'All but Tom Bluntesham, and he's sick with a bad back, so he won't be coming.'

Nor would he be missed, Ella thought, lecherous old goat that he was.

'I'll give Stewart Searle a ring.'

Thomas pursed his lips together. 'He'll not come. She's tried him already.'

Ella frowned. This wouldn't do. She'd have to have a word with Ursula. But perhaps not just at the moment. She swallowed another mouthful of water and tried to ignore the nauseous waves in her stomach.

'And she's wanting me to cut down on the feeds,' he muttered. "Level scoops, Thomas, not heaped," he mimicked, in a perfect imitation of Ursula's schoolmistress tone. 'What would she know? Those horses get fed for the work they do. No more, and no less. I can't cut back if they're in work. It's penny pinching, that's what it is.'

'Well, it's certainly strange,' Ella said. 'I wonder why she's never mentioned anything to me. I mean, it's not as if we've got any money worries. The livery is running at full capacity, and there's no shortage of bookings for lessons. In fact, I was under the impression that we were doing rather well.'

Thomas gave a loud 'harrumph', which sounded rather like one of his beloved horses.

Ella frowned. 'You don't think we are, do you?'

'It's not my place to say.'

'Thomas?'

He glanced up at her, and she could see the tired look in his eyes. 'You talk to your stepma,' he said. 'That's all I'm saying. She's the one you need to be dealing with.'

'But you do think we're in trouble, don't you?'

'Like I said,' he muttered, stooping to pick up the dripping hay nets. 'It's not my place to say.' He shook his head slightly, as he straightened up. 'I'll away and hang these in the stalls for you, Miss Ella.'

'Thanks, Thomas,' she said.

She winced, and wished, not for the first time, that she didn't have such a blinding headache. She could barely think straight. Why would Ursula keep something as important as money worries from her? That's if she had money worries, and it wasn't just a figment of Thomas's overactive imagination.

She'd never said a word to her about any problems with the farrier either. Yet a good working relationship with their farrier was essential, particularly considering the number of horses they had at the stables. With the livery business alone, he could be with them every week.

Perhaps Thomas was right. Perhaps she should have a chat with Ursula about the business side of things.

A chat with Ursula, however, was invariably one-sided, as Ella found, much to her annoyance. Her stepmother seemed to have perfected the art of dismissing any topic she didn't wish to discuss with the air of a politician at a press conference.

'Well of course it's difficult to get a farrier, darling. It's the show season,' she said. 'It's their busiest time of year. How was I to know that Mr Bluntesham was going to put his back out?'

Because he's ancient, and should have retired years ago, Ella thought crossly.

'And the reason I asked Thomas to cut back on the feeds was because of the recent flush of new grass. You know how rich that can be,' she added, implying that if she didn't, then she jolly well should. 'We don't want any of our horses coming down with laminitis, now do we?'

It was all perfectly feasible, Ella thought. Farriers were hard to get at this time of year, and horses on lush grazing didn't need as much hard feed as usual. So, Thomas's concerns were easily explained. But something wasn't adding up.

Despite her headache, which was turning out to be an unbelievably gruesome hangover of the worst variety, she had the strangest feeling that Ursula was keeping something back from her. She was being decidedly cagey, dismissive even. And when she had suggested taking a look at the books, Ursula had said they were with the accountant. Yet she was sure she had seen them in the office.

'It doesn't matter,' Ella said. 'The records will be on the computer, anyway.'

'Yes, of course, dear,' Ursula nodded. 'They will be, won't they? Oh, but you can't use it now,' she added, scurrying after her into the study.

'I can't?'

'No. No, I'm in the middle of something. Schedules and things,' she said, deliberately switching off the monitor as she spoke.

Ella didn't have a clue if she was being truthful, or just downright evasive. 'I'll go through them later, then,' she said. (Hopefully, when her headache had eased off a bit.)

'Yes. Yes, you do that,' Ursula said. 'I'll let you know when

I'm finished in here. But there's really nothing to worry about,' she added, giving her a forced smile. 'Everything's fine.'

Ella decided to reserve judgement on that until she had studied the accounts for herself. In the meantime, she would make a few discreet enquiries of her own, and that included contacting some of the local farriers the stables had employed over the past few months.

The results were not very reassuring. Of the two farriers she managed to get hold of, both confirmed that they were owed money. One man hadn't been paid for the remedial work he had done three months previously, and confirmed that he would not be coming back to Hollyfield Stables. Neither, it seemed, would the other man. 'Not unless I'm paid in advance,' he added.

'I'll write you a cheque myself,' Ella said.

'No way, love,' he said. 'It's cash or nothing. I'm not taking any more rubber cheques.'

'Cash, then,' she agreed. 'But can you come this week? I've got six horses that need doing?'

'I could do them on Thursday,' he said. 'I've got a slack day. Mind you, I was planning to take the wife shopping...'

'Oh, please,' Ella said.

'Yeah, I suppose,' he said at last. 'But it's got to be cash.'

'Of course.'

'Right then. I'll see you about nine thirty.'

Ella replaced the receiver with a scowl. How could Ursula have forgotten to pay them? Even worse, how had she managed to give them a cheque that bounced?
Surely their credit status with the bank was better than that?

'Darling, it was merely an oversight,' Ursula assured her firmly. (For some reason her stepmother didn't see it as any great disaster.) 'We had a slight cash flow problem that month. If I recall correctly, we had payments to the insurance company, and the feed merchant, plus the new loan payments on the sand school. All the silly man had to do was return the cheque to me and I would have written him another one.'

'But his bank charged him for it.'

'What can I say?' Ursula sniffed.

'Well, sorry might help.'

'Fine, right. Well, I'll apologise to him. Thursday you say?' She flicked noisily through the pages of her desk diary. 'See. I'm writing it in here. Farrier, Thursday. I'll grovel, and pay the man, if that's what you want.'

'No,' Ella said quietly, 'I'll pay him.'

'Ella, it was an oversight, a misunderstanding. Goodness, child, if you knew the juggling and sorting I had to do to keep this place running smoothly...' Ursula patted the coiled bun at the back of her neck with her fingers as she spoke.

'That's exactly what I want to know.'

Ursula gawped at her. 'What?'

'Well,' she said. 'As you so rightly pointed out, this is my business. I think it's about time I became more involved in the running of it, don't you?'

The expression on her stepmother's face, told her exactly what she thought of that idea.

'But Ella. Ella, darling,' Ursula sighed. 'You know how much you like working with the horses. I'm sure you'd find the accounting side of things boring, and it would leave you with so little free time.'

'No more boring than doing an inventory of tack,' she snapped.

Ursula fiddled with the pins holding her bun in place, an implacable frown on her face. 'Yes, well, in hindsight, perhaps I should have given that job to Kelly,' she muttered.

'Or Vanessa. Or Caroline.'

Ursula's scowl deepened.

'Anyway, it doesn't matter. All I'm saying is that I want to be more involved in the running of the stables, and I expect you to keep me informed. Particularly,' she added pointedly, 'if we have any more cash flow problems.'

'Oh, all right, though I don't see...' (Ella's withering glare stopped her in mid sentence.) 'Oh, fine,' Ursula said crossly.

Over her dead body, she thought. Some things were better

off kept quiet. At least until they were resolved, that is. This business with the Blackwater Film Company, for one.

'It's no good, mother. He just won't do it,' Vanessa complained, as the bay horse veered sharply away from the jump, almost unseating her in the process. She whacked her whip down on Majesty's rump, and jerked his head around. 'Come on, you stupid beast – jump!'

Ella tried to stifle a groan of dismay. Curiosity and a spare half hour in her busy schedule had given her the opportunity to watch her stepsister ride Majesty. It was the first proper chance she had had, since the past few days had seen her shut in the office, trying to make head or tail of the business accounts.

According to Ursula an unexpected computer crash had wiped out several of the records, so it was a bit of a hit and miss affair. Especially as it transpired that there were no back up copies, (although her stepmother did assure her that the accountant had all the details).

Bored with trying to make sense of meaningless columns of figures (which, unknown to her, had been meticulously altered by Ursula), Ella decided to take a breather, and see if the rumours she had heard about Vanessa's riding skills were accurate. Some of the girls were getting increasingly concerned about Majesty. They said that Vanessa was being too heavy handed with him and that the horse was becoming difficult (some said uncontrollable) and finally, that he was losing condition.

Now Ella was taking the time to assess the situation for herself. And what she was seeing, it had to be said, was a truly diabolical performance.

She sat next to her stepmother on a bench overlooking the sand school, her thoughts churning. If only she would stop yanking him in the mouth. Majesty was perfectly capable of clearing the jumps with ease, but every time he approached one, Vanessa dug her heels in, and then jerked hard on the bit. No wonder the poor horse kept backing off. She was giving him mixed instructions.

'Be positive, darling,' Ursula said. 'Make him go forward.'

'I can't,' Vanessa moaned. 'Ahh!' She gave a screech, as the horse swerved to one side again, momentarily unbalancing her. 'Bloody animal!' she swore. Her face was red with anger and frustration. 'I'll make you go forwards.'

Her whip lashed down on his hindquarters at the precise moment that his owner, Heather Hutchins, chose to stroll onto the viewing platform (a raised area frequently used by the judges when jumping competitions were taking place), in order to see how he was progressing.

'What the hell do you think you're doing to my horse!' she shrieked. Her face blazed with anger, as she vaulted over the rail, and ran across the sand school. 'Get off him!' she yelled, catching hold of the reins, and glaring furiously up at Vanessa. 'I said, get off him!'

'Mother?'

'Do as she says, darling,' Ursula said. She stood up, and brushed some imaginary fluff from her trousers as she did so. 'Miss Hutchins,' she began, in her most appeasing tone. 'I appreciate how this must have looked to you…'

'I know how it looked,' Heather snapped. Her normally pale cheeks were crimson with rage. Ella had never seen her so angry before. 'Do you know how much this horse is worth?'

'Well, yes, but…'

'This horse,' Heather continued,' is probably the most valuable asset your stable possesses, and I will not – I repeat – will not, have him ridden by amateurs.'

'Amateurs?' Vanessa said indignantly as she slithered off the horse, removed her riding hat, and tugged her blonde hair free of the hair net she had stuffed it in to. 'I'll have you know…'

Her words tailed away as she found herself almost nose to nose with Heather's furious face.

'You,' she said, jabbing her pointedly in the chest with the tip of her finger, 'are not to go near my horse ever again. Do I make myself clear?'

Vanessa cast a despairing glance at her mother. If she didn't get to ride Majesty, and Lewis Trevelyan came back to the stables (although they hadn't heard anything from him in over a week now), he would never believe she was the right person for the film. None of the other horses was a patch on the huge bay gelding.

'Now let's not be so hasty,' Ursula said, in her most wheedling tone, as she pushed past Ella and opened the small gate into the ménage. 'I mean, let's be honest here, Miss Hutchins. I agree that Majesty is a special horse. Indeed, he's one of our finest jumpers, but, like all top show animals, he can be highly spirited and, at times, difficult to control.'

She discreetly elbowed her daughter out of the way, and patted the horse fondly on the neck. Majesty tossed his head up and down and snorted through his flaring nostrils. Ursula stepped hurriedly to one side. 'I think you happened to catch Vanessa at a particularly troublesome moment, that's all.'

'No, I don't think so,' Heather said, in a voice that was clipped and horribly precise. She ran up the stirrups, and unfastened the girth. 'You see, I know that you've stopped Ella from riding him. Oh yes,' she said, nodding firmly. 'I have been kept reliably informed of what has been going on around here.' She lifted the saddle off the horse, and placed it on one of the guardrails around the arena.

Ursula glared at Ella, who gave her a helpless shrug. Whoever had told Heather, it hadn't been her.

'I was upset at the time, but I thought no, I'll give them the benefit of the doubt. They must have other riders who can do him justice.' Heather undid the bridle as she spoke. It was almost as if she was talking – or at least, ranting - to herself. 'Then I find out they've put the most ungainly lump of lard they can find on his back. An ignorant, heavy handed, cretin, who shouldn't be let loose on a pit pony, let alone an animal of such obvious worth.'

'Heather...Heather,' Ursula soothed. 'If there's been a

misunderstanding...'

'Only on my part,' she snapped, glaring over the horse's withers at her. 'Ella? Can you fetch me a head-collar? I should never have trusted you with him,' she added quietly, in a voice that was pure ice. 'Never in a million years.'

Ella saw the sharp, angry look in her stepmother's eyes.

'Hollyfield Stables has a reputation second to none,' she said huffily.

'Had!' Heather said. 'The operative word here is "had". Thanks, Ella,' she added, as she took the head collar from her and slipped it over the gelding's nose.

'You won't find a better livery yard than Hollyfields,' Ursula said.

'Actually, I doubt I'd find a worse one.'

'I beg your pardon?'

Heather finished fastening the head-collar around Majesty's neck and took hold of the lead rope. 'This place reeks of incompetence and penny pinching, and I'm not the only person to think that.'

'What? What?' Ursula looked stunned. Her mouth opened and shut like a landed fish in its final death throes. How could she say that, when she had spent a small fortune on the new sand school, to say nothing of the repairs to the stable block?

Vanessa was leaning against the guardrail, looking sulkily at the circular pattern she was making with her boot in the soft dry sand of the aforementioned arena.

She made a point of pretending to ignore Heather, who was leading Majesty out towards the stables. Ursula was flapping along behind her like an indignant chicken.

'Now look what you've done,' Ella groaned.

'Me?'

'Who else,' she said, picking up the saddle and bridle. She shook her head in disgust, before hurrying after them.

'Oh dear, oh dear,' Caroline announced cheerfully, from her vantage point over by the paddock gate. She had seen everything, and thoroughly enjoyed every single, humiliating moment 'Looks like you won't be riding him again.'

'Shut up!' Vanessa snapped, hurtling the whip in her direction. 'Just shut up! The stupid woman doesn't know what she's talking about.'

'Obviously,' Caroline said, as she hopped over the paddock rail, and crossed over to the sand school. She picked up the schooling whip, and twirled it between her fingers. 'I've always managed to do rather well on Majesty. Maybe I should go and have a little chat with her.'

'Don't you dare?'

'Or you'll do what?' Caroline's small white teeth gleamed between her thin, moist lips. 'After all, somebody's got to ride him, in case that film crew comes back to the stables.'

'I hate you!' Vanessa shrieked, chucking her rather expensive riding hat across the arena at her. 'I hate you!'

'Girls! Girls!' Ursula shouted, as she marched back to the arena. 'For goodness sake, stop acting like alley cats. What on earth will people think?'

'Who cares,' Vanessa muttered sulkily.

'I care!' The viciousness in Ursula's voice brought them both up sharp. 'I care what people think. And you should as well. Because someone – someone, and I don't know who - has been spreading rumours about this place.'

'What sort of rumours?' Caroline said.

'Nasty, malicious ones. The sort that gets people prosecuted for slander and libel.' Ursula's face had gone a rather worrying shade of ripe aubergine. 'Someone has been saying that we know nothing about horses, and that we're only in this business for the money. The cheek of it. Well, I,' she said, straightening herself up to her full height and glaring around as she spoke, 'intend to find out who it is.'

'Well, it wasn't us,' Caroline said shortly.

'Yes, I know that,' Ursula snapped.

'And it wouldn't be Ella.'

'No...no, I can see that.'

'So, it's bound to be one of the stable girls.'

'Or,' Ursula paused, thinking. 'Or one of the boys.' She never had liked that Thomas much, and she was under no illusions that the feeling was unequivocally mutual.

'What's happening about Majesty?' Vanessa said. She stooped to pick up her riding hat from where she had chucked it in her fit of pique, and then brushed the sand off the soft velvet cover with the sleeve of her white shirt.

'Oh, you can forget about him.'

'But ...'

'He's leaving,' Ursula said tersely. 'I have no intention of being spoken to like that. If people don't like the way I run this yard, then they are perfectly within their rights to go elsewhere. That's what I've told Miss Hutchins, and that is what she is at liberty to do.'

'Leaving!' Vanessa's mouth opened and closed like a goldfish. 'But...but you can't let him go. What about Lewis Trevelyan? What about the film? What about...?'

'Oh, do shut up,' Caroline snapped. 'This is all your fault. Now neither of us will get the chance to ride him.'

'No,' Ursula agreed. 'And nor will Ella.'

Vanessa and Caroline glanced at each other. A faint flicker of triumph flitted across Vanessa's face. A satisfied smirk spread across Caroline's.

'There are other horses, we could ride, I suppose,' Vanessa said.

'There's always Jasper.'

'Or Lady Ginger...or what about that dark bay, you know?'

'Mr Sticks.'

The sister's excited chatter reached Ella in the stable yard. She peered out of the barn door to see the two of them walking arm in arm with their mother towards the house. There was a jaunty swing to her stepmother's stride, and Vanessa appeared to be laughing. It was most odd.

She had expected Ursula to be devastated by Heather's announcement that she was removing Majesty from the stables, 'as soon as I can make other, more suitable, livery arrangements.'

Ella had fully anticipated a performance of apologetic grovelling worthy of an Oscar from her stepmother. To lose a client was bad enough, but to lose one with such a superb horse on full livery didn't bear thinking about.

She had practically cringed as she tensed herself for her stepmother's reaction.

But it never came.

Instead, Ursula had said, 'You must do as you think best,' and walked away.

Now, it seemed, she had even found something to laugh about.

It was all very strange.

'You do understand why I'm doing it, don't you?' Heather said, as she brushed Majesty's mane and tail. 'When Thomas phoned to tell me that she had stopped you from riding him, I was gutted. You're the only reason I brought him here in the first place.'

'Thanks,' Ella said. 'I appreciate the compliment. He's a real beauty. I got a lot of pleasure from working with him.' She rubbed his nose, and smiled as he blew down his nostrils at her. 'Where will you take him?'

'God knows,' Heather said, as she tugged the brush through a knotted piece of the horse's tail. She glanced over at Ella, and frowned. 'I honestly don't know. I mean, I thought I might take him over to River View, but it would mean doing everything myself, and I don't know if I can fit it all in, not now that I'm working full time. And I don't want to get a sharer. Or at least, not yet, anyway.'

'No.' Ella knew from experience that sharers sometimes caused more trouble than they were worth. It was often difficult to agree over routines and workloads, when two people tried to divide one animal between them. Many a time she had been obliged to act as an independent adjudicator, when two owners had almost come to blows.

'I mean, ideally, if I can get someone experienced to ride him during the week, then I can manage the rest myself,'

Heather said. 'Mucking out and feeding isn't a problem. I can see to that in the mornings and after I've finished work. And Peter, bless him, will always help if I ask him. It's just this business of exercising him,' she sighed. 'Willing though they may be, I can't ask any of the village teenagers. I need somebody responsible – somebody who isn't a novice rider – somebody...' She paused and Ella knew exactly what was coming. 'Somebody like you.'

'Heather, I can't,' she said.

'Why not?'

'Because of Ursula,' she said. 'She'd think I was consorting with the enemy. You do realise she's not going to forgive or forget what you said to her.'

'Good.' Heather said. 'And I hope she pays heed to it too, because I'm telling you, Ella. I meant every word. She's turning this business into a shambles, and you need to do something about it before she ruins the place completely.'

Ella was shocked. 'It's not that bad, is it?'

'Not yet, no. But don't say you haven't been warned. Ursula has about as much knowledge of running these stables, as I have of flying to the moon. If it wasn't for you, Ella, this place would have gone under by now.'

'That's some compliment,' she said, her cheeks colouring rapidly.

'It was meant to be.' Heather's warm smile turned into a wicked grin. 'So, now will you ride my horse for me? You'd be doing me an enormous favour,' she added. 'I trust him with you, and I've seen you ride together. You make a brilliant team.'

'I know, but...'

'And, I'd pay you.'

'It's not that,' she protested weakly. 'I mean, I wouldn't want money for doing it. Honestly, Heather, there's nothing I'd like more than to exercise him for you, but you're placing me in a very difficult position.'

'I know,' she said. 'And I'm sorry. But please tell me you'll think about it?'

Majesty nuzzled into Ella's shoulder, and blew warm, hay

scented breath over her face. She stroked his neck, and sighed. He really was a beautiful creature, and she had always loved riding him. 'Oh, all right,' she said at last. 'I must be mad for agreeing, but I'll do it.'

'You will?' Heather gave a screech of delight. 'Oh, that's brilliant, Ella. Thank you so much. You won't regret this.'

'Won't I?' she said, with a wry smile. That remained to be seen. Thinking of a reason to slip away from the stables for a couple of hours a day would be tricky, if not impossible. It would mean taking one of the other horses out and riding it over to the farm, exercising Majesty, and then riding it back again. That was the only feasible excuse she could think of, for disappearing for hours every day.

The trouble was that Ursula's beady eyes didn't miss much that went on around the place. She would have to be careful if she were to avoid arousing her suspicions.

Ursula, however, was otherwise preoccupied in the days following Majesty's unscheduled departure from the stables. A rather snotty phone call from the bank manager's secretary had put her in a foul mood.

'No, I cannot come into the bank this afternoon,' she told the girl firmly. 'It's not convenient.'

'Mr Jenson says it's imperative that he speaks to you. He's rather concerned you haven't responded to any of his letters.'

'That's because I haven't had time,' she snorted. 'Tell him I'll ring him, sometime.' She slammed down the receiver. Bloody bank managers. They were quick enough to offer her cash, and even quicker to demand it back again. The new surface to the all-weather sand school had cost her a small fortune. To say nothing of the regular visits from the farrier and the feed merchant. All she seemed to get these days were bills, bills and more blasted bills.

She scrolled down the screen of her computer, carefully examining the pages of accounts; the real accounts that she had kept stored on a back up disc, well out of sight of Ella. Things were not looking good for the stables. Losing Majesty was bad enough, but now two other horses had been removed from the livery yard. Rumours of bad management and lack of care were rife. Someone was stirring up trouble. She was going to have to do something drastic to stop the rapid decline of her fortunes. The publicity generated by the film company would have been priceless, if the filming had gone ahead, but even their interest seemed to have faded like a damp squib.

Petunia Fitzgerald had told her, quite imperiously, that she had heard they were planning to use the annual agricultural show as the setting for the riding scenes. (This was over coffee and cream cakes at the Disabled Riders Bazaar, when Ursula had been trying to brag to her about having the film crew over at Hollyfield).

'My Gerald is on the organising committee,' Petunia said. 'So, he should know.'

'I'm sure he's right,' Ursula replied sweetly. 'Nevertheless, I am still in negotiations with the film company. The facilities we have at Hollyfield, you see, are quite superb.'

'As are the ones at the County Showground.'

Ursula hoped Petunia would choke over her freshly percolated coffee and cream horn. This wouldn't do at all. If the film company backed off, she would be made to look a laughing stock. She had told everyone – well, mostly everyone - that Hollyfield was going to be featured in the latest Simon De Silva movie. Even the obnoxious kids from the Saturday pony club were bringing their autograph books to their lessons, in case one of the films stars happened to walk by. Something would have to be done.

Back in her office, Ursula scrolled down the columns of figures on her computer screen. Her reading glasses were perched on the end of her narrow nose, so that she looked like a stern headmistress glaring down at her pupils.

The figures in red seemed to far outnumber those in black. Where and when had it started to go wrong?

Ursula thought back to the early days when money, or the

lack of it, had never been a problem. Her first husband, Clive – a corpulent businessman with a stress filled job in the City - had keeled over and died of a massive heart attack when their daughters, Vanessa and Caroline, were both small.

His ample life insurance fund and generous widow's pension had softened the blow of his untimely demise, and she had been able to indulge the girls and herself in the lifestyle to which they had all become accustomed.

The girls had attended private schools, and each had their own pony, which they took to various rallies and pony club events.

It was at one such event that she had first laid eyes on Robert Johnson, the talented show jumper. He was two years older than her; a widower, whose wife had tragically died from cancer, leaving him to bring up their only daughter, Ella.

The child, Ursula decided, needed a mother. And she needed a husband. The life insurance lump sum was running low, and she wanted some security for herself and her daughters. Marriage to Robert Johnson was the ideal solution.

Luckily, it was a doddle to convince him to feel the same way.

The marriage was satisfactory for both of them. Ella gained a mother, and the siblings she had never had, and Robert was able to leave the business side of the stables in his wife's (supposedly) capable hands whilst he toured the world.

Ursula could not have been happier.

Even Robert's death in a tragic car accident so soon after their marriage took place, did not trouble her unduly. Apart from the inconvenience of having his daughter to look after, and the petty conditions attached to his will, life could not have been more perfect. She had money, power, and prestige, everything that came with being the business manager of Hollyfield Stables.

And now, five years down the line, it looked as if everything was going wrong again.

Two letters had arrived on the very same morning. One, in a muddy brown envelope, was from the bank, complaining about the current state of her business account. (Immediate action was required to reduce the size of her rather sizeable overdraft). Ursula had ripped it in half and tossed it into the bin.

The other one - a white envelope embossed with silver swirls, and a pressed seal on the reverse – had been put to one side whilst Ursula answered the phone call from the bank manager's snooty secretary.

It stood propped against the phone, as she peered at the figures on the screen. The only solution, she decided, was to put up the livery charges. Either that, or cut the wages bill, but she couldn't see that going down very well with the staff.

Distracted, her gaze rested on the pristine white envelope, that she had almost forgotten to open. It looked infinitely more interesting than the figures on the screen.

She picked it up, and turned it over between her fingers. It wasn't a bill, that much was for sure. No one wasted money sending bills in fancy, decorative envelopes. It felt like a card, or some sort of invitation.

Now whom, she wondered, running her fingernail along the flap, and ripping it open, could this be from?

Chapter Eight

Whilst Ursula was shut in her study pondering over the accounts, Ella was enjoying an after-work drink with her friend Kate in the lounge bar of the village pub.

'We could eat here, if you like,' Kate suggested. 'Otherwise, it's beans on toast for me. My folks have gone to visit Aunt Margaret in Southwold.'

'Don't you ever cook?' Ella said.

'Not if I can help it.' Kate picked up the menu. 'Believe me, if you'd tried my cooking, you'd understand why.'

Ella smiled. 'I'll need to phone Ursula. She'll be expecting me.'

'My God, you mean she feeds you?'

'Actually, she's a pretty good cook.' Ella groped in her bag for her mobile. 'I have a feeling she went to cordon bleu classes when she was younger. She thought it would come in useful for all the entertaining she used to do. You know – posh dinners for businessmen and their wives – that sort of thing.'

Kate drained her glass. 'That woman never ceases to amaze me. I bet she…'

'Shush.' Ella waved Kate to be quiet as she jabbed out the numbers on her phone. 'Oh hi,' she said as the call was answered. 'It's only me. I thought I'd better let you know I'll be late back. No, I won't be home for supper.' She paused, and then said 'No, you don't need to leave me anything. Thanks anyway. Bye. Well,' she said, glancing across at her friend. 'Was *she* in a good mood?'

'I don't know. Was she?'

'Yes, oddly enough.' Ella pulled a face. 'She was positively foul earlier on. In fact, she's been bad tempered all week. If I didn't know better, I'd say she'd been drinking.'

'Maybe she's drowning her sorrows.'

'What sorrows?'

'I thought you said she'd lost some prize horse from the livery yard,' Kate said, handing her the menu. 'I'm going to have the home cured gammon and egg.'

'Hmm, that's right.' Ella mulled over the menu. 'Majesty's gone. Heather's taken him to River View Farm. You know, Mr Dobson's place. Think I'll have the lasagne,' she added. 'Do you want me to order?'

'No, I'll do it.' Kate picked up the glasses. 'Same again?'

'Yes, please.'

Two glasses of wine later, and Ella found herself confiding in her friend about the worrying situation at the stables.

'I thought it was just Thomas at first, you know, being a bit melodramatic. He doesn't get on with Ursula. In fact, I don't think he ever has done. But when Heather said virtually the same thing, I began to wonder if there was something in it.'

'And is there?'

'I don't know. That's the funny thing. I've gone through the records and everything seems fine, but Ursula's definitely trying to cut corners.'

'Maybe she's spiriting a bit away for her retirement,' Kate said. 'After all, she wasn't very well provided for in your dad's will, was she? He left almost everything to you.'

'Not quite everything,' Ella said. 'Yes, I got the house and the business, but Ursula got a tidy sum as well. More than enough, I'd say, to see her through a wealthy old age.'

'Ah, but she's not a frugal lady.'

'Nor are her daughters,' Ella giggled. 'Did I tell you how much Vanessa's hair had cost?'

'Yes, and if I'd paid that much, I'd be wanting a makeover

as well. Nice hair, shame about the face.'

'Honestly, Kate. You can be so cruel.'

'Truthful, I'd say.' Her eyes were looking rather glassy, and she was grinning profusely. Ella too, was feeling slightly tipsy. Must have been a good bottle of wine. No doubt they'd both be suffering the after effects of it in the morning.

'We need to find some men,' Kate announced cheerfully, as she peered around the lounge bar. 'You need to find a man.'

'Don't start that again,' Ella groaned. The memory of the debacle at the Jazz Club was still pretty fresh in her mind. As was the last attempt Kate had made to pair her off with someone. An ex-boyfriend, to be precise, who had spent the whole evening casting puppy-dog-eyes rather forlornly at the sight of his lost love, draped around the latest in her long line of male conquests.

'Leave it with me, Ella.'

'I'd rather not,' she groaned. She was doing quite nicely on her own, thank you very much. She didn't need a man to complicate her life, despite what Kate seemed to think. Besides which, her friend didn't seem to be doing very successfully in the man-hunting stakes herself. If she was so good at matchmaking, where was the great love of her life?

'You've gone very quiet,' Kate said, as she slapped her credit card down on the bill, slipped discreetly onto the table by the waitress.

'Have I?' she said, 'Oh here, let me pay my share.'

'Rubbish.' Kate waved her hand away. 'This was my idea. In any case, you've saved me an evening slaving away over a hot stove.'

'I doubt that.'

Kate looked mortally offended. 'One of these days I might surprise you,' she said. 'I might invite you over to mine for dinner.'

'I didn't know they delivered takeaways to your neck of the woods.'

'Ha ha,' she said, smiling up at the waitress. 'Thanks,' she said. 'That was lovely.'

'It was. It was delicious,' Ella agreed.

'Worth every penny,' Kate glanced at her watch. 'Goodness, is that the time? We've been here for hours. It's a good job I ordered us a taxi.' She yawned. 'I wish I didn't have to go to work in the morning?'

Ella smiled. 'Think yourself lucky you can sleep in till eight. I'll be up at six.'

'Yes, well you know what I think about that. Get those two other lazy toads out of bed. Let Vanessa and Caroline do some of the work.'

'I like the horses too much for that,' she said, grinning. 'I wouldn't wish their happy morning faces on anyone, man or beast.'

Kate shook her head. 'Ella, you're too nice, and that's half your trouble. You need to toughen up, my girl. It's the first rule of business, learn how to delegate'

'If you say so.'

'I do.' She slipped her arms into the sleeves of her jacket, and wrapped a long, silk scarf at least twice around her neck, before leaning forward to kiss her fondly on the cheek. 'Now then, where's that taxi driver got to?'

He was standing by the bar, where he had been for the past ten minutes. It was a well-known fact that whenever Kate rang for a taxi, it would involve a long delay before she got in to it. The drivers were used to her by now.

'Sorry,' Ella murmured, by way of apology, as she followed her friend to the waiting car.

'He'll have left the meter running,' Kate said, as she settled herself into the front seat, and tossed her hair back over her shoulder. 'They always do when they know it's for me.'

The driver, a middle-aged man with a full head of grey hair, grinned at her as he climbed in and slammed the door shut. 'Marsh Lane Cottage, ladies?'

'That's the one,' Kate said. 'But stop at Hollyfield Stables on the way, thanks. And you,' she peered over her shoulder at Ella, and waggled a finger at her. 'You think about what I've said, and

I'll ring you tomorrow, okay?'

It was almost eleven o'clock, and way past the time Ella would normally have gone to bed (on a work day, that is), when she waved goodbye to Kate from the sweeping driveway at the front of the stables. The lights were still on in the house, and the sound of animated conversation, when she turned her key in the door, signalled that Ursula and her daughters were still up.

Not wanting to disturb them, she clicked on the hall light, and headed quietly for the stairs.

'Ella? Is that you?'

Oh damn. 'Yes,' she said, as she hung her jacket on the banisters.

Ursula's florid face appeared in the lounge doorway. She appeared to be slightly inebriated. A half-drunk glass of something dangled from one hand. The other was hanging on to the doorframe.

'Had a good evening?'

The stench of gin was horribly apparent.

'Yes, thanks.'

'Good. Good.' Ursula paused, and blinked at her. 'Good,' she said again.

Ella wondered if she was supposed to say something. There was an expectant look on her stepmother's face.

'I had a meal with Kate.'

'Ah.' Ursula took a mouthful of her drink. 'Was it good?'

'Yes, it was. Very good.'

'And did she...er... say anything?"

'About what?'

'Oh,' Ursula waved her hand in the air. 'Anything.'

'Not really.' Ella was well and truly puzzled by now. 'We just chatted. You know?'

'You girls,' Ursula smiled. 'You like to have your little chats, don't you?' She raised her eyebrows, and winked at her.

This was ridiculous. Ella didn't have a clue what she was going on about. Nor did she want to stay and find out. Ursula was well away, if the lopsided smile on her face was anything to go by.

'I think I'll go up to bed now,' she said, pretending to stifle a yawn. 'I'm really shattered.'

'Yes…yes, you do that. You've got an early start tomorrow.'

As usual, she thought. 'Well, goodnight, then.'

'Goodnight, Ella.'

She padded slowly up the stairs. The lounge door closed, and she paused on the landing, listening to the sudden shriek of laughter, which sounded as if it came from Caroline.

'You mean she doesn't know?' (That was from Vanessa)

'No.'

'You're sure?'

'Positive.'

'You mean it's our little secret.'

The voices grew quieter, and the conversation faded as Ella strained to listen. It was obvious that something was going on, something they were trying to keep from her. And it had to be something important for Ursula to hit the gin bottle. But it can't have been bad news. She hadn't sounded unhappy. The total opposite, if that was possible. She had been remarkably cheerful.

It was with a certain degree of apprehension that Ella undressed and got ready for bed. She didn't like secrets, especially ones that she wasn't supposed to know about. But she was equally determined not to lose any sleep over the matter. Whatever it was, she reasoned, she would find out soon enough. Vanessa and Caroline were the last people to be trusted to keep their mouths shut. And if they didn't tell her, she was quite sure there would be someone else out there who would.

Breakfast in the Johnson household was a rather subdued affair. Ursula was suffering from the after effects of half a bottle of gin, and by the look of Vanessa and Caroline, they had matched her measure for measure.

Ella came back from feeding the horses to find the three of them sitting round the kitchen table, looking rather pained and delicate. The smell of burning toast filled the room. She kicked off her wellies by the back door, and padded across the stone flagged floor to the sink. 'Anyone want a coffee?' she said brightly, as she filled the kettle.

Vanessa groaned.

'Black, and strong,' Ursula muttered.

Caroline sighed, and shook her head.

'Just the one, then,' Ella said, reaching for the coffee jar. 'Any post today?'

Three pairs of eyes swung round and stared at her.

'What?'

'Post. Letters. I saw the postman as I was coming back from the yard.'

Ursula breathed out steadily. 'No. Well, nothing important,' she said. 'Why? Were you expecting something?'

Ella shook her head as she poured hot water over the coffee and stirred the steaming mugs.

Ursula was looking rather bleary-eyed, morose even, as she ladled a heaped spoonful of sugar into the proffered mug. 'All I seem to get these days is junk mail,' she muttered. 'Nobody ever writes to me. Well, nobody interesting, anyway.'

'I had a note from Mrs Whitten,' Ella said. 'She left it with Thomas. She wants to enrol all three of her children for the Pony Club Camp in August.'

'Oh joy,' Vanessa said. 'Some more little brats to run riot round the place.'

The Children's camp in the summer was the highlight of the Pony Club's calendar. The organisers descended en masse to Hollyfields, to stage gymkhanas, and lessons and fun events for their young members. The four-acre paddock was turned into a campsite for the week, and hordes of excited children, accompanied by their, usually, badly behaved Thelwell style ponies, shrieked and giggled and cried their way through the programme of events.

What was fun for the children was a nightmare for Vanessa, who couldn't abide the little brats, and Caroline, who gagged at the sight of anyone who reminded her of herself, in her formative years.

'I suppose they'll want to use the bathroom at all hours of the day and night again,' she groaned. The memory of grubby, mud-stained children queuing for the one and only toilet was not something she wished to be reminded of.

'Not if we get those portaloos installed in time,' Ursula said. The summer camp was a good money-spinner for the stables. Like it or loathe it, the event would be going ahead.

She heaped another spoonful of sugar into her coffee. 'Um, Ella,' she said, clearing her throat, and glancing slyly at her daughters. 'Next weekend....'

'What about it?' Ella popped a couple of slices of bread into the toaster, and reached into the fridge for some butter and marmalade.

'I know it's, technically, your weekend off.'

'Yes.'

'Well, I was wondering...' She paused, and took a sip of her coffee. 'You're not doing anything special, are you?'

'Me?' Ella glanced back at her. The three of them were staring at her with an expectant, almost hungry look on their faces. 'No,' she said. 'Why?'

'I'd like to change it, if that's all right with you?'

Now she was seriously beginning to get worried. Ursula didn't usually ask her permission if she wanted to make changes to the duty rosters. She normally went ahead and did it, and told her about it afterwards.

'Perhaps you could have this weekend off instead,' she said. 'I know its short notice, but the girls and I have something planned.'

'For next weekend?'

'Yes.'

The toast popped up out of the toaster, and Ella rescued it before Wilson, the Great Dane, could snatch it from the work surface, and gobble it down, a habit he was fond of doing, if he could get away with it.

'I suppose it'll be all right,' she said, patting the huge

grey lump of a dog fondly, and tossing him a crust as way of consolation for his disappointment.

Vanessa gave a small, smothered giggle, which drew her a withering glare from Ursula.

'So, you'll be able to work all next weekend,' she said, confirming what she had already said.

'Yes. Why?'

Ursula smiled. 'Well, it's the County Show, you see. I thought it would be a good idea if we took a few horses along, for publicity purposes. Vanessa and Caroline are going to ride in a couple of events, and I thought I would make an appearance, a public relations exercise, if you like.'

'Hmm. Whatever.' Ella buttered her toast, and crunched into it hungrily. One thing about these early mornings, they certainly gave her an appetite. She glanced up and caught Caroline's queasy face. She appeared to have gone quite green.

'I wouldn't be able to go if I couldn't leave you in charge,' Ursula said. 'These days it's difficult to know who to trust to take care of things, so I'll be relying on you, Ella.'

'Fine. I've said, it's not a problem.'

Ursula beamed. It quite transformed her face.

'Good. Good – well, that's excellent – isn't it, girls?'

Vanessa and Caroline nodded dutifully.

Ella had the strangest inkling that something was going on, but if it meant she could have the weekend off, she didn't care. After the hectic week she had had, trying to fit in Majesty as well as her other jobs, she was quite looking forward to a couple of days off.

'It means I won't be able to do the children's ride tomorrow morning, though,' she said. 'Not if it's my Saturday off.'

Caroline's face went a sicklier shade of green, as she caught her mother's eager look. 'Mother, I can't,' she groaned.

'Course you can,' Ursula insisted. 'It's only for one morning, after all. And you'll do it if it means you're free to ride at the Show next weekend.'

This thought seemed to cheer Caroline up immensely

(though she found it a bit unfair that Vanessa hadn't been roped in to help her).

Ella munched the last mouthful of her toast, and then carried the plate over to the sink to wash up.

'You can leave those, if you like,' Ursula said. 'You go and get on with your jobs round the yard. The sooner you're done, the sooner you can finish for the weekend.'

'Thanks,' she said, genuinely pleased. It was unlike her stepmother to want to give her any time off at all, let alone telling her to finish early, but she wasn't going to argue with her.

She slipped her feet back into her boots, and picked up her jacket, before heading out, in blissful ignorance, to the stable block.

Back in the kitchen, Ursula was beaming proudly at her two girls. 'Done it,' she said, 'and she doesn't suspect a thing.'

'She'll find out,' Vanessa said, reading the heavily embossed and personal invitation card, for about the hundredth time.

"The Blackwater Film Company is delighted to invite you to take part in the Simon De Silva Show-jumping Stakes. The winner of this prestigious event will be featured in the action film, 'No Turning Back,' featuring Simon De Silva. Short-listed candidates will be introduced personally to Mr De Silva, in the Keynes and Bain hospitality marquee. Please read the attached conditions of entry before applying. Names to be submitted to the competition secretary, care of the County Showground, by the morning of the event."

'So, what if she does?' Caroline said. 'She's agreed to work next weekend. You heard what Mother said? She won't go back on her word.'

'No,' Ursula said, smiling. 'That's something Ella would never do.'

Flattery and persuasion had succeeded, as she had known it surely would.

'We'd better start thinking about what you're going to wear, girls. We want it to be something special, something that will make you stand out from the crowd. I think I'll give that saddler over at Millhouse a ring.'

And sod the expense. The bank would have to wait a bit longer for its money. It could afford to. Ursula couldn't.

Chapter Nine

Filming of the latest Simon De Silva movie, 'No Turning Back', was making steady progress. A good proportion of the location work had been completed, and most of the studio scenes in London had been shot.

Miles Davison, the director – a stout little man - strutted across the cluttered studio floor clutching a clip board, and waving directions to the lighting and camera crews.

'Yes, over there – to the right – no, the right. I want the shot coming from behind the door.'

'Everything okay, Miles?'

Blood dripped from the gash on Simon De Silva's forehead. A livid red mark above his right cheekbone showed where a bruise was starting to form.

'Simon!' Miles chuckled gleefully, and patted him on the shoulder. 'Ready to give it another go?'

'Absolutely.'

'Great.' He waved his clipboard in the air. 'Listen everyone. We're starting this shot again,' he called.

'Places please,' came a voice from behind one of the sound monitors.

Simon sat himself down on the corner of a white Formica-topped table, and clutched a stained and damp cloth to his face. A woman in a nurse's uniform was leaning over him, poised and ready to bandage the cut on his arm.

'Ready folks?'

Simon winked at his co-star.

'And... action.'

The woman's hands worked quickly and efficiently,

winding the strip of gauze around his wrist. She glanced back at the closed door. 'You can't stay here.'

'I don't intend to.' He flexed his fingers, as if testing to see if they were still intact.

The woman straightened up, and pressed a clean gauze pad over the cut on his temple. 'Any idea how they found you?' she asked.

His hand closed over her wrist, and she gasped as he tugged her against his chest. 'No,' he said, 'not yet.'

He kissed her, long and hard, before releasing her with a reluctant sigh. 'Watch my back, Tanya,' he said, as he flicked the metal catch on the window.

'Don't I always?'

'Nearly always.' He pushed open the window, and scrambled onto the sill. A roguish grin transformed his rugged features. 'You were cutting it a bit fine this time, my love. Don't leave it so late in future.' He glanced from one side to the other, and then readied himself to jump. 'See you in Kensington.'

The girl released her hair from its tightly pinned knot and shook it free. 'I'll be waiting,' she said.

'Cut!'

Miles Davidson clapped loudly, as Simon jumped back into the studio, and took a playful bow in front of the assembled camera crew and sound people.

'I think that's what they call "a wrap",' he said. 'Well done, Simon, and well done, Molly. Right, folks.' He turned to the crowd of onlookers who had gathered to watch the take. 'That's it. Show's over. You can go now, but I want you all back here at seven on Monday, understand. Seven o'clock – a.m. That means morning, you lot. I don't want to see anyone crawling in at midday.'

The technicians were dismantling the lights, and moving furniture. Simon took a long cool drink from a bottle of chilled water, and splashed some of it over his face and hands. One of the make-up girls was attempting to wipe away the smears of fake blood from his forehead with a piece of cotton wool.

'It's okay, I can do that,' he said.

'You're sure?'

He nodded, and took it from her.

'Simon, my man.' Miles ambled towards him with a genial grin on his face.

'What?' he said, wiping his forehead with the damp piece of padding?

'Don't look so suspicious,' he said. 'It's about the riding scene. Thanks, Molly – yes, I'll see you on Monday – sorry sweetie, but we do need to start shooting first thing.'

'Bye, Moll,' Simon said, giving his co-star a wave. 'Well,' he said, after a considerable pause, when it seemed as if Miles had forgotten he had started up the conversation.

'Well, what? Oh.' Realisation suddenly dawned. 'The riding scene.'

Simon gritted his teeth. 'Yes?'

Miles looked worried. 'There isn't a problem, is there, Simon? I mean, I take it you can ride?'

'Um, sort of.'

'What?' Miles bushy eyebrows lowered a fraction.

'Well, it was a long time ago.'

'How long?'

Simon took another swig from the water bottle, and wiped his mouth with the back of his hand. 'Do donkeys on Blackpool beach count?'

'Jesus Christ!' Miles spluttered.

'Come on, Miles. It can't be that hard. Can it?'

'We're talking galloping horses, here,' he groaned. 'Not piddling little donkeys on a pleasure beach.'

'Well, I'll have a few lessons,' Simon said agreeably.

Miles shook his head in despair. 'We're shooting in a week,' he groaned. 'Lewis has got us the backing of the County Agricultural Show. We,' he said, producing a folded leaflet from his inside jacket pocket, 'or at least, you,' (He pointed to Simon's name in bold heading on the top of the glossy flyer) 'are holding our own show jumping competition as part of the programme of events. The winner will be featured in the film. Trevelyan's team thought that one up,' he added. 'They're after some show jumper they've seen, but can't quite pin down. Anyway,' he said, folding up the leaflet and stuffing it back into his pocket. 'It's quite a plus as far as I'm concerned. It means that any footage we include will be real live action, as opposed to the staged variety. Invitations have been sent to every equestrian business in the area, and the ad has gone into all the local papers, so we're expecting a lot of talent. And,' he added, 'I am reliably informed that it's all over social media, and that flyers have gone into every shop window for miles. And now you tell me you can't ride.' He sighed and gave a helpless shrug. '*Now,* you tell me.'

Simon drained the last few mouthfuls of chilled water from the bottle. 'It's not a problem, Miles,' he said calmly.

'You're damn right it isn't. Because I'm going to get some proper riders in.'

'No way,' he said. 'You know the score, Miles. I do my own stunts.'

The director shook his head wearily. 'Quite frankly, Simon. I'd like you to survive this film. I do have other projects in mind for you. Let me talk it over with Lewis.'

'Fine.' He shrugged. 'But I won't change my mind.'

Miles reached for his cell phone. Donkeys on Blackpool beach – Hah! Was the man insane? The scene asked for him to leap from the first aid building, sprint across the arena, and vault onto the nearest horse, before galloping into the distance. Sure, they could have a stunt rider for the final shots, but he wanted to get a few close ups. Not of a novice rider on a placid animal, but of the hero on a supremely fit and spirited horse. A handful of riding lessons was hardly going to achieve that.

'Jesus!' Lewis swore, as he listened to Miles' tirade on the other end of the phone. 'Why didn't he tell you?'

'Why didn't he tell you?' Miles said. 'You sent him the script. He must have known what was expected of him.'

'He did,' Lewis said, thinking back. (It had been a long time ago.) 'Yes, I'm sure he did. And if I recall, he didn't make any negative comments.'

'Right,' Miles said smugly. 'So, you sort it'

Thanks very much, Lewis thought, replacing the receiver with a scowl. That was all he needed. A novice rider as the hero in a scene that was absolutely crucial to the plot. Brilliant, bloody brilliant.

'Problems?' James said.

'Nothing insurmountable,' he said. (Or so he hoped).

The day was not exactly going according to plan. His business meeting with one of the film's sponsors had been difficult, to say the least. Since money ruled most aspects of film-making, unless one was hugely talented and wealthy in one's own right, the support of sponsors was crucial to a film's success.

'Are Keynes and Bain going to pull out?' Matthew asked.

They were seated in Lewis' office, where he had gathered the other three members of his production team together to discuss the slight hitch in plans.

'No, it's too late for that now. Let's just say they've got a case of the jitters.'

'Which you've managed to put right. Right?' Matthew said.

'Well, sort of.' Lewis uncorked a bottle of Chilean wine, provided for by Lucy, this time, and poured it into their glasses. 'I've told them about the planned publicity at the County Show, and they've agreed to foot the bill for the hospitality suite, as long as their name gets a mention, of course.'

'Of course.' James raised his glass to him.

'But then there's the slight problem that we haven't got a show-jumper yet.'

'So?' Matthew looked puzzled. 'You've said yourself; there'll be plenty of talent at the Show.'

'Yes,' Lewis agreed. 'But we want unknown talent, and I've been reliably informed that some of the big names in the horse world will be taking part.'

'Not in the Simon De Silva Stakes, surely,' Lucy sniggered.

Lewis gave her a pained glare.

'Hang on a minute,' James said. 'I don't understand. Why has it got to be unknown talent? Loads of sportsmen and women have had cameo roles as themselves in films. From racing drivers to footballers. They've all done it.'

'Yes, but...'

'You're still after that girl,' Matthew said, a knowing glint in his eye. 'That's why you're on about finding unknown talent. You think if she was well known, you'd recognise her.'

Lewis frowned. He was nearer to the truth than he cared to admit. 'What do I know about show-jumping,' he muttered. 'She could have won dozens of things, and I wouldn't know.'

'Exactly,' James said. 'And neither will Jo-public.'

'Yeah, yeah.' He conceded that they were probably right

'So, when are we going back?' Matthew asked.

'Next week.' Lucy flipped open her phone. 'I've booked us into the same hotel, and the mobile film unit will be up there from Thursday.'

'Any problems in that direction?'

'No, everything's arranged,' she said. 'And Simon's free to fit in with whatever we decide.'

'Oh good,' Lewis said, his voice heavy with sarcasm. 'Because I've got plans for that young man.'

Lucy tilted her head quizzically to one side. 'Do I need to make a note of them here?'

'No,' he said. 'But I do want you to find out how much an intensive course of riding lessons is going to cost.'

'You're joking?' Matthew spluttered. 'He can't ride?'

'Not yet he can't.' Lewis said, leaning over to top up their glasses. 'But I'm working on it.' He drained the last few drops from the bottle into his own glass. 'So now all we need is for this girl to show up, and we're sorted.'

'As easy as that, eh?' James raised his glass, and winked at him.

'Not quite,' Matthew said. 'She's got to win the competition yet.'

Lewis gave him a thoughtful look.

'It is part of the publicity. You said the winner would get a part in the film,' he said. 'If she turns up and doesn't win, I presume that's tough luck.'

'We'll see,' Lewis said. He hadn't bargained for that eventuality.

'What's that supposed to mean?' Lucy said.

'It means,' he murmured, draining his glass, 'That we'll see.' And that was all he intended to say on the matter.

With no further business to discuss, the meeting ended, as it usually did, with a resume of the plans for the next few days, and then they all adjourned to a restaurant in the main street for dinner.

Lewis declined the invitation to continue the evening's festivities by going to a nightclub. Instead, he left the three of them in a pub, and took a taxi back to his flat on his own.

The view from the apartment window was stunning. The lights along the Embankment glistened on the murky water of the Thames. A floating barge, with music, and lights flashing drifted downstream, the occupants enjoying an expensive, and unique evening pleasure cruise.

Lewis stood by the fourth-floor window, his fingers holding the stem of a wine glass, watching the evening turning slowly into night over London. The stream of traffic along the Embankment had eased. It never ceased entirely. People strolled along the length of the riverside, pausing, and watching, seemingly engrossed in their surroundings, or marching steadily and purposefully as they went about their business. A jogger ran by, fluorescent stickers glinting on the back of his shoes. A late-night dog walker stooped to pick up what his pet had deposited (in the plastic bag he, no doubt, always carried). Then held his offering at arm's length, as he searched for the nearest poop scoop bin.

Lewis drew back from the window, hesitated for a moment, and then drew the blinds. The light from the Art Deco lamp in the corner spilled onto the polished wood floor.

The cream leather sofa, glass topped table, and state of the art sound system indicated that the current occupant had stylish taste. Not his taste, Lewis thought. The decor was described as 'minimalist.' Or at least, that's what it said in the agency brochure. He just considered it bare.

'You're only renting it,' Matthew told him. 'What does it matter what it looks like?'

'It's not exactly home,' he complained. Home, for Lewis - his real home, that is (though he spent precious little time there) - was in the heart of the Yorkshire Moors. He had invested in an old farmhouse, where he could enjoy splendid isolation in comfortable, cluttered surroundings, and a decent pint in the village local, where the regulars ignored his glorified status, and treated him as one of them.

'Well, you're welcome to come and stay at my place if you're feeling lonely.'

'Thanks, but no thanks,' he said. 'I like my own space.'

It was true. Despite being associated with actors and the tabloid press for most of his adult life, Lewis had never felt comfortable with the trappings of fame. He hated the glitzy parties he was expected to attend, the social gatherings of the glitterati.

As a film producer renowned for working with some of the country's most talented actors, he sometimes received more attention than he felt was justified. The fact that it seemed to make him public property was something he could not easily come to terms with. He would shun publicity at all costs if it concerned his private life, though he was more than happy to talk about his work.

'People want to know who you are, Lewis,' one newspaper journalist told him. 'What makes you tick? Christ, they even want to know what you eat for breakfast.'

'Toast, like everyone else,' he muttered.

'Can I quote you on that?'

'Please don't.'

At least here, in the apartment, with its glorious view

over the Thames, he could watch the world go by and not have to worry about the flashing of cameras, and the lurking paparazzi. The roller coaster ride of fame was not for the faint-hearted. Sometimes he, like everyone else, needed to take time out for himself.

He swallowed the last mouthful of wine in his glass, and padded through to the luxuriously designed, Swedish style kitchen, to get himself a refill.

As he passed the huge, flat screen television in the corner of the lounge, his attention was diverted by the mention of, "Robert Johnson, riding Fools Gold..."

'What?'

He clicked the sound up on the screen. He hadn't been watching the programme. It was some cable channel, and he had only put it on to drown out the awful emptiness of his barren (but apparently stylish) apartment.

'It's five years since Robert Johnson was killed in a car crash,' came the polished tone of the programme presenter. 'And his record for completing the course in the fastest time has never been beaten until this week, when Peter Van Dryden, riding Wings of a Dove...'

'Robert Johnson?' Lewis peered at the screen. The footage showed the legendary show-jumper flying round the course on a magnificent bay horse with a flaxen mane and tail, and then changed to that of the current champion, Peter Van Dryden, a thirty-one-year old from Basel, in Switzerland.

'I always wanted to beat Robert's time,' the Swiss, was saying, in broken, and heavily accented English. 'He was a great rider. A great man.'

The camera zoomed in on Robert Johnson's face. Lewis was intrigued. This was a picture of a handsome and talented rider. What the hell did he see in someone like Ursula? Surely, she hadn't changed that much in five years. And yet, the woman he had seen at Hollyfield stables looked much older than he would have imagined Robert Johnson's wife to be, even bearing in mind the obvious grief and trauma she had been through.

Perhaps that's what was meant by the saying, "love is blind".

Not that he had much to compare with. His love life had taken a definite nosedive recently. He was tired of shallow fawning females, only interested in being with Lewis Trevelyan, the producer, and not Lewis Trevelyan, the man.

Serena had been the last in a long line of adoring females, who were only interested in getting their picture printed in the gossip pages of the latest celebrity magazine. When he discovered that she had given an interview to 'The Latest' – a no holds barred, spill the beans type of interview (most of it lies, because he really wasn't *that* interesting) - it signalled the end of their relationship.

Serena came out of the encounter rather well, several thousand pounds richer, in fact. But it made him even more determined to keep his private life private. Hence the lonely apartment on the fourth floor of this prestigious block of flats overlooking the Thames.

He watched the television footage of the show jumping with an expression akin to admiration and disbelief on his face. Some of the jumps were huge – taller than a normal man - and yet both horse and rider seemed to sail effortlessly over them. That took skill, he decided, swigging off another glass of wine, and guts of steel. He couldn't do it. Christ! He couldn't even ride. Dealing with financiers, film executives and dramatists every day was a cinch in comparison to that. Yet what did they get paid? Peanuts, unless they were at the top of their profession. And how many broken bones and broken hearts did it take to get there?

Enthralled, he watched the programme to its conclusion; learnt several interesting, if not to say thought provoking facts, and was surprised to discover it was after twelve o'clock by the time it ended. His colleagues would probably still be out clubbing, and hitting the high spots of London. Well, he could live without that. He had something much more important on his mind.

At seven fifteen the following morning, he made one of

many phone calls.

'James? Pick up the phone, James. I know you're there.'

'Jesus, Lewis,' came the weary groan from the other end of the line. 'Do you know what time it is?'

'To the minute,' he said cheerfully. 'I take it you had a good night? Better than the Jazz Club, I presume?'

'Don't remind me.'

Lewis smiled. The fact that both Matthew and James had been virtually ignored by their respective dates on the same night must have come as something of a body blow to the pair of them. Country girls obviously had more sense than their city counterparts, or maybe they were just plain choosy. 'I saw an interesting documentary on television last night,' he told him.

'You haven't phoned to tell me that?' James groaned.

'Actually, yes, I have.'

'You what?'

'Robert Johnson has a daughter.'

A long pause followed. 'I take it you're talking about the show-jumper, Robert Johnson?' James sighed.

'Naturally.'

An inaudible groan echoed down the line. 'Lewis, its seven-o-clock in the morning.'

'I know. Now listen, James, this could be important.'

'It could?' He didn't sound convinced.

'Yes. Those two girls at the stables were his step-daughters, right?'

'Right.'

'Well according to the documentary, Robert Johnson had a daughter. She was fifteen when he died, so that would make her about twenty or twenty-one now.'

'She's probably at college, then,' James said sleepily. 'That's the right sort of age. You would think if she were still at the stables, her stepmother would have mentioned her.'

'Hmm. That's what I thought,' Lewis said, scratching his unshaven jaw thoughtfully. 'But I can't help wondering if she was the girl I saw on the cross country course.'

'The mystery blonde?'

'Yes. Look, I know it sounds daft, but I'm sure I could see a certain resemblance between her and the man I watched last night on the telly.'

'So why wouldn't Ursula want us to know about her?'

'That, my friend,' he said. 'Is what I intend to find out.'

At eight fifteen precisely on that Saturday morning, Lewis Trevelyan drove his silver BMW from its covered parking space in the basement of the apartment block, and headed for Hammersmith, where he picked up Simon De Silva.

His personalised number plate, LEW 15, drew many an admiring glance, as he weaved through the London traffic, and hit the motorway at speed. He should have waited until he could have picked up a hire car, but he was anxious for them to be on their way.

'At least take a bloody minder with you,' James said, when he heard of his plans for the weekend. 'You'll have every female under fifty going nuts.'

'I doubt it,' Lewis said. 'This is Suffolk we're going to. They're a pretty reserved lot out there in the sticks. Besides which, if we turn up with loads of bodyguards, we're bound to attract attention. And in any case,' he added. 'I haven't given them Simon's real name. As far as they're concerned, his riding lesson is booked under the name of Adam Lansing.'

'And you don't think, for one minute, that they'll recognise him?'

'It's a possibility,' he said. 'But it's a chance we have to take.'

'Jesus, Lewis. You must be mad.'

'Desperate, more like,' he said. 'Don't worry, James. I'll keep in touch.'

He eased his foot off the accelerator pedal, and glanced across at his companion.

Simon De Silva was dozing in the passenger seat, having been rudely awoken by an early morning phone call.

'Riding lesson? Yeah, I'm up for it,' he had murmured sleepily, giving Lewis the distinct impression that he probably didn't know what he was agreeing to. He no doubt thought he was still in some kind of dream. A dream that had ended abruptly with him banging on the door and insisting that he dress appropriately for the occasion.

It was definitely a case of killing two birds with one stone. Whilst Simon was getting in some well-needed riding practice, Lewis intended to pay Ursula a visit. Because, one way or the other, he was going to find out the identity of the illusive blonde girl, whether she was Robert Johnson's daughter or not. And he had no intention of leaving the stables until he did so.

Chapter Ten

Saturday was usually the busiest day of the week for the staff at Hollyfield Stables. Apart from the weekly children's pony club for the under-twelve's, there was also the 'Own a Pony Day' sessions for willing teenagers, who could pay to have the joy of mucking out, feeding and grooming the horse of their choice.

It was a cost-effective way of securing cheap labour for the day, and the girls (and occasional boy), who took part, had no complaints about the fact that they were being used as unpaid workers. For one entire day they could pretend that they actually owned a horse. They were allowed to brush it to their hearts content and plait tails and manes, and oil hooves until they gleamed. A riding lesson was also included, and if they were lucky, an informal hack over the fields as well. In between, they would muck out stables, sweep the yard, fill hay nets and water buckets, and generally do all the tasks the regular stable girls did, and they even paid for the privilege of being allowed to do so.

Ella thought it was a bit of a rip-off, but Ursula insisted it was good practice for the participants. After all, they were being trained in stable management techniques. Where else would they get such an opportunity, and at such reasonable prices? (And it saved her having to fork out wages for weekend staff, when she could rely on the youngsters to do all the work).

This particular Saturday, Caroline was in charge of the smaller children's riding lessons, and Vanessa had been given the task of organising the 'Own a Pony Day' helpers.

'It's all right for you,' Caroline muttered crossly, as she tightened the girth on a fat little pony, which barely reached the height of her waist. 'I've got eight riders under the age of twelve, accompanied by their doting parents, who all want to see little Henry, or Jasmine do something other than trot round in a boring circle. They have no idea what it takes to teach some of their kids. And if I have that little madam Sasha Wilkes in my class again...'

'You have.' Vanessa scanned the list of names.

'Oh shit.'

'Why? What does she do?'

'Nothing I tell her to, that's what,' Caroline said. 'And if she tells me one more time that, "mummy says I should do this, that or the other," I'm likely to throttle the little blighter.'

'Precocious child, isn't she?' Ella said, with a wry smile, as she poked her head around the barn door. It was almost worth missing her day off, just to stay and watch the proceedings.

But she had plenty of things to do, and hanging about the stables was not one of them. 'I'm taking the Range Rover,' she said, dangling the keys in front of them. 'Ursula says she doesn't need it today and you two will be too busy.'

'Rub it in, why don't you,' Vanessa said sulkily.

Ella had no intention of rising to the bait. 'See you later, then,' she said, giving them a cheery wave.

In the car park, various cars were depositing children, from toddlers in top heavy riding hats, to tweenies, as Ella considered the under tens, wearing lycra jodhpurs and brightly coloured sweatshirts. The teenagers, complete with muddy boots and padded jackets, were assembling by the barn door, chattering excitedly.

'...But I want Minnie – you had her last week.'

'I'm going to ask if I can have Shannon today.'

'I don't care. I want Minnie...'

'Oh, hi, Ella.' Several pairs of eyes swivelled towards her, as she unlocked the door of the metallic blue Range Rover. 'Aren't you taking us today?'

'No. It's my weekend off,' she said cheerfully. 'I'm going into town. I think you've got Vanessa.'

Somebody groaned.

'She's no fun.'

'Old bossy boots.'

Ella tried not to smile. Out of the corner of her eyes she could see Vanessa making her way down from the tack room, her ample thighs squeezed into a pair of too tight breeches, which only served to accentuate the parts she would have been better off trying to hide. A large burgundy sweatshirt, with the Hollyfield stables motif on it, covered the unsightly spread of her spare tyre, which had been forced up above the waistband of her trousers. Dark navy suede chaps, and a polished pair of stable boots completed her outfit.

'She's gone blonde,' observed one of the sharper-eyed teenagers.

A titter of amusement rippled through the group.

'Looks more like her Mum than ever, now.'

'Maybe she's trying to look like Ella.'

'No. Oh my God.'

Vanessa scowled as she approached the gathered party. She had the sneakiest suspicion that they were talking about her, and she didn't like that thought one little bit. 'Now then, you lot,' she said, in her most authoritative tone. 'We haven't got time for you to stand around chatting all day. All the stables need to be mucked out. Come on, get a move on.'

Ella switched on the radio, and hummed to herself as she negotiated the narrow twisting country roads that led away from the stables. She was going into town to do a bit of shopping, and then she had arranged to meet Kate for lunch.

Normally, she would have used her free time to head over to River View Farm to exercise Majesty for Heather. But she stayed away at weekends, since that was the only time Heather herself could ride him.

Ella had to admit that she was pleased with his progress. Although the farm lacked the facilities of Hollyfield stables, with its superb cross-country course and all-weather sand school, she found she could keep him equally fit by riding him over the vast area of bridleways and tracks that surrounded the farm.

One day she had taken him down to the beach, and galloped him along the curving bay of sand. Another day they had headed over the fields, and popped over a few hedges and gates, by way of jumping practice. The horse was a natural, enthusiastic, eager, and willing. She was sure he would fulfil all of Heather's hopes and ambitions for him.

'I've waited a long time to own a horse like this one,' Heather told her one evening, when she had popped round to discuss his exercise programme with her. 'It's funny, but when I saw him, I just knew he was the horse for me. I had this inner intuition, that he was the right one. Have you ever had that sort of feeling?'

'No, but I know what you mean,' Ella said. 'I've ridden dozens of horses over the years, and you learn to know when you've found a good one. Majesty, I'm sure, is going to be a star.'

It was just a shame that he wasn't still kept at Hollyfield, she thought. Ursula had done herself no favours by letting Heather take him away.

She drove past the entrance to the farm, and turned left onto the road leading down to the end of the village. It was a back road, often used by locals as a short cut, and by horse riders and cyclists. Other traffic rarely went that way, since it was a narrow lane, with passing places, and if one got caught behind a tractor, the journey could take twice as long as on the main road.

Ella wasn't in any hurry. The reason she was driving that way was because it was convenient for the end of the village, and the junction leading to the road into town.

The driver of the silver BMW, however, *was* in a hurry, and he was going far too fast for the twisting, country lane.

Ella saw him in the same, shocked second that he suddenly saw her vehicle.

'Christ!' She wrenched the steering wheel hard to one side. The Range Rover bounced over the grass verge, through a ditch, and grazed down the length of a hawthorn hedge.

The screeching of metal as the wing mirror of the silver

car connected with the rear end panel of the Range Rover set her teeth on edge.

The dull thud it made as it ground its bumper into the grassy bank, and came to an abrupt stop a few yards further down the lane, made her swear profusely.

'You stupid, bloody idiot!' she yelled, as she banged open the door of the Range Rover, and scrambled out to inspect the damage. A nasty gouge was missing from the metallic blue paint of the rear panel. Ursula would go mad. This vehicle was her pride and joy. She always said she felt like royalty in it, when she was driving around the countryside. (The fact that she often acted as if she were royalty, was neither here, nor there).

Ella glared furiously at the occupants of the silver BMW.

They had made no move to get out of the car. Her heart skipped a double beat. Oh my God, they could be injured. Here she was, shouting about a tiny scratch, when they could be dead, or dying.

Lewis and Simon were neither hurt, nor incapacitated. They were, however, frantically wondering how they could get themselves out of what could possibly be a very embarrassing situation. The newspaper headlines flashed in front of Lewis' eyes. "Speeding film star and producer force local person off the road."

Shit! 'Simon?'

'Yeah, yeah, I'm fine.' He was reaching for his dark glasses. A denim baseball cap had already been jammed down over his head. 'Get us out of here, Lewis.'

'Don't worry. I intend to.' He fumbled in his pocket for his wallet.

'Are you all right?'

The tentative knock on the tinted glass of the window had Lewis reaching for his sunglasses as well. He hadn't even seen the person he had hit, and nor did he want to. Carefully keeping his head averted, he wound down the window a fraction.

'Yes, we're fine. I'm so sorry. It was my fault.'

'Too right, it was.'

With his head bowed, he thrust a wad of notes through the narrow gap above the window. 'Like I said, I'm really sorry. Here, take this. That ought to pay for any damage.'

'I think you'd better give me your insurance details,' the girl's voice said.

Ella was blowed if this boy racer thought he could just fob her off with a handful of money and a mere apology. He didn't have to face the wrath of Ursula, when she showed her the damage to her cherished vehicle.

She crouched down to get a better look at the driver, but all she could see was a pair of denims, and a pale cream shirt. His companion was slumped to one side in the passenger seat, a baseball cap pulled low over his forehead.

'There's no need for my insurance company to get involved,' the man said, pointedly turning away from her. All Ella could see was the side of his head, and a glimpse of sun-streaked hair.

'I take it you have got insurance,' she said scathingly.

'Yes, but I don't want to lose my no-claims bonus over a mere scratch. Now, if you'll excuse me, we're in a hurry.'

He switched on the ignition and revved the engine loudly.

'Hey! Wait a minute.'

Ella stepped backwards in surprise, as it became obvious that he had no intention of doing any such thing. He reversed rapidly over the grass verge, slammed the car into first gear, and then shot forwards again.

'You idiot!'

She shook her head in exasperation, and watched his brake lights come on as he took the next corner with a squeal of burning rubber. Heaven help them if there was a tractor heading their way. Their fancy powerful car with the personalised number plates wouldn't save them then.

She glanced down at the bundle of money the driver had practically thrown at her. Good grief! She fanned the notes out in her hand. They were mostly all fifty-pound notes. Hundreds of pounds worth. Her head jerked up again. And that number-plate

Surely, it couldn't have been…? No, it couldn't be. Could it?

'Lewis Trevelyan!' Kate shrieked, causing several heads in the pizza restaurant to turn and stare at them. 'You're kidding.'

'No, I'm not,' Ella said, in a hushed whisper. 'I'm sure it was him. And look. Look what he gave me.' She discreetly unfolded the wad of notes, which she had stashed away in the zippered part of her handbag (they wouldn't fit inside her small purse).

'Bloody hell!'

Ella blushed and wished, (as she'd wished on many previous occasions in the past), that her best friend wasn't quite so loud and over-excitable.

'Well, I hope you told him who you were.'

'I didn't get the chance to say anything,' she said, carefully replacing the money in her bag, and slipping it down the side of her seat, where she could keep a close eye on it. 'He was desperate to get away. I don't think he even looked at me.'

'Hmm. Strange.' Kate picked up a triangle of pizza with her fingers, and chewed thoughtfully on it for a moment. 'Wonder where he was going, in such a hurry.'

'Where *they* were going,' Ella said. 'He had somebody with him.'

'Male or female?'

'Male.' Ella cut herself a portion of garlic bread, and scooped up a forkful of green salad. 'I couldn't see much of him either, but I think he was young. He was wearing a baseball cap and dark glasses. You know,' she added thoughtfully, 'I can't help wondering if it was Simon De Silva.'

'No!' Kate almost choked over her food. 'Really?'

'Course not, you idiot,' she laughed. 'I was only teasing. How the heck would I know what he looked like.'

'Hmm. I suppose,' Kate said. 'Still, it's worth a thought. It could have been him. I mean, they are supposed to be filming round here, aren't they?'

Ella shrugged. 'I don't know. They never got back to us after that last visit, and to be honest, I didn't really expect them to. Not after they'd seen Caroline,' she added, with a rueful smile.

'Well, they must be up to something.'

'Yes, well, I'm sure we'll find out what it is soon enough,' Ella said, reaching for the large wooden pepper grinder.

At the precise moment that she was grinding a generous serving of mixed peppercorns over her pasta, the slightly scratched and mud splattered, silver BMW, was turning into the grounds of Hollyfield Stables.

Lewis Trevelyan was on a mission.

So too, was Caroline.

In her case, she wanted obedience, respect and cooperation from her motley group of junior riders, but sadly, it wasn't forthcoming. She had come to the conclusion that she had more chance of winning the Grand National on a Shetland pony than getting any of her class to ride properly.

True, it wasn't her fault that Jemima had tumbled so spectacularly backwards over the rump of her short-legged, fat little pony.

The blame lay squarely with Sasha Wilkes, who had insisted on twirling her scarlet whip around her head whenever she got excited (rather like a mounted majorette on parade). A slight misjudgement on her part had sent the whip hurtling skywards, and then plummeting back to earth again. Unfortunately (for Jemima, that is) it landed right in front of Mr Magic's nose. The normally bomb proof pony had spun round and shot off, promptly depositing its little rider in a crumpled, wailing heap on the ground.

'Oh, my poor darling!' Jemima's mother leapt over the rail and sprinted to her sobbing daughter's side. 'Are you all right? Tell Mummy where it hurts?'

Since the child was padded out with every available kind of body protection that money could buy, Caroline suspected that she wasn't hurt at all. 'Now then, Jemima,' she said, in as caring a voice as she could muster. 'You just sit quietly for a moment, while I find somebody to catch your pony for you.'

She glared at the precocious Sasha Wilkes, who was looking innocently around the arena, as if none of this drama could possibly be attributed to her.

'Sasha. I want you to dismount, please.'

'Why?'

'Because I say so. Now, Sasha, please!'

Caroline felt her cheeks burning. All eyes were upon her, to say nothing of those of Sasha's mother and father.

'I want you to pick up your whip and give it to your parents. You don't need it in this lesson, and perhaps if you'd listened to me in the first place, Jemima's accident would never have happened. That's right. Now hand it over to them, yes, over the rail. I know it's hard for you to reach...' She breathed out slowly and steadily as the child, obviously in a strop, thrust the whip at her mother. 'Good,' she sighed. 'And now, you can get back on Honeybun. Thanks Kelly,' she added, as the young stable girl who was helping her with the class lesson, brought back Mr Magic, from where he was standing snorting, rather nervously, at the furthest end of the arena.

'Don't want to ride that one,' snuffled Jemima miserably.

'He'll be all right now,' Caroline said. 'He had a fright, that's all. Come on, Jemima. I'll lift you up.

'No!' A petulant foot stamped itself down hard.

'You need to get back on.'

'I don't see why,' the mother retorted, clutching her child to her side. 'That animal's obviously dangerous. It's hardly suitable for a novice ride.'

Give me strength, Caroline seethed. She attempted to smile at the distraught child and mother. 'Little tumbles like this happen all the time, Mrs West...'she began, in what she hoped was a conciliatory tone of voice.

'Indeed!' The mother straightened her shoulders determinedly. 'Well perhaps you should take another look at the sort of animals you use in children's lessons. Come on Jemima. We're leaving. And we won't be coming back,' she added loudly.

'We'll be going to New Hall Equestrian Centre from now on. I've heard they're much more experienced with younger children.'

Caroline was fuming as she caught the anxious looks the watching parents were giving each other, obviously wondering if their offspring were safe in her hands. Somebody murmured, 'I've heard that, too,' well within earshot of her. Another muttered, 'She's not as good as Ella, that's for sure.'

'Now then, children,' she said briskly, through gritted teeth. 'If you're ready, we'll carry on with the lesson. Pick up your reins, and prepare to move off. Oh, and Kelly,' She beckoned over to the young helper. 'Perhaps you could walk alongside the lead pony. We don't want any more accidents, do we?' At this, she glared at Sasha, who was looking smugly satisfied with herself. 'Right then,' she said. 'Walk on.'

Meanwhile, in the stable yard, Vanessa was suffering from mutiny in the ranks. The teenagers were getting bored with the endless mucking out of stables.

'When are we going to get to groom the horses?' asked a rather thin girl, with a pale face and a bad case of acne.

'Soon,' she said, glancing up from her latest copy of "The Horse Owner" magazine. She was in the middle of a particularly interesting article about dressage riders. And her coffee was getting cold, she realised, as she slurped a tepid mouthful of it. 'Have you filled all the hay nets, like I told you?'

'Ella lets us do that after we've ridden,' said a rather pretty girl with dark, shiny hair, which had been cut into a flattering chin length bob.

'Well, Ella's not here,' she said, flicking over the pages of her magazine.

'Don't we know it,' muttered a sulky looking child of about fourteen.

Vanessa glared at her. 'Weren't you supposed to be filling the water buckets?'

'Done it.'

'Oh.' She looked at her watch. Goodness was it that time already. She supposed she had better let them bring the horses in from the paddocks, or they wouldn't have a chance to ride them.

'All right,' she said, standing up, and laying her magazine to one side. (She would continue with that article later). 'You can go and get a head-collar, and fetch your horse in from the field. Do you all know who you're supposed to be catching?'

'Yes,' came the rather bored reply. They had known from the moment they set foot on the yard. That was the first thing they did when they arrived; read the list to see which horse they had been allocated for the day.

'Good,' Vanessa said, because she, for one, didn't have a clue. Her mother normally picked the horses. She tended to know what one would be suitable for which teenager. Barring a few half-hearted arguments, she usually got it right. 'Off you go, then,' she said.

The scrum to get out of the barn door nearly sent her flying.

Bloody kids, she thought, as she picked up her magazine and sat down again. With any luck, the horses would be so difficult to catch that she would be able to finish the article she was reading before they got back to the yard.

Three quarters of an hour later, and she had finished the whole magazine, and was sitting drumming her heels on a wooden tack trunk, wondering where her unruly tribe of kids had disappeared.

She supposed she had better go and look for them.

The shrieks and giggles of laughter coming from the car park seemed like a good enough place to start her search.

The girls were standing beside a silver-coloured car talking, or at least, laughing, with someone. Not a single tethered horse or pony was in sight. In fact, the head-collars seemed to have been draped on the fence, or tossed to the ground.

Annoyed that they had so blatantly disobeyed her, Vanessa stomped through the gate to the car park, intent on giving them a piece of her mind.

The personalised number-plate on the silver BMW caught

her eye first; the sneaky, sideways glance from one of the girls, and the furtive whispering came second.

'Here she comes.'

'Don't tell her we told you.'

And then there was the giggling.

Vanessa's eyes widened and the breath caught in the back of her throat, as the car door swung open, and Lewis Trevelyan – *the* Lewis Trevelyan (all six foot four of gorgeous manliness) - stood up, and held out his hand.

'Ah,' he said. 'You must be Vanessa.'

She tried to say yes, but her mouth was so dry, it sounded like a squeak, and her legs were shaking so much she could hardly stand still. Her head bobbed up and down like a nodding toy, as his warm, firm fingers, closed around her sweating palm. (Don't faint. Don't pass out, she told herself sternly).

'We didn't get a chance to talk, the last time I came.'

'No,' she sighed. She felt as if she were about to swoon.

'The girls have been telling me all about their 'Own a pony' day. Sounds good to me.' He winked at his adoring audience, who all seemed to be clutching tatty bits of paper to their chests.

A crowd of interested on-lookers were starting to appear from all corners of the yard. (Vanessa sincerely hoped that they noticed it was *her* hand he was holding).

'I was wondering if your mother was at home?' he said, tilting his head in the direction of the house. A shock of sun-streaked blonde hair tumbled forward over his forehead. 'I had to bring a friend up here for a riding lesson, so I thought I'd take the chance and drop in on her.'

Friend? Riding lesson? Vanessa glanced back towards the sand school, where she could vaguely make out Stella giving instruction to someone on Jester. (Why, oh why hadn't she paid attention to the names booked into the diary for lessons that day?)

'I didn't think it would be fair to stand and watch,' he added. 'It might put him off.'

'Um, yes,' Vanessa said. 'Who is it, exactly?'

'Adam,' Lewis said, grinning broadly. 'Adam Lansing.'

Never heard of him, Vanessa thought.

'So, if your mother's in, perhaps I could have a word with her?'

Vanessa cheeks had gone crimson, and her eyes were wide and bulging in their sockets. For once, she appeared to be at a loss for words.

One of the girls tittered.

Vanessa shot her a warning look. 'Yes, of course,' she said, as she struggled to regain some of her composure. 'Come with me.'

'No, its okay,' he said, casually withdrawing his hand from her vice like grip on his fingers. 'You carry on. I don't want to interrupt your work here with the girls.'

'It's no problem...'

'No, really.' He gave her a reassuring pat on the shoulder. 'You stay here. I insist.'

Vanessa watched, rather forlornly, as he strode up the gravel drive towards the house. The way he walked, with those long, rangy legs, the firm muscles rippling beneath the neat cut of his jeans – the casual stride; the windswept, but undoubtedly expensive, cut of his hair...oh God, he was so gorgeous.

'Look! Look, he's signed it to me. To Mandy, it says!'

The pretty girl with the dark hair waved a scrap of paper under Vanessa's nose.

'He's put, "Love Lewis" on mine,' crowed the girl with bad acne.

'Oh, he's so nice.'

Vanessa scowled at the gaggle of teenagers, with their irritating giggles and excited chatter. Jumping up and down like...like lovesick adolescents, (and like she would have done, if she had been given half the chance).

'Yes, well, show's over,' she snapped. 'You're supposed to be catching some horses, aren't you?'

The group of girls gathered up the head-collars, which had been abandoned in such haste, and carried on chatting and laughing as they ran towards the fields.

Vanessa stared up at the house where, a moment earlier, Lewis Trevelyan had stood waiting to be let in. What did he want, she wondered anxiously? And why was he so keen to speak to her mother. More importantly, she thought, with a twinge of panic, where the hell was Caroline?

Ursula Johnson was in the process of baking a cake for the weekly Charity Club coffee morning. It was her duty, as an upstanding member of the community, to let it be known that she was always willing to do her bit for charity. The fact that she loathed baking, and couldn't give two hoots about whatever charity they were supporting this week, was neither here nor there. Duty had to be seen to be done.

She prodded a skewer into the middle of the fruitcake, which she had just removed from the centre of the oven, and examined it dubiously. She never knew when these things were cooked or not.

The doorbell rang at a most inconvenient moment.

Cursing, she slid the cake tin back into the oven, and turned the heat up. A few more minutes to finish it off should do, she thought, as she wiped her hands clean on a damp cloth, and went to open the door.

Lewis Trevelyan was the last person she expected to see standing on the doorstep (and the last person she would have wanted to see *her*, all red-faced and harassed from baking, and wearing a large apron that was smudged with flour and egg whites). But it was too late.

'Oh.' Her mouth opened like the proverbial goldfish, as she yanked open the door and found him grinning down at her.

'Hello again,' he said brightly. 'Not interrupting anything, am I?'

'No. Well, just a spot of baking,' she said, wiping her hands on her apron. 'I like to do a cake for the Charity Club. I do one most weeks,' she added.

'Smells good.'

Ursula blushed. Behind him she could see a gathering horde of people, staring up towards the house. 'Come in, Mr Trevelyan,' she said, opening the door a bit wider. 'Oh, and ignore the dog. He's harmless enough.'

Harmless he may be, but Lewis had never seen one quite so huge. The Great Dane must have been almost four foot at the shoulder. It's huge, drooling mouth tilted sideways, as it gazed up at him with inquisitive eyes. A deep, thunderous 'woof' rumbled from the back of its throat.

'Basket, Wilson,' Ursula said. The dog slumped to the floor in front of the warm oven, and pointedly ignored her. It lay its head down on its huge paws, and closed its eyes.

It seemed to have accepted his presence in the house, but Lewis felt one could never be too sure where strange dogs were concerned. He kept a careful watch on the slumbering grey bulk, as he sidestepped past it and then followed Ursula through into the coolness of the lounge.

'Now then, Mr Trevelyan,' she said, patting the cushion of a chair for him to sit on. 'What can I do for you?'

Lewis felt distinctly uncomfortable, as he perched on the edge of the bottle green armchair. He wasn't quite sure how he was going to phrase this. His gaze scanned the walls for photographs, mementoes, and reminders, anything that might prompt the thread of his intended topic of conversation. He could see nothing.

No pictures of Robert Johnson; no cups, medal, trophies; not even a photograph of his most famous horse, Fool's Gold. And certainly, no photos of his daughter.

A framed portrait of Vanessa, Caroline and their mother, however, hung in pride of place over the fireplace. A watercolour of a mill cottage hung from another wall, and a picture of two children's ponies was propped up on the oak sideboard. And that was it.

'As you know,' he said, 'we're not going to use Hollyfield Stables for our location shots.'

'I had heard,' Ursula said huffily. Though why they hadn't

had the decency to tell her before Petunia Fitzgerald found out was something she would be enquiring about in the very near future.

Lewis nodded, and then shook his head. 'It wasn't my idea. Believe me. I think Hollyfield Stables would have been perfect.'

(Ursula resolved to savour those words and store them for future retelling, perhaps at the next charity luncheon.)

'Anyway, we're going ahead with the County Showground shoot. I take it you've had your invitation card?'

'Oh yes, yes,' she nodded agreeably.

'And the girls will be coming?'

'Of course. They wouldn't miss it for the world?'

'Good,' Lewis said. 'We obviously want as many experienced riders as we can, at the show.'

Yet another observation to make at the charity luncheon, Ursula thought gleefully.

'Your husband,' he said, glancing back at her, with a practiced smile.

(Ursula nearly said, 'which one?' but thought better of it). 'Yes?' she said.

'He was a show jumper, wasn't he?'

'A British champion show jumper,' she said proudly.

'And I'm right in thinking its five years since he died?'

'Five years this month,' Ursula said, with a suitably pained expression on her face. 'He was killed in a car crash. It was tragic. He was on his way home to spend some time with me and the girls.'

'Vanessa and Caroline,' he said thoughtfully.

Ursula looked pleased he had remembered their names.

'And his other daughter? I don't think I've met her.'

Ursula's eyes narrowed slightly.

'Your stepdaughter,' he added airily.

'Oh, you mean, Ella.'

'Ella. That's right.' He leaned back in the armchair and stretched his long legs out in front of him. This was getting interesting. Ursula was looking quite flustered. 'Is she here?'

'Here? No. Well, I mean, she's not here now, because... she's out,' she said falteringly. 'But I'm sure you probably saw her the last time you came. She's usually hanging around the yard, helping out, you know.'

'Does she ride?'

'Um...not really. No.'

Lewis raised an eyebrow at her. His doubting expression was all too clear to see. Robert Johnson's daughter did not ride. Oh, come on, woman. Did he look like a fool?

Ursula rapidly lowered her gaze. 'What I mean is – um - she sometimes rides, but not like her father.'

'She's not a show-jumper, then?'

'No. Although, she does try, bless her. But she's not very good. I mean, I've tried coaching her, but some things can't be taught, can they? And these young girls, well, they hate being told what to do.'

'I can imagine,' Lewis said. 'Still, she's lucky she's got you to help her.'

'Yes...yes, she is.' Ursula beamed.

'And I'll look forward to seeing her at the County Show next weekend.'

His words had the same effect on Ursula, as a sudden drenching of icy cold water would have done. Her eyes almost popped out of her head; her jaw locked open, and the colour rapidly drained from her face.

'Next weekend?' she repeated.

'That's right.' Lewis stood up. At six foot four, he towered over the rather squat Mrs Johnson. Smiling, he patted her on the shoulder. 'Don't forget to tell her, I told you so, will you?'

She gazed helplessly up at him. 'No, no I won't forget.' Oh, my goodness. 'Wilson! Basket!' she shrieked, as the huge Great Dane came bounding into the hallway, having been disturbed from its comfortable nap in front of the cooker, and nearly sending her honoured guest flying.

'He's all right,' Lewis said, quickly recovering his balance, and stroking the large, silky head. 'Aren't you, boy? Good lad.'

Overgrown dogs were now the least of his worries. He eased open the front door a fraction. Several people were congregating around his car. Others were sitting on the arena fencing, watching the lesson in progress. Yet more people were loitering on the driveway. Miles had been right. They should have brought a minder with them.

They all looked innocent enough, but if they found out it was Simon De Silva having the riding lesson, they'd be lucky to escape with their clothes intact. He'd seen it happen before. Poor Bradley Gulliver had stepped outside the Regent to sign a few autographs, and ended up in hospital with several broken bones and concussion, and none of his fans had been older than fifteen either.

'Is there a problem, Mr Trevelyan?'

'A slight one, yes,' he said. 'I don't suppose you could get rid of those people outside, could you? Tell them my car's broken down and I've left in a taxi.'

Ursula gave him a reassuring smile. 'Of course. You wait here. I won't be a moment.'

Lewis ducked back out of sight as he heard a stampede of footsteps trampling over the gravel the moment the front door opened.

Shrieks of 'Lewis!' were soon silenced as Ursula stood her ground, the huge Great Dane standing resolute at her side.

'Mr Trevelyan has gone,' she said loudly. 'He left by the back door, and a taxi picked him up at the end of the lane. There's no point in you all hanging about here.'

'What about his car?' came a high-pitched voice?

'He's sending someone to collect it.'

'You mean he's not coming back?'

'That's exactly what I mean. If you want to see him, you'll have to go to the County Showground next weekend. I have it on good authority that he's going to be there.'

'Excellent stuff,' Lewis said, as he peered around the corner of a curtain, and watched the crowd thin and drift away. 'You even had me convinced.'

Ursula shrugged, as she came back into the house and took off her jacket. 'Oh my God!' she suddenly shrieked. 'What's that smell?'

'Smell?'

'Something's burning.' Her face fell. The cake! The bloody fruitcake! She rushed into the kitchen, and flung open the oven door. A thick pall of black, sooty smoke puffed out at her.

'Well, thanks again,' Lewis said. Now was the time, he decided, to make a quick exit. Snatching up his keys, he hurried out of the house and managed to reach the car without being spotted. He scrambled into the driver's seat, and flung open the passenger door. Simon was strolling nonchalantly towards him; a silk covered riding hat tucked under one arm.

'Get in!' Lewis hissed.

'What's the rush?'

'Just do it,' he said, switching on the ignition.

As he was reversing rapidly out of the car park, Caroline was doing a steady jog towards the house.

The fire alarm was bleeping loudly and incessantly as she burst through the front door, desperate to find out if the rumours circulating the yard were true.

How could Lewis Trevelyan be here, and she not know about it?

She paused in the hallway, sniffing the air, and listening curiously to the frantic beeping noise. What on earth was going on? 'Mother?' She pushed open the kitchen door. 'Mother, what's burning?'

Ursula was sitting at the table, consuming a generous measure of medicinal brandy from a soot-stained glass.

Wilson was throwing up on the floor, having gobbled the best part of the charred fruitcake, which had dropped out of Ursula's hands when she tried to extricate it, in flames, from the oven.

And Lewis Trevelyan, apparently, had gone.

Chapter Eleven

'Christ, Lewis, I ache.'

Simon hobbled his way into the canteen, and levered himself into the softest looking chair he could find. 'Get me a coffee, will you?'

'Blimey,' Lewis said. 'I thought you said you could do this.'

'I can.' Simon winced. 'Believe me, I can. It's just a bit painful, that's all.'

Four consecutive days of riding had left him feeling a little bit sensitive in certain areas of his anatomy. The lesson at Hollyfields had been bad enough - lots of sitting trot on the lunge (to get his balance, apparently) - with an instructor who had never learnt the art of compassion. Then three days at a riding school near the studios, with a woman who looked old enough to be his mother, and treated him like the child she probably never had.

'Still, you've managed a canter,' Lewis said.

'That was the easy bit,' Simon groaned. 'I tell you what, mate. I'm not doing this again, not for any film. I want that written into my contract.'

Lewis grinned. 'At least Miles will be pleased.'

'Stuff Miles,' he muttered.

With the bulk of the studio work completed, Lewis had been previewing some of the final takes with the film's director, and he had to admit that they were good. In fact, they were very good.

Miles' vast experience in the film industry had gained him a worldwide reputation for excellence in his field. This latest effort proved why. The critics would not be disappointed. His insistence that he had the final say when it came to the casting of the main characters had evidently pulled off. The chemistry between Simon and Molly was clear from the start. They made a perfect working team.

Miles chuckled merrily, as he watched her take a swipe at the side of his face. 'See that, Lewis?' he said. 'That almost connected, and maybe it did. The angry look in Simon's eyes seems real enough.

'Find something that pleases you?' came a sardonic drawl from the doorway of the studio.

'Chemistry, my boy,' Miles said, drawing back from the camera, and grinning at the film's main star. 'You and Molly in action. Want to see?'

'No thanks,' Simon said. 'I'll wait for the premiere, if it's all the same to you.'

'Spoken like a true star.' Miles waved to the crew, to let them know he had finished, before turning back to Lewis. 'I gather you had no luck in Suffolk.'

He frowned, as he sat down in one of the folding chairs. 'News travels fast,' he muttered. 'I didn't get to see the girl, if that's what you mean. But she does exist. She's called Ella.'

'Ella. Ella Johnson.' Miles repeated the name, as if it might mean something to him, but it didn't.

'I'm hoping she'll turn up for the competition.'

'Well, whether she does or not, the filming will be going ahead. The event has been advertised in all the local papers, and the television people are doing a feature on it as well. You know the sort of thing; film star comes to Suffolk. Which reminds me,' he added, leafing through a pile of papers on the arm of his chair, and turning back to Simon. 'Your agent called. The BBC has been in touch. They want to do an interview with you.' He handed him a yellow post-it note, with a number scribbled on it. 'Can you give Estelle a ring?'

'What, now?'

Miles nodded. 'She did ask.'

Simon pocketed the note with a frown. A long and involved

conversation with his slightly neurotic and highly excitable agent was not what he had in mind just now.

'Oh, and Roger's booked the Ivy for tonight. You haven't forgotten, have you? The limo's coming to pick you and Lewis up at eight.'

'Just as well,' Simon remarked, with a knowing smile.

Miles looked at him quizzically. 'How come?'

'Pranged the BMW, didn't he.'

'What?' Miles swung round to face Lewis. 'You did?'

'Yes, unfortunately. But don't worry, no one was hurt.'

'And he managed to pay off the girl before she spotted who I was,' Simon added. 'It was only a scratch, Miles,' he added, seeing the director's disapproving stare. 'We couldn't hang about and make polite conversation, now, could we?'

'No, I suppose not.'

'Anyway, he's had Tony take it to the garage for repairs. He reckons it'll be fixed in a couple of days.'

'And in the meantime?'

'I guess I'll be taking black cabs, like the rest of you,' Lewis said.

Simon stood up, and patted the folded post-it note in his pocket. 'Think I'll give Estelle a ring,' he said. 'I'll see you guys later.'

'At eight, remember?'

'Yep, at eight.'

Ella didn't have the luxury of being able to take black cabs whilst she put the car in for repairs. She needed to get Ursula's car fixed fast, before the scratch was noticed.

Consequently, she spent the remainder of her Saturday off work trying to do just that.

'Two days?' she said, gawping at the phone receiver, as if she couldn't believe her ears. 'I can't leave it with you for two days. I need the job done today. This afternoon.' (This was the third garage she had tried and all to no avail).

'Sorry, my love,' the mechanic told her, in an accent that

was pure Cockney. 'By the sounds of things, it will need cutting out and refilling. Then there's the spraying, and these metallic paints are one hell of a job to match up...'

'Forget it,' she said, replacing the receiver with a sigh. She had thought it would have been a simple enough task to get a paint repair shop or a garage to touch up the nasty gouge in the back of Ursula's Range Rover. With the money she had been given, she could have paid for the job in cash, and her stepmother would never have known any different.

'Try Gary,' Kate said helpfully, as she stirred a spoonful of sugar into her coffee.

'Gary who?'

'Gary Holdsworth. You know. We were at school together. Oh, you must remember him. A gawky looking lad with ginger hair. He works over at Epson's garage in Rutherdale.'

'Gary Holdsworth?' Ella repeated, trying to conjure up a face to fit the name. 'Oh, him! God, is he a mechanic?' The youth she remembered had been so clumsy, (even going so far as to drop the prized football trophy on Sports Day, in front of a horrified audience of parents and children) that she didn't know if she dared trust him on Ursula's beloved car.

'Apparently so. He did the bodywork on Laura's mini when she had that shunt last February, remember? The week when we had all the ice and snow, and she was hit from behind by a white transit van.'

'And he fixed that?'

Kate nodded, and wipe the creamy froth from her coffee off her lips. 'Did a good job too.'

'What's his number?'

'Blowed if I know. Google it.'

Ella put the name of the garage into her phone and waited. 'Found it?'

'Yes,' Ella said, nodding.

'Here. Let me have it,' Kate took the phone from her. 'Hello? Is that Epsons? Yes, I'd like to speak to Gary, please. Gary Holdsworth.' She winked at Ella, and mouthed, 'He always used to fancy me.'

As did most of Ecclesfield High School, Ella recalled.

'Hi, Gary,' she said, after a short pause. 'It's Kate here. I was wondering if you could do me a favour...'

Ella listened intently, as her friend explained the urgency of the situation.

'...Yes. At three o'clock. Yes, we'll be there. Thanks, Gary.' She clicked off the phone, and grinned at her. 'Sorted,' she said.

'Really?'

'Well, he's going to take a look at it, anyway. He says he should be able to do a cover up job, if nothing else.' She glanced at her watch. 'We'd better get going. It'll take us half an hour to get there. You lead, and I'll follow.'

The 'Gary Holdsworth' from school bore little resemblance to the 'Gary Holdsworth' of Epson's garage. Either that or her memory had deserted her, Ella thought.

The man in question was lying prostrate under the front end of a battered green Fiesta, his legs encased in dark brown overalls, and his feet sticking out at right angles. He was wearing steel capped boots.

'Gary?' Kate said warily, even though the man in reception had waved them over to the workroom with a gruff, 'He's over there,' so they knew it had to be him.

The figure scooted out on a trolley board. 'Hi,' he said, from his horizontal position at their feet. 'Thought I heard voices.' His face was streaked with oil and dirt, and wore a lopsided kind of grin.

Ella was surprised to see that his ginger hair was darker than she remembered it to be. It could almost be described as a warm brown, and all traces of adolescent gawkiness had disappeared. He jumped nimbly to his feet, and brushed his oil-smeared hands down the side of his overalls.

'Nice to see you again, Ella,' he said. 'I'd offer you my hand, but you probably wouldn't take it.'

Kate grinned. 'I can't believe you're proposing already, Gary?'

153

'Ha ha,' he said. 'I'll ignore that remark.' He turned back to Ella. 'I gather you've had a spot of bother with your car.'

'Yes, but it's not actually my car,' she said, glaring at Kate. How could she joke at a time like this? 'It belongs to my stepmother, and she'll go berserk if she sees the damage.'

'Which one is it?' he asked, glancing over at the crowded forecourt.

'The blue Range Rover, the one over there.' She pointed to where she had parked the car next to Kate's sporty little hatchback.

'I'd better take a look,' he said. 'I'll wash this oil off my hands first.'

'See,' Kate whispered, grinning, as they waited patiently on the forecourt for his return.

'See what?' Ella said. 'You're such a flirt, Kate.'

'Yes, well, it sometimes comes in useful, don't you agree? Anyway, by the way he was looking you up and down; I think he's taken a shine to you.'

'Don't be so ridiculous.'

Kate tapped the side of her nose. 'You mark my words. I can see these things a mile off. He was impressed. The question is, are you?'

'Me?' Ella choked. 'Kate, he was such a gormless idiot at school.'

'So? That was then. And this,' she said, nudging her, as he strolled back across the forecourt. 'This is now.'

Gary certainly didn't seem anything like the clumsy youth she remembered from her school days. He was perfectly confident and capable.

'You've got two choices,' he said, as he ran his hand over the gouged paintwork on the Range Rover. 'A professional job, which involves cutting out, filling and respraying, or a touch up job.'

'Whatever's quickest,' Ella said. 'I need it done today.'

'That could be tricky.' He paused, and crouched down to examine the scratch from a different angle. 'But I reckon I could do it,' he said, glancing sideways up at her. 'You'd have to leave

154

it here for, say...' He glanced at his watch. '...Two hours? It'll probably be ready about half five.'

'Half five would be brilliant,' she said, her face beaming. Ursula wouldn't need to know anything about her little mishap if that was the case.

'Right, then. 'He straightened up, smiling. 'I'd best get started.'

Kate linked her arm in Ella's, and winked at him. 'Do a good job on it, Gary, and we'll take you out afterwards for a drink to celebrate.'

'Thanks for the offer,' he said, 'but I don't think my wife would appreciate it, if it's all the same to you.'

'Wife?' Kate spluttered in disbelief, as she reversed her car out of the garage. She put her foot down as they turned onto the main road.

'That's what the man said.' Ella smirked.

'Well, I never knew he was married.'

'No, and you thought you could twist him round your little finger with those feminine wiles of yours, when truth be told, he's probably a decent bloke trying to earn a bit of extra cash with some overtime.'

Kate balanced one hand on the steering wheel, as she flicked her lighter underneath the end of her cigarette. 'Bet she was pregnant,' she muttered, breathing out a steady stream of smoke.

Ella wound down the window. 'Who?'

'The girl he married, of course.'

'That's a bit uncharitable of you,' she said.

'True.' Kate grinned wickedly across at her. 'I just hate seeing a good man go to waste. And he has definitely improved with age.'

'Hasn't he just,' Ella laughed.

Two hours later, and the Range Rover was looking as good as new. Not perfect, Gary told her, (and the paint was still a bit tacky), but it should pass any inspection from a casual observer.

'How much do I owe you?' Ella asked, feeling in her

handbag for the wad of money.

'Let me see,' He stroked his chin thoughtfully. 'Let's say fifty quid?'

'Fifty quid?' she choked.

He looked concerned. 'Do you think that's a bit too much?'

'More like too little,' she said. 'Come on, Gary. It must cost more than that. You can't see the mark or anything, and the touch up paint is spot on. Let me give you at least a hundred pounds.'

'Bet you don't get many customers offering to pay you more than you ask,' Kate observed dryly.

Ella ignored her. 'Look, you managed to get it done in one day, and that was really important to me,' she said. 'So here, take it. I insist.'

'Well,' Gary scratched his head. 'If, you're sure.'

She handed over two of the fifty-pound notes with a firm nod. 'I'm sure. And thanks, Gary. I don't know what I would have done without you.' (Nor did she know what she was going to do with all the leftover money in her handbag, either).

'Found somebody else, I expect,' he said. He slipped the notes into his wallet, and pocketed it with a smile. 'Anyway, I didn't mind doing a favour for an old school mate. It was good to see you again, Ella. You too, Kate.'

'Likewise,' Kate said.

'Wonder who he married,' Ella said later, as they sat drinking coffee in Kate's bedroom. They had gone back to her house, so that Kate could get changed for her 'big' date. The man in question had been the object of Kate's fancy for well over a month now. Persistence and guile had eventually paid off. He had sent her a text message that afternoon, inviting her out for a drink. Ella was going to help her decide what to wear. Though goodness knows why, she thought, since Kate looked fabulous in everything.

'I'm surprised you didn't ask him,' she added, flicking through Kate's wardrobe. Her friend wasn't usually so reticent. 'What about this one?' She held out a powder blue lacy top. 'With black trousers?'

'No.'

'I know, this red one.'

Kate frowned. 'Put it on the pile of possibles.'

'You've got more in that pile than you've got left in your wardrobe,' she observed dryly. 'Who is this guy, anyway?'

'Mark? He's one of the managers from head office, and he's absolutely gorgeous.'

'You say that about everyone you go out with,' Ella said.

'No, I don't. The peach top, that one.' She wagged a finger, sticky with fresh nail varnish, at her.

'Very pretty,' Ella murmured, holding it up and examining it with a critical eye. 'It's a bit see-through, though.'

'Perfect for a first date.' Kate grinned. 'Shall I ask him if he's got any nice single friends?'

'No.' Ella retorted crossly.

Kate blew on her fingernails. 'Pass me that bottle of perfume, will you?'

Painted, preened, and dressed to perfection, in a black leather mini skirt, peach (see-through) blouse, and black boots, Kate was finally ready for her date.

'Think I'll make a move,' Ella said, picking up her bag.

'You could wait. He'll be here in a minute. I'll introduce you if you like?'

'No, I'd better go,' she said. 'Thanks for everything, Kate. I mean, for lunch, and the car and helping me get things sorted.'

'That's what friends are for.' She stood up and straightened her tight leather skirt as she spoke. 'You don't think this is too short?'

Ella grinned. 'I'm sure this Mark, whoever he is, will be bowled over by it. I'll see you tomorrow, Kate.'

'Yes, I'll ring you,' she said. 'And remember we've got the Jazz Club tomorrow night. You did say you'd go.'

'Blimey,' Ella said. 'I can't believe it's a week since the last time we went.'

She left Kate contorting herself from every angle in front

of the full-length mirror in her bedroom. It never ceased to amaze her that her friend, who seemed so supremely confident in everything she did, was always so uncertain when it came to deciding what to wear. Ella didn't have that problem. She had work clothes, riding clothes, and a few 'going out' clothes. Normally she chose whatever was closest to hand. Perhaps tomorrow night, she thought, she would make more of an effort.

In the meantime, she had better get home. It was getting dark, and it would be darker still by the time she got back to Hollyfields. If she were lucky, there would be no one around to notice the paint job she'd had done on the rear panel of the Range Rover. She could always plead ignorance at a later date.

But she was worrying needlessly, because back at the stables, Ursula had much more pressing concerns on her mind.

The entire day had been a public relations disaster from the start.

An irate Mrs West had removed her daughter Jemima from the children's pony lesson class, and loudly announced to anyone who would listen, that the whole place was a disgrace and a shambles, and they would not be coming back

Consequently, three other children did not book lessons for the following week, and Sasha Wilkes' mother insisted that her daughter would only return if she could have her usual instructor, and not the incompetent Caroline.

If that wasn't bad enough, Vanessa then found that her group of willing teenagers were no longer so willing, since they had had their brush with stardom. All they wanted to do was talk about their encounter with Lewis Trevelyan, and they had spent half the afternoon phoning their friends on their mobiles to do just that.

When one of the livery owners subsequently discovered her horse had been put in a stable that hadn't been mucked out properly, she was justifiably furious.

The trouble was she complained so vocally, that some of the other owners started to protest as well. (The water buckets hadn't been cleaned out, the hay nets were half empty, and some

158

idiot had given the wrong feed to a laminitic pony on starvation rations).

Ursula spent the best part of the afternoon either cancelling bookings, or consoling ruffled feelings. The worst part was when she counted up the week's takings, and discovered they were way down on the week before, and horrendously low, compared to the same period the previous year.

It was no wonder that the bank manager, who had personally authorised the business loan for the sand school, was starting to doubt her ability to pay it back.

The future of the stables lay in clever marketing and advertising, and in events guaranteed to attract new customers.

Ursula drummed her fingers on the top of the desk, and peered morosely out of the window. She needed to think of something new, something different. They already had the children's Pony Club camp, but perhaps they could cater more for the older riders, the bored housewives with time and (hopefully) money on their hands, or the middle-aged men who fancied themselves as Clint Eastwood?

She picked up the invitation card, which was tucked behind some bills in the drawer of her writing desk, and read it through again. Simon De Silva may not know it, she mused, but the future success of Hollyfield lay in his hands.

The stables needed some favourable publicity, because good publicity (as her bank manager kept telling her) was the key to business success.

This film could be the making of them.

It had to be.

Chapter Twelve

Preparations for the annual Agricultural Show were in full swing. On the County Showground, marquees were being erected, and stands assembled. Various catering companies had already been allocated their pitches, and the final timetable of events had been printed and published. The addendum was inserted meticulously into every programme: 'Extra event; the filming of the Simon De Silva Show-jumping competition'.

The posters, which had been displayed around the surrounding towns for weeks now, were hastily amended to carry the extra flyer, and the local radio station devoted an entire chat show programme to it.

Everyone, it seemed, was talking about the filming, and the effect it would have on the scattered and mainly rural community.

'We'll have sightseers flooding into the place.'

'It won't be a local show.'

'They'll ruin the atmosphere.'

'But think of the trade benefits.' (This from Gerald Fitzgerald, head of the organising committee, and husband of Petunia). As a businessman himself, he could see the advantages of having a huge crowd in attendance at the show.

'I'm thinking of the traffic,' grumbled William Daley, whose property boarded the ring road around the town, and who found it almost impossible to get out of his driveway at the best of times.

'A minor inconvenience,' agreed Gerald. 'But it is only for two days.'

Two days, where the pride of the County's cattle, sheep,

pigs and other livestock were put on display, alongside trade stands of every description. The Women's Institute would be there in force, displaying their varied talents from cake-making to flower arranging, (Mrs Fitzgerald was hotly tipped to win the dried flower class), and various stalls, from country clothing to crafts would be open for business.

The show jumping was one of the main attractions for many people. That and the heavy horses. Some people never got beyond the grand arena, preferring instead, to secure their place at the ringside, in a coveted seat, complete with rugs, picnic and binoculars.

If the filming took place inside the arena, it was a guaranteed fact that most of the seats would be filled within an hour, if not less, of the gates opening.

'Well, I'll be going,' Jimmy Mulligan announced, as he read the amended poster on the notice board outside the village church. 'I've always fancied myself in a film. What do you think, Thomas?'

'Sure, and I think you'd have made a fine star, Jimmy my boy, but sadly, they don't make silent movies any more.'

Thomas Button ducked quickly, to avoid the half-hearted punch the young stable lad swung at him.

'I don't care. I'm still going. That Lewis Trevelyan might recognise me. He spoke to me, you know.

'Indeed, he did,' Thomas said, as he stepped forward to read the poster for himself. They had strolled into the village on the pretext of buying fresh rolls, ham and cheese for lunch, their morning duties having been completed early, giving them a couple of hours free before the afternoon shift of feeding and grooming.

The posters for the show were everywhere, attached to lampposts, nailed to fences, and in every shop window they passed. (Someone was going a bit overboard with the publicity, Thomas thought). The additional flyer had been slapped diagonally across the top corner of the notice.

"The Simon De Silva Stakes, to be held on Saturday at two

o'clock," he read aloud. 'Wonder if Ella knows about this?'

Jimmy shrugged. 'I don't see how she couldn't. Vanessa and Caroline are talking about nothing else. Apparently, Ursula has treated them to new show jackets and breeches, and riding boots that cost the earth. Oh, yes, and get this; she's ordered a new saddle and bridle for Nero.'

Thomas raised an eyebrow at him. 'In the hope of achieving what, exactly?'

'A horse that behaves itself,' Jimmy chuckled. 'She thinks he's bad tempered because his saddle doesn't fit properly.'

'And we know it's because he's such a cantankerous beast.'

Thomas smiled as he stared thoughtfully at the poster. It was strange that he hadn't seen any similar notices in the tack room, the most likely place for any to be displayed. Nor had he seen any lying about the stable yard or house. He had the sneakiest feeling that Ursula was trying to keep this from Ella.

'What are you doing?' Jimmy said. He watched, surprised, as Thomas carefully unpinned the notice from the board, folded it in half, and then half again, and slipped it into his pocket.

'Borrowing this poster.'

'Borrowing it?'

'Just in case,' he said, tapping the side of his nose. 'Come on, lad. It's time we were back at the yard.'

Ella didn't know when she had enjoyed a weekend off more. If it hadn't been for the slight mishap with Ursula's Range Rover, it would have been perfect. The Sunday night jazz club had once again been a total success. Her old friends had been as good as their word, and had all turned up at the same venue for another evening's drinking and dancing. It had been great fun.

Now, however, she was reaping the consequences of her own over indulgence. She really must stop drinking so much, she resolved, swallowing a couple of painkillers with a large glass of water. It wasn't doing her any good at all.

She had missed the morning feeds again. Not that Thomas would object. He was as reliable and capable as they come. But it wasn't fair of her to take advantage of him. She would need to apologise to him – yet again.

'There's no need for that, lass,' he said, when she finally made her appearance on the yard, looking somewhat the worse for wear. 'Everyone needs a social life. Mind, I'm glad to see you back,' he added. 'We've had one hell of a week-end.'

'Really?' Ella said. 'Why? What happened?'

By the time Thomas had filled her in with the details, her headache had eased a bit, and she was feeling marginally better. It was immensely satisfying to know that Vanessa and Caroline were both as incompetent as she believed them to be. The sad thing was that Ursula couldn't see it for love or money. Her daughters could do no wrong in her eyes. She would always find someone else to take the blame.

'...And then, that producer chap turned up,' Thomas said, as he poured himself a cup of coffee. 'And he caused mayhem in the yard. Those Saturday kids didn't want anything to do with horses after they'd spoken to him.'

'Lewis Trevelyan came here?' she said. That would explain how she managed to collide with him on the back road outside the village. It didn't explain, however, why he had been driving like such a lunatic on the narrow country roads. 'What did he want?'

Thomas shrugged. 'Search me. He went up to the house. That's all I know. My guess is, he was looking for you.'

Ella blushed. 'Don't be so daft.'

'Ah, but I'm not that daft,' he said, his voice becoming more serious, as he groped in his pocket. 'See this, Ella.' He handed her the folded-up piece of paper. 'There are posters all over the village, but there's none of them here. You read that, and then tell me why.'

'It's for the County Show,' she said, scanning the notice quickly. 'That's all. The County Show.'

'Indeed, it is,' he said. 'And what's that?' He jabbed a finger at the attached flyer. 'The Simon De Silva Show-jumping stakes.'

'So?'

'For goodness sake, lass. Are you so hung over that you can't see what I'm getting at? They're filming at the show. Lewis Trevelyan is going to be at the show. He's looking for a rider at the show. Get my drift?'

'And Vanessa and Caroline are going to be at the show,' Ella groaned.

It suddenly dawned on her, what was going on. No wonder Ursula had been so keen for her to have this weekend off. She had manoeuvred things so cleverly, that she hadn't been suspicious of her in the slightest. And now she had agreed – no, promised, to cover for her the next weekend – the weekend of the County Show.

Thomas was nodding severely at her. 'Now you understand my meaning. She's had this planned from the start. She knows, as well as any of us, that if you turn up at the show, her precious daughters won't stand a chance. That film company will only have eyes for you and you alone.'

'Thomas, I think you're exaggerating...'

'Am I?' He shook his head as he spoke. 'No. I don't think so.'

'Well, even if it is true, it's not going to make any difference,' she sighed. 'I won't be going.'

'It doesn't seem right to me,' Thomas muttered, tipping the dregs of his coffee into the enamel sink, and rinsing his mug under the tap.

If Ella hadn't felt so wretched, she would have been inclined to agree with him. But she couldn't help thinking that there would be thousands of people at the show, and dozens taking part in the show jumping. It seemed highly unlikely that Lewis Trevelyan would miss her, when he would have plenty of other riders to choose from.

She left Thomas muttering to himself, and headed down to the sand school, where Stella was holding her advanced dressage class. This was one area where Hollyfield stables excelled. Stella was a stickler for a properly turned-out horse and rider. Appearances counted, and she had been known to refuse to teach any client who turned up without a proper hairnet and necktie. The fact that she was a stuck-up snob with manners above her station was neither here nor there. She got results, and that, in Ursula's eyes, was what mattered most.

'...And straight down the middle, and stand. And bow. Thank you, Meghan. That was very good. Do that on Saturday and you're bound to be placed. Now then, Gemma. Let's see you do the same.'

Ella perched herself on the end seat and watched as Stella put her select group of riders through their paces.

The dressage movements asked for in the arena aimed to test the quality and level of training of the horse and rider, and had six main objectives; rhythm, suppleness, connection, impulsion, straightness, and collection in all areas.

A good dressage rider's aim was to restore the natural grace and beauty of the horse, without tension or resistance.

Gemma Pearson was a skilled rider, but she did not have the ability to feel the horse's movements to the level required for such a demanding discipline.

'No, no, no!' Stella said, whacking her whip against her thigh. 'You're letting him fall in on the forehand. Half halt. That's it. And again. Good. He's listening to you now.'

Ella was suitably impressed. She gave Gemma a reassuring smile, before hopping down from the seat, and heading back to the yard.

Thomas had finished hanging up the hay nets, and was mixing the feeds in the storeroom.

'Feeling any better?' he asked.

'Not much,' she said. 'It's my own fault, though, so I'm not going to moan. I thought I'd take Star out. I gather his owner isn't coming up today. Her name's missing from the exercise sheet.'

'No. She's on holiday,' Thomas said. He straightened up and glanced over at her. 'You think about what I said, Ella.'

'Much good it will do me.'

'There's always a way or a means of doing things.' He scooped a measure of chaff into a bucket, and mixed it with some soaked sugar beet as he spoke. 'That's if you've a mind to do it.'

Oh yes, she could just see it, her, abandoning her responsibilities at the stables to ride in the show jumping stakes. Ursula would have a fit if she spotted her name appearing on the competitors list, especially as she had gone to such great lengths to keep the event such a secret.

'Dream on, Thomas,' she muttered, as she fastened her suede chaps over her riding boots. 'If anyone asks, I've gone for a long ride.'

'Going to see Majesty again, are you?'

She gaped at him, appalled.

He was whistling softly as he sliced up a handful of carrots. His eyes glinted mischievously at her.

'How did you find out?' she sighed.

'I'm not daft, Ella.'

'Promise me you won't say anything.'

'I won't say anything, lass,' he said. 'You go and enjoy yourself.'

He was already scooping up the feeds for the next bucket.

Ella stared at him for a moment. How did he know? Had he spoken to Heather? Had she told him? She watched silently, as he measured out the scoops of feed.

Well, it didn't matter, one way or the other. She knew he wouldn't say anything to Ursula. He disliked her more than anyone else did.

'See you later, Thomas,' she said, picking up her jacket.

'Aye,' he said. 'That you will.'

The sun was warm on her back as she rode Majesty out of the farm entrance and along the narrow tarmac road. A bridleway led through the woods, and over the fields. It was a track often used by ramblers and bird-watchers. If they followed it far enough, they would come to the salt marshes, where hides had been built with money sponsored by a local shipping company.

The tall cranes of the dock could clearly be seen in the distance. The sunlight glittered on the glassy surface of the estuary, and to the right, she could see the masts and rigging of dozens of yachts, tied up in the marina.

She rode on a loose rein, enjoying the peace, and the stillness of the afternoon. Majesty walked briskly, his head tucked under him, despite the lack of rein contact.

Her fingers patted the warm silkiness of his glossy neck.

'You'd be good at the show,' she murmured. 'You miss jumping, don't you boy.'

Heather had invested in some poles and stands, and had erected a course of jumps in one of the farmer's fields, but the ground was boggy in places, or too hard, or too uneven for any serious work.

Perhaps she could persuade Heather to let her take him back to Hollyfield the following weekend, and put him through his paces there. She'd never get a better opportunity, what with Ursula, Vanessa and Caroline performing at the County Show.

She relaxed in the saddle, and enjoyed the gentle swaying motion of the horse's steady walk.

'Next weekend, boy,' she said, rubbing his withers fondly. 'You and I are going to do some proper jumping.'

One of Majesty's ears twitched to the side. Ella laughed. 'That's right, my beauty. Proper jumping.' She gathered up his reins. The track was long and sandy, and perfect for a canter. 'Which means keeping you fit,' she told him, as she urged him into a loping stride.

In the distance, the brown sails of an old sailing barge flapped weakly in the gentle stillness of the breeze. As it made its way up the river a large container vessel, fully laden, moved slowly away from its mooring. The tugboats were guiding it past the marker buoys, and out towards the open sea.

And five miles away, in the Grand Arena of the County Showground, the first camera crew had arrived, and were busy checking view points and angles, and selecting their optimum positions, in readiness for the planned filming of the event.

* * *

'My roots are showing,' Vanessa complained, as she combed her blonde hair into a centre parting, and tied it back with an elastic band.

'Rubbish,' Ursula said, glancing up from the ever-growing pile of paperwork on her desk that needed attention. 'And even if they are it doesn't matter, because you'll be wearing a hat.' She had no intention of forking out another small fortune at the hairdressers, to cover up the miniscule line of mousy brown hair that her daughter was complaining about.

'I won't be wearing one all the time,' she said sulkily.

Ursula gave her a warning glare.

'I want to look my best, mother. You know how important it is.'

Not just important, imperative, Ursula thought, dividing the bills into two piles; the essential, and the not so essential. The bank was still threatening to call in its loan, so she had better give them a sweetener. The vet's bill was well overdue, but she had known Simon Percival for years, and reasoned that he would be willing to wait. The important thing being he wouldn't let any of the horses suffer because of non-payment of his bill.

'Mother. You're not listening, are you?'

'I am, my sweet, but I really don't think there's anything wrong with your hair. You'd be far better off practising your jumping skills.'

Vanessa pulled a face. 'I'm fed-up practising. Nero never does what I ask him to, and that stupid saddle hasn't helped.'

Yet another thousand pounds down the drain, Ursula thought wearily. 'All right, well try riding Jasper again.'

'I can't,' she muttered crossly. 'Caroline wants him.' She pulled her hair free from the elastic band, and decided to plait it instead. 'It's a pity we don't still have Majesty,' she said. 'He would have been perfect.'

'If you had been allowed to ride him,' Ursula said. The memory of her argument with Heather was still pretty clear in her mind. That unfortunate incident, she was certain, had heralded the start of their downturn in fortune. Losing so many livery owners in one week had been nothing short of disastrous for the business. Now it looked as if the children's lessons would be going the same way. 'Try Minstrel,' she suggested. 'He's a good jumper.'

The grey Arab was a fine-looking gelding with wonderful paces. Stella used him regularly in her class. Indeed, she had high hopes for him in the dressage event at the County Show. She had put Meghan Middleton forward to ride the Intermediate Freestyle Test, and was confident that she would win a place in the final line-up.

The scheduling was always tight at the County Show, so several events tended to run simultaneously. The three horse riding arenas made this possible, with the Grand Arena being used for major events, and the smaller ones being used for children's ponies, or in-hand classes, or (as in this case), the dressage tests.

Unfortunately, the timing of the Simon De Silva Show Jumping Stakes was going to clash with the timing of the dressage event, a fact that Stella made all too clear.

'Your daughter cannot ride Minstrel,' she said, in the snooty tone that Ursula had often aspired to, but never managed to pull off. 'You'll have to find something else for her. I've arranged for Meghan to compete on him, and I can't change the arrangements at this late stage.'

'I'm sure you can,' Ursula said, equally determined. Who did Stella think she was, telling her what to do? Who owned the stables, anyway?

'Mrs Johnson,' Stella sounded imperious, as she raised herself to her full height, 'I'd like to point out that, as an instructor, I've seen both girls ride, and in my opinion, Meghan has the better change of winning the trophy for dressage, than Vanessa has for competing in the show-jumping.'

'You're entitled to your opinion, Stella,' Ursula said. 'But that's all it is, your opinion. I happen to think that Vanessa could do rather well on Minstrel, which is why I want her to be given the opportunity to ride him.'

The normally stern face of the instructor grew more cross and implacable by the second. 'I'm sorry. I can't agree with you.'

'Then don't,' Ursula said, effectively dismissing her. She turned and marched down to the stable block, where Vanessa was loitering nervously; awaiting the outcome of what she was sure was going to be a heated debate.

'You can't do this!' Stella shouted, her voice rising.

'Who can't,' Ursula muttered. She did not look back. 'Vanessa, get Thomas to saddle up Minstrel. You can try popping him over a few jumps now.'

'Now?' Vanessa peered warily over her mother's shoulder. Stella was in a furious temper. She had tossed her whip to one side, and was yanking off her pristine show jacket. The spotted necktie was following suit.

'Yes, now. Just ignore her. She'll calm down in a moment.'

'I don't think she will,' Vanessa observed.

Stella was goose-stepping across the sand school in her knee high black shiny boots like a Nazi storm trooper on parade. Her normally serene and unflappable expression had been replaced by one of red-cheeked fury.

'I quit!' she yelled.

'Mother,' Vanessa tapped her on the arm. 'Stella said...'

'I heard what she said,' Ursula snapped. God in Heaven, when was it all going to end. 'I'm sure she doesn't mean it,' she added hastily. She was, however, beginning to have her doubts. A quick glance behind her had shown her that Stella was tossing her jacket and hat into the boot of her car. And the duty list indicated she had a class at three, an advanced class, which no one else was qualified or skilled enough to take.

'Perhaps you ought to talk to her,' Vanessa said.

'I'll do no such thing,' Ursula stuffed her hands into the pockets of her padded body warmer, and looked positively mutinous. 'Do you want to ride Minstrel, at the show, or not?'

'Yes.'

'Right. That's all I need to know. Thomas! Thomas?' Her voice raised itself by a full octave. 'Where is that damn

170

Irishman? Thomas!'

The man in question was swilling down the yard with the hosepipe, and whistling loudly as he did so. The sudden slamming of a car door and the revving of an engine were the first things that disturbed him, and he glanced up in time to see Stella's car screeching off down the driveway, leaving a scattering of gravel and stones in her wake.

The second thing that disturbed him was the sound of Ursula's bad-tempered caterwauling.

For the love of Mary, he muttered, as he turned off the tap, and coiled up the hose. What now?

'Didn't you hear me calling?' Ursula demanded, as he strolled nonchalantly into the stable block, a strand of straw stuck firmly between his teeth.

'That I did, Ma'am,' he said. 'And that's why I'm here.'

His jaunty stance infuriated Ursula. His knowing look infuriated her more.

'I want Minstrel tacked up and ready for my daughter to ride in less than five minutes, understand?' she snapped.

'Yes, Ma'am.'

'Well?' she said. 'What are you waiting for?'

Thomas scratched his forehead. 'Minstrel? That's the grey Arab, right?'

'You know it is,' she responded crossly. The man was an idiot.

'Only he's already tacked up,' Thomas explained. 'It's on the list, you see. He's down to do a class at three.'

'Well tack up something else, then, and bring Minstrel to me.'

'Right you are, Ma'am.'

The grey Arab was a distinctive looking horse with a pale cream mane and tail and an intelligent looking face. The straight-sided dressage saddle it was wearing was not the most suitable tack for a jumping lesson, but Ursula had neither the patience, nor the inclination to change it.

'Take him into the four-acre field,' she told her daughter,

giving her a leg up into the saddle. 'The poles are already set up.'

Vanessa fidgeted uncomfortably in her seat. 'I don't know if I can jump him in this,' she complained. 'There's no knee support.'

'Nonsense. You'll be fine,' Ursula assured her. 'What now?' She glared at Thomas, who was standing idly by the barn door.

'I was wondering,' he began.

'Yes?'

'The three-o-clock lesson.'

'Yes?' she snorted. 'What about it?'

'Well, it looks to me as if Stella has gone home,' he said. 'So, I was wondering who was taking it.'

Ursula exhaled loudly. 'Find Ella. She'll have to do it.'

'She's out.'

'What do you mean, out?'

'Out riding,' Thomas explained. 'She's taken Star, and I don't reckon she'll be back in time.'

'Oh, brilliant. Just bloody brilliant.' Ursula handed Vanessa a whip and waved her away as she considered what to do next. There wasn't anyone else to take the class, and yet she couldn't afford to cancel the lesson. Not the way her finances were going. 'Thomas,' she said, managing a weak smile. 'You ride, don't you?'

'I've been known to,' he said cautiously. What on earth was the old crow planning now?

'An instructional hack,' she announced, beaming. 'That's what we'll do. We'll tell them the horses need to relax, prior to the Show. You can do that, can't you Thomas?'

'I can,' he said, somewhat dubiously. 'But won't they be wondering why Stella isn't with them?'

Ursula scowled. 'Stella has a migraine. That's why she's gone home'

Migraine, my foot, Thomas thought. Not by the way she had hared down that driveway. Something else was amiss here, and something serious, if the worried look on Ursula's face was anything to go by. Still, he didn't have time to speculate at the moment. He had to find a suitable horse to ride.

Meanwhile, in the four-acre field, Vanessa was putting the grey Arab through his paces. Minstrel was a gentleman, a generous horse who could forgive inadequate riders their faults, since he was so well schooled himself.

Vanessa was more than impressed to find that at the slightest tweak, or pressure from her, the horse floated through a variety of transitions, with seemingly little effort. His turns were exact, his stride relaxed, and his carriage superb. Why on earth hadn't she ridden him before, or was this one of Stella's best-kept secrets?

She turned his head and cantered towards the first set of jumps, a double consisting of two sets of poles, a couple of strides apart. Minstrel's ears pricked forwards, as he sailed effortlessly over the pair of them, made a perfect landing, and turned expertly towards the next jump.

It was like flying, Vanessa thought. The horse was wonderful.

Her enthusiasm grew along with her excitement, and she completed the course with no faults. Not one single pole fell, or even wobbled. He didn't refuse, swerve, or run out of any of the jumps. He was fantastic.

As she pulled him up and patted his neck, she felt her cheeks flush with pleasure. For the first time she suddenly realised that she stood a very real chance of making Lewis Trevelyan sit up and take notice of her. It was quite an exhilarating thought.

'How many riders?' Lewis said, tucking the phone between his ear and his shoulder, as he leafed through the pages of the script.

'Dozens of them. More than they say they can handle,' James said. 'The secretary thinks we should limit the numbers. They've been inundated with entries.'

'No way,' Lewis said. 'We can't do that.'

'We've got to think of something, if only for safety reasons.'

'Okay.' He paused, considering the problem. 'What about if

we narrow the age range again – say, from eighteen to twenty-five.'

'Possibly.'

'There can't be that many blonde haired, female riders out there, surely?'

James laughed. 'I hope not. Oh, and Lucy says you're still being sexist.'

'Tell her to get real,' Lewis sighed. 'Even she wouldn't send a dwarf to audition for the role of a giant.'

'I'll tell her,' he said. 'Oh, and Matt says we need to be careful we don't offend the locals. Apparently, there's a kind of film hysteria building up. With the exception of a couple of documentaries, there's been nothing of this scale in these parts for years. Hence the number of entries for the competition.'

'Fine. Well, tell him we'll use everyone else in the background shots. That should keep them happy.' (Though whether the shots would get past the cutting room floor was another matter entirely. No director or producer in their right minds would film a showground full of blonde-haired young women, all the same sort of age, unless they were doing a re-make of something like the Stepford Wives.)

'This girl's really getting to me, James,' he sighed. 'I need to find her. She's even in my dreams. I'm telling you I'll know her as soon as I see her.'

'If she turns up.'

'She will,' he said.

After the way Ursula had reacted when he had mentioned Robert Johnson's daughter, he was ninety nine percent certain that she was the girl he was looking for. And he had left Ursula in no doubt that he wanted to meet her. If she didn't pass the message on, then the woman was a fool.

Then again, he thought ruefully, perhaps she was.

Whilst Lewis was making his phone call, Ella was sponging Majesty down. The horse was supremely fit, but he was sweating after their long, fast ride, and she didn't want him to catch a chill. She sponged around his ears, and under his belly, before fastening a string sweat rug over him and leading him into his stable.

'You wait there,' she murmured, patting his neck, 'while I go and catch Star.'

The piebald gelding was having a lovely time, having been given an unexpected break from his exercise routine. It wasn't often he got the chance to unwind in a lush and muddy farmer's field. Consequently, he was making the most of it.

Ella groaned as she saw the caked in mud encrusted over most of his black and white coat. 'Did you have to roll?' she said. Clumps of matted soil hung from his forelock and mane, and his face looked as if he was having a mud mask beauty treatment. It would take forever to brush all the tell-tale bits off him.

She fastened a head-collar on him, and led him out of the field. Ursula would be wondering where she was, but she would just have to wonder. These things couldn't be rushed. Star would have to be spotless, before she could saddle him up for the long ride home.

Majesty whinnied softly when she led the piebald gelding into the stable yard, and Star gave an answering whicker.

'Don't know why you're looking so pleased with yourself,' she muttered. 'God, but you're filthy.' She tied him to a tethering ring in the wall, before going to search for a body brush.

As she was hunting through the small shed, which served as a tack room on the farm, she heard the sound of a car. It was probably the farmer, she thought, poking her head around the wooden door. But it wasn't. It was Heather.

'Hi,' she said, strolling over to greet her. 'I didn't expect to see you today.'

Heather climbed out of the car, and straightened her knee length skirt. 'I didn't expect to be here,' she said. 'But I had to deliver a document over at Mainwarings, so I thought I'd pop in to see how my beauty is doing.'

'Majesty?' Ella said. 'He's doing fine, unlike this old nag, here. Talk about taking advantage of the situation.'

'Hmm. He is a bit muddy, isn't he?' Heather looked Star up and down. She didn't step any closer, perhaps because she was wearing a smart, tailored jacket, and a pale pink blouse, which weren't the most practical garments to wear, when dealing with a mud-stained horse. 'Anyway, I'm glad I caught you,' she said, leafing through the pockets of her handbag. 'Ah, here it is.'

Ella tilted her head to one side. 'What?'

'The entry form for the show on Saturday,' she said. 'I picked it up in the village. I thought I might take Majesty along. What do you think?'

'Brilliant,' Ella said trying hard to hide her disappointment. She had hoped to take Majesty to Hollyfield at the weekend. 'Vanessa and Caroline are going.'

'So, I believe.' Heather smiled. 'Who are they riding?'

'God knows.'

'What about you?'

'Me?' Ella shook her head. 'I'm not going. I have to work.'

'You're kidding?' Heather said, dismayed. 'Ella, they're doing the filming for the latest Simon De Silva movie at the show. They're specifically looking for show-jumpers to include in the film. You've got to be there. I mean, you of all people, just have to be there.'

'Why?' she sighed. 'Because Robert Johnson was my father?'

'Well, there's that, of course, but...'

'Forget it, Heather,' she said, turning to walk away. 'I won't be there. It's as simple as that.'

The older woman glanced at her watch. She ought to be getting back to work but she could see Ella was upset. Had she touched a sore point? Was there something going on at Hollyfields that she didn't know about?

She followed her to the yard and stood by Majesty's stable door, stroking his neck (at least he was clean), as she watched Ella attempt to brush the mud off the piebald gelding. 'I'm sorry,' she said.

'It's not your fault.' Ella stooped to brush the horse's belly.

Star rubbed the back of her neck with his hairy, mud-encrusted chin. 'Ursula obviously didn't want me to go. She's re-scheduled the timetable so that I'm working that day. I should have realised she was up to something, but it never crossed my mind.'

'The cow!'

'Well, you know what she's like,' she said. 'She wants to put Vanessa and Caroline in the limelight, not me.'

'But it's so unfair,' Heather said crossly. 'Don't you think it's unfair?'

'A bit,' Ella said. 'But there's not a lot I can do about it.'

She laid the brush to one side, and lifted the saddle down from the stable door. Star fidgeted as she tried to tighten his girth. 'How much did you manage to eat?' she groaned, poking a finger into his swollen and well-satisfied belly. 'It's the starvation paddock for you when I get you back, old man.'

Heather smiled. Ella was such a sweet young girl. She glanced again at her watch. But she couldn't stay. She really did have to get back to work. A few pressing matters, that had been brought to her attention, needed investigating.

'Look, I'll try and catch up with you during the week,' she said, reaching for her car keys. 'Perhaps you could give me a ring, say, on Thursday? You can let me know if you think Majesty will be fit enough for the Show.'

'Oh, he'll be fit enough.' She grinned, as she swung herself up into the saddle, and gathered up Star's reins. 'The question is, Heather, will you?'

'Yes, I know. I'm one of those dreaded week-end riders, and no doubt I'll ache for England the following day, but I aim to give it a go. If only to wipe the satisfied smirk of Ursula's face when she sees me there.'

'Go for it,' Ella said. 'I wish I could.'

As she rode along the track leading back to Hollyfield Stables, it might have surprised her to know that someone else was also thinking along those lines.

Chapter Thirteen

Ursula spent the best part of the following two days cajoling, pleading and grovelling to Stella Watkins. She could not afford to lose her one and only dressage instructor, particularly since she had heard, on the grapevine, that New Hall Equestrian Centre were looking for a suitably qualified person to take charge of their dressage team.

On the subject of Minstrel, however, she refused to be swayed. Vanessa could, and would, be riding him at the County Show.

'But I've had a word with Mary Rose,' she told Stella, (having taken the chance to phone her the moment she had finished discussing the matter with Mary) 'and she's quite happy for Meghan to ride Lady Jane. She's not taking her to the show because she's abroad next weekend. Paris, I believe.'

Lady Jane was a top-class Hanoverian dressage horse, kept at livery at the stables, and ridden only by her owner. It had cost Ursula the promise of free livery for a month, (and much imploring on her part), before Mary could be persuaded to allow Meghan to compete on her. (And then, only because she had seen Meghan ride for herself, and knew how competent she was).

'Lady Jane?' Stella queried. 'Are you sure?'

'Quite sure,' Ursula said.

A long pause followed, as Stella considered the matter.

Ursula started to doodle on the notepad beside the phone. Hurry up woman, she thought. I haven't got all day. The doodle grew into a large, black spiral, which spread down the page and became a vine, with leaves hanging off it.

'I happen to think that Meghan would do better riding Lady Jane than she would on Minstrel,' she added, ripping the page from the notepad and screwing it into a small ball. 'You have to admit, that that horse has a natural talent for dressage.'

'Indeed,' Stella agreed. 'She has beautiful paces.'

'And it would be a shame to miss out on the opportunity to ride her. You know how possessive Mary can be.'

'Yes, quite.' Even she had to admit that it was practically unheard of for Mary to allow anyone else on her horse. (Which was probably why she got such good results from her). They had been placed in several recent events, and taken the trophy at the previous year's County Show.

'So, what do you say?' Ursula said. 'Will you reconsider your decision?'

'Possibly,' Stella said. 'I'll need to think about it.'

Ursula was incensed. What did the woman have to think about? She was being offered a prize-winning horse on a platter. If Meghan won the dressage event, a lot of the credit would go to her instructor. Why was she hesitating?

Stella, however, knew when a carrot was being dangled under the end of her nose, and she was quite prepared to let Ursula sweat for a while. She had every intention of returning to her rather comfortable post at the stables. Until this unfortunate business with Minstrel, she had virtually ruled the roost there. None of the other riding instructors were a match for her, and Ursula didn't have a clue when it came to showing horses. So yes, she would be going back, but only on her terms.

Ursula was starting to panic. She thought Stella would jump at the offer. Now she was beginning to think that New Hall Equestrian Centre had been in touch with her after all. 'There is the chance,' she added hastily, 'that I may be able to arrange a small pay rise for you as well. A token rise, to show how much we appreciate all the hard work you put in.'

'That's very kind of you, Mrs Johnson.'

Oh, how she hated the subtle sarcasm in her tone. 'It's no more than you deserve, Stella,' she said, through well-gritted teeth. 'Hollyfield Stables' excellent reputation for dressage is entirely down to you. I really don't know what we would do without you.'

Stella could hazard a guess. The term bankruptcy sprang to mind. She smiled serenely, as she cupped the receiver to her ear. 'Maybe I was a bit hasty,' she said.

Ursula's spirits leapt. 'Not at all,' she said. 'I should have been more sympathetic to your needs.'

'It was a dreadful misunderstanding.'

'I couldn't agree more.'

'So, we'll say no more about it?'

'Not a word.'

'Good,' Stella said, with a somewhat triumphant pitch to her voice. 'Then I'll see you tomorrow at ten, as usual.'

Ursula replaced the phone with a scowl. Thank God for that. Stupid, pompous ass of a woman. Well at least that was one problem sorted. Though how in heaven's name she was going to afford the pay-rise she had hinted at was quite beyond her. The farrier had demanded cash on his last visit, due to a mix up at the bank. Her last cheque had bounced, and he didn't want a repeat of that episode. Neither did Ursula. It wouldn't do for rumours like that to leak out into the business community. The fact that she had a slight cash flow problem at the moment was inconvenient, but not insurmountable. She had already taken steps to improve the current situation.

A notice had gone out to all livery owners, informing them of the small rise in rent, which would take place from the following month. The price of both class and private lessons was also going up, and an advertisement had been placed in the local newspaper, offering stabling and schooling facilities at competitive rates.

Ursula flicked through the pages of the evening paper until she found the Classified Ads. Under 'Horse and Rider' was the entry that had cost her a small fortune to insert. Still, it looked good. The caption, "Quality livery available for the discerning horse owner," stood out from the rest of the print, and was followed by a short description of the facilities on offer.

Unfortunately, New Hall Equestrian Centre was also advertising its business, and on the same page. Damn and blast! Ursula folded up the paper, and pushed it to one side. Perhaps she should think about starting up the stud again. Since they had lost their finest stallion a few years back, she had given up on a breeding programme. It had always seemed to be more trouble than it was worth. The vet's bills alone were prohibitive. But Thomas was experienced with quality bloodstock. Maybe she should have a few words with him, and see if he was enthusiastic enough to give it another go.

The phone rang as she was contemplating this new train of thought.

'Good afternoon, Hollyfield Stables, how can I help?' she said, in her telephone voice, which was uncharacteristically bright and cheerful.

The male voice on the other end, however, was not. 'Ursula Johnson?'

'Yes,' she said warily.

'Hello, Mrs Johnson. Andrew Jenson, here, from the bank. I've been trying to get hold of you for some time.'

'Really?' She tried to express surprise.

'Yes. It's about your overdraft.'

'Oh?' Ursula sucked in a deep breath. 'Is there a problem with it?'

'You tell me, Mrs Johnson,' came the caustic reply.

'Well, I'm quite happy about it,' she said brightly. 'With the new business, and the latest press release – oh, and the filming, of course – you've heard about the filming? You can see why I have such high hopes for the future of Hollyfield Stables.'

'Yes, but sadly, high hopes don't pay bills, and the bank needs to see some kind of return on its investment.'

'I appreciate that, but...'

'Good,' he said crisply. 'Because I'm giving you one month, Mrs Johnson.'

A cold sinking feeling settled itself in Ursula's stomach. 'One month?' she echoed.

'One month. If you don't start repaying some of the loan, the bank will have to decide whether to foreclose or not.'

'But the new rent increases don't take place until next month, and the advertisement has only just gone in the newspaper,' she groaned. 'Mr Jenson, I do think you're being a trifle unreasonable.'

'Do you,' he said coldly. 'Well, isn't that a shame. One month, Mrs Johnson. Good day.'

Good bloody day, my foot. Ursula slammed the receiver down.

'Mother?'

'What?' she barked, glaring over her shoulder at this unwarranted interruption?

Caroline stood in the doorway, a rather petulant frown on her sulky face. (Unlike Ella, she wasn't used to being shouted at.) 'It doesn't matter,' she retorted. 'I can see that you're busy.'

'Oh, for goodness sake, child. What do you want?'

'Well, if you must know,' she said. 'I was wondering if I could get some new riding gloves before the show on Saturday.'

'You want new riding gloves?' Ursula positively spat out the words at her.

'Yes.'

'Mother, I really do need them, and there's a sale on in that new saddlery shop in town. And Vanessa says...'

'Just get them.'

Caroline's face brightened. 'You mean it?'

'Yes. Yes. Go and buy them, and while you're at it, get anything else you think you might need. Because one way or the other, you or your sister have to win on Saturday. I don't care who does it, but one of you has to be in that film.'

'It'll be me,' Caroline announced triumphantly. 'I know it will.'

Ursula had her doubts about that, but wouldn't dream of hurting her daughter by voicing them. It was Minstrel she was pinning her hopes on, Minstrel and Vanessa. Together, they could pull this off. She was sure of it. Failure was not, and could not, be an option.

Saturday morning dawned bright and sunny, with only the faintest wisps of an overnight mist left hanging in the air.

Preparations at Hollyfield stables had started early. The horses had been fed and groomed, before being bandaged and wrapped for travelling. The horsebox could take up to eight horses, but on this occasion, only four were using it to go to the County Show. Minstrel and Jasper, for the show jumping, Lady Jane for the dressage, and the fourth horse, Holly, for the working hunter class.

Ella had been up since six, plaiting manes, and wrapping bandages around tails, and sorting out the tack and grooming boxes for each horse. The excitement was buzzing around the yard. Several of the livery owners who had their own transport were going, and a variety of trailers, and small boxes were appearing from all corners of the yard. Not all of the classes were ridden classes. There was everything from 'in hand' to 'mountain and moorland.' And one girl was taking her horse purely for the sake of getting him used to large crowds, prior to entering him in future shows.

Ella couldn't help wishing she was going with them. Loading Jasper onto the box, she felt a sudden pang of envy. She knew she was a far better rider than Vanessa or Caroline. It would have been nice to take part in the show, if only to prove it to them. Still, it was her own fault she couldn't go. She was the one who had readily agreed to change shifts. She couldn't blame anyone else for that mistake.

'Be good,' she murmured, fastening a hay net up for the horse, and patting him gently on the neck. Jasper snorted, and tugged at the lead rope. He didn't like travelling. It would take him a while to settle down at the other end. (Which was another reason why she wished she were going. Caroline was not renowned for her patience.) 'Right. You can load Minstrel now,' she said, sliding the partition shut, and standing to one side.

The grey Arab was a seasoned traveller, and showed no

hesitation in walking up the rubber-matted ramp and into the box. Ella made sure he was secure, before folding the partition shut.

Jasper was starting to paw restlessly at the straw covered floor. A squeal from Minstrel showed he was not impressed.

'Next,' Ella called.

Lady Jane's coat gleamed like black silk as she strutted proudly up the ramp, her neck and head held high. She looked stunning, even with her padded travelling boots and bandaged tail. This horse was worth a small fortune, she thought, taking the lead rope from the young stable girl, and fastening it to the piece of baling twine that hung from a ring on the box wall. She hoped Meghan appreciated the honour she was being given. No one, not even Stella Watkins, had been allowed to ride Lady Jane.

'Right,' she said, closing the next partition and sliding the bolt across. 'We're ready for Holly now.'

With the last horse securely loaded, it was time to carry on the tack and grooming equipment, plus several containers of water and hay nets full of hay.

Vanessa and Caroline took no part in the actual loading of either horses or equipment. They were far too busy getting themselves organised. They had both been up since dawn, arguing over whose turn it was to use the bathroom, the hairdryer, and even the toilet, at one point. Tempers were short, and nerves were frayed.

'I feel sick, Mother,' Caroline complained, chewing half-heartedly on a dry piece of toast.

'No, you don't. It's the excitement, that's all.'

'I do. I feel sick.'

'Good,' Vanessa said, liberally coating her toast in butter and marmalade. 'You won't want to ride, then, will you?'

'But I do want to ride.' Caroline sounded quite pitiful.

'And so, you shall, my darling,' Ursula murmured, pressing a mug of hot sweet tea into her hands. 'You and Jasper make a lovely team.'

Vanessa opened her mouth to say something, but caught the warning glare in her mother's eye. She scowled, and then crunched into her slice of dripping toast. Wilson, who was slavering under the kitchen table, nudged her knee. She tossed him a crust, which he failed to catch, and it landed sticky side down on the tiled floor. Ursula stepped on it a moment later.

'I'm sure you'll be fine, darling,' she said, glancing down, and wondering why the floor suddenly felt tacky. 'You mustn't be nervous.'

'I'm not nervous,' Vanessa announced, reaching over to pluck another slice of toast out of the rack.

Caroline looked as if she were about to cry. 'That's because you've got Minstrel,' she said.

'So?'

'Well, he's heaps better than Jasper. You know he is.'

'Is he?' Vanessa tried to look surprised.

Caroline muttered something unintelligible under her breath.

'Girls, girls,' Ursula soothed. 'There's no point in arguing. It doesn't matter who wins, as long as one of you does. And this way, we've got two chances.' She smiled fondly at the pair of them. 'Oh, my dears, I am so proud of you, so very proud.' A moist tear was starting to form in the corner of her eye. 'This is going to be so worthwhile. I know it is.'

'There goes Lady Muck and her two poisonous daughters,' Thomas said, watching thoughtfully as the dark blue Range Rover swept down the gravel drive after the huge horse-box, and scattered the neatly clipped verges with dozens of small stones. He gave a twirling wave as the vehicle sped past. 'Well,' he muttered, glancing over at Ella, who was sweeping the yard free of hay and dirt. 'Acts like bleeding Royalty, doesn't she?'

Ella managed a weak smile.

'So, lass,' he said, ambling over to her. 'What are your plans for today?'

'Not a lot,' she said, pausing for a moment to lean on the

handle of her broom. 'I've got the children's class at ten, but there are only four names on the list, and no one's booked in for this afternoon. I reckon most people are going to the Show.'

'And that includes your teenage helpers, right?'

'Right,' she nodded. 'Only Kelly and Tamsin turned up this morning. The others are all hoping to see Simon De Silva, or, failing that, Lewis Trevelyan again.'

'Ah, the fickleness of youth.' Thomas picked up the muck scoop, and removed a heap of droppings from outside one of the boxes. 'It's going to be a pretty quiet day, then.'

'Busy, though,' she said. 'Between us, we've got to muck out all the stables, and prepare the feeds for tonight.'

'Best get started, then,' he said. 'Tell you what, I'll muck out, and you bring in the ponies for this morning's lesson. Kelly and Tamsin can help you tack up.'

The girls were bursting with enthusiasm. Their devotion to the horses, and everything connected to them, meant that Saturdays were the highlight of the week for them. Nothing was too much trouble. They lugged heavy water buckets from stable to stable, polished tack, groomed and brushed and plaited the ponies' manes, and even put up with the odd nip or kick, just to be near the creatures they so adored.

Both volunteered to lead in the children's pony class, so that those youngsters wishing to trot could do so safely.

Sasha Wilkes was in her element. 'Look, Mummy, look!' she yelled, as she bounced up and down in the saddle like a wobbling sack of jellybeans, whilst Tamsin clung on to the side of her padded jacket to hold her securely in place.

'And walk,' Ella said, lowering her voice. The four ponies plodding round the arena slowed to a gentle amble.

'Again! Again!' Sasha shrieked, her legs flapping wildly against the little Dartmoor pony's sides. Biscuit got the message, and sprang forwards, and it was purely by luck that Tamsin managed to keep a hold of her charge, thus preventing her from tumbling backwards over the pony's hindquarters.

'Well sat, Sasha,' Ella said. The little girl beamed. 'Don't kick so hard, next time, though,' she added, kindly. 'I don't think Biscuit likes it.'

The rest of the lesson passed without incident, and Ella was pleased when all four children booked lessons for the following week. Ursula would have no cause for complaint on her account, she thought.

By twelve o'clock, the stables had all been cleaned out, and fresh straw, hay and water put down for the evening, when most of the horses came in. A few hardy types lived out, native breeds, mostly, who could cope better when the weather was inclement. The thoroughbreds and finer ponies tended to be better off if stabled overnight.

It was a never-ending round of putting out, mucking out, and then bringing in again. Such were the joys of horse ownership. No wonder those who could afford it paid for private livery, Ella thought, as she tipped yet another laden wheelbarrow on to the muckheap. Her clothes were filthy and her boots were starting to smell. She longed for a soak in a hot bath, but she couldn't leave the yard unmanned. Thomas had left for the village a good half hour ago, saying he needed to pick something up. Maybe she had time to take a quick shower. As Kelly had so politely pointed out, she really did hum a bit. She glanced at her watch. Thomas was due back at any moment, and she was sure the girls were capable of taking any phone messages in his absence.

'Give me ten minutes,' she told them, 'And then you can go and get some lunch.'

She stood under the warm shower and let the force of the water cascade over her hair. It was pure bliss. She lathered it up with shampoo, and rinsed it thoroughly, before wrapping it in a towel to dry. Barefoot, she padded through into the bedroom, and sorted out some clean jodhpurs, and a white blouse. Dressed and refreshed, she hurried downstairs, dragging a comb through her damp hair. She didn't have time to dry it properly, so she pinned it up, and reasoned that the warm sun would do the job for her. Stuffing her feet into her riding boots, and snatching up her jacket, she opened the door to head back to the yard, and nearly trampled over Thomas, who was standing on the doorstep, one hand raised as if about to knock on it.

'That was good timing,' he said.

'Christ, you gave me a fright.' She stopped short, and caught her breath. Thomas was grinning at her. Why was he grinning at her? She looked suspiciously over his shoulder to where a small sporty hatch back was parked with its engine running. It looked like Kate's car. Her eyes narrowed slightly. It *was* Kate's car.

'Thomas,' she said. 'Isn't that…?'

'Aye, it is, lass.' He gave her a wink. 'And it drives like a dream.'

'But why?' she spluttered dazedly. 'I mean, what are you doing with it?'

'I'll explain that on the road, me darling. Come on,' he said, catching hold of her arm. 'We haven't got much time.'

'What do you mean, we haven't got much time?'

'To get to the Show, of course,' he said, holding open the car door for her.

'Thomas, I can't leave the stables.'

'Sure, you can,' he said. 'It's all arranged. Now get in, or do I have to throw you in myself.'

Bewildered, she glanced back at the yard. Tamsin and Kelly were standing laughing and waving at her. 'Good luck,' they yelled. 'Get us an autograph.'

'They know about this?' she said, her voice shaking.

Thomas nodded and grinned, as he revved the engine.

'Who else knows?' she croaked, sliding into her seat and fastening the seatbelt.

'Only Kate and Heather,' he said.

She glanced across at him. 'Heather Hutchins knows?'

'Well, you need a horse to ride, lass,' he said simply, 'and there's none better than hers, that's for sure.'

Ella was stunned. 'You're being serious, aren't you? I'm going to ride Majesty.'

'That you are me darling.' He winked at her as the car accelerated onto the main road. 'That you are.'

Chapter Fourteen

The Keynes and Bain hospitality marquee was swarming with people. The film crew, actors and actresses mingled with technicians and extras, as Miles Davison gave a run down of how he foresaw the scheduling for the day ahead.

'Simon, I want you on next, running from the first aid post. That's all we need at the moment. And Molly, you'll be standing by the window. Jason?' He scanned the list of names on his clipboard. 'Where's Jason?'

'Gone for a leak,' came a shouted reply.

'Okay, well forget that for now. Lewis?'

'Yep?'

'I want you and your team in the grand ring for the jumping competition. You can be extras, members of the crowd, whatever you like.'

'Me?' Lucy yelped, running a hand through her perfectly styled hair. 'God, I wish I'd known. I must look a sight.'

Lewis gave her a withering glare. His patience was wearing rather thin. Three hours, he had been stuck in this glorified tent, when he had really wanted to be outside and watching the proceedings.

Matthew had managed to get hold of a list of entrants for the show jumping competition, and a quick scan of the names had not revealed an Ella Johnson on it. Vanessa and Caroline were there, but not Ella.

'Lewis Trevelyan, Hi. I'm Christopher Simmons.' (The tall man with the bald head and the seriously unfashionable grey suit flashed an identity badge at him.) 'I'm from the local press.

Can I have a few words?'

'Sure.' Lewis motioned him over to a table, and pulled up a chair.

'I gather Blackwater Films are running this competition,' the man said, switching on a small, hand-held tape recorder and placing it on the table in front of them. 'You don't mind if I record...'

'No, go ahead,' Lewis said. 'And yes, Blackwater Films are in charge of this particular event.'

'Can you tell me why?'

Lewis shrugged. 'We're looking for talented riders. What better place to find them, than at the County Show?'

'Indeed.' The reporter nodded. 'But aren't you going to a lot of trouble for what, admittedly, is only a very minor scene in the film?'

'Possibly.'

'In fact, I think I'm right in saying that this scene is only going to be about three minutes long.'

'Give or take a few seconds,' Lewis confirmed.

'And it's not a big budget movie, is it? I mean, it's not on the scale of Hollywood films.'

'Neither was "The Full Monty", Mr Simmons,' Lewis said, drumming his fingers on the table as he spoke. 'Quality doesn't necessarily come with a high price tag. We're after realism here; real emotions, real nerves, and real endurance. And that's why we're using real people.'

'So, it's not just a publicity exercise?'

'No,' he said, and then added quickly, 'but naturally any publicity we get will be an added bonus.'

'Naturally.' The reporter grinned. A double page spread in the daily paper would not do the production team any harm at all, particularly if the footage included shots of local people, which it was bound to, given the circumstances. 'Well, thanks for your time, Mr Trevelyan,' he said, switching off his recording. 'I won't keep you. I can see how busy you are. Perhaps if I could have a word with Mr De Silva?'

'He's on set,' Lewis said. 'They're shooting one of the scenes outside the main arena, but you might be able to catch him later.'

'I see. Well, thanks again.' He stood up and shook his hand. 'Local paper, you say?' Lewis said, as a sudden thought occurred to him.

'That's right.'

'Have you been with them long?'

'Longer than I care to mention,' the journalist laughed.

'Then you might be the person I need to speak to,' he said. 'Do you remember the show-jumper, Robert Johnson?'

'Indeed, I do.' Mr Simmons beamed. 'Yes, I was fortunate enough to interview him on several occasions. He used to own a stable and stud not far from here, Hollyfield Stables, outside of Ecclesfield. The family runs it now. You do know he died?' he added, giving him a sudden sharp look.

'Yes, I heard about the car crash. Five years ago, wasn't it?'

'Hmm. Must be. Tragic,' he added, shaking his head. 'That poor girl. To lose her mother, and then her father, and her barely fifteen at the time.'

'Tragic,' Lewis echoed.

'Of course, she was a good little rider as well. Gabriella Johnson,' he sighed. 'Pretty young thing. She was a regular winner in the Junior Ponies UK Championship events.'

'Does she still compete?'

'You know, I'm not sure if she does.' Christopher Simmons pocketed his recorder as he spoke. 'I think she mainly teaches now. She could well be here, you know. You'll have to ask her that for yourself.'

'I will,' he said. 'Thanks.'

Gabriella. Of course – Gabriella – Ella!

'Matthew! Let me see that list of riders again.'

Got it! He jabbed his finger at the sheet and gave a low whistle. 'She's here, Matt. See here. They've crossed out Heather Hutchins, and put in Gabriella Johnson. That's her.'

'Who?'

'Robert Johnson's daughter, you idiot,' he said, grinning.

Lucy gave a loud and imperious sniff as she examined her immaculately polished fingernails. 'Of course, she might not be who you think she is.'

'I'll lay odds on it that she is,' Lewis muttered.

'Fifty quid and you're on,' Matthew said cheerfully.

'Done.'

Lucy gave a cluck of disapproval. 'Well, I'm off,' she said. 'If I'm going to be an extra, I need to get to make-up.'

Lewis glanced at his watch. 'And I need to go check out the competitors. Where did you say they were again?'

'Mother! Mother! Oh my God! I've just seen him,' Vanessa shrieked, as she bounded across the paddock to the horsebox. The horses were standing tethered to separate rings on the side of the lorry, whilst their travelling boots and bandages were removed. Jasper shied and Lady Jane snorted and tossed her head as Vanessa hurtled past.

'Who, darling?' Ursula said, ducking underneath an overhanging hay net. Wisps of hay clung to her hair and padded fleece jacket. 'No, don't hang it up there,' she said, to one of the over-keen youngsters, who were helping them unload. 'Use a bit of baling twine.'

'Simon De Silva,' Vanessa panted, clutching at her side. 'They're filming him now.'

'Where?' Caroline said.

'Over there.' Vanessa waggled her hand in the direction of one of the marquees. 'I saw loads of cameras and sound equipment and stuff.' And truckloads of security guards too, though she failed to mention that fact. Indeed, her one fleeting glimpse of Simon De Silva had been as he sprinted across the grass, and even then, she'd only seen the top of his head.

'He was gorgeous!' she enthused breathlessly. 'And he smiled at me.'

'Liar!' Caroline snapped.

'You weren't there.'

'So?' Caroline was struggling to fasten the catch of her riding hat under her chin. The blonde wig she was wearing, courtesy of one of the charity shops in town, was making things difficult, to say the least. 'I bet he didn't even see you,' she sneered.

'He did so...'

'Hadn't you better be getting Minstrel tacked up?' Ursula said, somewhat diplomatically. 'They'll be starting the warm up soon.'

Vanessa glowered at her sister. 'Did so,' she muttered.

Caroline gave her a dismissive shrug. 'Where are my new gloves, Mother?'

'In the trunk,' Ursula said. 'Meghan?' She turned her attention to their star dressage rider, who was so much more agreeable than her own daughters when it came to competitions. 'Meghan, have you got a necktie pin? Stella says you must always wear one. Yes? Because I've got a gold one if you need it. You don't? Oh good. Good. Now then, where's the show sheen?'

As the horses were being brushed and groomed in readiness for the competition, Vanessa and Caroline were making a point of eyeing up their rivals in the show jumping event.

Marsha Wilmot's daughter Amelia had entered, riding White Star.

'She's never eighteen,' Caroline said loudly, as the chestnut filly trotted past them with her young rider on board. 'She can't be more than sixteen.'

'Fifteen,' Ursula said, peering over the top of her gold-rimmed glasses.

'And there's Sally Mason. She must be at least thirty.'

'They'll have to be disqualified,' Vanessa said. 'They will be, Mother, won't they?'

'Yes, of course,' Ursula said. Or at least, they would be once she'd passed on the relevant details to the judging panel. 'Don't worry, girls. Something tells me you're going to do rather well here today.' (Please God) 'Now then,' she added, glancing at her watch. 'It must be nearly time for you to walk the course.'

The jumps had to be taken in a set sequence, and all riders were required to familiarise themselves with the layout, before tackling it for real. This was the only opportunity they would have to measure the distance between each set of jumps, the angles and degree of turns, and the areas where they could make up the most time. If it came to a jump off, this sort of knowledge would be of paramount importance.

Ursula watched anxiously as Vanessa and Caroline strolled round the course. They didn't seem to be paying much attention to the matter in hand. Vanessa seemed more intent on staring over at the camera crew than the jumps, and Caroline was pouting and putting on a provocative wiggle as she walked. In her skin-tight jodhpurs and blonde wig, it was not an endearing sight.

'God give me strength,' Lewis groaned, as he stood at the side of the arena and studied the riders walking the course. 'Look at those two.'

'Don't tell me. Let me guess,' Matthew said. 'Ursula Johnson's daughters?'

'The same.' He gave a half-hearted raise of his hand in response to Vanessa's frantic wave.

'And no sign of the other girl?'

Lewis screwed his eyes up and peered into the distance. 'Not so far,' he said.

'There are a few fit young ladies out there,' James observed, as he came to stand behind them. 'What is it about girls in jodhpurs, carrying whips, eh?'

'Pervert,' Lucy muttered. She tapped Lewis on the shoulder. 'I've got a message from Miles. Apparently, the weather's looking bad for tomorrow, so he'd like to complete the outdoor shots today.'

'You're kidding,' Lewis choked. 'We haven't got him a rider yet. And by the looks of things, this competition could go on all afternoon.'

'Well, you've got plenty to choose from,' she said, waving a well-manicured hand at the arena. 'Any one of them would do. All Miles needs is someone to hold the horse for Simon.'

'Yes, I know,' Lewis said. He glanced back at her, agitated. 'I know.'

Lucy pouted. 'Where is Simon, anyway?'

'Still shooting, I think. He is, isn't he, James?'

'What? Oh, Simon, yeah, think so.' He returned his gaze to the bevy of lovelies wandering the course in front of him. 'This is going to be difficult, Lewis. Very difficult.'

It would be, if the right girl didn't show up. Lewis glanced anxiously at his watch, and then back into the Grand Ring, where the compere was making an announcement.

'Ladies and Gentlemen, we welcome you to the Grand Ring, where we shall shortly be starting the Simon De Silva show jumping stakes. For those of you who don't know – and I suspect most of you do -' (A titter went round the crowd), 'filming is taking place during the competition. I have been asked by the organisers to make several requests...'

'Don't stare at the cameras,' Matthew chuckled, glancing at Lewis. 'They all will, you know. It's a risky business shooting at a live event.'

'Cynic,' he muttered.

'...And please remember to switch off all mobile phones during the competition. We also request that you do not use flash photography, though the taking of photographs is, of course permitted.'

'Unless, of course, its photos of the film crew.' James nudged him gently and pointed at Lucy, who was applying her lipstick with the utmost of care. 'Guess there was no room in the make-up trailer,' he whispered.

Lucy glared at him as she clicked shut her mirrored compact, and slipped it into her handbag. 'I'm going to take my place in the audience,' she said primly. 'Anyone coming?'

'Why not?' Matthew said agreeably. 'Lewis?'

'No.' He shook his head. 'I need to speak to Miles.'

'He's not in a good mood,' Lucy said.

He wasn't the only one. Tempers on set were becoming distinctly frayed.

Problems with the sound recording meant that Simon de Silva had been required to do the scene outside the first aid post several times.

He was, he said, getting rather fed up of sprinting over the same piece of grass.

'It's not my fault the bloody announcer keeps chipping in with some new instruction for the crowd,' snapped the boom operator. 'This thing pretty sensitive you know. It picks up everything.'

'Yes, well I'm not Linford Christie,' Simon said. 'There's only so many takes I can do, before I start to look knackered.'

'Okay, okay, you can have a break,' Miles said. 'Get Jason and we'll shoot his scene. Lewis,' he said, spotting him hovering in the background. He waved him forwards. 'Rain's forecast for tomorrow.'

' Lucy told me,' he said. 'Is that going to cause problems?'

Miles shrugged. 'I'd like to get finished today, if at all possible. How long will it take to find me a girl, or shall I just use one of the extras?'

'The competition's starting now,' he said. 'We can't go back on our word, Miles. It would look bad for the company.'

The director shook his head. 'Not my problem, Lewis. You know what they say about time being money. I take it you've found us a suitable horse?'

'Yes.' Lewis lied through his teeth. A suitable horse. What was that? Simon had been taking lessons, but he was still only a novice rider. The horses he had seen so far looked pretty spirited and highly-strung for his liking. What they needed was a magnificent looking beast with a laid-back temperament.

'Simon?' he called, waving him over.

'Yes?'

'Be honest with me,' he said. 'Do you think you can manage the riding scene? I mean, honestly?'

'No problem,' he said, grinning. 'Whether I survive it is another matter entirely.'

'I'm not joking,' Lewis muttered.

'Neither am I.'

'Christ.' He glanced around the showground. Where could he find a placid animal at this late stage in the day? 'Come with me,' he said, catching hold of his sleeve. 'And bring some of your minders.'

'Where are we going?'

'To find you a bloody horse,' he said. 'Preferably one that's not likely to kill you.'

In the warm up ring several of the competitors were testing their paces over the practice jumps. Caroline was having problems with Jasper, not least because he was nervous. The crowds, tannoys and unaccustomed noises were unsettling him. He was used to shows, but not one on this scale. The aerial display by a paragliding club did not help either. Brightly coloured silk canopies floating down from all parts of the sky was enough to unsettle the calmest of horses, and Jasper was not a calm horse.

A child's scarlet helium filled balloon sailed over the practice ring. A moment later came the hysterical wailing of the balloon's small owner. Jasper shied into another horse, which promptly lashed out with its hind legs, and caught Caroline's left thigh a hefty blow.

Ursula winced as she watched. 'Are you all right, darling?' she called.

Her daughter's face had gone rather pale. 'Can you still ride?'

Caroline managed a weak nod.

'Can't you keep that horse under control?' shouted a loutish youth in a dirty denim jacket and a pair of baggy combat trousers. 'See her, she's useless,' he added, sniggering at his mates.

'Why don't you shut up,' Ursula said, rounding on the unfortunate heckler with a furious glare. 'Or perhaps you think you could do better? Ever ridden a horse, sonny?' She peered down at him like a predatory hawk.

'Uh, no,' the youth said, smirking at his friends.

'Want to give it a try?'

'Uh...'

Ursula's hand descended on his shoulder in a grip of pure steel. 'Caroline. Bring Jasper over here. I've got a young man here who thinks he can do better than you. Now then,' she said, smiling thinly. 'Let's see how you do on him.'

'Gerroff!' the youth said, twisting away from her. Jasper was foaming at the mouth and showing the whites of his eye. 'I'm not getting on that.'

'Thought not.' Ursula said, straightening up with a satisfied smile.

'Bloody animal's mad,' he muttered.

'Hmm, and do the words yellow, and chicken, spring to mind?'

The guffaw from the crowd of teenage boys drowned out the youth's sullen response.

Smugly satisfied, Ursula turned her attention back to her daughters. Surprisingly, Vanessa seemed to be managing rather well. Minstrel had the most delightful of paces, and when she popped him over a couple of jumps, he made it look so effortless and easy.

'Oh well done, darling,' she said.

Vanessa beamed. For the first time ever, she felt she had a chance of winning. The horse was a natural, with a fearless, bold jump and a lightning turn of speed. He far outclassed any of the other horses. She trotted him serenely around the collecting ring, her head held high. This was her turn to shine, her turn to show everyone what she was made of.

'Nice horse,' Simon said, as they stopped to watch the proceedings from a safe vantage point outside the arena.

'Shame about the rider,' Lewis muttered. 'Come on, and keep those dark glasses on,' he added crisply. 'I don't want anyone recognising you.'

In the swarming throng of people, it was easy to remain anonymous. The crowds were jostling to secure their seats around the Grand Ring. No one paid much attention to the group of men making their way to the area reserved for horseboxes and trailers. Everyone else appeared to be going in the opposite direction.

'She's got to be here,' Lewis said, scanning the crowds.

'Who?' Simon said, munching on a tasty snack from the hog roast stall. 'This is really good,' he said. 'Better than the stuff they dish up in that catering van. Hey Marcus, get me another of these, will you. Yeah, with apple sauce, and crackling if they've got it.'

'There!' Lewis announced triumphantly, stopping dead in his tracks. Simon and two of the minders trundled into him.

'What?'

'Where?'

'Over there,' he said, pointing to a maroon and rather tatty looking horsebox which had a large bay horse tethered alongside it. The girl was standing by the horse's head, fastening the bridle. Her long blonde hair had been fastened into a shining plait which hung down the back of her navy-blue show jacket, and she was wearing cream coloured breeches and black, polished knee length boots.

'That, my friends,' he announced, grinning profusely, 'is Gabriella Johnson, and if I'm not mistaken Simon,' he added slapping him heartily on the shoulder. 'She is going to be the answer to all your prayers.'

Chapter Fifteen

'You were cutting it a bit fine, weren't you, Thomas?' Heather Hutchins said, as she sorted through her things for a spare pair of riding gloves.

'Aye well, I did my best,' the small Irishman said, twirling the car keys around his finger, and winking mischievously at her. 'She's here, isn't she?'

'Yes, thank God.' Heather picked up the leather gloves and a smart new whip she had bought especially for the show. 'Ella, have you got a hat?'

'It's here,' Thomas said, opening the boot of the sporty blue car he had borrowed for the afternoon. 'Hat, stock, tie pin, the lot.'

Ella ducked under Majesty's head, and smiled at her co conspirators. 'Honestly, you pair,' she sighed. 'You'll get me shot.'

'Rubbish,' Heather said. 'You deserve to ride, and that's all there is to it.'

Ella smiled as she pulled her hat on, and tightened the strap. 'You're sure you don't mind?'

'Of course not. Besides,' Heather said, plucking at a strand of her light brown hair. 'This is hardly classed as blonde, is it? I would have probably been disqualified. No, you ride, Ella,' she insisted. 'Only make sure you win. I've already walked the course,' she added, 'and it's not bad at all. It's a tight turn between seven and eight, but Majesty should cope with that. Clear the final double and you're home and dry.'

'What's the water jump like?'

'Okay. A slight rise to the brush beforehand, but other than that, it doesn't look a problem. Not for him, anyway.'

Ella checked the girth, and adjusted the stirrups.

'God knows what I'm going to say to Vanessa and Caroline,' she said, as she swung up into the saddle.

'How about "hello",' Thomas suggested.

'Oh, just ignore them,' Heather said. 'It doesn't matter what they think. If you want to take part in the competition, there's no earthly reason why you shouldn't.'

'Only duty, loyalty and management of the stable yard....'

Thomas frowned. 'They'd not get anyone more loyal than you, Ella. But seeing as how you mentioned it, I'd better get back to Hollyfield. Best of luck, lass,' he added. 'I'll be rooting for you.'

'Thanks,' she said checking the girth again. Now that she was here, she was looking forward to taking part. It had been a while since she had competed, but the familiar rush of excitement and anticipation was there, as if it had been only yesterday.

She rubbed Majesty's head and stroked his neck. 'We can do it, boy,' she murmured. 'We can show them.'

'Ready?' Heather said.

Ella sucked in a deep breath, and nodded.

'I'll leg you up on the count of three. One, two...Oh my God!'

Ella's foot was poised in the stirrup, her knee bent ready to spring up on the third count. 'What's wrong?' she said, as Heather promptly dropped her leg and straightened up. 'Heather? What is it? Is something wrong with Majesty?'

'I don't believe it.'

'What?'

'It's him,' she blurted, tugging at Ella's sleeve. 'It's Simon De Silva.'

'Oh, so what,' she said, plainly irritated. 'He's bound to be here, isn't he? I mean he's being filmed at the show. Now come on and give me a leg up.'

'No, I mean, he's here,' Heather said, her cheeks turning a ripe shade of cherry red. 'He's right here. He's behind you,' she hissed.

'Miss Johnson? Miss Gabriella Johnson?'

Ella glanced round in surprise. 'Yes?' she said, gazing blankly at the group of men who were assembling beside her. Two of them were dressed in dark suits and black jumpers. They looked like security men or bouncers. The other two were more casually dressed in jeans and shirts. One of them looked vaguely familiar. Oh my God! She yanked her foot out of the stirrup, and spun round. It was him, the man she had seen peering into the window of Ludlow's Antique Emporium. Blimey. Her cheeks flushed scarlet. What was he doing here?

'Hi,' he said, stepping forwards. 'We haven't met, but I'm Lewis Trevelyan from Blackwater Films.'

Ella's eyes widened in surprise. Her mouth had formed into a silent 'oh.'

'And this is Simon De Silva, the star of our latest production.'

'Hello there.'

'Um...hello,' Ella said, finding her hand grasped and shaken warmly by the dark-haired young man in front of her. So, this was the infamous film star that all her friends were swooning over, was it? *The* Simon De Silva. Well, he was certainly good-looking – quite dishy, in fact - but not half as interesting to her as this other man was, this Lewis Trevelyan. He had a sort of rugged attractiveness about him that was making her feel quite giddy. The fact that he was perusing her with such obvious interest wasn't helping matters either. She detected a determined, but mildly amused glint in his eyes.

She glanced sideways at Heather, who gave a puzzled shrug of her shoulders. She seemed as perplexed by all this as she was.

'You're a very elusive woman, Miss Johnson,' he said.

'I am?'

'I'll say.' He grinned, and Ella felt her heart give an unexpected little thud against her ribcage. 'I've been trying to track you down for days.'

'You have?' she said.

'Oh yes.' He nodded grimly. (If she only but knew.) 'The

thing is,' he said. 'You're exactly the sort of person we need for this film.'

'That's what I said,' Heather crowed gleefully. 'She wasn't going to come, you know. We practically had to make her. Thomas and I planned it all between us.'

Ella blushed, and wished Heather would shut up. She wanted to hear what else this man had to say.

'She's a top-class rider, you know. Her father was...'

'Robert Johnson. Yes, I know,' Lewis said. He stuck his hands in the pockets of his jacket, and gave a slight shrug. 'The thing is,' he said. 'I've got a bit of a problem. It's not about the competition,' he added, glancing sideways up at Ella. (God, she was gorgeous.) 'Although, I suppose, in a way it is. To put it bluntly, I've got about ten minutes to find a horse for Simon to ride that won't ditch him in the nearest hedge the moment he digs his heels in. Not only that, but I need someone to help him while we're filming.' He smiled ruefully down at her. 'I was kind of hoping that person would be you.'

'Me?' Ella croaked. She couldn't believe it. Why would he want her, when she had never met him, let alone spoken to him, before?

'Oh, go on, Ella. You can do it,' Heather was saying cheerfully. She was looking as star struck as Kate had done, when she had first heard about the proposed filming at Hollyfield. 'Majesty's a real sweetie,' she said, smiling up at Simon. 'He'll do anything you want him to do.'

'He doesn't kick or buck, then?' Simon said, strolling round to the front of the horse and eyeing him up, man to beast. Majesty's ears pricked forwards and he blew down his nostrils at him. Simon laughed, and rubbed the horse's velvety nose with the palm of his hand.

'No, no, he's very laid back. But he can jump,' she added, glancing back at Lewis. 'He'd win this competition by a mile.'

'That's a pity,' Lewis said.

'Why?' Ella looked at him, puzzled.

'Because I doubt if he'll be able to take part. Not if you agree to help us,' he said. 'There won't be time.'

Not take part? Ella glanced at Heather. But surely that was the whole point of them coming here.

'It's a lot to ask, I know,' Lewis said. 'And I wouldn't ask, if I wasn't desperate.' He sighed, and shook his head. This was all going wrong. He was saying all the wrong things. He had been so overwhelmed with actually finding her, that for some insane reason, he had naturally assumed she would leap at the chance.

Ella ran up Majesty's stirrups, and patted him on the neck. Her thoughts were racing. 'Let me get this straight,' she said, swinging back to face Lewis. 'You want me to help Simon ride this horse now, this instant?'

'Hmm. That's about the size of it,' Lewis said.

'And we're going to be filmed doing it?'

'I guess so.'

'And the winner of the show-jumping competition, what will she get?' she said. 'I mean, I thought that was the prize, a part in the film with Simon De Silva.'

'Ah, but we didn't say what part,' he said. 'I'm sure we'll be able to think of something for her.'

'Well, it's all very strange,' Ella said, taking off her hat, and shaking her blonde hair free. 'If all you had to do was ask me, why are you bothering to run the competition?'

'Why?' Lewis choked. 'Because…Because…oh never mind. It'll take too long to explain. You'll do it, right?'

'Yes, okay,' she said. Though goodness knows why. She'd never hear the end of it from Vanessa and Caroline. This was their dream come true and she was going to be part of it. 'What do you want me to do?'

Simon De Silva was not a natural horseman. That much was apparent the moment he sat on Majesty. His legs stuck out in front of him, and he was slouched back in the saddle as if he were sitting in an armchair. The reins dangled loosely between his clenched fists.

'Like this?' he said, straightening his back.

'Um, not quite,' Ella said, walking round to inspect his position. 'Try pulling your legs back a bit, and gathering up the reins. 'That's better,' she said. It couldn't get much worse.

'Well?' Lewis said.

Ella grimaced.

'That bad, huh?' He frowned. 'Simon, can't you try and look as if you know what you're doing?'

'You want me to act the part?'

'It might help,' he said.

'Okay.' Ella caught hold of the reins. 'Let's try him at walk.' She clicked her tongue and Majesty sprang forwards. Simon swayed backwards like a rag doll.

'Steady on,' he muttered, clutching at the horse's mane. 'Caught me a bit off balance there.'

'This is hopeless,' Lewis groaned.

'No wait, I'm getting the hang of it,' Simon said. 'It's all about control. I can do this, Lewis.'

'Yes, but we haven't got all week,' he said. 'Miles wants you on set this afternoon.' He glanced hopefully at Ella. 'Got any suggestions?'

'I'm thinking,' she said, pursing her lips. Majesty wasn't the problem. It was Simon's lack of coordination that was causing him to lose his balance. If he could sit securely in his seat, he would be fine. What he needed was something to hold on to. Or someone.

'This scene you're shooting,' she said. 'I don't suppose it could be changed, could it?'

'I suspect it's going to be cut altogether,' Lewis muttered.

'No way.' Simon jerked on the reins, and Majesty stopped in mid stride, almost catapulting him over the horse's head. 'Whoops!'

'My point exactly.' Lewis said, scratching behind his ear.

The two burly minders were standing leaning against the horsebox watching the proceedings with detached interest and trying not to smile. Every so often, they would walk around, keeping an eye on anyone venturing too close. Heather was sitting on the grass, twirling her whip between her fingers, and enjoying every minute of the performance.

'I've got a suggestion,' Ella said. 'Why can't I ride with him?'

'How?' Lewis said. He was getting rather weary of all this. Simon De Silva deserved to be shot. He had taken the part knowing what the script entailed. No actor in their right mind should agree to do an action scene, if they weren't up to the job. And Simon's refusal to let stuntmen take over was only hampering things for everyone.

'He can sit behind me,' Ella explained. 'I'll be the one in control, and all he has to do is hold on.'

'Can you do that?' Lewis said, detecting a small glimmer of hope in her idea.

'I don't see why not,' she said. 'Let's try it and see.'

This time things went much more smoothly. Apart from an undignified scramble to get on, Simon managed to sit rather well behind her, and when she urged Majesty into a loping canter, the two of them moved in unison together.

Ella trotted Majesty in a half circle, and brought him back to the horsebox.

'Well?' she said.

Lewis was thinking. His face was set in an expression that was both stern and distant. This might just work. It would mean re-writing part of the script, but changes like this were made all the time. No one liked them, but sometimes they were essential to the smooth running of a film. If Simon ran from the first aid post and found Ella riding the nearest horse, all they would have to do is script him leaping up behind her, leaping being the operative word. They'd have to have a hidden ramp or something, judging by his ungainly scramble a moment ago. But yes, yes it might just work.

'Brilliant!' he said.

'Really?' Ella glanced over her shoulder at Simon, who was still hanging onto her waist as if he had been welded there. 'Well done,' she said.

'Thanks,' he replied. 'Although I'd like to make a small

suggestion. Could I have a bit more padding, please?' He winced, and a pained expression flitted across his face. 'This saddle's a bit hard.'

'Good,' Lewis said, somewhat unsympathetically. 'Because it serves you bloody well right.' He winked at Ella. 'And you, Miss Johnson, are a genius.'

The unaccustomed praise, combined with the way he was smiling up at her, was making Ella feel quite bashful. 'Thanks,' she said. She turned to help Simon dismount, which he did with a lot more style and finesse than he did when mounting. 'Are you okay?' she said.

'Hmm.' He nodded, but his drawn face indicated precisely the opposite. 'I'll live.'

'That's what we like to hear,' Lewis said, thumping him heartily on the back. 'Well done, Simon. Now then, about this change of plan...'

Ella watched as the two of them strolled across the grass, heads bent in earnest discussion. Her heart was thumping erratically and she was feeling all hot and flustered.

'Wow!' Heather said, coming forward to hold Majesty's reins. 'You were great. I can't believe you rode with Simon De Silva,' she sighed. 'Isn't he gorgeous?'

'Who? Oh Simon? Yes, I suppose so.' She swung her leg over the back of the saddle, and jumped down. 'I rather like the other bloke myself,' she added. 'That Lewis Trevelyan.'

Heather turned and squinted over at the two men. 'To be honest, I hadn't really noticed him,' she said. 'But yes, I can see what you mean. He looks a bit film starrish, doesn't he?'

'He's the producer,' Ella said. 'The one who's been coming up to Hollyfield all this time. I'm not surprised Vanessa and Caroline got in such a dither about seeing him.' She slid up the stirrups and patted Majesty on the neck. 'Wonder if he's married?' she said.

Heather raised an eyebrow at her and smiled. 'Want me to find out?'

'No.' Ella gaped at her aghast. 'No.' Her voice lowered. 'I was just wondering, that's all.'

Lewis was watching her as he spoke to Simon. No wonder Ursula had been so keen to keep her out of the way. She was stunning. The way she moved, the way she talked, in fact, everything about her, was beautiful. In comparison to her stepsisters, she had it all, looks, talent, the lot. He had a good feeling about this.

'Right then, folks,' he said. 'If we could make our way over to the Grand Ring, I think it's time we told Miles about the change of scene.'

The final call for competitors in the Simon De Silva show-jumping stakes was being made over the loudspeakers.

Lewis caught Ella by the arm and gently pulled her to one side. 'You're sure about this?' he said. 'I mean, I know I've put you on the spot, but I'll understand if you want to change your mind?'

His touch on her arm was like an electric shock against her skin. She could smell the faint scent of his aftershave as he bowed his head close to hers. For this man, she thought dazedly, she would do anything.

'No, its fine,' she said. 'I haven't competed for ages, anyway.'

'Why not?' he asked. His dark eyes glittered warmly. 'I'm sure you'd be good at it.'

'I am. Or at least, I was. Time, I suppose,' she explained. 'Work, the horses, running the business.'

'Isn't that Ursula's job?'

Ella looked up at him. Her voice was starting to waver. 'She makes it hers,' she said. 'But technically, it's mine. Ursula's not that good with horses,' she explained. 'But she is good at dealing with people.'

'I can't say I'd noticed,' Lewis responded, with a knowing smile.

Ella felt her heart melt. It was almost as if he knew what was going on over at Hollyfield. Maybe he was more astute than he looked.

'Come on, we'd best get moving,' he said. 'Simon, do you

want to ride over?'

The star of the film gave an abrupt and firm shake of his head. 'Think I'll give it a miss, if it's all the same to you.'

'Saving your strength for the real thing, huh?'

Simon pulled a face. 'Whatever.'

Ella looped the reins over Majesty's head and started to lead him, with Heather following on behind, flanked by Simon and the two bouncers. Lewis walked beside her, his long legs striding to keep up with the horse's steady plod.

'Rider number 607, that's Caroline Johnson riding Jasper, is disqualified,' came the announcement over the tannoy. 'Sixteen faults and a refusal. The next rider is number 382, Maxine Wallace on Pepperpot...'

'Oh, that's a shame,' Ella said, pausing to listen. 'Caroline's out. I wonder what went wrong.'

'Putting her on a horse in the first place, I suspect,' Lewis said. 'Well,' he added, catching sight of Ella's surprised stare. 'Be honest, she's not the most able of horsewomen.'

'Ursula thinks she is,' Heather said, hurrying to catch up with them.

Lewis smiled knowingly. 'There's the problem.'

'Have you got children, Mr Trevelyan?' she added airily.

Ella's gaped at Heather. Crikey, she was worse than Kate when it came to getting to the point of the matter.

'None that I know of,' he assured her. 'I'm not married.'

Heather gave Ella a triumphant "there you are" look, before lagging behind again in order to continue her little chat with Simon.

'You must work long hours,' Ella said. Then wished she hadn't, as it sounded like she was making excuses for him not being married.

'So must you,' he said, an amused smile crinkling the corner of his eyes. 'All that mucking out and rising at dawn to feed the horses must put a damper on your social life.'

What social life, she felt tempted to say? But she didn't. She merely smiled, and nodded. 'I don't have many late nights,' she said.

'I'm not surprised.'

They had reached the area that had been cordoned off for the film crew and their associates. Huge catering trucks stood side by side with caravans and trailers, and portable loos.

'Won't be a moment,' Lewis said, flashing his pass to one of the security men stationed at the entrance. 'I need to set things up with the team. Kenny will get you a cold drink while you're waiting, won't you Ken?' He pointed over to one of the trailers. 'You can tether the horse over there, if you like.'

'It's okay. I'll hold him,' Ella said.

'Sure?'

'I'm sure,' she said. The last thing she wanted was Majesty being startled by all the unusual activity going on around him, and taking off in fright with a trailer attached to his lead rope.

She loosened her hold on the reins, and Majesty – ever one to seize an opportunity - lowered his head and began to munch quite happily on the flattened area of grass around them.

Ella rubbed her hand on his withers. 'He's being very calm about all this, isn't he?' she said. The brightly coloured trucks or the noise from the generators would have unsettled most other horses.

'That's the beauty of keeping him on a farm,' Heather said, standing on tiptoe in an attempt to peer over the high security fencing. 'Once he'd seen his first combine harvester and realised it wasn't going to hurt him, everything else became acceptable to him – tractors, trailers, you name it – he doesn't bat an eyelid.'

'What about the lights?' Ella said. 'Do you think he'll be all right with them?'

Heather peered at the huge floodlights, set up on scaffolding outside the arena. 'Yes, he'll be fine.' She nudged Ella's arm. 'What about you, though? Are you all right about it?'

'What?'

'Riding with Simon, of course. Lucky cow,' she added.

'That's going to be the easy part,' Ella said. 'It's what happens next, that worries me.'

'What do you mean? You're not still concerned about Ursula, are you?'

'A bit.' Ella murmured, stroking Majesty's neck.

'For God's sake, why? Heather spluttered. 'She had no right to stop you coming here.'

'Well, she didn't exactly stop me.'

'Rubbish. She made damn well sure you couldn't come. You know she did.' Heather shook her head. 'All that talk about leaving you in charge. It was a ploy to keep you away. Honestly, that women,' she seethed. 'She makes my blood boil. She's ruining the business for you and everyone else that uses the stables. She's on another planet, Ella. It's high time you opened your eyes and saw what she was doing.'

'I know,' Ella sighed. She straightened up and brushed a strand of hair out of her eyes. 'I do know,' she added quietly. 'I guess it was just easier to pretend not to.'

'Ladies?'

One of the technicians peered his head round the high security fence and waved over at them. 'Lewis says can you come through, now.'

'This is it!' Heather said, scrambling to her feet.

Ella gave her a weak smile. 'I can't help wondering what I'm doing here.'

'Having your moment of fame,' Heather said, looping the reins over Majesty's head, and handing them over to her. 'You go for it, girl.'

The scene behind the fence was one of frantic activity. Technicians were busy assembling a special track to mount the camera on. It was to run alongside the ramp of the horse trailer, where Simon De Silva would vault onto Majesty. A stand-in actor was playing the part as the various lights and cameras were erected, using a pile of hay-bales for the horse.

Simon, meanwhile, was sitting by one of the caravans, having his makeup hastily re-applied, a bloody gash on his forehead, and smudges of dirt on his brow.

'Ella?' He beckoned her over. She handed the horse's reins to

Heather, and made her way across the crowded set towards him.

'You might need a touch of this,' he said.

'What, make-up?'

He nodded. 'What do you think, Sarah? Does she need a bit of colour?'

The woman, who was dabbing blood spots onto the front of his shirt, glanced up at her and smiled. 'She'll look like a ghost if she doesn't.'

'Make-up it is, then.' He grinned, and Ella suddenly saw why everyone was so besotted with him. He had the most gorgeous smile.

'Ella!' Lewis Trevelyan came striding towards her holding a clipboard and a sheet of paper in one hand.

(Whereas he, she thought shyly, was in a different league altogether.)

'I've got one of the scriptwriters doing a quick rehash of that scene. Should take about thirty or forty minutes. Then we'll be ready to rehearse the shot. Miles isn't happy about it,' he added. 'But he realises it's our only option if we want to finish filming today.'

'Thirty minutes?' she said.

'Is that a problem?'

His eyes glanced sideways at her, and Ella felt her stomach quiver under their thoughtful stare. Why was he having such an effect on her? She wasn't a silly star struck teenager. And yet she felt weak just being near him.

'Um...no,' she said. 'Well, not really. I mean...'

'What?' His thoughtful gaze continued. Ella thought she was going to faint, or keel over, or do something equally stupid.

'It's Majesty,' she blurted. 'He needs to be kept moving.' She sucked in a deep breath. This was ridiculous. She had never felt like this before. 'I need to keep him warmed up.'

'Ah, right,' he said. He smiled, almost knowingly, and Ella felt a surge of heat flood through her veins.

'I'll take him to the practice arena. Do a few circuits with him,' she said, in as matter-of-fact a tone as she could muster.

'We'll come back in, say,' she looked at her watch, 'twenty-five minutes?'

Lewis nodded. But as she turned to walk away his hand on her arm stopped her in mid-stride. Ella felt her heart leap to her throat as she glanced back at him.

'I really appreciate what you're doing for us, Miss Johnson,' he said.

She blushed. 'It's nothing.'

'Oh, it's far from that,' he said softly.

His gaze lingered on her as she made her way back to the horse. 'Far from that.'

'Lewis!'

Distracted, he glanced round. Mathew was sauntering towards him munching a hot Suffolk sausage in a home baked bun, (courtesy of one of the farmer's stalls in the Food Hall.) 'I gather you've found your rider,' he said.

'Better than that,' Lewis said. He pointed to where Ella was swinging up into the saddle. 'That's her,' he added, jabbing him good-humouredly in the ribs. 'And you owe me fifty quid. She's agreed to be filmed with Simon.'

'When?'

'In about thirty minutes.'

'You're kidding!' Mathew gulped back the last mouthful of his sausage. 'Have you forgotten about the competition? Lewis,' he groaned. 'This is not going to look good. There's still a dozen or so riders to go. You can't pick a winner before the event finishes.'

'Who can't?'

'Lewis. We agreed...'

'I know what we agreed, Matthew, but Miles won't wait,' he said. 'You heard what he said to Lucy. He wants to finish the shoot today. I've found him the perfect girl, and the perfect horse.'

'Right, but what happens to the winner of the competition?'

'She'll get a part,' he said. 'Any part. Just not this one, okay?'

214

Matthew grimaced. 'The public won't like it.'

'The public won't know.' Lewis lowered his voice. 'They won't, Matt. There's no reason why they should. As long as we stick to our promise made in the publicity flyers that the winner gets to appear in the latest Simon De Silva movie, we're home and dry.'

'And you'll honour that,' Matthew said, jerking his head in the direction of the Grand Ring, where Vanessa Johnson was about to make her entrance on the striking grey Arab, 'no matter who wins?'

'Of course,' Lewis said. Though whether the shot got past the cutting room floor was neither here nor there.

Matthew thought about it for a moment, his brows furrowed, and then he reached inside his jacket pocket for his wallet. 'Suppose I'd better pay up, then,' he said.

'Yes,' Lewis said, holding out his hand. 'I suppose you had.'

Chapter Sixteen

Ursula Johnson was almost beside herself with excitement as she watched Vanessa trot into the arena on Minstrel. After the disappointing performance from Caroline, she was pinning all her hopes on her other daughter.

She crossed both sets of fingers, and everything else she could think of. A silent prayer wouldn't go amiss either, she thought.

'And now we have Miss Vanessa Johnson riding Minstrel,' came the announcement over the tannoy. Ursula felt a surge of pride.

'Very nice,' observed the immaculately dressed woman in the scarlet dress and matching hat sitting alongside her.

'That's my daughter,' Ursula blurted. She couldn't help herself. Her cheeks felt as if they would burst under the pressure of her beaming grin. Vanessa had popped over the first jump as if it had been a pole on the ground. Minstrel was flying round, as sure footed as they come.

'Quality blood line,' said an elderly gentleman in a bowler hat a little further along the rail. 'You can tell that with Arab's. Pure class.'

The crowd gasped as Minstrel nudged the top pole in the double, but it stayed put. An audible sigh echoed round the arena.

Ursula was on her feet and clutching at the white railings as horse and rider headed for the water. 'Come on, come on,' she hissed, her knuckles pinched white under her skin.

Minstrel cleared it with ease, and Ursula let out a sigh. The horse was magnificent. That's where they'd been going wrong all these years. She'd been putting the girls on sub-standard animals, ones that had no hope of a clear round. Why hadn't she realised it before now? It was all Stella Watkins fault. Using the horse for dressage when it clearly excelled at show jumping. She would be having words with her.

Vanessa had reached the final turn and was heading for the last jump. Ursula felt her heart thumping madly against her chest. 'Please do it,' she prayed. 'Please, please do it.'

The roar of applause from the crowd as Vanessa sailed over the jump and galloped for the finish had everyone out of his or her seats.

'Oh my God!' Ursula shrieked, punching the sky with her fist. 'She's done it. She's done it!'

The woman in the red dress gave her a disdainful stare. Such unsightly shows of exuberance were not the done thing in the chairman's stand.

Ursula couldn't care less. 'Wasn't she brilliant?' she enthused. 'My goodness, that girl's got talent. It's in the genes, you know. Her stepfather was a champion show-jumper.'

'Then it's hardly in her genes,' the woman retorted crisply.

Deflated, Ursula gave her a withering glare, before snatching up her bag, and pushing her way through the rows of interested spectators. 'Excuse me…excuse me.' She shoved her way out of the seating area, and made towards the arena's main exit.

The commentator was still talking as she left. 'That's a clear round for Vanessa Johnson riding Minstrel. We now have three riders in the jump-off. Let's see if we can make it four. Our next competitor is number 217 – that's Hilary Frampton on Pegasus…'

Ursula had reached the collecting ring, where Vanessa was draping a sweat rug over the steaming and snorting Minstrel.

'Mother!' Vanessa practically threw herself into Ursula's outstretched arms. Her face was scarlet from her exertions. Beads of sweat trickled down her neck and into the stock of her shirt. 'We did it!' she shrieked. Her voice was on the verge of hysteria. 'We did it! We did it!' She slapped Minstrel heartily on the side of the neck. 'Did you see him jump? Mother, he was magnificent. Oh my God,' she panted breathlessly. 'I don't believe it. Mother, we're in the final.'

'Well done, darling,' Ursula said.

'Yes, well done,' muttered Caroline, somewhat begrudgingly, as she toyed with Minstrel's reins. Even she had to admit that her sister had done better than anyone expected her to do. The chances were that she could now win this competition. And if that were the case, she had better keep on the good side of her.

'Could you sponge him down for me?' Vanessa said sweetly.

'Yes, of course.' Caroline said. She'd do anything, if it gave her the chance to meet Simon De Silva. Of course, if she'd been given a better horse to ride herself, instead of that stupid Jasper, she might have done equally as well. It wasn't fair the way Vanessa had got the best horse. She brooded sulkily as she filled a bucket of water and carried it back to the still sweating Minstrel.

'Who's riding now?' Vanessa asked, as she shook her hair free from the sticky confines of her hat, and loosened the buttons on her neat fitting show jacket.

'Jessie Mason,' Ursula said, peering through the gap in the arena fence. 'But she's got four faults already. Whoops, that's another four. One hoof in the water.'

'And there's about six riders left to compete.' Vanessa took a long swig from a bottle of chilled water, and sprinkled some of it on her hands and sweaty brow.

'Yes, but so far you've got the fastest horse,' Ursula assured her. 'The others aren't a patch on Minstrel when it comes to speedy turns.'

'Oh my God!' Vanessa thumped herself down on a straw bale, and wiped her brow with the back of her hand. 'I could win this, Mother.'

'You could,' Ursula said, beaming. Her smiled faded slightly as she patted her on the shoulder. 'In fact, for the sake of the stables, I really think you must.'

Caroline smirked. 'No pressure there, then,' she observed dryly.

'Oh, do shut up,' Vanessa snapped. 'You're only jealous. But I'll show you. In fact, I'll show everyone.' She stood up and brushed the straw from her show breeches with the back of her hand. 'I'm going to win this competition,' she announced proudly. 'You see if I don't.'

A mobile camera unit was filming in the Grandstand as Ella rode Majesty into the collecting ring. Miles had wanted plenty of crowd scenes and background shots which would be cut into the main action. To this end, he had despatched small teams of cameramen and sound technicians to all areas of the Showground.

'Capture the atmosphere of the event,' he said, peering at a preview of some of the days' rushes through a small monitor. 'I want loads of close-ups. We're after tension here, the drama and excitement of the show jumping circuit. Good, yes, that's excellent.' He paused to examine a still of one of the riders falling at the water jump. 'Get me more like that, Adam,' he said, waving his hand at one of the crew. 'I can use those shots before we switch to the first-aid post. And talking of first-aid posts, how's Simon doing?'

'Still in make-up,' came the reply.

'How long before we shoot?'

'Fifteen, maybe twenty minutes.'

'Right. Jason? Can someone find me Jason?'

Ella was oblivious to the fact that she was being filmed as she trotted Majesty round the practice ring. She was more concerned about bumping into her stepmother, or one of her stepsisters.

'Oh, so what,' Heather said. 'It's none of their business what you do. You've as much right to be here as they have. More right, I'd say,' she added, under her breath, as she stood to one side and watched Ella pop Majesty over the jumps.

It seemed such a shame that she wasn't going to compete on him. He was obviously enjoying himself. The horse was a seasoned veteran of shows, since his previous owner, Janey Lake, had been a keen competitor. Pregnancy had lessened her enthusiasm for riding, and after the baby was born, she had decided to sell him. Janey's loss was her gain, Heather thought smugly. She had been right to buy Majesty when she did. The horse had a promising future ahead of him. His ears were pricked forwards, his eyes were intelligent, and his conformation and paces were quite superb.

'Heather!'

She turned to see Linda Bannister, one of the girls from the farm stables heading her way, carrying a grooming kit under one arm, and a plastic cup of something in the other. 'Thought that was you,' she said, coming to stand alongside her. 'I'm just taking a breather before the working hunter class. Debbie's keeping an eye on Millie for me.' She took a slurp of her hot drink. 'Yuck,' she said. 'No sugar.' She nodded her head in Majesty's direction. 'I thought you were riding him today.'

'That was the plan,' Heather said.

'But?' She placed her grooming box at her feet and turned expectantly to look at her.

'They changed the conditions of entry,' she said. 'So, I asked Ella to compete on him instead.'

'In the Simon De Silva stakes?'

Heather nodded. 'Well let's face it; she's the one with the blonde hair.'

'Oh yeah, I heard about that,' Linda said. 'It's for a part in some film, or something. I suppose that explains why Vanessa's dyed hers such a fetching shade of yellow. She did pretty well on Minstrel, though, didn't she?' she added.

'I don't know. Did she?'

Linda nodded as she stooped to retrieve her grooming kit. 'She got a clear round and she's through to the jump-off. Anyway, I'll catch you later, Heather. Got to do a quick brush up and polish on Millie.'

'Good luck,' Heather said. Clear round, hmm? She glanced at her watch, and then over at Majesty, being expertly ridden around the ring. Seemed a shame to let this opportunity go to waste. 'Ella?' she called. 'Ella, come here a minute.'

'Ladies and gentlemen, we have five riders through to the final jump-off, and two riders left to compete in this, the Simon De Silva show jumping stakes. Now, as you all now, the producer of Blackwater Films has agreed to let the winner feature in Simon's latest movie. So, let's give a rousing round of support for our next competitor, Miss Camellia Brown on Silver...'

'No!' Ella said. 'I can't, Heather. I don't have time.'

'You do,' Heather insisted. 'It'll only take a few minutes. Ten minutes at the most. You know you want to.'

'Yes, I know I want to,' Ella said, staring over at the gates leading to the entrance into the Grand Ring. It was what she wanted more than anything. It hadn't bothered her before, the lack of competitions. She hadn't had time to compete. But now that she was here – now that she could feel the atmosphere and the growing tension - she knew she desperately wanted to take part.

'Ten minutes,' Heather repeated.

Ella ran her hand down Majesty's neck. He was stamping his foot up and down, as if he too was eager to get going. 'It won't even take that long,' she said breathlessly. 'I can go straight in, ride the course, and come straight out again.'

'Course you can.'

She glanced back over her shoulder. The previous contender was heading for the last jump. There was no one else left to ride. If she was going to compete, she had to do it, and do it now.

'Right!' she said, her mind made up. 'What number am I?'

'249,' Heather said, frantically groping in her pockets for the label. 'And I've even got the pins. Lean over and I'll clip it on.' She waved over at one of the jump judges. 'Yoo-hoo!' she called. 'We're over here! Number 249 – Gabriella Johnson? Yes, she's just coming.

Go for it,' she added, hurriedly pinning the black and white label onto the back of Ella's show jacket.

'Wish me luck,' she said, gathering up the reins.

'You don't need it,' Heather said. 'But good luck anyway.'

The last rider, a chubby faced girl with pink cheeks and a flighty looking palomino pony, trotted out of the arena.

Ella gave her a polite nod as she passed. This was it, then. She took in a deep breath, and exhaled it slowly, before urging the horse forwards. 'Come on, Majesty,' she murmured. 'Let's show them what you're made of.'

The atmosphere around the Grand Ring was highly charged, as spectators crowded into the main Grandstand, or stood jostling by the railings, eager for front row positions. The fact that the film crew was in evidence no doubt added to the large number of people clamouring for places.

Ella trotted Majesty around the arena, and tried to get her bearings before the whistle signalled the start of her turn. The jumps were fairly evenly spread out, with two doubles, a triple spread and a few brush hedges. One of the turns would be tricky, but she could make up time in the run for the water.

'Steady boy,' she murmured, sensing Majesty's excitement. He had started to prance rather proudly with his tail held high and his ears pricked forwards in anticipation.

'Get this,' the cameraman muttered, as he peered through the lens. 'Miles is going to like this one. Jack, see if you can get the sound.'

'And our final competitor in this, the first round of the Simon De Silva show-jumping stakes, is Miss Gabriella Johnson, riding Majesty...'

'What! What!'

Ursula's deranged shriek drew more than a passing glare from the boom operator, who was trying to record the scene.

'There's got to be some mistake,' Ursula blurted, leaping to her feet and peering short-sightedly at the distant horse and rider, her quivering frame conveniently blocking out the view from Adam Spencer's lens.

She had returned to the spectators' stand in order to study the rest of the competition. As far as she could see, none of the other riders were a patch on Vanessa. Her daughter, she was sure, was going to walk it. So much so, that she was already deciding what she was going to wear at the film's premiere. (Something stylish and expensive, naturally). The announcement of the name, "Gabriella Johnson" over the loudspeaker threw her daydreams into total disarray.

'It can't be Ella!' she shrieked.

'Madam, please. If you don't mind.' The sound engineer pointed at the overhead microphone.

'Mind! I'll give you mind!' She gave him a withering glare as she tossed her handbag over one shoulder and stormed past him. 'Vanessa! Caroline!'

'This is hopeless,' Jack muttered.

'I guess that means we don't have sound,' Adam said.

'Oh, we do,' Jack sighed. 'But not the sort of background sound that Miles wants. We'll need to cut that bloody commentator out as well.'

'On the other hand,' Adam swivelled the camera round. 'This could be better.' He motioned to one of the other technicians positioned at the entrance to the arena. 'Let's keep recording, Jack. We could be on to something here.'

'It's not fair!' wailed Vanessa, her plump cheeks blotchy and tear-stained. 'Why did she have to show up? Mother, you promised!'

'I know, darling, I know.' Ursula was trying her best to be supportive, but had never been very good at dealing with tears and tantrums.

'She's cleared the double,' Caroline informed them smugly. 'And the water. In fact, I'd say she's doing rather well.'

This prompted another heart-rending sob from Vanessa that even had the sound engineer (who was furtively trying to record their conversation) feeling sorry for her.

'She's trying to steal my glory. I know she is.'

'Hush darling,' Ursula soothed. 'You've still got the jump-off, and we don't know if she's going to get through to that, yet.'

'Oh yes she is,' Caroline announced, who had been watching the proceedings with glee. She turned round to face them with a sickly sweet smile on her face. 'She's got a clear round. Ella's going to be in the final.'

'Brilliant! Absolutely brilliant!' Heather jumped over the barriers and ran to catch hold of Majesty's reins as Ella came trotting out of the ring.

'Wasn't he just,' Ella said, patting his neck. Her face glowed with delight. 'You've got a real star here, Heather. He wasn't fazed by anything.'

'It was you, I meant,' Heather chuckled. 'I knew he could do it.'

'Cheek!' Ella said as she swung her leg over the saddle and jumped down. Still, she had every right to be pleased with her performance. If someone had told her that morning, that she would be riding a Champion horse in the Grand ring in front of thousands of spectators, she would have thought they were off their heads. It was years since she had done any competitive jumping, and yet it had felt so right and so natural. She had moulded herself to the horse and they had formed a true partnership, one of total trust and belief. It was quite exhilarating.

She rubbed Majesty's damp brow and smiled as he nuzzled her cheek. 'How long do you think we've got before the jump-off?' she said.

Heather shrugged. 'I don't think it'll be very long. They're adjusting some of the poles now. My guess is that they'll want to get it over with as soon as possible.'

Ella glanced at her watch. But would it be soon enough? She'd promised the film crew she would be back on set in – Crikey! Five minutes. She would hardly have time to ride over there in that time, let alone compete in the final beforehand.

Heather saw her worried look, and caught hold of her arm. 'You can't back out now,' she said.

'I can't do anything else,' Ella sighed. She glanced up at the sky, already thickening with clouds and the promise of rain. 'They've got to finish the outdoor filming today.'

'Fine,' Heather said, nodding. 'I appreciate that, but half an hour isn't going to make much difference, is it?' She squeezed her arm. 'I know how much you want to do this, Ella. I'm sure the film crew will understand.'

'I don't think they will,' she said. From what she had seen of it, filming seemed to operate on a tight schedule, with everyone expected to be in set places and allocated positions at set times. Far be it for her to upset the equilibrium. And yet she felt as if she was being torn in two directions. She desperately wanted to take part in the final. She had come this far and now she needed to see if she could win. But how could she, when she was supposed to be at the other end of the Showground at the same time?

'Ella, for once in your life,' Heather sighed, 'do something for *you*. The world isn't going to end if you're a few minutes late.'

'Yes, I know. It's just that I said I'd be there.'

'And you will be,' Heather assured her. '*After* you've done the jump-off.'

'Where is she, Lewis?' Miles demanded, pacing backwards and forwards across the set, his tweed jacket looking more crumpled than usual.

The cameras were in position, the microphones and sound engineers on standby, and the dolly all set to roll.

A ramp with springs had been crudely assembled under the guise of a loading ramp, to assist Simon when he vaulted onto the horse. Except, that there was now no horse. No horse and no rider.

'It's your money, Lewis. But it's my time.'

'Yes, ok.' He glanced irritably at his watch. 'She'll be here.'

'The thought of "when" springs to mind,' Miles muttered. 'Ok team, we'll take a break. I want you all back here in fifteen minutes. Dave, let me see those shots of the crowd. Yes, on that monitor. Oh, and Molly, I want you to hang around for a bit longer. We may need to do that window scene again.'

Lewis swore beneath his breath as he jabbed at the numbers on his mobile phone. 'Lucy? Get back here. Of course, it's bloody important. Yes, I do mean now.' He clicked off the call, and then rang the next number. 'James? James, where are you? I need you on set...'

'Lewis!' Matthew came running from behind the scenes. 'I think you should...'

'Shut up a moment. No, not you, James.' He motioned at Matthew to be quiet. 'Yes, it is a crisis. Yes.' He clicked off the phone. 'Well?' He glowered over at him. 'I hope it's good news.'

'Hmm. Sort of,' Matthew said.

'What do you mean, sort of?'

Matthew volunteered a smile. 'She's in the final.'

'Who is?' Lewis' eyes widened. 'You don't mean Ella?'

'I certainly do.' He grinned. 'And, rumour has it, that she stands a very good chance of winning.'

'Bloody woman!' Lewis gave an exasperated groan. 'So that's where she disappeared to. She was supposed to be keeping the horse warmed up.'

'Oh, it's warmed up all right. You should have seen it, Lewis. It was magnificent. She made it look easy. Some of those jumps are pretty formidable.'

'And she's riding in the final?'

Matthew nodded. 'There are six of them competing. The same course, but it's against the clock.'

'This I've got to see,' Lewis said, making a run for the gate. 'No wait.' He pointed over at one of the trailers. 'Fetch Miles. Oh, and make sure we've got a film unit in the ring.'

'We have,' Matthew said. 'A couple of teams are already down there getting a few background shots.'

'Then warn them!' Lewis yelled. 'I want them ready for this.'

'Why, exactly?' Matthew said, reaching for his mobile

phone.

'Don't ask,' Lewis said. 'Just do it.'

'That's right, ladies and gentlemen. We have six riders in the final jump-off, and I must say we're in for a thrilling competition. This will be against the clock with time penalties incurred for any faults....'

'Where is she?' Lewis said, pushing his way to the front of the ring. The roar of the crowd was deafening as the first rider cantered into the arena.

'Over there.' Matthew pointed to the small group of riders circling the collecting ring. 'On the bay horse with the flaxen tail and mane.'

Lewis squinted into the distance. A commotion of sorts was going on just outside the arena, and Ursula Johnson appeared to be in the thick of it.

'Zoom in on them,' he instructed one of the cameramen. 'May I?' he added, snatching at an elderly gentleman's pair of binoculars, which hung on a strap around his neck.

What appeared to be a war of words was going on between the girl on the grey Arab, and the owner of Majesty. Vanessa and Heather, he decided, handing back the field glasses with a curt 'Thank-you.'

'Well, I must say...'muttered the elderly gentleman.

'Jack, get a sound crew over there,' Lewis said. 'Matthew, come with me.'

'It doesn't matter who wins,' Ursula was saying, in the soothing tone she reserved for inconsolable children at their first gymkhana.

'It does, Mother,' Vanessa sniffed, pointedly glaring at her stepsister. 'She shouldn't be here.'

'Well, she is, so just accept it,' Heather snapped. 'Just because your mean little plan failed...'

'What mean little plan?' Ursula snorted. 'Ella was left in charge of the stables...'

'Ella *is* in charge of the stables,' Heather said. 'The business is hers, remember?'

'Well, that's neither here, nor there.'

'You would say that.'

'For goodness sake!' Ella swung Majesty's head round until she sat facing the squabbling group. She had had quite enough of this senseless bickering. Vanessa and Caroline were looking at her as if she had crawled out from under a stone, Ursula was trying to be agreeable, and failing miserably, and Heather was just being plain bolshy. 'Can you stop arguing for one moment?' she demanded.

Her loud and determined voice had them all staring up at her in shocked surprise. Ella didn't usually answer back. In fact, Ella never raised her voice, not to anyone.

'Thank you,' she said firmly. 'Now then, I've as much right as anyone to take part in this competition, and it's up to me whether I ride in it, or not.' She stared pointedly at Ursula as she spoke. 'As it happens, I've made up my mind to compete. Majesty did well in the first round, and I'd like to see if he could do better in the next. I'm not doing it to spite you, Vanessa, and I'm sorry if that's how you feel about it. I'm here because I intend to do my best,' she added softly. 'Just as I expect everyone else to do the same.'

'Well said,' Ursula announced, clapping her hands together loudly.

'What?' Vanessa looked aghast. 'Mother!'

Ursula shot her a warning look. 'This is for Hollyfields,' she said. It didn't take an idiot to see that if Ella won; they would receive the same, if not more, publicity, than if Vanessa won. Ella was Robert Johnson's true daughter after all. And show jumping was in her blood.

In fact, Ursula decided, this might be an angle worth milking for all it was worth. Particularly as she, the unfortunate widow, was instrumental in encouraging Ella to resume her career after several years' absence from the show-jumping circuit. She could see the newspaper headlines already. "Grieving widow encourages daughter to take up father's reins". She patted her coiled bun reassuringly. Things might work out even better than she had originally planned.

'I think it's wonderful that you've both done so well,' she said, beaming up at the two riders. 'And I think Ella's made a very valid point. I know we've had our little differences in the past, but it's time to put all that behind us. We need to work together now. And I must say, having the two of you in the final is very gratifying, considering all the hard work we've put in at the stables...'

'Oh, give it a rest, woman,' Heather snorted. Ursula's sanctimonious warbling was making her stomach turn. 'Ella's here because she's a naturally talented rider and the only reason Vanessa's got through is because she's on a bloody good horse.'

'Excuse me?' Vanessa sniffed down her nose at her. 'I'll have you know...'

'Listen!' Caroline shouted, waving her into silence.

'What?'

'It's your turn,' she said. 'They're calling your name.'

Which, indeed, they were. Vanessa went a ripe shade of cherry red as she fastened her hat and fumbled with the reins. How could she have missed it? Her one important moment, and she hadn't even heard the announcement.

'...Vanessa Johnson riding Minstrel,' continued the commentator. 'I repeat, do we have Vanessa Johnson?'

'Yes! Oh my God!' she said. She was flustered now.

'Good luck,' Ella said.

'Yeah, right,' she sneered. She'd probably done this on purpose.

'I mean it,' Ella said softly. 'Minstrel's a good horse. Make sure you do your best for him.'

'Yes, good luck, darling,' Ursula called, giving her a genteel little wave. She was past caring one way or the other. If Vanessa didn't win, she was quite sure Ella would.

Chapter Seventeen

'Did you get a close up of that?' Lewis said, peering down at the collecting ring, where harmony seemed to have been restored between the various parties.

'Yes, and we've got sound, courtesy of Trevor,' Adam confirmed, pointing out one of the sound engineers perched rather precariously on a mobile crane unit.

'I don't think family squabbles are what Miles is looking for,' Matthew said. 'Not for an action film, anyway.'

'Who says I wanted it for Miles?' Lewis said, tapping the side of his nose.

'All right, all right, what's the big crisis,' Lucy demanded, elbowing her way through the throng. Her russet-coloured hair had been piled on top of her head and fastened with an expensive looking silk scarf. A mass of gold jewellery dangled round her neck and wrists. She had never been one for dressing down, but even she had to admit, albeit to herself, that her attire was not very practical for an Agricultural Show.

Matthew grinned. 'Better late than never, eh, Luce?'

'I'll have you know I scuffed the toe of these rather expensive shoes rushing over here,' she snapped. 'They're Jimmy Choo.'

'We've found our horse and rider,' Lewis told her, pointing down at the ring.

'How?' Lucy said. 'They haven't ridden the jump-off yet.'

'Told you,' Matthew gloated. He could see trouble looming, even if Lewis couldn't.

'That's irrelevant,' Lewis said.

'Not from where I'm standing.' Lucy leant one hand on his shoulder, and peered into the ring. 'That grey Arab's doing pretty well. Isn't she one of the Johnson sisters?'

'Yes,' Lewis muttered. Never before had he wanted a rider to fall off more keenly than he did at this moment.

'She's gone clear,' Matthew said.

The tremendous applause from the crowd signalled the worst. Vanessa was amongst the finalists. It was all down to timing now.

Lewis shook his head in despair. 'She can't win, Matthew. She can't.'

'Well, she jolly well might, so you'd best think of an alternative part for her, if you're determined to stick with Ella.'

'That goes without saying.'

'Right,' he said. 'Lucy, get your thinking cap on. This is important.'

The team from Blackwater Films were not aware of the journalist from the local press, who had entered the enclosure. Peter Marchant had come to get the story on the finalists for the morning paper. He already had a photographer down in the arena taking snapshots of the contestants. Now he wanted to get the film crews' version of the event. He drifted surreptitiously through the crowds, picking up titbits of conversation here and there. Gabriella Johnson was the favourite to win. Rumour had it that she was the daughter of Robert Johnson, a famous show-jumper in his own right. The other girl, Vanessa, was her stepsister, which made things even more interesting – a bit of sibling rivalry – that sort of thing.

'Ah, Mr Trevelyan,' he said, producing a notepad and pencil from his breast pocket. 'Could I have a few words?'

'Not now.' Lewis pushed past him.

'It's about the finalists,' he continued, jogging after him. 'I gather you want Miss Gabriella Johnson to win?'

'I said, "Not now".'

'Is there any reason for that?'

'Excuse me, please.' Lewis ducked into the hospitality tent, his thoughts racing. Miles wasn't going to be happy about this. It was turning into a farce. If the press got hold of the story that they favoured one rider over any of the others, and that rider didn't win, they would have a field day if she subsequently appeared in the film

'I've got it!' Lucy said, trotting after him on her mud splattered pink satin shoes. Kitten heels were not appropriate for outdoor events. She would remember that in future. 'Sod the horse,' she said.

Lewis rounded on her, his eyes widening in incredulity. 'What?'

'Simon can't ride anyway, so what's the point?'

'The point being,' he muttered, 'that this scene calls for action.'

'Correct.' She caught hold of his sleeve and gave it a tug. 'Come with me, Lewis. I've got something to show you.'

'I don't believe she just did that,' Heather said, as Vanessa came cantering out of the ring, a grin as wide as the English Channel on her face. 'She's only gone and got another clear round?'

Ella smiled. 'It doesn't surprise me. Minstrel's a good horse.'

'Yes, but too good for her.' Heather frowned as she patted Majesty's neck. 'You will beat her, won't you?'

'I'll certainly try to,' she said. She glanced again at her watch, conscious of the unravelling passage of time. She hoped Heather was right about this, and that the film crew would understand. She hated letting people down. Punctuality and reliability were something she believed in.

'Maybe you could get a message to Mr Trevelyan,' she suggested.

'What? And miss all the fun?' Heather shook her head. 'I'm not leaving until this is over, Ella. Besides, I don't expect you'll have to wait much longer. There are only two riders left.'

Apart from Vanessa, only one other girl had managed a clear round, but in a slower time. The penultimate rider was Hilary Frampton riding Pegasus, a flighty chestnut thoroughbred who had performed magnificently in the first round.

Ella knew Hilary from years back, when they had both competed in the Junior Ponies UK championships. She was a formidable opponent, with an impressive competition record behind her. The horse she was riding was fast and sure-footed, with a natural talent for jumping. This, Ella decided, was her main rival.

'That's four penalty faults for Camellia Brown on Silver...' the commentator was saying. 'Miss Brown is now out of the competition. Our next competitor is Hilary Frampton, on Pegasus. If you recall, this horse had the fastest time in the preliminary round, which wasn't against the clock. Let's see if she can do equally well in this round. A big hand, please for Hilary Frampton.'

'Stuck up little madam,' Ursula said. 'You do know who her father is, don't you.' She pointed to the Chairman's box. 'Only his right-hand man, no less. Oughtn't to be allowed,' she added.

'Why?' Heather rounded on her. 'I don't see how having an influential father is going to affect her riding ability, do you?'

Ursula's ferrety eyes narrowed slightly. She might have expected a comment like that from Heather Hutchins. She was another troublemaker, and no mistake. It was her decision to remove Majesty from the stables that had caused the business to almost collapse. Still, she would forgive her that, she decided with equanimity, but only if Ella managed to pull this one off.

'And that's the fastest time so far,' boomed the commentator, to the rapturous applause from the crowd. 'Miss Frampton beats Miss Johnson's time by five point two seconds.'

'No-oo!' Vanessa wailed, her hands going to her mouth. 'Oh no!'

'Oh shit!' Caroline muttered.

'That's a good time,' Heather said, giving Ella a leg-up. 'Think you can better it?'

'Only one way to find out,' she said, urging Majesty forwards. 'Come on, boy. Let's see what you can do.'

The applause greeted her as she trotted into the ring. The

commentator was making his introductions. 'And now we have Miss Gabriella Johnson riding Majesty. And yes, in case you were wondering, she is related to Vanessa. I have been informed that the two girls are stepsisters. So well done the Johnson girls, for putting on such a splendid performance today. Now let's see if Gabriella can snatch the prize from under the nose of Hilary Frampton, our current leader.'

'She's on,' Matthew said, nudging James. They were wedged behind one of the ringside barriers, to the right of the main entrance. 'Where's Lewis?' he added, peering back over his shoulder. 'I thought he wanted to see her?'

'God knows,' James said, glaring at an elderly woman with a shooting stick, who seemed determined to spear him in the foot with it. 'He took off with Lucy about five minutes ago. No, it's not a problem,' he said to the woman. 'No, it did miss me. Come on.' He tugged Matthew's sleeve. 'Let's move over here. Otherwise,' he added, under his breath, 'I'm in danger of losing a toe. No, no, not a problem,' he announced loudly. 'We can see better from this spot.'

'He should be here,' Matthew fretted, glancing round the crowded arena.

'You're right. He should be,' James said. 'This is his ball game. And you know what, Matt? I think he's lost the plot.'

'What?'

'All this business about that blonde haired girl.' He jerked his head in the direction of the ring. 'How he had to have her and no one else. Doesn't it strike you as a bit over the top?'

Matthew shrugged. 'You know Lewis. When he gets a hunch...'

'Yeah, but this is more than a hunch,' James said. 'This is a bloody obsession. I mean, the girl's not an actress.'

'Not that we know of.'

'But she is a good rider.' James opened his arms and waved his hands around the Showground. 'And how many of those have you seen out there.'

'Dozens.'

'My point exactly,' he said. 'And we need one for the scene. Just one.' He shook his head, despairingly. 'I tell you what, Matt, Miles was doing his nut back there. He wants the scene shot and the filming wrapped up today. For two pins I think he'd cut the horse chase from the film altogether.'

'But he's happy to use the Showground?'

'Oh yeah, yeah, that's not a problem. In fact, he's got some good footage. Did you view any of the rushes?'

'Didn't have time, mate.'

'Yeah, well, they're excellent.' He paused as a gasp from the crowd drew his attention back to the arena.

Majesty had brushed against the final pole in the triple and it was wobbling slightly. It stayed put.

'She's doing all right,' Matthew told him.

'Hmm. And she looks fast. Maybe she'll be the winner after all.'

'I certainly hope so.' Matthew said. 'It will solve a lot of our problems if she does win. Especially as our esteemed, and currently absent, producer has already ear-marked her for the part.'

'It's not going to happen, Lewis,' Lucy said, guiding him through the quagmire of a field with as much decorum as she could manage. 'You've got to be practical about this.' She stopped and balanced on one foot as she tried to remove a splodge of mud from her once pink shoe. 'Simon's having trouble vaulting onto a stack of hay bales, let alone a horse.'

'Which is why Ella's going to be up there to help him?' He stood patiently as she leaned one hand on his shoulder for support. 'Where in God's name are we going, Luce?'

They seemed to have wandered into an area cordoned off for agricultural vehicles. Everything from combines to tractors and trailers. He could see hedge trimmers; fancy gleaming ploughs, seed sowers, the lot. But unfortunately, the heavy machinery had dug up much of the soft, rain sodden ground, and unless they stuck to the tarmac road, which Lucy seemed unwilling to do, they were going to get coated in mud.

'Over here,' she said. 'I want you to meet Charlie.'

'Charlie?' Lewis felt his temper starting to rise. 'Who the hell is Charlie?'

He peered crossly at the groups of people wandering around the site. Most of them looked like farmers, either that or show officials. The Barbour wax jacket and green wellies were '*de rigueur*' apparently. So, he was patently out of place.

Besides which, he should be back at the Grand Ring watching the final of the show jumping. That was infinitely more important as far as he was concerned.

He stumbled into Lucy, who had stopped suddenly. 'What the heck...'

'This, my dear Lewis,' she said, standing smugly to one side and pointing a well-manicured finger out in front of her, 'is Charlie.'

Ursula was gnawing on a well-bitten fingernail as she watched Ella take a fast right hand turn and head for the double. 'Come on, come on,' she urged.

She let out a sigh of relief as Majesty sprang over the jumps and headed for the brush hedge. 'How's her timing doing?' she said, shooting an anxious glance at Heather, who was looking equally as tense.

'Neck and neck,' she murmured.

It was going to be close.

Vanessa dabbed at her eyes with a clump of soggy tissues. She didn't want Ella to win – that glory should have been hers - but she didn't want her to lose either.

She hung her head and sniffed loudly. She couldn't bear to watch.

'There's only the water jump left,' Caroline said. 'Oh my God!'

'What? What!' Vanessa's head jerked upwards.

'Majesty slipped – no – no, he's all right...he's ok.'

Heather shook her head.

The roar of the crowd surged around the arena.

'Well?' Ursula was on her feet and staring up at the huge black and white clock. The seconds were ticking away far too fast. 'Has she done it? Has she?'

The crowd were clapping and shouting. Surely that must mean?

'Ladies and gentlemen...'

Ursula clutched at Heather's arm.

'...We have a winner. By one point two seconds...'

'Is it her?' squeaked Vanessa, her voice high pitched and panicky.

'Shut up!' hissed Ursula.

'...Miss Hilary Frampton and Pegasus. Can we have a big hand please, for our champion. Hilary, if you'd like to do a circuit. Ladies and gentlemen, I give you Hilary Frampton, on Pegasus.'

'What the hell do you mean, "This is Charlie"?' Lewis spluttered, staring in the direction of Lucy's waggling finger. 'It's a bloody machine, for Christ's sake!'

'A quad bike, to be precise,' she said. 'Which doesn't buck, bite, bolt or kick. Plus, it's fast, nippy, and easy to ride. What do you think?' she added, standing back and folding her arms rather smugly in front of her.

'What do I think?' choked Lewis.

'Ye-es.' Lucy smiled up at him. 'Because, personally, I think it's rather a brilliant idea. Simon can run from the first aid post as planned, jump on this, and ride into the distance. Voila!'

'But we need a horse-rider!' Lewis circled the squat four-wheeled buggy warily.

'Not necessarily.'

'It's in the script.'

'Which can be changed.' She flashed her gleaming white teeth at him in a delighted little smile. 'Go on, Lewis, say it's a good idea. It won't kill you.'

'It might kill Simon,' he muttered. 'For all we know he might be as useless at driving one of these as he is at riding a horse.' He glanced over at the smartly dressed sales executive, who was eyeing him up with barely suppressed excitement, and then back at the shining machine. 'How much is this going to cost us?' he sighed.

'Not as much as you think,' Lucy said. 'And if we do use it, we can come to some arrangement with the company. They'll be getting free advertising, after all.'

'Right.' Lewis nodded.

'You mean it?'

'Yes, yes,' he groaned. 'Why not.' He pulled his mobile phone out of his pocket. 'You sort it out with these guys, Lucy. I need to talk to Miles.'

And, he thought, glancing over at the distant Grand Ring, he needed to find out what had happened to Ella.

It was a disaster, a total, unmitigated disaster. Ursula couldn't believe her bad luck. Two girls in the final – not one, but two - and still neither of them had managed to win the coveted first place. She was ruined. Ruined! She had bills for tack and equipment to pay, vets bills, farrier's bills, God-only-knows-what bills, and demands from the bank that could no longer be ignored. Well, that was it. That…was…it!

'We can still go and meet Simon De Silva, can't we Mother,' Vanessa said, snuffling into her sleeve. It was her one and only consolation. 'I mean all the runners up have been invited to the hospitality marquee.'

'Oh, do what you like,' Ursula snapped. She was beginning to wish she had never heard of the name Simon De Silva, nor Blackwater Films.

'Ella, are you going?' Vanessa asked, fervently hoping that she was. For once in her life, she could do with a bit of moral support.

'Hmm, what?' Ella said, lifting Majesty's reins over his head and using them to lead him to the gate. She glanced back at her stepsister. 'Me? No, I don't think so.'

'But why?' Vanessa wailed.

Heather darted her a quick look. She wasn't going to tell her, was she?

'I need to get Majesty sorted,' Ella said. 'He's a bit sweaty so I thought I'd walk him round a bit to cool him off. Maybe later,' she added, seeing Vanessa's crestfallen expression. 'I'll see how I feel.' She winked at Heather. 'Coming?'

'But I don't want to go on my own,' Vanessa whined.

'I'll go with you,' Caroline said.

Vanessa gave her a superior stare. 'You're not allowed,' she said. 'You weren't one of the finalists.'

'No...no, but I did take part. Oh, go on, please?'

'Not likely.' She'd rather pair up with Hilary Frampton, than give Caroline a chance to show her face.

'Mother! Mother make her!' Caroline gave a petulant stamp of her foot. 'Mother! It's not fair.' She lunged at her sister. 'If you don't take me...'

'And I won't.'

'Ooh!' Caroline was beside herself with frustration. She whacked her sister on the arm. 'I hate you. I do. I really, really hate you.'

'Bet you're glad to be out of it?' Heather said a short time later as she and Ella strolled towards the film set, one on each side of Majesty.

'Just a bit.' She sighed. 'I'm sorry I didn't win, though. I really thought I might, until he lost his footing.'

Heather shrugged. 'It's just one of those things. I thought he was the better horse, but then I'm biased, aren't I?'

'He is the better horse,' Ella said, smiling. She patted his neck. 'He's a real star.'

'A film star,' Heather added proudly. 'Aren't you, boy?'

Peter Marchant, fresh from his interview with the show's winner, and now on his way to have a chat with the director, pricked up his ears at the mention of the words "film star". He was surprised to see the girl he assumed to be the runner-up leading her horse towards the trailers surrounding the film set. Puzzled, he decided to follow them. This had all the makings of a fix, if he wasn't mistaken. A pretty blonde girl and a striking looking horse. Interesting. He chewed on the butt of his pencil as he watched them talking to the security guards. The girl was very pretty, much more so than the show's actual winner. Hilary Frampton was blonde, but she was hardly what he would call photogenic. Her angular jaw was rather masculine, and she had a nose like Julius Caesar. Whereas this girl – he glanced down at his list of names, Gabriella Johnson – she was stunning. And she had been the favourite, the one Lewis Trevelyan had his eye on. No, no this wasn't right. He watched with interest as the two girls lead the horse through the entrance in the high security fencing. They were obviously expected, be they winners or losers. This had all the makings of a story, and one he intended to get to the bottom of.

'Press,' he said, flashing his pass, and then standing impatiently as his card was scrutinised by the burly security guard on the gate. 'Can you tell me where I can find Miles Davison?'

The man eyed him up and down, studied the photo card again, and sullenly handed it back to him. 'Third trailer along on the left,' he said.

'Thanks.'

Peter Marchant had every intention of speaking to the director, eventually. But first, he wanted to see what was going on with the two girls and the horse. He followed them at a discreet distance, wishing fervently that he had brought a photographer with him.

Ella and Heather were unaware of his watchful presence. They were more concerned with finding Lewis and explaining why they were so late.

'He doesn't seem to be here,' Ella said. They had reached the area where filming had been scheduled to take place. The cameras had been set up on a running track beside the ramp, and men were busy laying cables and wires, and setting up lights.

'Lewis? Nah, haven't seen him?' said a youth in overalls, who was lying on the ground trying to fix a cable under one of the lighting stands. 'You could ask Miles.'

'That's the director, right?' Heather said.

'Yep. He's over there.' He waved them over to a catering van, where people were milling about with hot drinks and sandwiches.

'I'll go,' Ella said, handing Heather the reins. 'You wait here.'

For all she knew, she had messed up the filming schedule for the entire day, so she felt that an apology was expected first and foremost. After that, she would see if they still wanted her to continue with the scene. It would have helped if she could have seen Lewis Trevelyan, or even Simon De Silva, but she didn't see anyone that she recognised.

She took off her riding hat and tucked it under her arm, shaking her long hair free as she did so. In her show breeches and tailored jacket, she was feeling distinctly out of place. It was as if she had gate crashed a fancy-dress party, and been the only person not in fancy dress.

'Hi,' she said, smiling, as she approached the catering van. A woman in a white overall and with a white cap on her head peered down at her through the serving hatch.

'I'm looking for Miles, the director. I don't suppose you could point him out to me, could you?'

'Miles? He was here a moment ago. Effie? Do you know?'

A stout woman with tightly permed hair ducked her head up from a cupboard. 'I think he's gone to meet Mr Trevelyan,' she said. 'He took a call from him on his phone. Left his drink, he did, and I'd made him a nice cappuccino too.'

'Thanks,' Ella said, turning away. Now what? She scanned the small groups of people milling around the set. Everyone seemed to be busy, and no one was paying her much attention. She shrugged at Heather. This was hopeless. They may as well take Majesty back to the horsebox and get him loaded.

'Miss Johnson?' The man in the ill-fitting jacket and beige trousers came up behind her, catching her unawares. 'It is Miss

Gabriella Johnson, isn't it?'

'Yes,' she said warily.

'Peter Marchant.' He flashed his pass at her. 'I'm from the press. Do you mind if I have a few words with you?' He took his notepad from his breast pocket.

Ella wasn't sure what this was about, but some sixth sense told her it wasn't good. Not good at all.

'I take it you're here for the filming,' he said, his grey eyes perusing her steadily. 'Is that right?' His pencil hovered over the pad of dog-eared paper.

'Um,' she said. 'Well, actually...'

'Ella!'

The shout caught her off guard.

'Ella, my darling!'

The endearment surprised her even more. To say nothing of the shock she got when Lewis Trevelyan suddenly appeared as if from nowhere, and swept her into his arms, with a, 'Thank God you're here. I've been looking everywhere for you.'

What? What? She blinked up into his face in stunned disbelief. She was clamped hard against his chest, with one arm pinned across the small of her back. His head was bowed to hers and his breath was warm and intoxicating against her ear.

'Tell him nothing,' he whispered.' Understand?'

She managed a feeble nod, and was almost disappointed when she felt his grip lessen slightly. But not for long. His lips came down on hers in a kiss that was warm, passionate, and totally unexpected.

'Mr Trevelyan!' she croaked, finally coming up for air. It was a good job his arms were still around her waist, because her legs were giving way beneath her. She had been kissed before, but never quite like that. Her senses were reeling all over the place. In fact, if she didn't know better, she would have thought she was going into shock.

His eyes crinkled at the corners, and he gave her a reassuring wink. 'Now then, Mr Marchant,' he said, turning to face the gentleman of the press. 'What can we do for you?'

For one who was normally rather vocal, Peter Marchant appeared to be quite speechless.

'Ah...Um.' He glanced down at his paper and pencil.

'You've come about the filming at the Show, I take it?' Lewis suggested helpfully. 'Well, it's all in hand.' He gave Ella's fingers a reassuring squeeze.

'And you're going to use Hilary Frampton?'

'Of course.' Lewis smiled. 'In fact, Simon and I will be heading over to the hospitality marquee in about an hour. Perhaps if you could arrange for a photographer to be there, we could have a photo shoot with all the finalists.'

'An hour, you say.' Peter Marchant was jotting the details down as he spoke. 'Right, then.' He glanced up and gave what seemed like a knowing smile to Ella. Her cheeks were burning, and she was quite convinced that guilt was showing all over her face.

'I'll be there,' he said, tucking the pencil behind one ear.

'Excellent.'

Lewis continued to grin as he watched the journalist stroll away. 'That was bloody close,' he whispered, glancing sideways down at her. 'Ella? Ella, are you all right?'

Ella didn't know if she was, or she wasn't. Her head was buzzing, and every nerve in her body was tingling. They tingled even more when he swung round to face her and tilted her chin up with his fingers.

'You look flushed,' he said in a voice that was immediately concerned.

'Hmm,' was all she managed to say.

'I'm sorry for leaping on you like that,' he said ruefully. 'But it was all I could think of doing at the time. Peter Marchant's a bit of a weasel. I could see he was snooping round after something.'

'That's okay,' she mumbled. It was more than okay. It was unbelievable, incredible, earth shattering.

'Ella?' he said. 'Hey, I'm sorry.' He shook his head as he pulled her into the warm and comforting security of his arms. 'I really gave you a shock, didn't I?' He could feel her shaking through the thin cotton of his shirt. His chin rested on the top of her head, and the fresh scent of her newly washed hair gave him such a surge of longing, it was like a kick between his ribs. 'Jesus,' he thought, gently pulling away from her. It was a long time since he had felt like that.

'What's going on?' Heather said, abruptly breaking the spell. 'Are we taking Majesty back, or what?'

Lewis felt reluctant to let Ella go. Yet, let her he must. He stepped to one side and ran a distracted hand through his hair. 'Ah…yes. There's been a slight change of plan.'

'We're ready to rehearse that scene, Lewis,' came a shout from one of the film crew.

He acknowledged the call with a thumbs up sign. 'Simon's not riding,' he said. 'Or at least, he's not riding a horse. We've got him a quad bike,' he explained. 'Miles thought it might be safer.'

'So, you don't need us?' Heather said.

'Ah…no. Well, not right now.' His gaze rested on Ella as he spoke. But God, did he need her.

'We might as well take Majesty back, then,' Heather said, disappointment evident in her tone.

'Yes,' Lewis agreed. 'Look, I'm sorry to mess you about like this. We've got some good shots of him jumping, and we'll need to put a piece together with the winner of the competition, so maybe we'll get back to you.'

'I won't hold my breath,' Heather muttered. 'Come on, let's go.'

'No wait.' Lewis caught hold of Ella's arm. 'Stay. I mean, you can watch, if you like.'

She was staring up at him like a bewildered faun.

'Please?' he said.

'Lewis! Are you coming to this rehearsal, or what?'

'Ten seconds,' he called. His gaze returned to Ella. His voice was slow and carefully measured as he spoke. 'I'd really like it if you came with me.'

Ella would like to do nothing more. It was almost hypnotic, the hold he had over her. She was being drawn to him even though she barely knew him. But Heather's irritated shuffling behind her was enough to distract her from her thoughts.

'I'm sorry, I can't,' she said. 'I need to help load Majesty.'

The look on his face showed that he wasn't sure whether to believe her or not. 'Then come to the marquee later,' he insisted. 'Please.'

'I'll try,' she said.

Heather had stomped off ahead, and was busy unfastening Majesty's reins from the railing where she had left him tethered.

Ella was conscious of Lewis watching her as she hurried to catch up with them. It was a wonder she managed to walk at all, since her legs felt like jelly, her lips were glowing, and her skin tingled where he had touched her.

'What a blinking fiasco,' Heather muttered. 'I should have known this would happen. It's a good job you rode in the show, Ella, because coming here has been a complete waste of time.'

'Oh, I don't know.' Ella said, gazing dreamily back over her shoulder. 'I wouldn't say that.'

Chapter Eighteen

'Okay, so run this by me again,' Matthew said, scratching the back of his neck as he spoke. 'We're not using a horse now?'

'No.' Lewis stood, legs apart and arms folded, watching the preparations for the rehearsal.

'And Simon's riding that thing. Where the hell did you get it anyway?' he said, stepping forwards to take a closer look at the gleaming quad bike.

'Lucy found it. Clever girl,' he added, winking at her. 'It's called Charlie.'

'Charlie?'

'An abbreviation of the company name, apparently,' he explained. 'Clopton Haverton Agricultural Rentals and Loans Incorporated or something like that.'

'Right,' Matthew said, nodding. 'And what about the girl?'

Lewis gave him a sharp look. 'What girl? Oh, you mean Hilary Frampton?'

'No.'

'Oh, *that* girl.'

'Yes. Yes!' Matthew repeated, probingly. 'The one you had us traipsing all over the countryside to find. The one you couldn't make this film without. Remember?' He gave an impatient snort. 'Honest to God, Lewis, if I didn't know better, I'd say you were infatuated by her.'

'Maybe I am,' he said quietly.

'What!'

'Quiet please,' shouted the assistant director, an animated little man in his forties. 'Turnover.'

The camera operator started up the camera.

'Speed,' called the sound recordist.

'And "Action",' shouted Miles.

Simon De Silva came running across the grass and leapt onto the quad bike. He revved the engine loudly and glanced back over his shoulder. Jason was sprinting towards him, his face set in an expression of single-minded determination.

With a kick of the engine, Simon tore off across the grass, the cameras following him on the specially constructed track.

'And "Cut". That was good,' Miles said, nodding at Lewis. 'Yeah, pretty good.' He peered into the monitor. 'Let's try that one more time.'

Matthew was staring at him as if he had gone mad. 'What?' he repeated dazedly.

Lewis shrugged. 'I said, maybe I am.'

'I heard what you said,' he hissed. 'I want to know what you meant.'

'I don't know,' he said. 'I don't.' He met Matthew's gaze with a confused look of his own. 'I can't explain it.' And he couldn't. How could he put into words what he could barely comprehend himself? All he knew was that he had been mesmerised by her from the start.

He thought back to the very first day he had seen her. It was all there, in his mind, the delightful merriment of her laughter, the sultry vision of her striding across the fields with that huge black horse behind her, and the gleaming silken sway of her hair. And he had wanted her. Not for the film – that was a means to an end – but for him. Yes, he had tried to deny it. He had convinced himself he was drawn to her for professional reasons. She had intrigued him – bewitched him – he needed to know more about her. And he had been prepared to risk everything to find her. Even his reputation, he realised.

'All that palaver about finding a specific horse-rider – setting up the competition – doing all this,' Matthew groaned. 'It was all because you fancied her?'

'Hmm. Yes, I suppose it was, really,' Lewis reflected.

'Bleeding idiot!' Matthew thumped him on the back.

'Couldn't you just have phoned her up and asked her out on a date, like the rest of us?'

'Didn't know her name, did I,' he said, with a rueful smile.

'Lewis!' Matthew despaired of him, sometimes. 'Does Miles know about this?'

'No, and I'd appreciate...'

'Yeah, yeah, no problem.' Matthew lit a cigarette and drew on it deeply. 'What about the script?' he said. 'I thought the setting was supposed to be in the horse-riding world.'

'Yes, well, it still is,' he said. 'I mean, we've got the Showground, which is a huge bonus. And Simon, or should I say his alter-ego, 'Brett' was brought here in the back of a horsebox.'

'Trussed and bound, and freed by the lovely Tanya,' Matthew said, positively drooling.

'That's right.'

'So where does the show-jumper fit in?'

'Hilary Frampton?' Lewis frowned. 'To be honest, Matt, I don't rightly know. But I'm working on it.'

He glanced at his watch. Where was the time going? In forty minutes, he was supposed to be in the marquee. Forty minutes. The press would be waiting for him, and all the finalists, and he'd need to take Simon along.... He jerked his head up. 'Matt,' he said, grinning. 'I've just had a brainwave.'

'Brainstorm, more like.'

'No, this could work.' he said. 'I need a script-editor, some props, and a handful of extras. And bring Miles when he's finished. I've got an idea.'

'What do you mean, he's not here?' Ursula demanded, peering through the huge encompassing folds of the entrance to the Keynes and Bain hospitality marquee. 'My daughter's supposed to be meeting him.'

'Simon De Silva is still filming,' explained the public relations officer, who had been sent to make sure the finalists were kept happy and comfortable.

Vanessa was certainly happy, having consumed several

glasses of complementary champagne. A rather stupid smile was tilting the corner of her face, and her cheeks were flushed and glowing.

'Well surely I can wait inside with my daughter,' Ursula said. She had caught sight of Vanessa slumped on a seat in the middle of the floor, and was rather concerned about her welfare. 'It's starting to rain out here.'

'I'm sorry, Madam, but extra guests are not permitted.'

'Well thank you very much,' she snapped. 'Come on Caroline,' she added, digging her sulky looking daughter in the ribs.' We're obviously wasting our time out here.'

'I hate her,' Caroline muttered, dragging her heels. 'She's so spiteful. Well, she is, Mother. You'd think she'd let me go in with her.'

'I expect you would have done the same if you'd got through,' Ursula said. 'Now give me that umbrella, darling. You know how I hate getting my hair wet.'

Sheltering beneath the huge, candy-striped brolly, the pair of them made their way back to the horse box area, oblivious to the small army of technicians, sound engineers and cameramen gathering outside the entrance they had so recently vacated.

'I want extra lighting here, here, and here,' Miles said, reeling through the list of requirements. 'And I want a camera on that crane by the entrance. Yep, up there. How soon will we be ready?'

'Twenty minutes,' the assistant director assured him. 'We've got mobile units on standby anyway.'

'How's the props department doing?'

'Better than expected.'

'And the extras?'

'All present and correct.'

The group of spectators that had been shepherded into the hospitality marquee had been hand picked to help swell the numbers. Lucy and James had been given the task of selecting suitable candidates – those of the well-heeled and country fraternity- and had instructed them to sit at the tables and chat with their neighbours.

'In other words,' James said, 'we want you to act naturally, and please don't look at the cameras.'

The finalists were told to mingle with the crowd.

'And mime,' James said, peering down a camera lens. 'We don't need sound. We just need you to look as if you're talking.'

This was fine by Vanessa, since she was finding coherent talk a bit of a problem. Her words were becoming increasingly slurry. She weaved her way over to the buffet table, and nibbled on a few canapés, before quaffing back another glassful of champagne. Where was Simon, she wondered, giving a soft hiccup? (A middle-aged woman in a silk twin set and pearls gave her a disdainful stare.) She just wanted to see Simon.

The star of the film was in the process of being dressed by the costume department in a dark suit with matching tie, and a crisp white shirt.

'Eat your heart out Daniel Craig,' Lucy said, standing back to admire him. 'You look good in formal attire, Simon.'

'Thanks,' he said, glancing hurriedly over the amended pages of script. The previous scene had seen him abandoning the quad bike and ducking through the folds of the huge white marquee. Shots of him 'borrowing' the clothes from an inebriated young gentleman, who had collapsed unconscious in the toilet, would be filmed later in the studio. Now all he had to do was wander round with a tray of drinks, making sure that he served the finalist, Hilary Frampton.

'Ready?' Lewis said.

Simon nodded.

'Right. Well, I've told Hilary what to do, so I think we're all set.' He peered through the flap into the main body of the marquee. Ella still hadn't put in an appearance. To say he was disappointed was a bit of an understatement, but he couldn't dwell on it now. The press, in the form of Peter Marchant and his photographer, had arrived, and Miles was signalling that he was ready to start.

'What about you, Lucy?' he said. 'Are you going to be one of the extras?'

'You bet I am,' she said, flipping open her compact and taking a last long look at herself. 'I take it that's real champagne in those bottles.'

'Of course.'

'Then lead on,' she said.

'Places please,' came the call from the assistant director. 'And...quiet.'

Vanessa clamped a hand over her mouth, and wished she could stop hiccupping. It really was too bad. Perhaps another drink might help. She slurped into her glass, and the bubbles shot up her nose, causing her to sneeze.

'Oops, sorry,' she said, blinking like an owl as the marquee was suddenly illuminated with powerful lighting.

Hilary Frampton, waiting nervously by the buffet table, decided that Vanessa was one person to be avoided, and pointedly took three steps away from her.

'Ready everyone...'

'Speed.'

'And...Action!'

Simon strode purposefully into the room, carrying a tray of champagne flutes. He was immaculately dressed in his dark suit and tie. His hair had been brushed back from his face, and the crisp whiteness of the shirt set off his tanned skin.

Vanessa was instantly and hopelessly in love. She was also more than a little bit tipsy. Grinning like a buffoon, she lurched to her feet, her sole intention being to get near the object of her affection.

'Cut! Cut! Sit down, woman,' bellowed Miles Davison. Can someone get her to sit? Thank-you,' he said, nodding at an elderly man in knee length breeches and a tweed shooting jacket, who had clamped his hands on Vanessa's shoulders and forced her back down into her seat.

'No wait...wait,' Vanessa protested, vaguely trying to wave her arms at her captor. 'See, I only wanted to...'

'Quiet please,' called the sound recordist.

'...I am allowed, you know. I wash...waz...in the final.'

'Shut up!'

Vanessa chewed on her lower lip.

'Places everyone, and... Action.'

Simon re-entered the room at a slightly brisker pace, with the confident, self-assured stride of a man who knows what he's doing.

'Ladies?' he said, offering the tray of drinks to Hilary and her companions. They were supposed to smile at him and remove a couple of champagne flutes. And they possible would have done, if Vanessa hadn't called out 'Waiter? I say, waiter. Over here.'

'Cut!'

'For pity's sake,' Miles muttered, through gritted teeth. 'Who is that bloody female? Can't we have her gagged, or something?'

'A couple more glasses of bubbly and she won't need gagging,' Matthew said wryly.

'Lewis, can we have her removed?'

'I think it's advisable,' he said, stepping forwards. Since no one else had volunteered, it looked as if he was on his own. 'Come on, Vanessa,' he muttered, placing an arm around her waist and hoisting her to her feet. 'Let's go and get a little fresh air, shall we?'

'But I want to shee Shimon,' she slurred.

'Yes, but I don't think he wants to see you,' Lewis said. 'Or at least, not right now,' he added hastily. Vanessa's face had crumpled at his words. Oh Lord, don't let her blubber on me now.

But crying was the least of his worries. It would have been preferable to the projectile vomiting, anyway. Vanessa's lunch came back to visit her in glorious technicolour.

'Jesus Christ!' Lewis swore, as he held the unfortunate girl over the nearest litter bin, sadly a little too late, since his feet and trousers, plus a wide surrounding area, had been splattered rather unpleasantly with what seemed to be mainly regurgitated champagne and canapés.

'I'm so shorry,' Vanessa snivelled. Huge fat tears were trickling down her cheeks.

'It's okay,' Lewis said, patting her reassuringly on the shoulders.

It was the precursor to another retching session.

'Matthew, get over here!' he yelled.

'Not bloody likely,' his friend said, from a safe vantage point at the entrance to the marquee.

'Well get her mother – or sister – or how about a real nurse from the first aid post,' he suggested. 'It's okay Vanessa. Yes, well, better out than in,' he muttered. 'That's what I always say.'

The blinding flash of a camera bulb caught him off guard. Peter Marchant was watching the debacle with interest, and capturing the moment for posterity with his photographer.

'Very nice,' he murmured, jotting down a few notes. 'A couple of Hooray Henry's, if I'm not mistaken.'

'Get lost!' Lewis snapped.

'Yeah, push off,' Matthew said. 'Give the girl a break.'

'I'm only doing my job.'

Lewis glared. 'Get rid of him, Matt.'

'Consider it done.' Matthew hopped down a couple of steps and squared up in front of the older man. At six foot four, and an ex-rugby player, he looked a force to be reckoned with. 'Mr Marchant?'

'Yes, okay, I'm coming,' he said. He glanced back at Lewis, who was still struggling to support the hapless Vanessa. 'Good luck, mate,' he said cheerfully. 'I think you'll need it.'

What Lewis actually needed was some help. Vanessa weighed a ton. Where was everybody?

He peered back towards the marquee. The filming was in full swing and no one was coming in or out. Matt was pre-occupied trying to get rid of the journalist, and God only knows where the rest of the team were. The stream of visitors wandering past had absolutely no intention of getting involved either. Most of them gave Vanessa a wide berth and a disgusted stare, or paused to gawp for a few seconds, before shaking their heads and walking on.

Lewis resigned himself to being stuck with her until she stopped throwing up, or passed out, whichever came first. He certainly couldn't leave her in the condition she was in.

'Oh my God! I don't believe it'

Lewis seethed inwardly. Not another ogling spectator. Yes, come on, roll up, and see the sideshow. He straightened up, ready to make some cutting remark, and found he was rendered speechless by the sight of Ella's horrified and panic-stricken face.

'What's happened?' she cried, dashing to Vanessa's side. 'Oh my God. How long has she been like this?'

'Since she drank about a magnum of champagne,' Lewis sighed. He had never been so glad to see anyone in his entire life.

'Vanessa? Vanessa!' Ella slapped her lightly on both cheeks.

'Oh. Hel-lo Ella,' she mumbled, her eyes narrowing as she tried to focus. 'I've been waiting for you.'

'Can you stand up?'

Vanessa gave a loud hiccup. 'No. No, I don't think I can.' She giggled. 'I'm a bit tipsy you know.'

'More like ruddy plastered,' Lewis muttered.

Ella shot him a warning look.

'Well, it was me she puked over,' he complained.

'Yes, okay. I'm sorry. Look, I'd better take her home.'

'How?'

'I don't know.' Ella hooked her arm under Vanessa's armpit. 'Perhaps if you took the other side, we could get her to walk. Oh, but that's no good,' she realised. 'Oh blast.'

'What?'

'Heather's gone,' she said. 'She's taken Majesty back to the farm. And Thomas dropped me off here in Kate's car, so I've got no transport. I was planning to get a lift back with Ursula.'

Lewis looked at the state Vanessa was in, thought of Ursula, and shook his head. 'Not a good idea,' he said.

'No.'

He sighed. What the heck. He was in no fit state to go back on the set, not with his trousers and shoes stinking to high

254

heaven. 'Come on,' he said. 'But if she so much as coughs in the back of my car...'

'She won't,' Ella said, wrinkling her nose. 'There can't be anything left inside her.'

Lewis remained unconvinced. Consequently, Vanessa spent the majority of the journey home with her head hanging over a borrowed horse bucket.

'I don't feel well,' she moaned, as they carted her up the drive and into the house.

'I'm not surprised,' Ella said, helping her onto the settee. 'You must have drunk enough to sink a battleship.'

'I only had a few,' she sighed. 'It was very nice.'

'Yes, will this is even better,' Lewis said, handing her a large glass of water. 'I suggest you drink it. Yes, all of it. And then I'll get you another.'

Vanessa peered blearily up at him. Puzzled she looked at Ella. 'Thash Mr Trevelyan.'

Ella smiled. 'So it is.'

'Whaz he doing here?' she murmured sleepily. Her eyelids were closing.

Lewis edged the bucket nearer, so that it was positioned closer to her chin. 'We'd best leave her,' he whispered. 'Let her sleep it off.'

Ella wasn't so sure. 'What if she chokes?' she said.

'I'm sure we'll hear her, but my guess is she's out for the count.' He straightened up and shook his head. 'I wouldn't want to be in her shoes when Ursula finds out what she's done.'

'Ursula!' Ella groaned. She had forgotten all about her. They had left the Showground in such a hurry that she hadn't given her stepmother a second thought. 'She'll be looking for her.'

'I expect Miles will be looking for me,' Lewis said, reaching for his mobile. 'Don't worry,' he added. 'I'll make sure they get the message.'

Ella left him making a series of phone calls, and went into the kitchen to put the kettle on. A hot cup of tea seemed like a good idea. It would give her something to do, something to occupy her and stop her mind from racing. Being here with Lewis Trevelyan was affecting her concentration. The memory of his passionate kiss was all too fresh in her mind, even if the passion had been somewhat one-sided.

She popped a couple of tea bags into the pot, and jumped a mile as he came up behind her, and tapped her lightly on the arm.

'No sugar for me.'

'Milk?' she said, trying desperately to stop the flush of colour that was spreading over her face, and failing miserably.

'Please.' He slipped his phone into his pocket, and sat down on one of the pine stools. 'So,' he said, resting his elbows on the table and staring over at her. 'What happens now?'

'Oh, I expect Ursula will have fifty fits, and somehow it'll be my fault for not going to the marquee with Vanessa, and then...'

'I meant, with us,' he said softly.

Ella nearly dropped the teapot. She clattered it onto the tray, slopping dregs everywhere. 'Us?' she queried, fumbling for a damp cloth.

'Do you want me to stay with you,' he said. 'I mean, I can if you like. There's no rush for me to get back. Matthew said the filming went well, and Lucy can handle the extra paperwork. And,' he said, pointing down at his stained trousers. 'I'd really appreciate it if I could get out of these. They're starting to hum a bit.'

'Oh. Yes, of course,' she said, turning to face him. She had managed to balance the tray between her shaking hands, and hoped he wouldn't notice. 'I'm sure I can find you something to wear.' Though for the life of her, she couldn't think what. He was so tall and slim. And muscular, she decided, running her eyes up and down, and then hurriedly averting her gaze before her cheeks went pinker than they already were. 'The bathroom's upstairs on the right,' she added. 'If you take those off, I'll give them a quick rinse and put them in the dryer.' She slid the tea tray onto the table as she spoke.

'Upstairs, you say?'

'Hmm.' Ella nodded.

His re-emergence a couple of minutes later with a towel wrapped round his waist and not a lot else, was doing all kinds of things to her self control.'

'I'll get you some overalls,' she blurted, rushing through to the laundry room. Green work overalls, the ideal cover-up. She blushed as she handed him a large, clean, and virtually new pair, last worn by Vanessa several blue moons ago. (Vanessa was not one who liked to get her hands dirty.) 'These should do,' she said. 'And I'll be as quick as I can with your things.'

'I can wash them,' he said. 'They're pretty disgusting.'

'You forget,' she smiled. 'I spend my time with horses. I'm used to muck. And it's no trouble. I owe you this much,' she said. 'I honestly don't know what I would have done without you.'

Lewis grinned as he shoved his feet into the legs of the baggy green overalls. Ella tried to ignore the sight of his firm, naked and muscular thighs, and pointedly reached over to help herself to a mug of tea.

'I could say the same thing about you,' he said. 'You've no idea how glad I was when you turned up.' He chuckled. 'I thought I was stuck there for the duration.'

'Poor Vanessa,' Ella sighed.

'Poor you.' He picked up his mug and took a mouthful of hot tea. 'Missing out on your moment of fame. I hear you did well in the competition,' he said, wandering over to the table and sitting down again.

'Yes, I was pleased with my performance,' she agreed, 'considering I hadn't competed for years.'

'Think you'll take it up again?'

He was watching her steadily over the rim of his mug. Ella got the impression that he was genuinely interested in what she had to say, that he wasn't making polite conversation because he felt he had to.

'Oh, I don't know,' she said. 'I'm so busy here. Ursula makes sure of that.'

'But I heard it was your business?'

'Well yes, technically, it is,' she said, sitting down opposite him.

'But?'

She sighed. 'It's complicated.'

'Tell me.'

'Oh, you don't want to hear about it,' she said lightly. She didn't want to dwell on it too much herself. The fact that the stables were in dire financial straits was only now becoming apparent to her. Heather had told her more than a few home truths, and Kate had said her piece as well. The books were in a dubious state, and she had already resolved that first thing on the Monday morning, she would speak to the accountant about the true state of affairs.

He leaned forwards and closed his hand over hers. 'Yes,' he said, 'I do.'

Ella looked up and found she was drowning in his dark and intense gaze.

'Well, if you've got all day, to listen,' she said.

'I've got as long as it takes,' he said, and meant it.

She wasn't sure how it happened, but over the course of two pots of tea and the spin cycle in the washing machine she found herself telling him about her suspicions. Ursula was running the business at a loss because she had debts coming out of her ears. She had overspent on alterations and building work, including the new ménage, and she wasn't taking in enough funds to cover her loans.

'We've lost a lot of business because of her attitude to the clients,' she explained. 'The livery yard is our bread and butter, really. If owners aren't happy, they won't pay to keep their horses with us. That's why Heather took Majesty away,' she sighed. 'And he was a fantastic horse.'

'And that's the one you rode today,' Lewis said.

'Yes.'

'So, his owner obviously has no problems with you.'

'No. Heather's a good friend.'

'But not good enough to keep her horse with you, when the

business is struggling,' he said, raising an eyebrow at her.

'It's not like that,' Ella sighed. But actually, when she thought about it hard enough, it was like that. 'Anyway, I'm going to get to the bottom of things. I know Ursula's been keeping a lot from me, and I intend to find out what it is. If finances are the real problem, I need to sort them out. I've got a trust fund due from my grandmother in the next month,' she added, 'and that will help.'

'Next month?' he said.

'When I'm twenty-one.'

'Right,' he said. His dark eyes were watching her with such concentration and interest that she was beginning to feel butterflies flitting about in her stomach.

'Well, if you don't mind me saying so, I think finances are the least of your worries,' he said. 'I think your stepmother is the problem and you need to deal with her first.'

"How", was the thought that sprang to Ella's mind? She had been trying to deal with Ursula since she was a teenager, and to no avail.

'Maybe I can help?' he said.

'You?' Ella glanced up at him, surprised. Why would he want to help? She had only known him for five minutes. And yet, the way she had been unburdening herself to him, she felt as if she had known him for most of her life.

'I'm a dab hand at dealing with difficult people,' he said, giving her an incredibly sexy and half slanting smile.

Ella felt her heart skip a beat, and wondered vaguely if he had any idea what he was doing to her.

'Talking of difficult people,' she said, reluctantly tearing her eyes away from him, 'I think I'd better go and see how Vanessa's doing.'

Vanessa was doing fine. She was sleeping like a baby, curled up on her side with a faint smile on her lips.

Lewis watched as Ella threw a tartan rug over her, and tucked it in all around her. 'I hope she appreciates this,' he said.

'I doubt she'll remember.'

He smiled. 'I doubt I'll forget.'

There was a warmth in his eyes that was making her heart beat quicken. But he wouldn't be interested in her, she told herself firmly. Not really. It was just the situation that had brought them together.

'Your trousers should be dry by now,' she said.

'Possibly.' He placed one hand across the doorframe, blocking her way.

Ella looked up at him, her heart thumping like mad. 'I need to get to the machine,' she said. She had the strangest feeling that he was going to kiss her. That the look she could see in his eyes was more than polite interest.

'Mr Trevelyan.'

'Lewis,' he murmured, reaching over to push a strand of hair away from her face. The touch of his fingers on her cheekbone was like a feather against her skin.

'Lewis, then,'

'That's better,' he murmured, slipping his arm around her waist and pulling her towards him. 'Gabriella.' She was transfixed, hypnotised, spellbound. Like a rabbit caught in the headlights of a car, she stared dazedly up at him. This couldn't be happening, surely it couldn't be happening.

His head lowered and his lips brushed against hers, gently at first, and then more insistent and demanding. His arms went around her, pulling her tight against his chest. Ella was powerless to resist him, helpless against the waves of longing surging through her veins. His kiss deepened, and the burning touch of his hands on her skin was sending tremulous shivers rocketing down her spine. She could feel the length of his firm and muscular body, moulded against hers, and could only wonder at the growing sweetness and intensity of his kiss.

For one bizarre moment, she wondered if the press had arrived. If this was another staged performance he was putting on to keep the journalists happy. But something in the way he was holding her told her that this was no act. This, she realised, with a sudden lurch of her heart, this was for real.

The frantic ringing of the doorbell shattered her illusions. The banging of fists on the door only confirmed it. He must have seen them coming. God, she was an idiot. She twisted her head to one side and placed a hand squarely on his chest.

'Ignore it,' he murmured, his voice husky as he nuzzled into the side of her neck. 'Please, Ella.' He pressed tiny kisses on her forehead, her cheeks, and the corner of her eyes, her lips.

She could feel herself weakening. Maybe it wasn't the press.

'Ella? Come on, open up. I know you're in there.'

It wasn't, she realised guiltily. It was Kate.

She lifted her gaze to stare up into a pair of dark and smouldering eyes. She had a thousand questions she wanted to ask him. A million, no, a zillion things she wanted to say. Most of them beginning with a "how" or a "why".

Lewis gave a sigh, and pressed his lips on the top of her head. His arms gave her a tight squeeze. 'You'd better let her in,' he said reluctantly. 'That's if you still value your front door.'

Ella thought that a broken front door was the least of her worries. She reached up and ran her fingers over the faint stubble on his cheek, before clasping her hands behind his neck, and gazing searchingly into his eyes.

'Is this for real, Lewis?' she whispered.

'Yep.' He kissed her gently on the nose.

'No, I mean, *really* for real?'

'It is,' he said, with a resigned shrug. 'And don't ask me how it happened. It just did.' He pushed her hair back from her face. 'I was sort of hoping you might feel the same way.'

'I do,' she said wistfully. 'Or at least, I think I do.' It was too soon and too unexpected to make any sort of rational judgement on the matter.

And Kate, it seemed, was not prepared to give her the time to do it.

'I know you're in there,' came her wheedling voice through the letterbox. 'I've seen the car. Ella! Come on, open up, Ella. Please?'

'Go on,' Lewis sighed, giving her a push. 'We're not going to get any peace now anyway. You might as well let her in, and I'll go and get changed.'

Ella could hardly bear to let him out of her sight.

'Hang on, Kate!' she called. 'I'll be with you in a minute.'

She gave Lewis a wistful smile as she handed him his trousers from the dryer. 'This could take some explaining,' she said.

'Oh, I don't know,' he said, giving her a wink. 'I always find the truth works best.'

And it probably would, Ella thought, as she reached for the front door – if she knew exactly what that was.

Chapter Nineteen

Six hectic and life changing weeks later, and the preparations for Ella's twenty-first birthday celebrations were well under way.

Kate and Lewis had organized a barbecue for her that involved inviting half the village, the regulars from the Jazz Club, and the team from Blackwater Films. Money, it seemed, was no object. Lewis had insisted that the four hundred pounds, left over from the repair bill for Ursula's Range Rover, be put towards the cost of catering, with any excess being invoiced to him.

Kate watched him fondly, as he stoked up the barbecue with charcoal, and thought back to those first few days after the County Agricultural Show, when Ella had been bursting with happiness. A happiness that had been short lived when a Debt Recovery agency had turned up at the stables, demanding to claim goods to the value of the outstanding bills. The feed merchant had finally had enough of Ursula's excuses. So too, had Ella. Her visit to the accountant had revealed the depth of her stepmother's deceit. Extravagance, laziness, and bad business management had brought the business to its knees.

Lewis, bless him, had been there to help her through the crisis, Kate recalled. God knows what Ella would have done without him.

She hummed softly to herself as she unpacked the cool box and carted packs of sausages, steaks and burgers over to him. 'How's it doing?' she asked, peering at the warm and glowing coals. 'Thought so,' she added. 'Looks like you're about ready for these.'

Lewis prodded the hot charcoal with a poker. His hair

curled over the collar of his white t-shirt. His long legs and slim hips, clad in faded denim jeans, and his sexily tanned skin, gave him the appearance of a film star. He was quite a hunk, really, Kate thought. Lucky Ella.

'I tell you what I could do with,' he said, glancing over at her. 'A cold beer.'

'Coming right up,' Kate said.

By the time she had retrieved a couple of bottles from the fridge; Lewis had slapped a couple of steaks on the grill, and was whistling softly as he watched them sizzle.

'Any sign of the gang arriving?' he said.

'They're in the yard,' Kate told him. 'Ella's showing off her latest acquisition.'

The black stallion had been his birthday present to her. Not that he knew anything about horses, but Thomas had assured him, in his own inimitable way, that a finer beast would be hard to come by. He had taken him at his word, and bought the horse. That, and the timely cheque from his own personal bank account to countermand the threat of bankruptcy, was a token of his love for her.

She had blossomed in these few short weeks. Hours of probing through Ursula's business records, and unravelling the legacy of her inheritance, had given her a determination he had found nothing short of admirable. Step by step she was taking over the running of the business and distancing herself from her stepmother and all she stood for.

'Looks like there'll be a few foals arriving here in the spring,' Kate said, nibbling on a stick of celery dipped in cream cheese.

'That's the plan,' Lewis said, flipping over a piece of steak. 'Ella's put Thomas in charge of the stud. He's the one with all the experience. Hey Matthew,' he called. 'What do you think of the new horse?'

His friend emerged from the stable block brushing the dirt from his immaculately tailored, and totally impractical, light grey suit. 'I'd risk a pound or two on him at Newmarket,' he said, 'that's for sure.' He picked a can of beer out of the crate, and sauntered up the steps towards them. 'Something smells good.'

'Hands off!' Lewis said, slapping his hand away from the sausages. 'They're not ready yet. Kate, can you get me the kebabs.'

Matthew sat down on the edge of the patio wall, and watched approvingly as Kate leaned over the open cool box. 'Miles has finished with the rough cut,' he told him. 'There's only the theme tune to record now, and that's in hand.'

Lewis nodded. 'So, we're on schedule for general release in, say, four months?'

'December the fifth,' Matthew confirmed. 'We're aiming at the Christmas market.'

'Sounds good.' Lewis skewered a well-cooked sausage and placed it in a roll for him. 'Help yourself to relish or sauce,' he said. 'And don't blame me if you get food poisoning.'

Ella listened to the sounds of laughter and conversation echoing from the gardens, as she hung up the hay-net in the black stallion's stable.

Kate had been as good as her word, and staged a memorable party for her. Even going so far as to invite Ursula and her stepsisters along, though it had gone against the grain.

'That woman is a parasite,' Kate told her. 'And it's only because of Lewis Trevelyan that Hollyfield Stables is still in business.'

'I know,' Ella said. 'But my father must have loved her once. Why else would he have married her?'

'Because he was blinkered like the rest of them,' Kate snorted. 'You know how devious she can be, once she sets her mind to something.'

Which was true enough, Ella supposed. She had taken plenty of people in, and Michael Lloyd-Duncan, a local solicitor and magistrate, looked to be the next person on her list.

'What does she see in him?' Kate said. 'He's an old, arrogant, and ugly little fat man.'

'With money,' Ella said.

'Right,' Kate nodded. 'So, I've got to invite him?' she said. 'Well, it goes without saying, I suppose. Got anyone in mind for Vanessa and Caroline?'

And now the day had arrived, and Ella could not have been happier. She had Lewis in her life – the most fantastic, and amazing person she had ever known - and she was hopelessly and irretrievably head-over-heels in love with him. She had a business that was starting to recover, and a horse that was worth more than most of the others put together. 'You're a real beauty, aren't you, boy,' she murmured, stroking his velvety nose.

'Aye, he's a good un,' Thomas said, resting his arms on the stable door. 'You'll not go wrong with him.' He jerked his head in the direction of the music and merriment. 'Shouldn't you be out there, lass, with your guests?'

'In a minute,' she said. 'I was just enjoying the peace and quiet in here.'

'It's been a long, hard slog for you, hasn't it, Miss Ella,' he said softly. 'But everything comes to those who wait. That it does.'

Ella smiled. He was right. Which reminded her, she had one thing left to do before the day was out, and she had waited quite long enough to do it.

'What do you mean; you're giving us notice to leave?' Ursula spluttered as she stared in disbelief at the letter Ella had ceremoniously handed to her. (In front of Michael as well. It really was too bad.)

'I think it's all made perfectly clear in the letter,' Ella replied. 'The house is no longer your home. As of next week, I want you, Vanessa, and Caroline to move into the groom's cottage.'

'The groom's cottage!' Ursula looked as if she was going to faint. Her face had gone rather pale, and she began to fan herself quite rapidly with the sheet of paper clutched in her hand. 'Ella, you don't mean it.'

'Yes,' she said. 'I do. According to the terms of my father's will, you should have been living there for the past three years.'

'Well, yes, I know but...'

'No buts,' Ella said firmly. 'And I'm relying on you to tell the girls.'

Ursula didn't know what to say. She clutched at her elderly companion's stout arm for support. 'Oh, Michael,' she sniffed.

'Ursula? Ursula, my dear, are you unwell?'

'Darling, I do feel rather weak,' she agreed.

'Can I get you anything? A drink of water?'

'No, just hold me, Michael,' she sighed, leaning her head on his shoulder. 'Just hold me.'

'You should have done it years ago,' Kate said, as she picked her way round the pile of packing crates that were stacked by the door. Two high backed armchairs and an oak bureau blocked the hallway.

Ursula was not leaving empty handed. Everything she rightfully thought belonged to her was being removed from the house.

'God knows where she's going to put it,' Ella said with a wry grin. 'The cottage only has two bedrooms, and there's precious little living space in it.'

'I don't expect she'll be there for long, though.' Kate took the offered coffee mug from her with a grateful smile.

'I don't suppose she will,' Ella said. 'Not now she's got Michael Lloyd-Duncan in her sights.'

'Poor bloke,' Kate chuckled. 'Should we warn him off?'

'Absolutely not.'

'Mother!' Vanessa's indignant voice echoed down through the ceiling. 'Mother, I need you to help me with this suitcase. I can't get it to close.'

'Then take something out of it, darling. I'm sure Ella won't mind if you leave a few bits and pieces behind.'

'Will you?' Kate asked, raising her eyebrows at her.

Ella shook her head. She didn't care what they left behind, as long as they removed themselves from her house, and her property.

Ursula's misguided ambition and incompetence had almost ruined her business. The stables would pick up, given time, but she wasn't sure if her supposed feelings of family loyalty and kinship would ever recover.

Wilson's deep, thunderous bark preceded him bounding towards the front door, his paws clattering on the wooden parquet flooring.

'Sounds like he's back from London,' Kate said, grinning.

'Lewis?' Ella felt her cheeks flush with colour. 'But he's not due until tomorrow.'

Kate held the curtain open for her to see. 'I'd say he couldn't stay away.'

The silver BMW was pulling up on the drive. Ella plonked her mug down on one of the packing crates and ran to the door.

He was lifting a parcel out of the boot of his car, a large, flat, brown paper wrapped parcel. On the top of it lay an elaborate bouquet of flowers.

Ella felt her heart give a sudden leap as he turned and caught her staring at him. His eyes crinkled, and his smile widened.

'Lewis!' She ran across the gravel, and flung herself into his arms.

'Steady on,' he laughed. 'You'll have me over.'

Wilson was barking up at him, and cavorting around like an overgrown puppy at his feet. 'Blasted dog,' he said, but he was stroking the huge, silky grey head and floppy ears as he spoke.

He handed Ella the bunch of flowers. 'These,' he said, 'are for you. And this,' he lugged the parcel out of the boot, and set it down on the ground. 'Is for the yard.'

'The yard?' she said.

'Yep. I had it made specially.' Grinning, he watched her ripping off the brown paper. The sign was painted in gold lettering on a dark green background, with the silhouette of a rearing horse as the centre motif.

"Hollyfield Stables, Livery and Stud. Proprietor, Mrs Ella Trevelyan."

Ella's eyes widened, as she read the inscription. She swayed unsteadily, and had to prop herself against the side of the car for support. He had put 'Ella Trevelyan' on the sign, 'Mrs Ella Trevelyan'.

'Well?' he said. 'What do you think?' He gave her a sheepish grin. 'I didn't see the point in putting "Ella Johnson" on the board,' he added, 'because hopefully, you won't be Ella Johnson for much longer.'

'Lewis,' she choked. 'Are you asking me to marry you?'

He shrugged. 'It's probably not the most romantic proposal in the world…'

'You idiot,' she sighed. 'It has to be *the* most romantic proposal.'

'Thank God for that,' he said. Relief was etched all over his face. 'Is that a "yes", then?'

'Most definitely,' she laughed.

At that moment, a sulky looking Caroline, and a cross looking Vanessa were carting boxes and bags of belongings out of the house.

'That could have been me, you know,' Vanessa muttered, staring over at the pair of them, locked together in a loving embrace.

'In your dreams,' Caroline said.

Lewis heard the raised voices, and smiled as he pulled Ella tighter against his chest. She snuggled her head on his shoulder, and hugged him close.

In the distance, the two stepsisters were still arguing.

'And I'm not having the bed by the window. It's too bloody cold in that pokey little bedroom.'

'What gives you the right to choose?'

'Because I said it first, that's why.'

Lewis ran his hands down Ella's long, blonde hair, and

curled a strand of it round his finger. He kissed her gently on the lips. 'I don't know how you put up with them for so long,' he said.

'I guess I just got used to them being around.'

'Will you miss them?'

'No.' She wrapped her arms around his neck, and gazed up into his eyes. 'Not as long as you're here.'

'Oh, I'll be here,' he said. 'It's as easy to base myself in Suffolk as it is in London. And if I sell my place in Yorkshire,' he added,' I'll have plenty of cash spare to plough into the stud. So yes, Mrs Trevelyan–to-be, I'll be here for as long as you want me to be.'

Ella smiled as she tilted her chin towards his. 'How does forever sound?'

'Pretty good,' he murmured, as his lips came down on hers.

Kate stood and watched them from her vantage point outside the front door of the house. Young love, honestly! It would be nauseating, if it weren't so perfect. She munched on a half-eaten ginger biscuit, and clutched a mug of lukewarm coffee in her hand, as she wandered down the gravel drive towards them.

'Blimey!' she said, peering down at the half-unwrapped signboard, and then up again at Ella, (who was in the middle of a passionate clinch at the time). 'I take it I'm going to be chief bridesmaid?'

Ella laughed. 'Naturally.'

'Great,' she said. (The opportunities at a wedding were endless.) She smiled sweetly up at Lewis. Her face was a picture of eager anticipation. 'So, tell me,' She added, 'Whom are you going to choose for best man?'

'Kate!' Ella groaned. 'Can't you just congratulate us, like anyone else would?'

'I could,' she said, tossing the remains of her biscuit to Wilson, who wolfed it down with gusto. 'But a girl has to plan for her future, doesn't she?'

'Indeed, she does,' Lewis said.

And Ella, hugging him close, could not agree more.

THE END

Books By This Author

The Coach Trip

Sometimes life is okay. Sometimes change is better.

Age is no obstacle to falling in love, as Gilly discovers when she joins her older sister, Angie, on a coach trip to France.
Angie is going through a humiliating divorce, (her husband ran off with a younger woman),and Gilly agrees to go with her, despite not always getting on. She's sure she can put up with her for a week. After all, she's put up with her own belligerent husband, Charles, for long enough. The change of scene will be the tonic they both need.
However, she hadn't expected to find herself on a coach full of pensioners, along with a hopelessly inefficient smuggler, and a driver who makes her feel like a lovesick teenager, despite being nearer to her fifties than her teens.
The week away leads to some hilarious misunderstandings plus some serious soul-searching, as the two sisters enjoy a holiday together that neither of them will ever forget.

Muddy Boots And Mishaps

Love isn't always blind, but sometime it's blinkered.

Tack shop owner, Vanessa, has a non-existent love life (though not through lack of trying), but when rugged American, Hank Raymond Jefferson, starts work at Hollyfield Stables and Stud for the summer, she thinks she has found the man of her dreams.

Her nephew, Adam, is not convinced. Determined to protect his Aunt from yet another dating disaster, he decides to do a bit of snooping, and the secrets he uncovers are not what any of them could have imagined in this hilarious romantic comedy.

Another fun filled romance at Hollyfield Stables.

Printed in Great Britain
by Amazon

43363328R00158